D.V. CHERNOV

SEVERED ECHOES

A NICK SEVERS MYSTERY

heathen

HEATHEN PRESS, LLC

heathenpress.com

ISBN 979-8-9863298-1-9

First Printing, 2022

SEVERED ECHOES

0

The boy's skull cracked, and the sound made Nick open his eyes.

1

The coffee shop was probably not the best place to do this. At 10:30 in the morning, the place was buzzing with customer chatter and intermittent ringing of the register. Nick leaned closer to the thin glassy slab of Mike's phone on the table between them.

"What am I listening for?" The running timer on the phone's screen was speedily counting up milliseconds of the audio recording. But all Nick heard was the muted track of college radio playing overhead and the credit card machine impatiently beeping at the order counter behind him. He tried to discern anything, something, but registered only faint whirring and crackling, like amplified dead air in-between the stations on the car radio.

He checked Mike's face for any sign of a prank, but Mike shook his head and put his finger to his lips. The timer kept rolling, and under it, the tiny tick mark indicating progress crept along on its razor-thin line across the screen. Five seconds. Six.

Above the timer, like the inky needle of an EKG machine, a squiggly line tracked the sound waves, lethargically scribing minor bumps and dips as it registered the static. Eight seconds. Nine seconds. The tick mark was now almost halfway on its journey across the screen. And then, the invisible needle jumped to the top – a woman's startled shriek. Short, sharp, and clear. With the phone's volume turned all the way up, the sound was enough to make Nick jump back in his seat. The scream was brief, almost instantly muffled into an unintelligible gurgling murmur, followed with a *thud* and loud static-filled rustling that made the invisible needle scribe madly from top to bottom over and over and over. Until there was another thud, uncomfortably loud, followed with silence. Twelve seconds. "*N-n-n-n-n-o*" – a woman's hoarse, strained whisper. Nick leaned over the phone and heard another, barely audible: "*n-n-no.*" A tingle ran down his spine. There was another thud and then something broke and scattered, like a bottle shattering on the floor. Fifteen seconds. More staticky rustling. Sixteen seconds. Seventeen. Silence. Twenty-four seconds. Footsteps. Silence. The sound wave flattened into a razor line. The tick mark stopped at the other edge of the screen. The timer read thirty seconds exactly.

Nick sat back in the booth, feeling a bit queasy. Mike's eyebrows were frozen in a distraught frown. He was biting his fingernail, his gaze still glued to the screen.

"What is this?" Nick asked.

"A Lexi recording."

"Who?"

Mike snapped out of his trance. "Lexi – the digital voice assistant. You know? Like Alexa or Siri."

"Where did you get it?"

"An intern. Our company does machine learning for the manufacturer."

"What?"

"Machine learning. We help make the AI better. Any time there is a failed interaction, the system sends the recording to us."

Nick digested the barrage of techno jargon and weird jobs Mike just threw at him. So far, his usual method of asking a lot of questions was backfiring and yielding only more questions in his head.

"Why?" In his experience, it was never a bad idea to ask that one.

"So that we can review it and try to figure out what went wrong. So that next time the AI can handle it better."

"And that is what this was? What you call a *failed interaction?*"

"Yes."

"These happen a lot?"

"Yeah. A *ton.* Maybe a person is trying to order a pizza or play a song, but they use the wrong word, or they are talking with their mouth full, or there is too much background noise. Whatever the reason, if Lexi can't understand the request, the system sends us the recording to figure it out. Oftentimes, we find that there was no real request at all – the system just got turned on unintentionally."

"What do you mean?"

"The device listens for the trigger word or phrase to fully turn on and begin the interaction. Sometimes, something else may sound like the trigger word. Maybe someone was talking on the phone, or watching TV, or having sex. Believe me – I've heard it all. Sometimes we find nothing at all – just thirty seconds of silence; no clue as to why it got turned on."

Nick winced. "And people don't mind you listening to these?" These virtual assistants were everywhere these days, and it seemed he had to turn off a dozen preferences to stop the one on his phone from constantly popping up and offering its services. Knowing that the little buggers could be turning on all on their own did not help their case in the least, as far as he was concerned.

Mike shrugged. "It's anonymized. The reviewer never sees the name or address – nothing like that. Just a case ID." He caught Nick's bewildered look. "What? Everyone does this: Amazon, Google, Apple. It's all in the terms of use. You accept the terms when you turn the damn thing on. It's not our fault no one reads them."

Nick had to begrudgingly admit that this was a fair point. He himself had never read the terms of use for anything. He may have to start now. But then again, he would never have one of these listening devices in his home. Definitely not now.

"So, your intern was reviewing these and came across this particular recording?"

Mike nodded. "The poor kid was white as a sheet." He stared at Nick. "Tell me this does not sound like this woman is getting murdered?"

Nick took a long exhale and tapped his fingers on the table, considering. The phone screen between them had gone dark and its black mirror surface reflected Mike's earnest face. He had not seen Mike in person since college, and this was not the Mike he remembered – charming, affable, self-assured, invincible. The Mike in front of him may have been grown up and wearing a business shirt that probably cost more than Nick's entire outfit put together, but behind those familiar eyes, he could see that Mike was panicked. Maybe even scared. Looking at this new Mike, Nick felt sorry for him. But then again, perhaps the Nick sitting at this table now also looked sorry compared to his nineteen-year-old self.

"Look, Mike, people do crazy stuff in their homes. She could have been rehearsing for an audition, or having rough kinky sex, or watching a violent movie. When I was a street cop in Kansas City, I'd been called in for all sorts of things the neighbors thought they'd heard. Nine times out of ten, it was not murder. Something weird, but not murder."

Mike shook his head. "Nick, I've listened to literally thousands of these. I've heard it all. This is not kinky sex or a movie. Trust me."

"Ok, even if we suspect this is for real, is there anything we can do? Didn't you say all this was anonymized? I mean, do we even know if this was recorded in the U.S.?"

Mike dug in his pocket and fished out a yellow Post-it note. He stuck it on the table next to the phone.

"What's this?"

"The address where this device is plugged in."

"But…you said it was anonymized. You said no one can see the address or name…just the case number?"

"I said the *reviewer* can't see it. As a director, I have other places I can look. Not that I'm supposed to, but I do know this tech inside and out." The old cocky Mike was peeking out from this collapsed shell. "You see, nothing digital is ever truly anonymous. There is always a trail, if you know where to look. I used the system log files to find the user account tied to the case number."

Nick looked at the yellow swatch of paper without touching it. He looked back at Mike. "That's in my jurisdiction."

"I know. That's why I came to you. To check it out."

Nick pulled out a small leather notepad and a pen from his jacket, fully aware of and ignoring Mike's bemused look. He flipped to a blank page.

"Do you know when this was recorded?"

Mike picked up the phone and swiped at the screen a few times. "Tuesday, September 7, 8:13 PM."

"OK, so, less than 48 hours ago. Are there other recordings? Before or after this one?"

Mike shook his head. "Nothing at all earlier in the day and nothing after."

"You checked?" This surprised Nick. The Mike he knew back in the day would not have gone this far out of his way for a stranger.

Mike nodded and hung his head.

Nick took the Post-it, stuck it to the page and flipped his notebook closed. "OK, I can go check it out. A welfare check, if you will. But I'll need you to call it in."

Mike shook his head categorically. "Man, I can't be mixed up in this. I could lose my job."

"I can't just go knocking on doors without a documented probable cause."

"Can't you say it was an anonymous tip?"

"Sure. Do you want to call in the anonymous tip? You can call the station from a burner."

"Jesus, Nick," Mike leaned back in his seat and grinned the type of smile grown-ups can't help in those unexpected moments when they find themselves face-to-face with the boundless, unjaded, naïve imagination of a three-year-old. "You think burners are secure? Are you sure you and I were born in the same generation? Haven't you heard of Snowden?"

Nick rewarded Mike's rhetorical curiosity with a humorless unblinking stare he had perfected over the years as a beat cop.

Mike lost the grin and sighed. "Can I send you an anonymous email?"

Nick shrugged. "*Can* you? I thought you said nothing is really anonymous?"

Mike rolled a short, nervous laugh. "Touché. Let's just say it would take a three-letter federal agency, hundreds of manhours, and blatant violation of international data laws to crack it. I seriously doubt your department has that kind of pull."

Nick couldn't argue with that. "OK. Send your fancy email, and I will check it out."

"Thank you."

Mike leaned back, trying to look relaxed, but Nick could still see the shadow of unease behind his eyes. Mike slipped his phone back into his jacket and took a sip of his coffee. He examined Nick.

"It's good to see you, man. In person. Instead of on Claire's Instagram."

Nick hung his head in shame. His reputation for being a social media recluse used to be a source of incessant chiding from his friends and family, until eventually they all gave up. "I know. I am terrible about keeping in touch. Just ask my mom. Hey, maybe you two should connect."

Mike shook his head. "I'm just giving you a hard time. We are as much to blame. You guys moved to Denver when? Six months ago? We should have had you over right there and then, in-between the COVID waves, before the lockdown ruined the year for everyone. But hey, let's fix this. Talk to Claire, and I'll talk to Amy – let's have you guys over. The weather is cooling off nicely. Firepit, scotch, cigars. How about this weekend?"

Nick finished his cup. It sounded like a nice break, and he would finally get Claire off his back about not having friends outside of work.

"Make it bourbon, and you've got a deal."

2

The silhouette of Pikes Peak crinkled with early snow – wedges of white and cerulean on the crisp azure horizon. Overhead, a pine branch framed the view. It was like looking through a 1930s travel poster. *See Colorado.* Nick breathed it in. After all this time, he still could not get enough of the air here – clear like the tolling of a bell, invigorating like a shot of glacier water. The mid-September sun baked hot from above, but every now and then, a cool breeze rolled through the trees, stirring up the scent of warm cedar. He wondered if higher up, along the Guanella Pass Road, the aspens had already begun to turn into gold. But here, in the low-rolling foothills of the Kenosha range, summer still reigned, oblivious of the cold that would soon descend from the higher elevations. Soon, there would be the first snow. Nick looked forward to it. He loved it here, probably more than Claire did. He never felt this free anywhere else.

The views were good here at Scraggy Ridge, but he still liked his part of the town better – it had more pine trees. He tore his gaze away from Pikes Peak and the distant horizon and walked back up the driveway toward the house from Mike's sticky note. It was quiet here. Secluded. All he could hear was the wind moving through the trees, the cries of a magpie somewhere nearby, and the measured crunching of his own boots in the crushed red shale – nature's gravel around these parts. The house was a simple light-gray bungalow with dark shutters and trim. Claire probably would have called it cute. It was set into the side of a mountain on a small clearing with the edge of the woods looming on the slope behind it. There were flower boxes on the front porch and a deck out back. Next to the driveway was an above-ground propane tank, freshly repainted to match the house. A tidy estate.

Nick looked at his watch – just after noon. He had already been here for almost two hours. The jagged line of bright-yellow crime scene tape serpentined from the mailbox at the end of the driveway up the slope toward the trees and around the house, slowly encircling it, foot by foot, like a python preparing to constrict its prey. At the other end of the tape was Jason, cautiously making his way on the rolling, rocky slope with the heavy spool in his hands. He was wrapping the tape around tree trunks, gradually angling the long, uneven arc back toward Nick.

Jason Birch was one of two auxiliary police officers in Pine Lake, supplementing the two full-time members of the PD. Auxiliary officers were not paid and were not issued a weapon. Typically, auxiliary officers were called on to help with town events. Typically, Nick would not have brought an auxiliary officer to a crime scene. But today was not a typical day. The crime scene needed to be secured, Chief Ray was tied up at the county, and the second auxiliary officer was Ruth – a feisty 72-year-old blue-haired librarian with a bad hip. Pine Lake was a small department, and they made do with what they had to get the job done. So, Jason got the call.

Nick liked Jason. He was a strapping local boy in his early thirties, an avid hunter and fisher, a Carhartt aficionado, and a university graduate from the Colorado School of Mines with a degree in electrical engineering. That was a no-joke degree, and School of Mines was a no-joke school. Unlike those questionable online universities that practically gave you the degree just for paying the tuition, or those preppy Ivy Leagues and the regional wannabes that gave you a degree just because your daddy was a senator, at the School of Mines, you had to have smarts to make it. And Jason was smart. But he was also easy to talk to and had a well-paying job with an energy company that funded his never-ending supply of grown-up toys. He lived alone and told Nick he did unpaid auxiliary policing just to keep from being idle, but Nick suspected he did it because Pine Lake was his hometown from the very first breath he took, and he liked watching over it. When it came to policing, Jason had a knack for being useful, and it did not hurt that he knew the town and the mountains like the back of his hand.

Jason managed to make it back down from the woods behind the house without taking a spill on the slippery shale slope. He pulled the final stretch of tape across the driveway, and Nick heard the opening click of the pocketknife Jason always carried clipped to the inside of his jeans pocket. He tied the loose end of the tape at the mailbox and stomped off to put the remaining roll in the truck. The circle was closed. Nick took in the view of Jason's handiwork. The yellow-demarcated scene was maybe too large, but he was OK with that, knowing now that the few things he knew (or thought he knew) about what happened in that house were only a pebble at the base of a mountain of things he did not.

Which was not to say that there was a shortage of things to consider. Earlier, while Jason was still on his way here, Nick made several rounds through the property, starting just outside the house and then circling on a sweeping spiral further and further out, until he was inside the tree line, which is where he found one boot print in the moist dirt near the creek. Hiking boot? Men's? Evidence? There was always something mystical about those first minutes at the scene, when the uncertain outlines of the developing picture were just beginning to emerge. When things that were just ordinary objects in this world only a short time ago now competed for their place in this picture. Some were evidence, some not. Some would be miscategorized. Some would be missed. It was like trying to reconstruct the plot of one play based on a closet stuffed with props from a dozen. All he could do was try not to screw up, not too badly, at least. He had shadowed a couple of death investigations during his probationary assignment with Kansas City PD but had never done one solo. The basic investigative method was mostly the same as with property crimes, and he had done plenty of those. Still, *mostly the same* was not *the same*, and this was most definitely not a property crime.

The footprint wanted to be in the picture. He photographed it, stuck a yellow evidence flag next to it, and tied a strip of tape on the nearby tree. Better let the County CSI lift it – they had nicer toys than what was in the back of his Tahoe. Further out, he came across a piece of a granola bar wrapper trapped in the rocks. Photo, evidence flag, evidence bag. He was almost to the ridge. He looked back toward the house. It was below him, maybe a hundred yards away. He was still alone on the scene. This really was a quiet, secluded, wooded area. No neighbors in sight, and he had not seen a single car drive past since he got here. He hiked up to the top of the ridge, to see what was on the other side, and found himself at a clearing – a curve in a single-track dirt road. No tire prints – only boots and dog paws. Must be an old forestry road that had been turned into a hiking trail. Based on the tracks, it did not appear heavily trafficked, but it was all the more reason to have Jason tape off a generous swath around the house.

By the time he had finished his rounds and was heading back down toward the house, the Jefferson County Coroner's truck pulled up. This momentary distraction was all it took for him to almost wipe out on the slope of rolling shale. A rough but sturdy trunk of a young lodgepole pine was the only thing that saved him from disgrace and a bruised backside. *"Slick as snot,"* he heard Chief Ray's vernacular in his head, and gave thanks to the chief's practical disposition toward the dress code. *"This is Colorado,"* Ray told Nick on the first day, chewing on a toothpick and evaluating Nick's suit, tie and dress shoes. *"You *just dress for the job, OK? Dungarees, tuxedo, Speedo – I don't care what you wear. Just make sure you have somewhere to put your badge and your weapon."*

Claire said the Levi's with a button-down shirt looked *hot* and pulled one of the barely worn blazers from his teaching days out of the closet for him to keep in the truck: *"for meetings, and such."* Nick actually found the jacket useful for when he had to carry. Ray carried his sidearm openly on his belt, but as a detective, Nick preferred not to make people feel uneasy before he needed them to. Claire joked – with a straight face – that she would get him a rodeo belt buckle and a Stetson for Christmas, but he nipped this idea in the bud (at least he hoped that he did). While he would readily concede that the cowboy hat added a trademark of ruggedness and manliness to Chief Ray's silhouette, Nick felt it best advised to leave the true western accoutrements to the true westerners. He took pride in the fact that at no point of his life could anyone accuse him of being a slave to fashion. He and fashion were never friends. Not even Facebook friends. Fashion always seemed disingenuous to him, felt like posing, and he was not a poser. A closet full of blue, gray and black did a fine job of representing the full rainbow of his fashion sensibilities.

A dog barked somewhere far away. Hikers or neighbors? Jason returned from the truck, carrying the drone he used for scouting his hunting spots. Unfolded, the thing was good three feet across. The propellers whirred to life, and the drone effortlessly lifted into the air. Jason leaned into Nick, sharing the view from the impossibly huge phablet phone in his hand.

Nick had never used a drone before. The image from the camera streamed in impressive high-definition clarity. Nick could see every nailhead in the decking and every shingle on the roof. Nick could see the back of his own head. While they were watching the live feed from the drone, the drone was watching them. There was something unnatural about seeing himself looking in the other direction. He found this experience to be a bit unsettling and disorienting. It was as if there were two of him. Two pairs of eyes watching. Was this what a soul saw when it left the body?

The drone climbed higher, filling the screen with treetops and the snaking ribbon of the road. About half of a mile away, another rooftop was nestled in the thicket of trees: a neighbor. Probably the one with the barking dog. Nick would have to pay them a visit, but he did not hold his breath. This area was densely treed and sparsely populated. Even if the girl had been shot, no one would have heard anything. And the girl had not been shot.

The dirt trail he had discovered on the other side of the ridge wound around and terminated in a small parking lot just around the bend up the road. Two vehicles were parked there – an SUV and a Jeep with its top off.

"Do you know what this trail is called?"

"Scraggy Ridge."

Naturally. "I'd better run over to the trailhead and take a look. Here is the sign-in sheet." Nick reached in through the open passenger side window of the Tahoe and pulled out the clipboard with the crime scene entry log. He thought about it. "Don't let anyone in the house except the CSI."

Jason nodded. "What about the Chief?"

"Tell him I said not till after CSI."

Jason nodded and stuck the clipboard under his arm. "Can I let Brenda *out*?"

Nick glanced at the Jefferson County Coroner's truck, whose hot manifolds were still ticking intermittently under the hood from the drive up from Golden.

"Yeah."

Nick climbed into the driver's seat of his Tahoe and headed down the curvy country road. This was the outskirts. Pine Lake was not complicated. The official population was 2,183. (2,182 – he corrected himself). The downtown had that Old Colorado mountain-town charm with tall Western-style shop facades and bells on the doors. There was a trailer home community to the east, and the sparsely homed wooded hills to the west – Scraggy Ridge included. And there were virtually no tourists, unlike in the ski towns higher up the mountains. Pine Lake was just isolated enough. To the north, a half-hour's drive away, was the town of Conifer. To the east were the foothills, and beyond them was Castle Rock and the rest of the sprawling suburbs of Denver. From time to time, Nick drove out to the foothills and watched through the binoculars the giant earthmovers of Richmond and DR Horton home builders crawling in the distance, clearing out space for new neighborhoods, edging farther and farther west from Castle Rock. Their build sites were still only expansive dirt fields, with a handful of model homes complete with freshly transplanted trees and peppered with bright flags like encampments of an invading army laying siege at the defensive line of the foothills. He did not like going east.

The trailhead was less than a mile away. He parked under the pines on the side of the road. The Jeep and the small SUV – a Subaru – were still here. The lot was a small dirt-and-gravel clearing with no trash bin, no bathrooms, and no park service signs. This was just as he had suspected – a semi-official trail converted from an old forestry or mining road. There were hundreds of these in the mountains – some minimally maintained by the park service, some not at all, and most not listed on any hiking maps or apps. The lot could fit maybe eight cars on a good day, and any overflow would have had to park up and down the narrow shoulder of the road. But he doubted this trail ever got *that* busy.

The entrance to the trail itself was marked only with two upright log posts. There were the expected tracks in the dirt – boot prints, dog paws, mountain bike tires and horseshoes – but nothing of real interest. The lot itself was also clean with the exception of a spent joint in the gravel. Likely unrelated, but why not? He bagged it just in case. Somehow, "mile high" was never high enough for some. He took a few photos of the lot and made a note to check with the Park Service to see if anyone had patrolled this area over the last two days. It was a long shot.

When he pulled up at the house again, CSI was still not there, and Jason was chatting with Brenda from the Coroner's office at the end of the driveway. His folded drone lay dutifully on the tailgate of his RAM truck like a loyal old hunting dog.

"So," Nick asked, ducking under the police tape stretched across the driveway. "What's the verdict?"

Brenda had her iPad and her scrunched-up hair cap in her hand. "Looks like a suicide to me. You still want an autopsy?"

She was a pretty woman in her 50s with dirty blonde hair and eyes the color of light-blue columbines that now squinted at him in the mercilessly bright high-plains sun. She didn't flirt with him when she first met him, like some of the ER nurses. He appreciated that.

"Yes," he said.

"You sure? September is not a homicide month."

He pondered for a moment if there was possible merit to Brenda's seasonality theory on homicide. It would certainly make his job easier if he could close cases based on the weather. But then again, given the heck of the time Denver TV stations had in predicting rain in the front range, the weather was probably not the most reliable measure to go by.

He nodded to the front porch, to several large brown paper bags by the door. "That's an Amazon grocery delivery. A week's worth of food. There's ice cream in there. Was. You ever seen anyone order Häagen-Dazs and then kill themselves?"

She shook her head. "Not yet. But that wouldn't be the weirdest thing I've seen." She squinted at her iPad.

"You got time of death?" he asked.

"I'd say around thirty-six hours. Depending on how hot the water was, I can give you about a four-hour window. So, I am putting it between 6 and 10 p.m. on Wednesday, September the

8." She vigorously swiped and tapped at something. "Who called it in?"

"An anonymous tip."

She wrinkled the corner of her mouth. "Well, that's never good but still don't mean homicide. You need help tracing the number?"

"It was an email. Secure. Swiss privacy and stuff. I'm told it's completely anonymous."

"Swiss, huh? Well, that's a first in my book. Don't know much about their email, but I do love their hot cocoa on snowy days."

For a second, Nick considered bursting her bubble with regards to the origins of the Swiss Miss packets at the county office. But he had to concede to himself that his own life experience with anything Swiss prior to receiving Mike's email was hardly more impressive and likely limited to the same delicious sugary packet concoctions of hot cocoa, cheese with holes, and to discussing Carl Jung's archetype theories in his grad school literature class.

"Can you hold off taking her till later? I want CSI to process the intact scene."

"It's your scene, hon. If you say later, then later it is." She tapped through something on the screen. "I'll work on finding the next of kin. Anyone else residing with her?" Her light blues flashed at him.

He shook his head.

"You going to be the primary on this one?"

"Yep."

A white Tahoe identical to Nick's whirred around the bend in the road and pulled up behind Brenda's truck. The door with the Pine Lake PD logo swung open and a pair of weathered square-toed Ariats hit the roadside dirt. This was the other half of the Pine Lake Police Department, otherwise known as Chief Ray Mitchell. The Stetson got seated in its rightful place before the door shut, and the chief's wiry, sturdy frame ambled toward them with an easy cowboy shuffle.

"Well, hi there, Ray." Apparently, Brenda's flirtatious smile was reserved for the chief.

"Hi Brenda. How's Gracie? She had that baby yet?"

"Next week," Brenda beamed. "May be my last grandbaby. She told Chip after this one she's done."

"Can't say that I blame her after four, but I do agree the new ones are cuter." He looked to the house. "You been inside yet? What d'ya think?"

"Looks like a suicide, but your boy thinks it might be staged."

"Well, he *is* my best detective." Ray gave Nick a hearty slap on the back.

Nick indulged them with a smile. At 32, he was a grown man rather than a *boy*, and he was also the first and *only* detective in Pine Lake, but if making him feel like a teenager on the farm gave these two a sense of kinship, he was willing to suffer through it with grace. Brenda was widowed, and Ray had been divorced for almost twenty years. It wouldn't have been the worst thing if the two hooked up. The thought of Ray retiring alone with all those guns in his house terrified Nick.

"How many years has it been since your last homicide?" Brenda squinted at Ray.

"Six," Ray nodded, not having to think about it. "Unless you count that John Doe some hunters found off Buffalo Creek Road two summers ago, but he wasn't one of ours."

"And this one? Is she?"

Ray nodded again. "New in town. Bought this place from the Hendersons about six months ago."

"Poor thing," Brenda shook her head.

Nick started back toward the house. "Well, I'm going to do another walkthrough before CSI gets here."

Ray smoothed his silver mustache. "You go ahead. I'll be there in a bit. Let me get the full report from Miss Brenda here first."

Having worked with Ray for almost a year now, Nick knew that *"I'll be there in a bit"* was shorthand for *"I've seen enough crime scenes in my 40 years on the force, and I don't believe I'll be looking at this one or any others, for that matter, if I can help it, as long as I live."* He also knew that *"getting the full report from Miss Brenda"* meant talking up the cute lady about the kids, the weather, church, and whatever wild gossip Brenda brought down from the county. In other words, this was Ray's way of confirming to Nick that he was on his own and had the chief's full confidence.

This was just fine with Nick. He put on his boot covers and a new pair of gloves and went back inside. There, the air was cooler and darker. Brenda's and Ray's voices melted away behind the closed front door. The place was small but clean and modern – grays and whites. Small kitchen with new stainless appliances. Food in the fridge. Green "Clean" light on the dishwasher; someone had cleaned up. Small living room with a reading chair by the window. Small bedroom with the barnwood accent wall that was all the rage a couple of years ago. A queen-size bed with a bookshelf headboard. Bed made. Clothes put away. Purse on the dresser. Everything in its right place.

He had walked through these rooms several times already and filled his notebook with notes and his phone with pictures, but he knew he was still missing something. He was not seeing something. He could feel it. And soon, the CSI techs would descend on the scene and leave fingerprint powder and yellow numbered evidence tents all over the place. This was his last chance to walk through this place and see it the way the last person who was here before him left it. Was it the victim or someone else?

He tried to absorb the scene, but the scene itself was just one part of the picture. In death investigations, there was also victimology to consider. Victimology was the carefully pieced together study of the deceased: their environment, habits, job, recreational preferences, circles of friends, tastes in pets – anything could hold a clue to what happened to them and why. Some of this he would gather from the autopsy, and some from the interviews. But some of this was right here, embedded in the surroundings. All Nick had to do was ask the right questions. It was methodical, analytical work, and it aligned well with how his mind worked.

On the fireplace, there was a framed 5x7 photo of a man, a woman, and a little girl on the porch of a log cabin with pine trees looming to the side. The photo looked older, faded. Could be somewhere here in the Rockies. No gaming console under the TV. No drug paraphernalia. *What did she do to unwind?* Sparse furnishings and decorations indicated someone who appreciated simplicity and order in life. *Was she a high-strung control freak or a chill minimalist?* The furniture was modern, with clean, predictable lines. Probably from IKEA. Except for one antique lacquered chair with curved arms, claw-foot legs and red and gold upholstery. Maybe it came with the place? Or was it an intentional statement piece from someone with a subdued flair for style?

Nick once more examined the spine of the hardcover book left open on the reading chair – *Data Science for Artificial Intelligence Systems Design.* Hardly a beach read for most people. The fridge contained an opened bottle of red wine and various healthy food. More healthy foods were in the brown Amazon bags on the porch, with the exception of the ruined pint of ice cream. She cared about what she ate but wine and ice cream showed that she had no qualms with indulging when she wanted to. What did this say about her relations with people? Most murder victims are killed by someone they know.

If this were a murder, this is the way the house was when the killer left it.

This is the way the killer left *her.*

Nick stopped at the threshold of the bathroom. Working as a cop, he had come to expect that death was not beautiful. Not usually. Not the way he used to think of it when he was teaching literature. He used to think of death the way Romantic poets had imagined it, like that painting – *The Death of Chatterton*: a pallid youth swooned on the bed; the poison vial rolled forward from his lifeless hand. Tragic but beautiful, poetic, meaningful. That painting used to mesmerize him in college. Real crime scenes didn't do that. Real crime scenes made most people want to look away.

Before today, he had seen 57 dead bodies in his life. He wasn't sure how he knew that. He did not make a conscious effort to keep track. But he remembered them all. Fifty-six were during his six years with Kansas City PD. Not from a distance or on video, but one-on-one, or face-to-face, so to speak, as a handful of them did not have faces. Some had been dead minutes, others – days or even months. None were beautiful.

Nothing beautiful happened once the heart stopped pumping blood, unless you took morbid pleasure in the ravages of biology. Nature did not fuss about with being tidy, as it set about disassembling and recycling our mortal remains. Our own enzymes and bacteria turned with indifferent efficiency on their own hosts in feasts of self-digestion. Heat, humidity and insects – all in plentiful supply in KC – accelerated and intensified the process. In death, we all turned bloated, colorful, oozing and foul-smelling. Each of Nick's five senses have been forever imprinted with a death scene. Most with more than one.

But not this one. This one was different. Like *The Death of Chatterton*, of all the senses it captured only his gaze. The girl's face was a pale moon over the still red pond of her bathtub. Her head was resting on her right shoulder. Her eyes were closed. Her face was peaceful – she could have been sleeping. Her right arm, white as alabaster, was draped over the edge of the tub. A crisscross cut on her wrist. Dried blood on her hand. A small pearl-handled folding knife on the dark slate floor tiles. Bloody fingerprints on the handle and a small puddle of congealed blood next to the white enameled clawfoot of the tub. The scene was neat, as if it were composed with the key details in focus in the foreground, contrasting from the background. A very clean bathroom. The cut. The blood. The knife. A forgotten college art term popped into his head – *Clair-obscur*. It meant selective use of light and dark in the painting. *Clair-obscur* was the artist's deliberate decision about what to show and what to obscure. If someone had staged this scene, what did they choose to obscure?

If this was murder, it was the cleanest one he had ever seen.

He studied her wrist. Impossibly thin and white. There were several cuts. A few shallow ones, just through the skin, and the long, decisive X from the wrist down to almost the middle of her forearm. The edges were now dry, shrunken and slightly curled upwards. He could see the thin layer of her skin, the light pinks of her tissue and the silvery-white threads of her sinews. *Down the road, not across the street,* as they say. These were not the cross-the-wrist cries for help. These cuts were meant. Deep enough to sever the radial artery.

He watched her motionless form for a moment, trying to decipher the answers in the lines of her face. The dead had a presence. Not their ghost – he'd never seen one of those. But it was something. Or maybe the absence of something. Like the pull of a void. Like the gravity of a black hole slowly bleeding energy out from this world and into the next. He could always feel it when he was around a body. He suspected others could not, and so he never told anyone. To them, the dead were inanimate.

"Lisa." He said her name out loud, as someone would when she was alive, calling her from another room in this house. For just an instant, he could see her alive, could feel her presence within these walls, like an echo. But then it dissipated again, like her last breath, and only the absence was left.

Lisa Benoche. Twenty-five years old, according to the ID in her purse. Educated. Neither rich nor poor. No evident vices to speak of, so far. Nothing to indicate the crime scene had been staged. Everything here fit and made sense. A textbook suicide, as long as he could ignore the recording.

Why would anyone in the world want to kill you?

He stood in the doorway of the bedroom and examined the small device of gray fabric and polished metal the size of a coffee cup nestled between the books on the headboard.

"Lexi?"

Lexi was playing dead. Or she just didn't talk to strangers.

Damn it, Mike! A copy of the recording would have been nice. Nick did his best replaying it in his head. There was the sound of a struggle, but there were no signs of a struggle here. There was also the sound of something breaking or scattering on the floor. It sounded like a hard floor, but the bedroom was carpeted. The bathroom was tiled, but there was nothing there. The rest of the house had hardwoods. He inspected the short hallway outside the bathroom and then moved toward the kitchen. Next to the front door was a small, tall wooden side table, like the one people put keys on. The curved front edge had a scuffed flat spot about an inch long. It looked like a fresh impact with a few lifted splinters and light unstained wood showing through. He turned on his flashlight and got down on his knees. Clean floor. Too clean? Not even a dust bunny. But from the thin gap between the baseboard and the floor, a sparkling sliver of glass glimmered back at him. He took a picture of the location and then used one of his business cards to nudge the shard out into the open. It was the size of a fingernail and had teal glazing on one side. He bagged it.

An unfamiliar male voice blared outside, breaking the serenity of the scene. CSI? Nick took one last look around and opened the front door. A black unmarked Explorer SUV was parked at the end of the driveway. A man and a woman, both in suits, were talking to Ray. City detectives, if Nick had to guess.

"Un-fucking-believable!" The man blew up, glaring in Nick's direction and clearly wanting to ensure Nick heard him. "We drive to the edge of the fucking BFE for nothing, and now your fucking rookie will tie up our forensics while he fumbles a fucking suicide!"

The man dropping the f-bombs threw his arms out in exasperation, and Nick watched him spin around and stride angrily back to the Explorer, where he shut himself inside on the passenger side and furiously thumbed at the screen of his phone.

The woman turned back to Ray, Nick and Brenda: "You'll have to excuse my partner. He is having a rough week."

"What's the matter with him?" Ray inquired with genuine amiability.

"Oh, take your pick – caseload, marriage, drinking. You've seen the movies." She tilted her head and studied Nick from behind a pair of Ray-Bans. She added a smile, to clarify this was a dry joke. "Hi, I am Jana Barnes," she stuck out her hand to Nick.

He shook it. Her touch was smooth, warm and firm. Her shirt cuff peeking from under the sleeve of her fitted navy jacket was pure white and starched. Her shiny auburn hair was pulled back into a neat ponytail.

"The county dispatch must not have updated their directory," Ray offered. "I did tell them we had our own detective now."

"Sorry you drove out all this way," Nick said, catching on to the cause of this conflict. "You are welcome to take a look. I think Jason has the entry log sheet." He looked to Jason who was eating a sandwich and taking in the spectacle from the tailgate of his Dodge RAM truck.

Barnes kept her gaze on Nick. "Oh, I think you've got it under control here. And I'd better take Davis back to the office before he blows." She glanced back at the Explorer. "A belated welcome to the county. We *are* glad you are here. God knows, we need help. And if *you* need help with anything, you just let me know." She handed Nick her card and walked back down the driveway. Nick wondered how she managed to walk on the shale driveway in her high-heel dress boots.

The familiar sound behind him was Ray chuckling. Nick turned around.

"*You just let me know, now,*" Ray nudged Brenda with his elbow and smoothed his mustache.

"What? She seems nice." Nick was already exhausted with where this was going.

"Oh, Jana's nice, all right." Brenda gave him a wink, and she and Ray burst out laughing.

Nick sighed. The CSI truck pulled in and the tech began unloading big black plastic Pelican cases from the back. Lights, camera, action. Jason, probably feeling bored, put away his sandwich and headed over to help the tech. What had been a quiet country road in front of this house just a few hours ago was now resembling a police convention.

Nick left the CSI tech to do his job and told Jason he could head home now. Thank God for Jason. Leaving Ray and Brenda to chat on the porch of the house, Nick headed back to his Tahoe and sunk into the sunbaked cabin. He checked his coffee cup already knowing the result – empty. He took a reticent sip of warm water from the plastic bottle in his other cupholder. This day was a blur.

When he put his phone on the console, he noticed it blinking at him with its tiny blue LED light – missed messages. The first one was a text from Mike: "*Anything?*" He left it unanswered. The second one was from Jason with a link to the photos from the drone. Nick clicked the link and scrolled through the thumbnails. One of them caught his eye, and he tapped on it. In the zoomed out, downward panorama, everything on the ground looked tiny. Tiny Nick and Jason stood in the driveway, inside the jagged noose of yellow police tape fixed around the tiny house, the final place on this earth where Lisa Benoche had been alive.

Thr33

"The fucker has twenty-five minutes left," the message from Roses blipped into the Tox chat window.

The link to download and install Tox was the second message Roses had ever sent Kat in the private support group on Facebook. The first one was "Wanna have some *real* fun?" just as Kat was half-way into a post on the power of positive affirmations for recovering from childhood trauma. Kat clicked the link and installed Tox, and the first message Roses sent her on Tox was "Don't ever click shit someone you don't know sends you." And then a smiley face.

Tox, Roses said, was the best she could do security-wise without getting her on Tor. Kat thought about asking what Tor was but figured it was one of those "if you have to ask, you're not ready for it" situations. She was fine with that – of all the words she could use to describe herself, *techie* was not one. *Trusting* was also not one, but somehow, she trusted Roses. Roses was different. Many people in the group overshared, and some were too new-agey for Kat, but she always liked Roses' contributions– short, pragmatic and with an edge.

That was over a year ago.

Since then, she had accompanied Roses on dozens of "cases" from the comfort of her couch or a coffee shop booth, glued to Roses' shared screen – a window into another world, one that beckoned her day after day and made her look forward to opening the clamshell of her laptop. Roses was in an all-female hacktivist group. Hacktivists, Kat learned, were hackers with a cause. Roses' group called themselves f8sabitch, and their cause was to *"take down perv scumbags."* When Kat first heard the group's name, she thought it was corny, but now she liked it. Fate – *f8* – was indeed *a bitch* in Kat's personal experience, but turning it around and pointing its business end at someone else was surprisingly empowering. And, so, time after time, she watched Roses do her craft. It was like being on a citizen's ride-along, vigilante style.

Today, they were *doxing*. Kat knew what that meant. It meant Roses had been snooping around some strangers' computers and cloud drives (and when was she ever not?) and had uncovered a cache of illegal porn or snuff. She then scraped up whatever personal information she could find on this poor schmuck, and usually it was everything he had – name, address, phone, email, date of birth, social security number, credit card accounts. It was amazing what Roses could dig up in a matter of just a few hours. And once she held in her hand this digital power of God over the unsuspecting moron's head, she would release it. No wicked schemes, no devious ploys. Just a concise post to 8chan or the Tor board, detailing the perv's list of offenses and including his complete personal information, the latter acting as blood in the water to ensure action. With that, Roses' part was done. The Internet would dole out its own justice, she said, and Kat believed her. Minutes after being doxed, the unaware moron would have his identity stolen ten times over. By the time he'd wake up the next morning, his world would have already changed zip codes several levels down into his personal hell. Someone would have maxed out his credit cards, his phone would be blowing up with an endless stream of anonymous texts and disgusting photos, his social media accounts would be hijacked and defaced, and if the web hooligans felt inspired, there would even be a pizza delivery guy with thirty pizzas at his door, expecting cash, and right behind the pizza guy would be a tire-screeching, siren-wailing squad of

SWAT cars responding to an anonymous call about an armed domestic hostage situation at his address.

The schmuck was fucked. Doxing would make sure of that. Child molesters and dirty cops probably had quicker and less painful deaths in prison showers.

But at the moment, this particular schmuck was not being doxed. Not yet. This schmuck was special. This time, Roses had hooked a *real whale* and sat on him for almost a week, listening in on his communications using a packet sniffer. This one wasn't just downloading contraband porn. This one frequented a sex trafficking service in NYC and had souvenir videos of underage girls tied to the beds to prove it. For this one, doxing alone seemed too meager and impersonal. For this one, Roses opened up a fresh level of hell.

This one, Roses wanted to rattle to his core before the swift axe of doxing fell. And, as Roses said, few things rattled a perv more than ransomware. And, naturally, she was right. Kat had seen this with her own eyes when Roses had hacked the pervs' webcams. It was all in that brief moment when they first turned on the laptop and were greeted with a red screen and a large 24-hour timer ticking down the seconds, the minutes and the hours with a polite message informing them that all their files had been encrypted and would be made public on their social media unless payment were made to the included bitcoin wallet. An honest trade – bitcoins for the decryption key.

23:59:59 – your move.

Kat relished watching their faces during that first brief moment. Unaware of being watched, they plunged head-first through the first four stages of grief – the initial paralyzing Shock, the brief disbelief of Denial, the involuntary outburst of Anger, and a few futile Bargaining attempts to bypass the doom, usually in a frenzied staccato of several keys – [Esc], [Backspace], [Enter] – followed by a hurried system reboot.

23:56:20 – hello again, fucker :).

By the time the screen returned to the unrelenting counter, the dizzying fall of emotions was over, and Depression had set in, in the sickly company of Anxiety and Fear.

Bitcoins, or else your life as you know it will be over.

It was as if they had lost a loved one. It was like cutting a junkie off from the supply. The precious device that had been their confidant, their enabler, their sidekick and guide on their perverse excursions had suddenly turned against them. Now, with their most private indiscretions crammed into this red ticking doomsday clock in front of them, they had hit their lowest low. They were exposed like a frat boy on hazing night. They'd been found out and they were powerless over what was to come next. In those moments, Kat's deep-seated anger would sometimes retreat, and she would actually feel sorry for them. It was as if all along there had been a good, law-abiding citizen in the back seat of this joyride drive-by, and she had just woken up. Despite what had been done to Kat herself, doing this to them did not always feel good. But Roses would always set her straight. This wasn't about the individual schmuck *du jour*, and it wasn't about Kat or even Roses. This was hacktivism, and hacktivism was about weaponizing anger. Hacktivism was anti-establishment. Hacktivism was about power, and power was about taking away someone else's.

And, so, this was the fate Roses was now in the process of administering onto her *whale*. Ransomware with the added threat of doxing always made for a potent incentive. But this whale was not biting. The neon-yellow seconds kept on ticking ominously on the blood-red screen.

00:18:50

She had never seen the counter get this low.

"Do you think 15 bitcoins is too much? That's over $750K," she typed.

"This douche is the CFO of a big fat bank," Roses' reply blipped in almost instantaneously.

The douche can afford 3/4 million – she finished Roses' laconic response in her head.

She used to wonder what Roses looked like. Her Facebook profile had no photos, videos or updates of any kind. No cats, dogs, babies, selfies or food. No linked Insta or Snap. No timeline, no birth date, no friends. She imagined Roses relished that last fact. Naively, Kat had actually tried to friend Roses on Facebook when they first started talking, only to be ignored. The only thing Kat knew for sure was that Roses' full online name was *Roses Are Red*, but everyone in the group called her just *Roses*. After all this time, Kat accepted that it didn't really matter what Roses looked like. She knew Roses valued anonymity above all, and so she never asked. She just pictured her in a black tank top, with tattoos, piercings, and neon orange spiked hair on some days or a pixie haircut on others. That was *her* Roses. But for all she knew, Roses could have been a suburban soccer mom sitting next to a labradoodle. What was that meme? *On the Internet, no one knows you are a dog.* She supposed that was true for everybody else, but she was certain Roses *would* know.

00:15:11

"How is *DearJohn*?" Roses pinged.

DearJohn was the codename Roses gave to Kat's personal project. Kat liked the name. It was an opening that foreboded the ending. A hello that meant goodbye.

"Good." *DearJohn* was now in phase two, the main event, so to speak. "But too early to tell," she added.

"OK. Let me know if you need any more help."

"Thx"

"You got balls."

"?"

"To do what you are doing. It's no basic smash'n grab hackjob. You're into serious shit, girl."

Being complimented by Roses was a mixed feeling – an acknowledgement of her talent coming from a career criminal.

Still, she could not push down elation. She did not want to. This was indeed *her* "case." She had come up with the plan all on her own and Roses helped her make it real. No, it was certainly not a basic smash'n grab. It wasn't something that could be done overnight, or even over a few weeks. Like a trap, it required planning and patience. It could very well take months, but she had time. She was playing the long game with this one. It had to be right.

The clock froze: *00:13:01*

"Cha-ching," Roses pinged.

"Get the FUCK OUT!"

"Hell yeah!" A wine glass emoji. She watched Roses open the TORwallet app, where 15 bitcoins sat cozily on the balance line. Kat did the conversion on her laptop – 785,070 U.S. dollars.

"And would the ladies care to make an anonymous donation this evening?" Roses typed.

Right now, Roses had an English accent in Kat's head.

"Yes, yes we would," she smiled, topping off her own glass and wishing she could really do a celebratory clank with Roses right now.

"And will this donation be to the Center for Child Abuse Prevention, the Battered Women Foundation, or the World Coalition to End Sex Trafficking?"

"Why not make it all three?"

"Excellent choice."

She watched Roses deftly divvy up the newly deposited 15 bitcoins into equal transfers to three accounts. And then, before Kat had time for a second thought, Roses hit *Send*. Poof – the small crypto fortune disappeared from her wallet and whirred across the web to its new homes.

Chills tingled up Kat's spine. $785K was the largest take she had ever seen Roses score. And she just watched her give it all away. She wasn't surprised that Roses could do it – *f8sabitch* upheld high standards of ethics and integrity when it came to hacktivism. That's not to say that Roses never pursued her own targets of opportunity (she had to make a living somehow, and Kat was pretty sure Roses did not punch in for an 8-5 like the rest of the mere mortals), but she had never seen Rose mix business with pleasure (although, to think of it, Kat was not entirely sure which was which for Roses).

The TORwallet showed a balance of 0 BTC. The wine and the freefall from $785K gave Kat a head rush. She wondered if she could have done the same if she was in Roses' shoes. $785K could have gone a long way. She could have run away. Become someone else. Again.

"Did you send him the key?" Kat typed into the chat.

A smiley face rolled in.

"You are going to dox him anyways?" Kat already knew the answer.

"Already done. Did you ever doubt me?"

Kat smiled, picturing the panic on the other side of the perv's screen. "Not for a sec."

"I hope the fucker gets swatted. Same time Tuesday?"

4

The boy's skull cracked. A thick, moist, squishy, sickly crack of breaking bone. It was this sound that instantly made Nick open his eyes. As if paralyzed by the vision, he listened, motionless and breathless, to the darkness of the bedroom, but all he could hear and feel was the racing drumbeat in his own chest. *It was a dream.* He drew in a slow, deep breath as his mind began to untangle from the clutches of the nightmare. *Wasn't it?* The echo of the crack was still ringing in his ears. The rock, rough and heavy, still felt real in his hand, familiar like a phantom limb.

Claire was breathing evenly next to him. *What the hell was this?* – he thought. He never had dreams. Not anymore. Well, maybe he did, but he never remembered them. Claire had dreams – vivid, dynamic, weird, and she was always excited to tell him over breakfast. But not him. He just sunk into a black void when he closed his eyes, and then he resurfaced again when his alarm went off. Given the things he had seen as a cop, he was OK with the black void.

Maybe it was something outside. Something real, like the phone ringing in your dream and in the real world at the same time, he thought and listened intently. The house was quiet, and so was the street. The neighbor's dogs weren't barking. He resisted the temptation to look at the clock – if it were an hour or less before his alarm, he knew he wouldn't be able to go back to sleep. Oblivion was bliss. He turned away from the edge of the bed and toward Claire's warm breath. He closed his eyes.

When his alarm went off, he was in deep sleep again. 4:50 am. It used to be 5:00, but he conceded the extra ten minutes of sleep to his workweek mornings as part of the New Year's resolution this year. He had done the mental math, and it added up to almost two extra days' worth of waking hours for the year. It seemed like a wise decision at the time.

He silenced his phone mechanically, without looking, and sat up on the edge of the bed. He wasn't awake yet, but he had perfected this reflex to the point where Claire didn't even register the one single *beep* the alarm was able to emit before he killed it. He squeezed and opened his eyes as his mind was still trying to claw out of the sleepy fog. The faint, watered-down glowing rectangle of the window was all the light he needed to make his way to the bathroom without knocking into things in the dark.

There, he turned on the hot water faucet. He wasn't sure why, exactly – he was never there long enough for the water to actually warm up. Maybe it was just a trick of self-deception: splashing the still-cold water on his face woke him up just enough to pull on his running clothes. By 5:10, he was outside the closing garage door, shivering in the morning chill and fitting in his earbuds. At the end of the street, the dirt trail began – a wooded shortcut to the lake. This was his time – the twilight before the dawn. This was a world that was no longer dark but also not yet illuminated. The world of shadows with no edges. As his breath settled into a rhythm and his feet found their beat, he could think. That's when he remembered his dream.

5

Nick returned from the run to find Claire already finishing up in the kitchen. He settled into his chair, relishing the burning sensation in his legs and the fading wave of post-run endorphins. Claire was hustling between the fridge and the sink, putting away her dishes and packing her lunch. She had her light-blue scrubs on today, which were his favorite. There was something enchanting about the combination of that color, her pale skin and her blonde hair. It made her glow.

"Your socks match," he noted. Lately, she had been in the habit of mismatching them. It started innocently enough one day when she paired two eligible units whose partners went MIA during the run-ins with the laundry appliances. But eventually, this progressed into a wanton rebellion against the most fundamental rule in Nick's fashion book (thin as it were). It was as if her left and right sides had different personalities.

She looked at her feet. "It's Friday." She shrugged one shoulder. "I have nothing against Fridays." She grabbed her coffee mug and keys. "I'll see you tonight," she leaned down and smooched his lips.

"OK, have a good day. Love you." He inhaled her lingering perfume.

"Love you too," she echoed from the entryway, getting on her shoes. "Bye." The door shut.

"Bye," he said to the empty house.

Today was autopsy day. His first since KC. He thought about this, as he showered and ate breakfast. Autopsy was in the natural order of things. Death was not the abrupt end of a chapter most people thought it to be. Even a violent death wasn't. There was nothing abrupt about it. People today were woven into the fabric of the world, wired into it with myriad synapses that kept on firing, oblivious that the person had already taken their final breath. The final breath was just the beginning of the end. The next morning, their wakeup alarms still would go off. The emails they sent to their coworkers the day before would still be waiting to be read and replied to. Their phones would *buzz* and *ding* periodically with their social media apps, which, panicked by the user's prolonged inactivity, would fire off one alert and notification after another, like the resuscitating jolts of a defibrillator, trying everything in their power to get the user's thumbs swiping again. The post office would keep delivering their mail. Telemarketers would keep calling. The inbound signs of life would be plentiful. But the person would have gone dark. It is as if they had gone on a trip out of the country, to unplug beyond the reach of cellphones and Wi-Fi.

And in a way, they did. Their souls may have moved on, but their bodies still had a journey of many days ahead of them, and many new people to meet. A journey of a thousand miles began with a single step, as the saying went. And for the recently departed, that first step typically meant a ride to the nearest medical examiner's office. There, like at a passport checkpoint in a foreign airport, their arrival would be officially documented, including an all-new set of photos, because no one ever looked quite the same as their IDs when they landed here. And you could be certain that Customs here would thoroughly go through all of your stuff.

For Lisa Benoche, this meant a ride to the County Coroner's office in Golden – a charming touristy town nestled in the foothills just west of Denver.

For Nick, this was his first visit as well. Golden was a forty-minute drive away from Pine Lake – first, down from the mountains on Highway 285, and then north on 470. It was an easy drive, compared to many others in the mountains, especially on a warm, bright, fall day. A town of Gold Rush fame, Golden was the gateway into the big mountains. The living came here for easy hikes, hipster eats and the Coors brewery tours. The dead came here because someone decided they had something to declare.

He drove around the large county government complex, following his phone's directions to the coroner's office. It ended up being a two-story edifice with a sign that identified it simply as the Dakota Building.

This was to be his second meeting with Lisa, and probably the last one. She was with Brenda now, who was assisted by the autopsy technician and the autopsy photographer. Lisa's three medically trained visitors were in full protective gear, with green scrubs, booties, face shields, face masks, and latex gloves. Through the glass of the long observation window, Nick watched them attend to her with choreographed efficiency, pausing their practiced movements just long enough to be punctuated with flashes from the camera's ring light.

At the center of this costumed gathering, Lisa herself was lying nude on the stainless-steel table. Seeing her thin, pale arm made Nick think of Claire, and how she always got so cold when they went into a store or a restaurant with air conditioning. The air in this building was cool, and it was probably even cooler inside the autopsy suite. The dead did not get the shivers or goosebumps, but the cold stainless-steel slab somehow still felt inhumanely unfair. At his first autopsy, he had resolved to the likelihood that he himself would one day end up on a table like this. But his mind refused even the possibility of a consideration of it happening to Claire.

By the time he got here, the long Y incision stemming from below Lisa's navel and branching out all the way to her shoulders had already been opened wide to let in the bright artificial light and for her attendants to take things out. She had herself now become a crime scene – to be inspected, documented, dictated into Brenda's recorder and thoroughly photographed.

He was glad he had missed the cutting and the opening. That was his intention. He was OK with most of what followed in the autopsy, but that initial incision and then the cutting and the opening of the rib cage always made him look away. It was a violent and intrusive act. Brenda looked up, noticing Nick standing in the window out of the corner of her eye. She gave him a nod with her face shield. Judging by the state of Lisa's disassembly, they were wrapping up.

He sat and waited, watching Brenda make a trip to the scale with Lisa's liver. He thought of the dream from last night. He could still vividly see that kid's face smeared with blood. The blood glistened, flowing from the rough, dark crevices of his caved-in skull. Somehow, the kid's face was familiar. But it was distant and uncertain, like a childhood memory. Weird. He rubbed his tired eyes. Last night's interrupted sleep was filling his head with fog.

Brenda tapped on the window and waved him in.

She met him at the door and pushed up the face shield with the back of her nitrile-gloved hand: "You alright, hon?"

Nick nodded and got out his notepad. The autopsy technician was closing Lisa up.

"So, what you got, doc?"

"Well, I'll wait to do the final report till the bloodwork comes back. But so far, this girl looks clean. Heart, liver, lungs, endocrine system – all unremarkable." Nick knew in Coroner talk, *unremarkable* meant good. "She could have lived a long, healthy life."

"So, if you had to call it now, what would you say?"

"So far, the manner of death is consistent with suicide."

Of course – the girl was clean, the crime scene was clean, there was no evidence of a crime, and Lisa was not talking. He much preferred meeting people while they were alive.

"Are you sure?"

She shrugged. "No evidence of struggle. Lacerations severed the radial artery on both wrists. Hesitation cuts on the wrists consistent with suicide."

"Can those be faked?"

She pushed her face shield higher, her faded blues looking at him from below the clear plastic visor. "Oh, sure, like most things. But given no evidence to the contrary, the simplest explanation prevails for now."

He wrote down *hesitation cuts*. "What's the going lead time on labs?"

"Four to six."

"Days?" It was worth a shot.

"Weeks."

He nodded. "Can we also order full toxicology?"

She gave him an amused look. "Hon, this looked like a suicide yesterday and it still does after the autopsy. But Ray says you are good, so I will go along. So…Do *you* think we need to do a full toxicology?"

He cursed Mike in his head again. He wished he already had the recording from Lexi, but it could still be days or weeks before the manufacturer would respond to the request. He could not hold the body indefinitely for no apparent reason. So, until he got the recording, he had to look like an idiot, doubling down on everyone's time and resources against the evidence. He sighed and realized he did it out loud.

"I do," he said. He felt out of sorts.

"OK, I'll order it."

"Thank you." He tapped his pen on the notepad. "Do you think it could have been staged?"

"For someone else to cut her wrists?"

"Yes. What would it take?"

"Well, there are no defensive wounds, no ligature marks, and nothing under her fingernails. She would have had to be unconscious for someone to do this to her without a struggle.

She could have been drugged, but I am guessing you already know that since you want full toxicology."

"Could she have been knocked unconscious?"

"There is no evidence of blunt force trauma to the head."

"Strangulation?" He was grasping at straws.

"We would have seen some external signs – bruising of neck tissue, petechial hemorrhaging in the conjunctiva of the eyes and on the eyelids. We don't have any of that."

This was turning out to be exactly as enlightening as he had feared. "OK, anything else you got for me?"

She went back to one of the tables and returned with a small plastic evidence bag.

"Just these," she said, handing it to him. Two silver stud earrings with amber-colored stones. "Forensics have already processed. You can release to the family, if you'd like."

6

By the time Nick pulled into the gravel lot in front of the station, the brain fog had condensed into a headache. The more he thought about the Lexi recording, the less plausible it seemed. Was it even real? Maybe it was a glitch. Glitches happened. Like the frequent flyer emails he kept getting for someone named Derek. Maybe the wires in the cloud got crossed. Maybe Mike did not trace it to the right account. Maybe it was from another address, and he was chasing something that wasn't there. The only thing he knew for sure was that he needed to get this elusive recording into evidence and analyzed. That was the only way to be certain. But there was still no word from the manufacturer. He decided that if he had not heard anything by Monday, he would put more pressure on Mike and get it from him. He was not above playing the bad cop.

The Pine Lake Police Department was headquartered in a pale-yellow ranch double-wide with lapboard siding and a large porch with two rocking chairs gifted to the department by a town artisan named Arnie. The same chairs and other Rocky Mountain crafts were on exhibit for sale at Arnie's shop further down on Summit Street, next to Millie's Café. Arnie was also the one to carve the large wooden sign that was installed in a timber frame at the base of three lodgepole pines in front of the station and that read *Pine Lake Police Department – est. 1885*. As Nick got out of his truck, cursing Lexi, he pondered what high-tech evidence looked like 136 years ago.

Seeing Nick walk in, Patty sprung up from her perch at the front desk and grabbed her keys. "You going to be in for a bit?"

She was a lively, plump lady with short curly dark hair and a disarming smile.

He took the trouble to reply even though she was already half-way to the door with her purse on her arm. "As far as I know."

"OK, I just need to run to the store real quick. We are all out of Peanut M&M's. You need anything?"

"Umm. Coffee?"

"The cupboard is full," she replied, already in the double glass entryway.

"Is Ray out?"

"He's in Conifer but should be back soon."

Besides providing dispatch services to the department, Patty also spent considerable time ensuring that everything at the station, including Ray, stayed on track. The Peanut M&M's in question were a critical component to this mission, with Ray being responsible for depleting her supplies, thanks to his mid-afternoon sugar-snacking safaris through the office, which he paired with extended social calls at Patty's desk, in Nick's office, or with Jason, Ruth, and whoever else happened to stop by. Ray liked people, and Nick would not at all be surprised if the chief opened a bar in town after retiring.

Patty vanished, leaving Nick in the silence of the empty station. He poured himself a coffee, popped two Tylenols from the drawer under the coffee machine, and went into his office. But as soon as he settled at his desk, car tires crunched through the gravel outside. He swiveled his chair around to catch a silver Jeep Cherokee pulling in. *Rental* – he noted the sticker on the windshield.

A stout old man with short gray hair got out of the driver's seat. He reached in the back, pulled out a Carhartt vest and put it on. A woman with long dark hair exited from the passenger side. She clutched her purse and pulled her cardigan tightly across her front. It was a bit breezy today, and people from out of state often thought the fall here to be chilly, despite the abundant sunshine.

Nick heard them walking up the porch steps – the old man's boots plodding heavily, concealing the woman's light, quick steps. The tin cowbell clanged on the door – Nick had visitors. He took his coffee to go and went out to the front. As soon as he saw the woman's face, he knew exactly who she was before she had to say a word.

"Hello, I'm Lori Benoche," she said and started crying.

***

The old man was Lori's father, Clint. Nick brought them into his office and let them get situated while he went to get a water for Lori and a coffee for Clint. Lori sipped her water, sobbing, and tears welled again in her eyes, as she told Nick about receiving the call from the JeffCo Coroner's office. They took the first flight they could from Omaha to Denver and drove from the airport straight to the coroner's office in Golden to identify the body. They must have just missed him there after the autopsy, Nick thought. Then they went to Lisa's house…

After mentioning her daughter's name, Lori could no longer continue her narrative, having completely given in to the gut-wrenching grief.

"The house is still taped off, so we didn't go in," Clint finished for her solemnly.

Clint's sad eyes and hardened face kept his grief locked away. His hand gently rubbed his daughter's back as she wept.

Nick wasn't very good with people's emotions, but his prior experience had taught him that the two best things to do in such situations were to listen and to give empathy. He knew he could be better at both. He moved the Kleenex box to the corner of his desk, closer to Lori. These two people had just spent the day in a breathless rush to get here, with no time to just sit and deal with this new reality of their lives. And now they were here, far from home, on what was probably the worst day of their lives. All he could do was give them some comfort and serve as a silent witness to their tragedy. The two generations of one family – the past and the present – having just lost their future.

"I just can't believe she would do this to herself. She was so excited about this job," Lori said, bunching up the soggy tissue in her hand. Nick moved his trashcan to the outside of his desk. "She loved the mountains. Her job contract was only a year, but she still bought a house. She said the real estate market was hot here, and she would make money even if she sold after the year. She was good with numbers and money like that. She got it from her dad – he was an engineer. He died when she was fifteen." She suddenly stopped this stream of consciousness, lost in the maze of sad memories, her gaze fixed on something beyond the walls of Nick's office. Her tears were dry for the moment.

"Mrs. Benoche," Nick said. "When was the last time you talked to Lisa?"

"Umm, early last week?" She pulled out her phone and scrolled through her call log. "Yes – last Tuesday."

"How did she seem to you?"

Lori shook her head, biting her lip to hold back the next wave of tears. "Good. I think. She was planning a hiking trip with a girl from work. Dani, I think was her name. Have you talked to her?"

"Not yet. Her employer is my next stop. Is it…C.V. Services?" he checked the note he made and circled in his notebook based on the business cards he had found in the victim's purse.

She shook her head. "No, that's just the consulting company. I think they are in California. She was contracting through them for an IT company here in Denver. If you call C.V. Services, I am sure they can tell you which one."

He nodded, taking notes. "I am sorry to have to ask this, but did Lisa have a history of depression or previous suicide attempts?"

She shook her head again. "She was always a happy kid. She went through a rough patch in high school after her father died. We both did. She did some drugs for a while, nothing hard. She told me everything, always. I helped her anyway I could and just tried to keep her safe. She went to counseling for a bit, and she pulled through. Got through college with good grades, got a great job. She was just starting to blossom, to become her own adult person. I find it so difficult to understand why she would…" Her chin trembled, and she pulled a fresh tissue from the box and pressed it into her eyes.

"This may seem like a strange question, but did Lisa have any enemies? Someone who was giving her a hard time or would want to hurt her?"

She raised her eyes, cloudy with tears. "Do you think someone did this to her?"

The last thing Nick wanted to do was give this grieving woman more unanswered questions and more cause for sorrow. He shook his head. "We have no evidence to suggest this, but we thoroughly investigate all unattended deaths to rule out any other possibilities before we decide on the official manner of death."

Lori bit her lip and turned her red eyes to the corner of the ceiling, forcing her brain through the mental Rolodex of people and events. She shook her head and her eyes settled back on Nick: "Lisa did not have enemies. Everyone loved her."

"What about relationships? Was she seeing anyone?"

She shook her head. "Not for a while. She was never very outgoing, and after college she really poured herself into her career. The last steady boyfriend she had was in high school. She dated a few guys in college, but nothing serious."

Nick nodded. He'd still want to check her phone for dating apps once forensics got it unlocked. He doubted most young people kept their mothers in the loop when it came to things like Tinder and Grindr.

The cowbell jangled in the entryway, and the unmistakable shuffle of the chief's boots announced his return. Shortly, his grinning face popped into Nick's doorway. Seeing Nick occupied, he turned away, but Nick called him back.

"This is our Chief of Police Ray Mitchell. Ray – this is Mrs. Lori Benoche and her father Clint. They just flew down from Omaha."

Ray's face melted, and Nick thought Ray himself would tear up. "Oh gosh, dear, I am so sorry for your loss," he took Lori's hand into both of his. "What a tragedy," he said, taking Clint's hand next and giving him a one-arm hug and a comforting pat on the back. "Where are you folks staying?"

Lori looked at her father and then back at Ray. "We don't know yet. Didn't have time to make arrangements before we left."

"Hey, don't you worry. Let me call Larry at Howard Johnson's. He'll put you up, no charge. It's just off I-25. Hot breakfast every morning. Let me get you the address."

And just like that, Ray had given them comfort. And it was genuine, not a canned platitude he could have perfected over the decades on the job. Nick could have hugged the old cowboy right then.

Lori looked back to Nick. "Should we go back to the coroner's office? Do you think they will release the body today?"

Nick shook his head. He could not tell them he was not ready to have Brenda release the body. Not yet. "You just go settle in, get some rest and freshen up. I will call and let you know when they are ready for you. And I can take you there when the time comes. I may have more questions for you, anyways."

7

The boy's skull cracked. A thick, moist, squishy, sickly crack of bone breaking under Nick's blow.

FUCK! was his first waking thought. He sat up and felt cold sweat rolling off his forehead. Claire stirred next to him in the dark.

"Are you OK?" she asked and cleared her throat.

"Yeah, sorry. Just a weird dream."

She put her warm hand on him. He felt around in the dark to find his water bottle on the bedside table and took a drink.

The dream was just as before. The same face, the same rock, the same crack. Why would he dream the exact same random thing twice? He was no expert on dreams, but a repeated dream seemed abnormal even for him. The same nightmare twice in two nights. *Maybe more?* He did not get nightmares. He did have his share of weird dreams when he first started with KCPD, but those dreams always had some anchor in reality, and they never repeated. This one was totally off the wall, and yet it left a cold sliver of unease in him.

He forced his mind to stop analyzing. What he needed now was sleep. His pillow felt hot and stifling, so he flipped it over to the cool, dry side. With his eyes closed, he focused on breathing: counting off slow, even breaths, trying to get his heart to settle down. He did not get far past *twenty* before he drifted back into the darkness.

***

Today was Claire's day off. Nick came down to the kitchen to find her still in her sweats, digging for something in the cabinet while the kitchen faucet was running and the TV in the living room was blabbing at half-volume through the morning news.

"Are you sure you need to go in today? It's Saturday," she asked, pouring him a cup of coffee.

"Yeah, I should. I need to read through the preliminary autopsy and forensics reports. And check on the victim's family while I am at it. Just a couple of hours, tops."

She looked at him seriously. "You're a good man, Nick Severs."

"I just don't want to mess this up. If I do, there is no one else to blame." He took a sip of coffee and thought of Lori crying in his office yesterday and Clint's stoic, grief-hardened face.

Claire sat down across from him with her coffee, and he gave her a smile.

"What are *you* doing today?" he asked.

She shrugged. "Thought about going to the gym but may work in the yard instead. Haven't decided yet. My flowers need some attention. Are we still on with Mike and Amy tonight?"

He nodded, drinking his coffee.

"What time? Seven?"

"Yep."

"OK. I'll be ready. It will be nice to meet them."

"They are dying to meet you, too. Thanks to your Instagram and Facebook, they think you are too good for me. At least that's what Mike said."

"I like them already," she smiled. "So...what's this nightmare you had last night?"

"Eh," he sighed. "Have you ever had a dream that you were killing someone?"

She raised her eyebrows over her coffee cup. "Umm...no. Whom were you killing? Not me, I hope?"

As a former English major, he adored her proper use of *whom*. He smiled and shook his head. "No. Some young kid."

"Anyone you know?"

"I don't think so."

"That's weird." She sipped her coffee, looking at the morning sky in the window.

"Yep. Which part?"

"That you don't know him. Do you think our brain can create people that don't exist, or does it only replay actual faces we've seen but maybe did not register or forgot, like from the crowds, traffic, or TV? Maybe this kid is real, and you just don't remember him?"

"I guess he could be," Nick gulped hot coffee, scalding his throat. The thought was unsettling.

"How did you kill him?"

"With a rock."

"That seems very personal."

"Yup," he took another, smaller gulp.

"Where did this happen? Somewhere you recognize?"

He thought about it and shook his head.

"You did not recognize anything in this dream?"

"It was dark. Nighttime."

"So, what could you see?"

Nick closed his eyes, reconstructing the disturbing image. "He is lying on his back in the grass. Short grass, like a mowed lawn. I am standing over him with the rock in my hand. That's it."

"Hmm. Weird. Is it bothering you? That you had this dream?"

Bothering was putting it lightly. The more he thought about it, the more he felt a bit shook up. "This is the second time this week. The same exact dream."

She raised her eyebrow again. "Hmm. If it's bothering you, maybe you should go see someone."

"A shrink?"

"Yeah, why not? It's probably just the stress of working on this case. It's your first body since KC. We moved here to get away from it, and we have, till now. Counselors can be surprisingly helpful. I am sure they can give you some tools to deal with the stress and make the nightmares go away."

And if they instead decide I am nuts? He could handle this himself, thank you very much.

Claire fixated on the TV behind him. He turned around to catch the photo of a clean-shaven, half-smiling, corporate white man with glasses and graying hair. The red ticker tape at the bottom of the screen typed out "BANK CFO COMMITS SUICIDE."

"Did you see this?" Claire asked, glued to the screen.

"No. What happened? Did the market crash? Did he get audited?" Nick said with a scowl and checked his watch – time to get going.

She gave him the obliging smirk. "No. Apparently, he was involved in a sex trafficking ring. Someone hacked his computer and publicly exposed him."

Nick stood up. "Wow. Hackers with morals and bankers with shame. Maybe this year *is* finally turning around."

She looked up at him with just a tinge of clinical concern in her gaze, and it made him realize he was feeling grumpy.

She set her mug on the table and came up to him. Her knees touched the floor. She moved her delicate fingers up the inside of his thigh. Her tongue slowly circled her lips and she put her mouth on the excited bulge growing in his pants. Her eyelashes fluttered as she looked up at him. He groaned. The crotch of his jeans grew torturously claustrophobic. The corners of her eyes were laughing. She rose back to her feet, leaving a moist bitemark as evidence of her crime.

"Thanks, honey, I hope this goes down before I get to the station." He feigned a grimace.

She stepped back to the table and picked up her coffee mug. Her messy blonde bun bobbed casually as she took a sip. Her big innocent eyes looked at him. He fought off the urge to set her on the kitchen table and pull up her T-shirt to get to those hard nipples he saw standing at attention under the thin fabric.

"Now you have something more pleasant to think about," she said. "You'd better get going, Detective."

"How do you know just what to do to drive me crazy?"

"It's my superpower, baby. Because I'm your destiny."

"How do I know you won't use your superpower for evil? Maybe I should run, while I still can?"

"Maybe you should. But then again, I am not the one dreaming of killing people. Maybe I should be the one running."

8

Nick ended up spending almost six hours at the station. He first went through Brenda's preliminary autopsy report and every single one of the attached autopsy photos. Then he clicked through all the crime scene photos one by one, studying them, as if for the first time. There were no signs of struggle, no signs of assault – neither on Lisa nor at the scene. So far, the absence of any evidence of foul play was overwhelmingly outweighing anything that could prove the contrary – an audio recording he did not have and a shard of glass that could have been anything and nothing.

The CSI techs lifted two sets of latent fingerprints at the scene. One set belonged to the victim. The other set was found on the wine bottle in the fridge. The prints from the bottle were still being analyzed. They appeared to be good enough to run through the FBI's identification system, but Nick knew better than to get excited about that. Most houses had multiple prints – friends, relatives, repair people. Everybody had somebody else in their house at some point. Still, these were another person's prints, and he hoped they weren't just from the clerk at the liquor store. Only the victim's prints were on the knife, and none were found on the shard of glass Nick fished out from under the baseboard. Still, he was encouraged by the fact that there were only two sets of prints found. Two was much too few. It *could* mean someone had wiped the rest.

Next, Nick checked his email for any news from the Lexi manufacturer – something that had become his almost hourly ritual over the last few days. Nothing. He thought about calling Lori and Clint, but struggled with what he would say, so he decided to wait till he had news. Maybe tomorrow. He checked the clock; somehow, it was already past 5 p.m., and he was the last one left in the building. Pine Lake was too small to have a graveyard shift; when Patty left for the day, the emergency dispatch rolled over to the county. It was time for him to get going, too. As he pulled away from the station – empty and dark in his rearview mirror – he tried to leave the case locked inside it. For Claire's sake, and for his own, Nick always tried to leave work at work. But driving home tonight, he thought it was going to be difficult with this one.

When he got home, Claire was getting ready in front of the vanity mirror in the bathroom. He changed his shirt.

"What time is it?" she checked in.

"Six-twenty."

"OK – I'm hurrying." She leaned closer to the mirror, rolled her eyes up to the ceiling and brushed on mascara in smooth, slow strokes.

"It's ok," he said. "It's just Mike and Amy."

Nick loved watching her get ready. Claire did not *need* make up. When they first started dating, he told her she did not need to put it on for his sake, to which she laughed and said she did it for herself. Her beautification process empowered her and mystified him. It was like witnessing a secret magic ritual. His strikingly pretty, familiar girlfriend went in, and through some witchery emerged as a stunning goddess who turned heads and could bring the world to its knees if she wanted to. This made him feel both lucky and unworthy. How did he trick her into being with him? He felt like a rough ogre next to her. Would she wake up one day and realize he was beginning to grow hair out of his ears like an old man? He wished he could transform like she could, but slipping on a nicer shirt seemed to be the extent of his glamor powers.

She put in her dangly earrings and turned to him. "How do I look?"

He took in the view of things. Jeans, T-shirt, long cardigan, and dirty blond hair straightened and pulled up in a clip.

"Hot. I think we should cancel on Mike and Amy." His mind entertained the scenario.

She rattled through her make up case for lip gloss and turned back to the mirror. "Don't smudge," she said, as he leaned into her for a kiss and a whiff of perfume on her skin. "C'mon – we are running late."

He followed her to the garage.

"Grab the wine!"

He made a U-turn back to the kitchen.

Claire drove. Her little Subaru carved down the darkening curves of Highway 285 in a dizzying descent into the Denver plains. She always drove like it was a getaway, even when they were just going to the grocery store. Nick could relate. There were many times in Nick's life when he had felt like the way she drove.

Mike and Amy lived in the older part of Littleton, off Belleview, in one of the ritzy brick-walled neighborhoods.

"Jesus, is that it?" Claire pulled up next to the stone pillars acting as the gateway. Beyond them, a paved path wound its way to the dramatically lit two-story Colorado chateau of timber, rock, glass and iron. "How much do you think this set them back?"

He thought about it. "Million-five? Two?" Mike had done well for himself.

The tall, heavy mahogany door rolled open to reveal Amy. She squeaked with delight and wrapped a hug around Nick. "The elusive Nick Severs," she said. "How long has it been? And Claire!" she moved on to his better half without waiting for an answer. "Girl, you are even more beautiful in real life. Come in, come in!"

Nick had not seen Amy in person since he was a groomsman in her and Mike's wedding. If it weren't for Claire taking charge of his social media relations, he probably would have had no idea what anyone looked like now and how many kids they had. In the warm light of the lobby, Amy seemed to glow with her golden late-summer tan wrapped in a crocheted burnt-orange cardigan. Her trademark sparkling eyes and dimples smiled at Nick just as they did in the countless Facebook posts Claire had shown him.

"This house is amazing," Claire complimented, absorbing her surroundings.

"And it smells amazing, too," Nick added. The smell of warm butter, garlic and pepper suddenly made him very hungry.

"Mike is cooking," Amy said, leading them through the house. "And the girls are having a sleepover at a friend's house."

"Ooh, so I won't get to meet them?" Claire was disappointed. Nick knew she adored the photos of the two grade-school girls with big brown baby-doll eyes and skin the color of creamy cappuccino. They *were* cute. Mike and Amy made pretty babies.

"You'll get your chance someday, but not tonight" Amy laughed. "Believe me, Mike and I are ready for some time with other grown-ups!"

"Not sure you can really call this guy a grown up," Mike piped up as they walked into the kitchen space. He gave Nick a half-hug on the account of his dirty apron and hands. "I am talking about myself, of course. Nick is a perfectly responsible adult. And you must be Claire! At last."

Claire got Mike's half-hug from the other side.

"I hope you guys like shrimp pasta. It's almost ready," he said. "What do you want to drink?" He directed Nick's attention to a row of bottles on the massive granite island with a gesture similar to a flight attendant demonstrating the path to the nearest emergency exit. The island was at least four times bigger than the little two-seater breakfast peninsula in Nick and

Claire's kitchen. "We have a Cab, a Merlot and a Malbec in the reds, and a Chard and a Pino in the whites, and of course if you want something stronger–"

"Maybe a Malbec to start with," Nick said. Perhaps one day he too could graduate from a peninsula to an island.

Amy was already pouring Claire a glass of the Pino, chattering something about schools and daycare. Claire caught Nick's look from the corner of her eye and gave him a smile.

"You always had great taste," Mike said. "I've been on a Malbec kick myself lately." He poured Nick a glass and they clanked cheers. Amy whisked Claire off, glasses in hands, into the depths of the house.

"I guess it's tour time," Mike said, smirking. "I'll show you the game room and the garage later."

"It's a nice place." Nick took in the expanses of granite, stainless steel and glass in the kitchen. "How long have you guys been here?"

"Umm, almost two years."

"You like it?"

"Yeah! And the girls like the school."

"That's great, man. I am happy for you guys." In the years since college, Mike had evolved into the image of corporate success. He always liked shiny expensive things and made it his mission in life to be able to afford them one day.

"Work treating you well?" Nick asked.

"Really good. Great money, benefits. A couple of business trips to Europe every year. It's a high growth tech market. There's talk of an IPO."

"Nice," Nick said, giving it the inflection Mike probably expected and trying to recall the last time the word IPO was mentioned in his work life. In his life.

Mike nodded, stirring something in the big stainless pot. "How about you? Did you ever check out that address I gave you?"

Nick sighed. "Yeah." He lost his gaze in the burgundy pool in his glass. "You were right. It was a death. Looks like a suicide, but more questions than answers right now."

"Damn." Mike stopped stirring, stared into the pot, then shook his head. "Hey, I'm sorry to bring it up. I'm sure you need a break from work. You just relax and forget about it for a while. Here," he slid an iPad to him on the island. "Pick some music. What are you listening to these days?"

Nick smiled, anticipating a snide remark. He loved music but would not call his tastes *current* under any circumstances. "Oh, I've been getting back into some oldies, Linkin Park, Alice in Chains, Soundgarden..."

"Jeez! You feelin' nostalgic? That's the music that speaks to you? That's angry white boy music. It can't be that good for you. I mean, didn't all those lead singers kill themselves?"

"I don't know..." Who said teenage angst had to end? "And what did angry black boys listen to? Biggie and Tupac? Last time I checked, they weren't exactly better off."

Mike rolled his head back and laughed heartily. "Touché, my man, you got a point. You can put on your metal."

"Nah, it's not really dinner music." Nick swiped through the infinite scroll of stations. "How about blues? Here – Joe Bonamassa. Claire and I saw him at the Red Rocks this summer."

"Right on," Mike nodded. "The dude's all right."

Amy and Claire returned with empty glasses and flushed cheeks. Nick put his arm around his woman, pulled her into his side and kissed her head. Her hair always smelled so good.

"OK, the food is ready." Mike took off his apron and tossed it on the counter.

"You guys want to eat inside or outside?" Amy turned to them. "We've got a fireplace out there."

Nick and Claire glanced at each other. Colorado had low humidity, mild temperatures and virtually no bugs, and she and Nick ate outside practically every night during the summer.

"You have to ask?" Claire grinned.

"Outside it is!" Amy nodded and started clanking through the silverware drawer, extracting shiny utensils.

The back patio looked expansive even in the dark. A pergola, an outdoor kitchen, a table, a fireplace, a burbling water feature, and a firepit with a cushy patio couch and chairs. Even the outside at Mike and Amy's was nice. They had an outside *living* space, compared to what Nick had – just *the outside*. It was like being on one of those TV shows where people were shown the houses they couldn't afford. He knew Claire liked it too. He wished he could give all this to her, but the best he could do was make a few mental notes of possible projects for when he would have the time to get creative with his tools.

The table was set under a string of lights glowing warmly against the deep indigo skies. The flickering flames of the fireplace made shadows dance, softened by the light of candles covered with the hurricane glass.

"This is amazing," Claire took a bite.

"I know, I won the lottery with this one," Amy winked at Mike. "Handsome, smart, and can cook."

"All I did was read and follow the recipe," Mike raised his hands in the air. "It's all about following the directions."

"So, he is trainable, as well." Claire made Amy snort, and they clanked glasses. "I am still working on Nick – he hates measuring stuff out when cooking."

Nick shrugged. "The recipe is just a general suggestion. I just go by taste. When it's right, it's right."

"So, *Detective* Nick Severs," Amy pronounced. "That does have a nice ring to it. How do you like the policing line of work?"

This was a simple question with a complex answer. Changing his careers on the verge of turning 30 was not exactly a point of pride. To make matters worse, people always seemed to want to know why he chose to be a cop. He was pretty sure no one quizzed lawyers, doctors and bankers about their career choices. But when it came to cops, people just had to know.

"Better than expected, given my shitty luck with career choices."

"What do you mean?"

"Well, look at my teaching career – by the time I got my master's and started teaching, higher education was already entering a nosedive. Budget cuts. Layoffs. I taught for three years, and then my contract was not renewed. So, I had two options. Either double down and go for a PhD, which would mean another five years of school and $50,000 in student loans, or – jump."

"And so, you jumped?"

"I did. Cut the losses and ran. I figured it was a good time to try something different."

"And the risk of it does not bother you?"

"No. I don't mind the risk." It's the mundane he dreaded. He didn't say it in front of Mike, but he wasn't the cubicle type. Even teaching was beginning to feel like a stale, canned cycle toward the end of his short stint. Doing the same thing semester after semester and year after year made him feel like he wasn't getting anywhere. It suffocated him to envision the rest of his life playing out in these measured-out cycles. It made him want to run. And he did.

"Can you believe this time six years ago this guy was teaching Shakespeare?" Mike folded his arms and shook his head. "And now he's got a badge and a gun, and he reads people their Miranda rights."

"And as always, my timing couldn't be less perfect – the protests, police defunding, ACAB."

Mike shook his head. "Things will settle down. People are naïve if they think they can have a functional society without police."

"As long as there are humans on this planet, someone will have to dole out justice," Claire added.

"I think you are thinking of superheroes, not cops," Nick smiled.

"Yes – cops!" Amy said. "Right now, we need good cops more than ever."

"Amen to that!" Mike lifted his glass. "Here's to good cops. Thank you, Nick, for doing what you do."

The three of them enthusiastically clanked their glasses, and Nick bashfully obliged them with a toast.

"But how come you are at Pine Lake? Doesn't Denver Metro pay better than a backwater PD?"

Nick did not miss the fiery sideways glance Amy gave Mike, as if protecting the dignity of a poor relative. But Mike was buzzed and oblivious to her cues. This failed interaction made Nick smile. "They do, but as someone said, money isn't everything. In my five years on the street beat in Kansas City, I've seen enough shit to last a lifetime. I'll take backwater for a change. Thankfully, Claire can get a job just about anywhere. I think she could get hired on the moon." He deflected the conversation onto his better half, tired of being the topic and confident she could handle it.

"Where do you work, Claire?" Mike credulously followed his lead.

"I am a nurse at the Children's Hospital South."

Amy lit up. "Do you like working with kids? It must be hard...given the circumstances." Her eyebrows formed a concerned wrinkle.

"It can be, but I am glad I can be there. They are going through a rough time, and I can help make things at least a little better for them."

"Aww, you guys are just perfect for each other," Amy beamed again. "And you met online? Right? How did it happen?"

Claire gave him an innocently naughty glance over the rim of her wine glass but did not put it down – he was it again.

He sighed with a smile. "Well, I was with Kansas City PD, and I hadn't really been dating for almost a year while I was going through the detective school and taking the exam. When I made it through field training, some of the guys from the department threw me a party and all their wives had a bit too much to drink and decided to set up an online dating profile for me. I must have been too drunk to resist. I totally forgot about it until about a week later when I noticed all the emails in my spam. I went in to close the account, and that's when I saw Claire's picture for the first time, at the very top of the list. Her eyes just drew me in. So, I contacted her. And for some reason, she wrote back. I still have no idea why." He pulled in Claire for a kiss.

"Don't sell yourself short, dude," Amy interjected. "The girl got a catch."

Dude – that word was a throwback.

"Shh," Claire said, "You gonna ruin him. He might get ideas."

"Not a chance, babe," Nick squeezed her hand. "You are it for me. If you leave me, I'll just move to the mountains, grow a beard, and talk to the animals."

"Now, that I believe," Claire laughed.

"You guys are so sweet," Amy cooed and grabbed Mike's hand, shaking him out of his buzzed stupor. "So, when are we going to see a ring?" She tilted her head, tightened her lips and gave Nick a penetrating stare.

"That *is* an excellent question," Claire turned to him and copied Amy's look.

Nick laughed under the pressure. "Hey, hey! I only get one shot at this, so I have to make it a sure shot. It hasn't even been a year!"

"Just don't wait too long," Amy shook her head at him and turned back to his better half. "So, Claire, you are from Kansas City too?"

"No, I am actually from Cape Girardeau. It's a small town about two hours south of St. Louis. But I was living in KC during my nursing practicum."

"Cape Girardeau? That sounds exotic."

"Hardly," Claire laughed.

"Do you still have family there?"

"Not anymore," she shook her head. "My parents passed a while back."

"Oh, I'm so sorry," Amy covered her mouth with her hand.

"It's OK."

Nick gave her hand a light squeeze. Claire had lost both of her parents to cancer, long before the two of them met, but whenever the subject came up, he always felt a little guilty that he seldom talked to his own, both of whom were very much alive. He took some comfort in the fact that they would most certainly claim Claire as their own when they would finally meet her.

His phone vibrated in his pocket, and he instinctively pulled it out to check the caller – *JeffCo RCL* – the Regional Crime Lab. "I am so sorry, guys," he put his hand on his heart and stood up. "I have to take this."

"No problem, brother," Mike gestured to the tall windows of the living room. "Just go in the house if you need privacy."

Nick nodded and swiped the screen. "This is Detective Severs."

The call lasted only a few minutes, but after he hung up, Nick had to sit down on Mike's living room sofa for a few more, just to get his head wrapped around the new facts.

When he finally walked back to the terrace, Mike, Amy and Claire were clearing off the table.

"Hey, you want that bourbon now, my man?" Mike greeted him. "I got some cigars."

"Yeah, that sounds good." He studied his friend. "You want to show me that game room?"

"Oh yeah!" Mike got visibly fired up.

He peeled the waxy ring off a brand-new bottle. "This stuff is cask strength, 120 proof! It's *damn* good." He poured a couple of fingers into two glasses, handed one to Nick and clanked with him. "Wait till you see this new 8K TV I got," he said, leading him down the curved staircase into the basement.

In the game room, Nick set the glass down on the edge of the pool table and closed the double doors. "WHAT. THE. FUCK. MIKE?" he shout-whispered at startled Mike. "You *knew* her?"

Mike's face turned ashen.

Nick stared him down under the bright LED lights of the game room. "Your prints were on the wine bottle in her fridge."

Mike took a gulp of his bourbon and folded himself onto a bar stool.

"It was a one-time thing, Nick. Well…two-time."

Nick kept glaring, letting Mike fill the silence.

Mike sighed and wiped his forehead. "Lisa came on as contractor, working on a project for me at Intergenix. Things just happened. You know how it can be at work? A few late nights, tight deadlines." He searched Nick's face for any sign of empathy but found none. "It was just two times, and we cut it off. It was mutual. But then, a couple of days later she did not show up for work. I got worried. I tried her phone a few times, but she did not pick up. I did not want to go back to her place, so I pulled her Lexi logs just to make sure there was still activity. There was only one recording for that week. So, I listened to it. I know I shouldn't have, but I did. It wasn't the intern – I did it. And that's all I did. And then I came to you. And the rest is all true, just as I told you. I swear, Nick."

"Does Amy know any of this?"

Mike shook his head emphatically.

"How can I believe anything you say? You lied to me. You withheld information related to this girl's death. You are lying to Amy."

He hung his head. "I know."

"Where were you that night?"

He recoiled on his stool. "Jesus, man. You think I had something to do with it? Nick, I was the one who brought it to you."

"Where were you? The night of September the Seventh?"

Mike wiped his forehead and pulled out his phone. "The Seventh…Tuesday…The girls had a play rehearsal at school…There are cameras there. I am sure you can pull video. You can check my phone's location data if you want."

Nick scrutinized Mike. Until about twenty minutes ago, he thought he knew his old friend pretty well. Now, he wasn't sure who was sitting across from him. Could Mike have done it? Nick wanted to believe that he couldn't. But this wasn't the Mike he knew in college. Cheating on his wife, lying, having a relationship with an employee. Could it have led to violence? Could Mike have changed this much? Or maybe he didn't? Nick had seen him as a college athlete. He had seen Mike's aggression flare up on the basketball court. Who knew? Maybe Lisa wanted more? Maybe threatened to go to Amy? Maybe he panicked?

Nick watched Mike's big hands. They trembled slightly, still clutching the glass of bourbon. Could he have staged a suicide? And clean up? The scene was too organized. Too perfect for a crime of passion. And why would Mike then tip him off that this was a possible homicide? Still, he would need to take a look at those school security cameras to be certain. He took a sip of the bourbon. It *was* damn good. He felt the fire spread down into his lungs.

"Mike, are you sure the recording is real?"

Mike wrinkled his face in puzzlement. "What do you mean?"

"I mean that this is the only piece that does not fit. So, could this recording be a glitch? A wrong address?"

Mike shook his head. "It's her voice, man. I know it."

"OK. But do you think she could have committed suicide?"

"No. Well, I guess, anything's possible, but I don't think so." He shook his head again. "She was smart, pretty, and had a great job – you should see the hourly rate we paid for her! Why would she kill herself? And you heard the recording. That sounded like someone else was there. Didn't it?"

"I don't know. I only heard it that one time. I'll need you to turn it over so I can have forensics analyze it."

"I can't give it to you, Nick. Not legally. There are data privacy laws. You'll have to go through the manufacturer and request the data release."

"I have. They still have not responded."

Mike nodded. "They can deny it and cite their privacy policy. I've seen it happen before."

The whole situation was beginning to seriously annoy Nick. "You are telling me their privacy policy allows them to make money off people's data but not help solve their own murder?"

"Pretty much."

"OK. So, you'll have to get it for me some other way then."

Mike shook his head again. "Nick, I can't. I am not supposed to be accessing it. If you get the recording through the unofficial channels, all they have to do is look at the logs and they'll see it was me."

A quiet rage seethed at the bottom of Nick's heart. He wanted to drag Mike to the station by the ear and get this whole tangled mess of lies and technobabble out into the open and on the record. He stared into his friend's sobered-up, sorry eyes.

"Damn it, Mike. You've put me into a terrible fucking position. I am either solving this case, or I am protecting you. I can't be doing both."

"I know, brother. And I am so, so sorry. I messed up."

"You'll still have to give me a formal statement."

"Oh, no, Nick. Why?" He pleaded like an overgrown schoolboy sent to the principal's office. "Amy will leave me if she finds out."

"Well, let's see. Lisa worked for you and your fingerprints were on a wine bottle in her fridge. Any cop in my shoes would want to talk to you."

Mike rubbed his forehead. "How did they know the prints on the bottle were mine? I've never been arrested."

"Did you renew your driver's license recently? Or get TSA Precheck? Or Global Entry?"

"Shit… OK, I'll do a statement but as her manager only."

"And the wine bottle?"

"I gave it to her as a thank you gift for finishing a project. That's what happened."

Nick did not know if this was the truth or Mike was practicing his lie. At this point, he did not want to know.

"How…how did she die?" Mike's hand trembled as he took another drink.

"Her wrists were cut."

Tears formed in Mike's eyes.

"What was her state of mind when you broke it off?" Nick pressed.

Mike sniffled and wiped his eyes. "She is the one that broke it off."

"That does not mean she was OK."

"Man, I am telling you she did not kill herself. You heard the recording."

"The recording I don't have? It's the only thing that does not fit in this whole case. And if I can't get my hands on it, it might as well not exist at all as far as the legal system is concerned."

Mike hung his head under Nick's glare.

"You have been to her house, right?" Nick inquired.

"Yeah. Twice."

"OK, by the front door, there is a small wooden table."

Mike scrunched the corner of his mouth. "Yeah, I guess."

"Was there anything on it?"

Mike squinted and shook his head. "I don't remember."

"Think, damn it!"

A glint sparkled in Mike's eye. "A dish. A fancy glass dish for keys and stuff, you know? Blueish green glass. Why?"

"Because it's not there anymore."

Mike lit up. "OK, see – that must be what broke on the recording. Right?"

Nick just stared at him glumly.

"Nick, look, I know this does not look good, but I promise you, I was nowhere near her when she died."

"Where was Amy?"

"What? Amy? You think she could...? No way!"

"You'd be surprised at what a scorned woman can do."

"She was at the girls' play rehearsal with me."

"She could have hired someone."

"Jesus, Nick! You think she ordered a hit on Lisa? Trust me, if Amy found out, the first hit would've been on me. Look. I will help you any way I can. I just have to stay anonymous as far as the source of the tip."

Nick finished his drink. The first week of the investigation was coming to an end, and the puzzle of this case was becoming only more complicated. He hoped this was the proverbial bottom and soon someone would have some helpful answers for him. He was tired. He looked at Mike.

"You know you'll have to come clean with Amy. She deserves better."

A shadow rolled over Mike's face again. "I know. I messed up so bad, man. It's a sick feeling. But I can't. It will kill us. Kill all of this. Destroy the girls."

Mike's gaze suddenly sharpened. "Hey, you know who you should check out? Lisa's ex. One day she got a text from him and got really upset. I think that was about two weeks ago. If you check her phone, it might still be on there."

***

They drove back home on the dark, empty mountain highway, Claire's Subaru downshifting confidently up the steepening grade.

"They are so good together," Claire said, watching the phosphorous dashed arc of the guardrail curving out of sight into the pitch blackness of the gorge. "The house, the girls. I am happy for them." She glanced at him, her eyes sparkling with the light of the dashboard. "What are you thinking about?"

He put his hand on the center console and she put hers on his.

"Mike cheated on Amy," he said.

She glanced at him again. "Jesus. What is wrong with him?"

Nick shook his head.

"Does she know?"

"No."

"Damn." She was quiet for a while, navigating the dark highway unwinding before them.

He interlaced his fingers with hers. "Do you think everyone ends up like that? Living in a lie?"

"I think people make that choice. But it doesn't mean they have to." She put her hand back on the wheel and accelerated into another blind turn.

9

The boy's skull cracked. Nick opened his eyes. The same damned dream. *Exactly* the same as the two times before. Maybe even more detailed this time. He could see the kid's eyes rolled back in his head. The blood was glistening in the light. And the lighting was strange. Like from a nearby bright artificial light – maybe headlights?

He looked at his phone – 4:20.

"Are you OK?" Claire mumbled sleepily.

"Yeah." He cleared his throat, trying to swallow down his pounding heart.

Why would he dream the exact same thing three nights in a row? This dream — it felt strangely familiar. And not just because he had already seen it two times before. This time it felt like recognition. Especially the boy's face. What if Claire was right? What if this kid was real? *Did this happen?* This thought was like a whisper, but it made his breath shallower. Until this moment, his past had always felt certain. He had considered himself to have good memory. But now, as he feverishly scrolled back in his head through the decades of past Nicks, he realized there were only a handful of memories he could recall with absolute and detailed certainly for any given decade. The rest was like a foggy, blurry, underdeveloped footage. What did he do between his twenty-third birthday and the 4th of July holiday in 2015? What about September of 2009? Sure, he could try to reconstruct the likely answer based on where he was living and working at the time, but it was not at all like rewinding a video to a clear freeze-frame. His memory was not the steel vault he had always assumed it to be. This was an unsettling realization. He didn't *remember* killing anyone, but apparently, that did not mean much, given how relatively little he remembered of the thirty-one years he had been alive.

But that wasn't even the worst realization. The worst was that he did recall that there were a few episodes in his past when he with absolute certainty *did not* remember what happened. These few times were the result of partying too hard in college. Too much drinking, possibly some weed, and zero recollection of how he got to his bed. That nauseating spinning-room sensation now gave him the cold-sweat chills again. The kid looked about the right age for that time in Nick's life.

A tiny panic lodged in his chest, but his brain hurriedly overran it, spinning up other plausible explanations. This wasn't real. He could remember nothing even remotely similar to this in his real life. He had never seen that boy in real life. He had never killed anyone with a rock. He would have remembered *that*. He had never doubted himself in his whole life. And yet, as he told himself this, he did not know if he quite believed it.

Nick needed to stop thinking, but it was too late to try to go to sleep again. His alarm would be going off soon. If he stayed in bed, he would just keep taking this damn dream apart over and over in his head. Instead, he got up, got dressed, and was soon in the driveway, ready for his run.

As he closed the garage, he realized that his phone and earbuds were still on the bench in the entryway where he put on his shoes. He was about to punch in the garage code again but changed his mind and set off on the dirt trail to the lake without music.

The woods were silent, save for the soft crinkling of pine needles under his feet. The rhythm of his stride and of his measured breathing helped reset his brain. The aroma of pine woods entered his lungs. Maybe it was the memory of all the childhood Christmases, or just his own unique chemistry, but he found the scent of pine both soothing and invigorating. If a place could have a soul, and the soul could have a scent, Colorado's soul would smell like pine. There were about a dozen different varieties of pine in Colorado. The pines, the spruces and the firs reigned here – from the prairie plains east of Denver to the rocky, windy cliffs at 12,000 feet of elevation where the tree line ended. Colorado was conifer country. It wasn't that Nick did not like other trees – he did. The oaks, the cottonwoods, the willows, the alders and the aspens all were nice to look at and to listen to their leaves rustle in the wind. But none of them had a scent. Not like the pines did.

About a mile from the trailhead, the forest path came to a rocky clearing above the lake. In daylight, this was a scenic overlook, but right now there were only the smooth, silver backs of the boulders demarcating the precipice. Nick slowed to a walk and approached the edge. The horizon to the east was beginning to glow, and the faint pink and gold first light was drawing the shoreline of the lake out of the twilight. Pine Lake was a dammed section of the Buffalo Creek – a glassy-surfaced reservoir encircled with thick pine forest, granite outcrops and a narrow sandy beach on the north shore. Everything was still and quiet here at this hour, except for his own rapidly pumping heart. Perhaps, because he was here, nature was on alert. He took a couple of steps to the edge of the boulder and sat down on the smooth surface sloping away gently into the long drop toward the treetops somewhere below.

This spot was called Echo Rock on the account of it being known to produce echoes, or more specifically odd echoes. Something in the acoustics of the rocks and the water trapped the sound and returned it after an eerie delay, distorted. The first time they had hiked here, Claire stood where he was sitting now and, without warning, screamed at the top of her lungs and got back a wild, blood-chilling cry of a banshee. It was as if something else had answered her. She egged him on to try it, but he was never much of a shouter. He was more of a listener, especially in nature. He did not try it. He just joked with her that he was too scared of what response he would get back.

The nature around him returned to life – birds were chirping, and something was rustling in the nearby trees. Maybe it was because he stopped moving and merged with the landscape. Or maybe it was the approaching sunrise. He sat there for a bit, watching the world imperceptibly inch out of the shadows. He could have sat there for hours, absorbed in the *now* that just was – without questions or recurring nightmares. But he had to go. Without his phone, he did not know exactly what time it was, but judging by the expanding light on the horizon, he guessed it had to be after six. Today, he had a lot to do.

T3n

Sometimes – *most times* – the easiest way in was not straight-on. Kat knew this from watching Roses. Say your target is a law firm in the Cayman Islands. It has an office building, and this building has layers of physical security around it: the lobby with a security guard; security cameras everywhere; an elevator with secure code access; locked office doors with key-card access; locked file cabinets; locked server room, etc. If you tried going straight-in, the way the employees did – through the front door – you would not make it far.

Digital security worked the same way: legitimate users logged into their laptops with secure credentials and multifactor authentication. This was their front door. Sure, you could steal the laptop from an employee's car, and maybe even crack the password and spoof the multifactor authentication and manage to grab some of the files from the hard drive, but you would still be in the lobby, so to speak. The laptop would soon be reported lost, and the company IT would send the kill pill to wipe it clean. Or *brick it*, as Roses would say. And bricks were worthless. Good hacks did not make bricks because good hacks did not announce themselves. Good hacks were stealthy. Great hacks took months for the target to discover. The best hacks were never discovered at all.

That's why good hackers stayed away from the front doors and found other ways in. And there were always other ways in. Just as the real buildings had unlatched side alley windows, propped-open service entrances and unmonitored sewer tunnels, so a company's network could have an unpatched server, or a network port carelessly left open during configuration. There was creativity in hacking that appealed to Kat. It was like trying to solve a puzzle. No fortress was impenetrable. Even stone walls had cracks.

Great hacking was elegant. And Roses was a great hacker. The way into the law firm in the Cayman Islands was actually not even through the law firm. It was through the IT company that had set up the law firm's email servers. The IT company's technician had carelessly pasted the administrator password into a spreadsheet in his project files. With this admin password, Roses got instant access to several years of the firm's email archives. With all the attachments. The attachments were the pay dirt: case documents, contracts, and invoices – with all the names named and all the signatures signed. The same confidential attachments were stored encrypted under high security in the law firm's records management system, yet they were emailed carelessly without encryption for the purposes of communicating with clients and suppliers. That's how Roses hacked the law firm.

And that's how Kat was hacking *DearJohn*.

DearJohn was number six on her list of seven. Seven links to one night all those years ago. Seven severed echoes of the past that always hung around her – sometimes muddled and distorted, and sometimes clear as a bell, but never far away. She never knew when one of these ghostly memories would resurface uninvited and whisper into her ear. In the early days, these echoes could stop her world from turning and could send her tumbling to a dissociative shutdown. She had lost many days of her life to such benders of isolation, compulsive chain-smoking and drinking. On days like that, all seemed to be lost, and she would cling to the affirmation mantras chanting in her head like the prayers of a pilgrim being thrown about in a small boat in the middle of the raging sea at night. But this was back then. She handled these echoes better now, keeping them at bay, but still never far away.

There were seven names on her list, and of the seven, the first three were dead. The fourth would be dead soon. The fifth was enjoying an extended stay in a federal incarceration facility, courtesy of Kat. And the seventh – well, she knew exactly where to find him when she was ready. Right now, *DearJohn* had her undivided attention.

DearJohn wasn't yet dead or behind bars because he was the only one she still felt the obligation to validate. The scales of retribution had not yet fully tipped against him. He was a specter inside a specter. He was connected to Kat's patchwork memory of that night, but she did not know exactly how. Not yet. She needed more information. Sensitive, buried information. And to get sensitive information, one had to hack the source.

But this wasn't Roses' type of hacking. This wasn't about blackmail, ransomware or doxing. This wasn't about the money. For Kat, this was as personal as it got. That one night all those years ago was a jagged, razor-edged shard stuck in her very core. *Kat* was the product of that night. And she was certain this same shard must have left a mark on *DearJohn*, too. A crack she could follow inward, to his very core.

At first, she tried to crack him with no technology at all. For months, she probed discreetly in his past, with him unknowingly under her microscope, but all without success. That's when Roses elevated Kat's game. A bit of tech changed everything.

Technology fascinated Kat. But it wasn't just about the technology itself. It fascinated Kat that technology could be used in vastly different ways. Most of the time, it was a surgically precise weapon that could strike an open network port on a server half a world away. But sometimes, equally amazing, it could be a crude blunt tool, like a battering ram bludgeoning a stone wall. Over and over. And now, in less than a week, cracks were finally appearing.

And therein lay another difference between Kat and Roses. The merry hacktivists of *f8sab!tch* would break in first and then snoop around, looking for anything of value, like burglars rummaging through the drawers. But not Kat. Not with *DearJohn*. With him, she knew exactly what she was looking for. She had the photo, after all. But she needed more. She needed his memory because she couldn't rely on her own. She would extract it from him like an archived file from a backup hard drive.

And then…what? Revenge? Reprisal? Retribution, justice, vindication? Closure came in so many ever-so-slightly-different flavors, and she hadn't quite decided on what form it would take. And why get ahead of herself? When the time came, she would know. Right now, she savored complete control. Right now, all she had to do was deepen the cracks and work herself in.

The address for Intergenix took Nick to a shiny new glass building in the foothills just off Highway 470. In the shiny new stainless elevator, his finger had to trace the labels on the double row of buttons up to the very top – the 14th floor. The elevator deposited him in a sun-lit foyer encased in layers of glass: glass walls, glass doors, and even a domed glass skylight overhead. The foyer was furnished with modern lounge chairs, vibrant-green, possibly plastic plants, and a pale young redhead at the reception desk.

"Hi! Welcome to Intergenix!" She flashed a blindingly white smile at him.

He flashed his badge. "Hi. I'm Detective Nick Severs." Her eyes widened. "I need to talk to someone about an employee of yours, Lisa Benoche. Is her manager here?"

The girl's chin trembled, and she reached for the box of tissues. "I'm sorry," she dabbed the corners of her eyes masterfully avoiding smudging her eyeliner. "I still can't believe she is gone."

"Did you know her well?"

She shook her head. "Just the small office stuff, breakroom talk. She was *soooper* nice." She sniffled. "Let me get you Bruce."

Her manicured finger jabbed a few buttons on her desk phone, and she conveyed Nick's arrival into her headset in calm, professional voice.

"He will be with you in just a few minutes," she said and sighed a crier's sigh. Nick nodded and settled into one the loungy chairs.

If he had to give the style of this lobby a name, he would have to call it Post-Corporate Modern. This wasn't the grandfatherly boardroom opulence of mahogany and dark leather. The new look of corporate was light and airy, like a hipster hotel lounge, rich in light textures – light-colored fibers, metals and woods. And, of course, glass. Through the glass walls and corridors, Nick could see shapes of people moving around like ants in a plexiglass ant farm. If some of the walls hadn't been made of frosted glass, he probably would have been able to see all the way through the building, from the lobby to the outside windows.

He turned his attention to the single non-glassy wall in the foyer which held a triptych of abstract corporate art and a row of smaller plaques and frames. The one closest to his chair was from the Greater Denver Chamber of Commerce, and the one next to it held a Denver Business Journal article titled "Top 30 under 30: Denver's Brightest Tech Execs."

The electronic lock behind him clicked, and when Nick turned around, there was a man in a light-blue suit standing next to him.

"Bruce Cogan," he held out his hand. "President and CEO."

Cogan looked to be in his late thirties. His suit had an athletic cut, and when Nick shook his vice-grip hand, he guessed those were not shoulder pads in his jacket. The rest of his appearance was equally taut – neatly-cropped light hair, cleanly-shaved face, and a muscular neck spreading open the top button of his blue-checkered shirt.

"You want to talk about Lisa? We can go to my office. Do you want anything? Water? Coffee?" His index finger paused in mid-air in the direction of the girl at the front desk. She looked up, stretching slightly at attention and shining that bright smile again under the teary eyes.

"No, I am good. Thank you," Nick replied and followed Cogan's lead into the glass labyrinth.

There was a sense of high energy about this place. Everyone looked busy and the keyboards were clicking away in rapid staccatos. Nick followed Cogan past an empty glassed-in conference room with a large whiteboard covered in dry-erase bulleted lists and cascading columns of multi-colored Post-it notes. The top of the whiteboard was inscribed *Release 11.5* in red marker, underlined twice. Beyond the windows of the conference room was the distant skyline of the downtown. Cogan turned the corner, and they entered a maze of low cubicle walls. Judging by all the heads Nick saw, this space was pretty much at capacity. On this side of the building, the windows faced the rolling foothills with a jagged sliver of mountains behind them.

"You've got nice views here," Nick said.

Cogan nodded. "Yes, it helps to be on the top floor. We used to be in the Denver Tech Center for five years, but it got to be too corporate there, and the lease costs…you wouldn't believe. The views are definitely better here." He pointed further down the hall. "We have a rooftop deck on the west side. You should see the sunsets from there."

At the proverbial corner office, Cogan let Nick in through the door first. Cogan's office was clean and organized, presenting a trim appearance without any excess, like Cogan himself. Nick appreciated that. He did not like messy people. Unless they were criminals, that is. Messy people made messy criminals. And messy criminals made his job easier.

Instead of settling into the executive chair behind his desk, Cogan invited Nick to a pair of leather conversation armchairs with a coffee table between them. Nick sat down in the one with its back to the corner – gunslinger style – with a good view of Cogan and his office behind him. Cogan was a minimalist decorator. There was one bookcase behind the desk and three framed ironman medals on the wall next to it. A framed photo on the desk showed four soldiers in light-colored camouflage with a mountain range behind them.

"You served?" Nick asked.

Cogan nodded. "Army Rangers. Two tours in Afghanistan. That's me and my buddies. Two of them did not make it back home. How about you?"

Nick shook his head. "Just five years with KCPD."

"I would imagine it's similar. A dangerous job, and you know what it's like to have people depending on you."

"It looks like you have quite a lot of people depending on you now." Nick sized up the sea of cubicles outside Cogan's office while getting out his notepad. "What is it that your company does?" In conducting investigations, Nick often found it illuminating to start with those questions he already had the answers for. In part he did this to get a baseline on reading the other person, like the first questions of the lie detector tests: *Is your name Nick Severs?* He also did this because sometimes he got new answers.

Cogan mechanically tugged down the side of his jacket so it would not rumple unflatteringly as he sat down. "We specialize in Artificial Intelligence – AI. We provide machine learning services for many very large companies you are familiar with, to make their products smarter. We have also developed our own proprietary AI engine, and companies can use it to solve business problems, automate processes, or find insights in large volumes of data." Cogan clearly was used to delivering elevator pitches to laypeople like Nick.

"You must be doing well."

Cogan's eyes squeezed lightly, and he studied Nick for an intense millisecond.

"We do well, and we also try to do good. When I started Intergenix, I also established a non-profit organization called The Code of Honor that helps veterans transition into technology jobs. For me, running this company has always been as much about building technology as it is about helping rebuild lives. We've been successful, but it has also been a humbling experience. We started with just six people, and now we have four hundred employees, and our apprenticeship program accepts four new veteran applicants per month. All these people now rely on me and my management team for their future and for their families' futures. They are my family, and Lisa Benoche was one of us." He shook his head. "Poor girl."

"How long did she work for you?"

"Umm…maybe seven months. I can get you her HR file if you need the exact dates. Technically, she was a contractor. But she was good. Very good. We most likely would have extended her an offer at the end of the contract."

"What kind of work did she do?"

"Data analytics. She was helping us fine-tune the machine learning algorithms."

"How was her project going? Any issues?"

Cogan shook his head. "Her manager said she was performing well. Very well, actually."

"What about her relations with coworkers? Any conflicts or tension you've noticed?"

He furrowed his brow and shook his head. "No. She was well liked from what I'd seen. Do you have any idea why she would commit a suicide?"

"First, we still have to confirm that it was indeed a suicide."

Cogan's eyes narrowed again, like a sniper's stare. "Oh? When we got the call from the coroner's office, I thought they said it was."

"They may have said *an apparent* suicide. And that's what it is right now, but we have to investigate every unattended death, regardless of what it looks like. Can I see where Lisa sat?"

"Of course." Cogan rose to his feet with controlled fluidity of an athlete. "Follow me."

Lisa's desk was in a cubicle in the middle of a large block of cubicles. It was empty except for the banker's box in the office chair. A folded sweater topped the box. One end of a blue network cable lay sadly on the surface, unplugged. Nick noted that the name tag on the cubicle wall was handwritten, unlike the printed ones on the surrounding cubicles, probably on the account of Lisa being a contractor.

"Dani packed up Lisa's things for her family," Cogan offered, seeing Nick contemplating the empty space.

In the adjacent cubicle, a young woman with a pair of hair sticks stuck in a dark brown messy bun stood up.

"Dani, this is Detective Severs," Cogan introduced. Nick shook her thin and very cold hand.

"Sorry," she apologized self-consciously and rubbed her hands together. Her gray eyes were sad. "With all the sun and the windows, the AC is going nonstop here," she pointed to the vent in the ceiling above her desk. "Lisa did not have a lot of personal stuff here. I was going to ship it to her family."

"I can take it to her mother. She flew in."

Dani nodded. "I've been watering her plant." She cast her gaze down to the small fat green leafy thing busting out of an oversized coffee mug on her desk. "Do you think I can keep it to remember her by?"

Nick nodded. "I am sure her mother would like that. Were you and Lisa close?"

"Not super close, but we hung out every now and then. She was new to the area, so I showed her around Denver. We went hiking a couple of times this summer."

Nick flipped to the page titled *People* in his notebook and added an entry for Dani. Like a growing cast of characters, the list of people in Lisa's life was beginning to flesh out.

"Did she have a computer here or did she bring her own?"

"She had a company laptop," Cogan said. "She just had access to our corporate systems. For security reasons, no personal devices were allowed on the network. Data privacy regulations are getting more and more strict...*Hey, Mike!*" Cogan suddenly raised his hand, flagging someone down the hall. Nick turned to see Mike's broad-shouldered frame lumbering toward them through the sea of cubicle walls.

"Mike, this is…" He did not finish as Mike moved in close and gave Nick a hearty handshake followed by a shoulder pat. "…you two know each other?"

"Nick and I went to college together." Mike turned to his boss. "Glad you finally stopped by. Wish it was under better circumstances."

Cogan observed them without a smile, his eyes tightened again. Neither hostile nor friendly. Evaluating. He checked his watch. "Detective, I apologize. I have a call I need to hop on. But I leave you in good hands with Mike. Ms. Benoche reported to him, so I trust he can answer any additional questions you might have. If you do end up needing me, I will be happy to chat after my call." He shook Nick's hand and gave him a small official smile. "It was a pleasure to meet you. Please convey to the family how saddened we are by their loss. Once we find out the funeral arrangements, I will send flowers."

He walked off with a prompt, purposeful pace and disappeared around the corner.

"Want to talk in my office?" Mike offered.

"Sure. Hang on a sec." Nick turned to Dani who had bundled herself in a gray cardigan in front of her computer screen.

She looked up and pulled out her earbuds by the wires.

"It was nice meeting you," Nick said. "I may have to call you if I have any additional questions about Lisa. Do you have a good number?"

"Sure." She reached into her desk drawer and pulled out a business card. She circled a number with a pen and handed the card to Nick. "The cell number is my personal phone, if you need to reach me after work."

Nick nodded to her and then turned back to Mike, ready for him to lead the way. Mike's office was in the inner bank of rooms in the middle of the floorplan. Mike did not have a window. He had a glass wall with a door. His only view was to the sea of cubicles. Nick supposed that the view served to remind Mike that he was fortunate to have more walls than the poor saps out there.

Mike closed the door behind them, and his wide eyes fixed on Nick. "So, any leads?"

Nick sat in the side chair and studied the family photo on Mike's desk. Amy looked so happy. "No." Nick looked back at Mike. "Let's take care of your statement really quick."

Mike cleared his throat and straightened up in his high-back managerial chair.

"How long did you know Lisa?"

"Umm, she started here in March. So, about six months."

"And you managed her directly?"

"She was a contractor, so I managed her project with us, but I wasn't really her boss. No HR-type conversations, you know?"

Nick nodded. "How was her project going?"

"Very good. She was very smart. Picked up things quickly, had great ideas." Mike's gaze drifted off past the glass wall to Lisa's empty cubicle.

"When did you last see her?"

"Last Tuesday."

"The Seventh? The day she died?"

"Yes."

"How did she seem?"

"Normal." Mike shrugged.

"Did she do anything out of the ordinary?"

"No. She left at the end of the day, said she would see me tomorrow, and never showed up the next day."

"Tell me about the working conditions here. Is this a high stress kind of place? High expectations?"

Mike sneered. "Man, this is tech. Expectations are always high. People work long hours. Blame the Asperger's idiot-savants that started the Silicon Valley. Now everyone's expected to perform to their level. Work hard, play hard, as they say. If anything, Lisa had it easier as a contractor. Her hours were capped."

"What about your boss – Cogan? Is he hard on people? He seems pretty high-strung."

"Bruce? Oh, hell no. I mean, he expects results, but he is a hundred percent committed to the people. He cultivates the team. I think he knows the names of every single person out there," he nodded to the sea of cubes. "The employees love him. At company events, he is like a rock star or a messiah, or both. People cheer when he gets up on stage, and not because they have to. He really cares about them. If he sees you burning out, he will be the first to tell you to take a few days off. And if you decide this gig is not for you, there are no hard feelings. He is not a vindictive asshole like some company founders tend to be. Now, if you *are* picking up on any tension, it could be this IPO process. Bruce has been all business for the last few months. We are having auditors and underwriters here every week. Looking at our financials, looking at our code. It's like a corporate equivalent of a colonoscopy."

Nick raised one eyebrow from his notebook. "Do you think he's got something to be worried about relating to this IPO process?"

Mike shook his head. "No, I don't think so. Investment bankers have been calling him for years. And he's already declined several buy offers. This company is hot property. But there are a lot of pieces to this process, and lots of variables can influence valuation."

"And how do the employees feel about the IPO?"

"Well, let me put it this way. A lot of people here have private stock options. When the company goes public, these options will mature, and these people will make a lot of money. Some will become millionaires overnight."

"And you?"

He smiled. "Not quite, but we will do well." He glanced at the family photo. "You found the ex-boyfriend yet?"

"No. But he is next on my list."

"I'm telling you man, check him out. I could tell it was bad news when he texted Lisa. Something was going on there, but she would not talk about it."

"OK, I will." Nick put away his notepad. "Does Amy know yet?"

Mike shook his head. "She just knows a coworker had died. Nothing else."

"When are you going to tell her?"

"I can't, man. It would end us."

"And what if it comes out as a result of the investigation?"

"I know. If it does, it does. It's my mess. But you won't let it happen, will you?"

Nick did his best to suppress the grating scratch of irritation. "Mike. You know I can't promise you that. I have no idea which way this investigation is going to go. I'll do what I can to keep you out of the spotlight, but I won't lie to protect you."

Mike hung his head. "I know, and I don't expect you to. This will work out, I just know."

"You mean for you? Because it didn't exactly work out for Lisa."

Mike closed his eyes and shook his head again. "I know. Poor choice of words. You just check out the ex. And tell me how I can help. Anything. Anything at all."

***

A box, a plant, a secret, a lie – the pieces we leave behind when we die. Things left for the living to fuss about, the delayed echoes of our decisions. As Nick sat in the thickening afternoon traffic, the needle-pressure of a headache was forming right between his eyes.

The car in front of him was stopped at a cross-walk – a high school was getting out, and the uneven trickle of teenagers was streaming across the street.

And then he saw *him*. Just a glimpse of the face, but he instantly recognized him. The lanky figure in a charcoal hoodie. Shaggy dark brown hair swooping over his eyes. It was *him*. But not lying on the ground. Not with a gaping blood-filled cavity in his skull. Not with his eyes rolled back in his head. He was alive and walking in the crosswalk. In front of the stopped cars. Talking to his friends. And now proceeding down the street away from Nick.

Nick's pulse revved up. He shoved the Tahoe's shifter into Park, jumped out and ran after.

"Hey," he caught up and put his hand on the boy's shoulder.

The kid turned around, and Nick instantly knew it was not him. The face was fuller. The eyes were brown. The chin was not clefted.

"Yeah?" The kid stared at him. "What's up?"

"Nothing. I thought you were someone else. Sorry."

"Pedo," his friend said, and the girls with them giggled.

Class clown. Nick sighed and pulled back his jacket to expose the badge on his belt.

"Shit. I am so sorry, man!" The class clown's smugness evaporated, and he pulled his friend's sleeve to go. Nick eyed the backpack the kid tucked out of sight. The clown backed off too easily. School drug dealer, Nick guessed, as he watched them scuttle.

The light changed, and the log line of cars behind the Tahoe began honking. The headache was really pounding at his temples now. He climbed back into the driver's seat and popped a couple of Tylenols from the bottle he took from the station.

12

Claire made lasagna. He was too distracted to feel hungry when he first pulled into the driveway, but as soon as he walked through the door and smelled the intoxicating mix of tangy tomato sauce, garlic, and warm cheese, he suddenly was absolutely starving and remembered that he never got lunch.

The TV in the living room was turned to the news. From the brief snippets of overly engaged reporting, Nick gathered that the breaking news was that some big law firm he had never heard of in the Cayman Islands got hacked, and their data was being held for a ransom of $10 million. That wasn't the breaking part of the story. The breaking part was that the Cayman Islands were a tax haven for the rich, and the hackers had already released the names of a dozen politicians and industrialists who were on the firm's client list and now threatened to release the full files. Unless the ransom were paid, naturally.

Nick considered for an instant if he cared in any possible way about the outcome of this ordeal. The people on that list operated on a completely different level of existence than the mere mortal plain on which he and the people he knew lived. A million, ten million, a billion – it all was equally astronomical from his situation in life. The hackers could have asked for a lot more, and they probably would have gotten it. Whichever way this scenario would play out would not make the smallest ripple in the lives of the rest of the world. What he did find amusing, however, was that evidently no one seemed to doubt for a second that this law firm's high society clients had something to hide.

He set the table and poured the wine. When Claire slid a plate with a mouth-watering slice in front of him, he could feel himself salivate like one of Pavlov's dogs. If he had to pick his final meal on Earth, this would have to be it. There was just nothing else quite as heavenly as the warm layers of lasagna. He may have had German and English family heritage, but Italian was definitely his comfort food. Claire knew this and had the recipe down to a science. He wondered what Lisa's favorite food was. Favorite music? He knew so many details about her life now, but still did not really know her. Not the way normal people knew each other. Living people. Under normal circumstances. He realized that Claire was watching him and that he was not talking.

"Thanks for making this, babe." He gave her a tired smile. "You're too good to me."

"You are welcome. And don't worry, you'll pay me back." She winked.

"Care to tell me how?"

"Oh, you'll know it when the time comes."

He chuckled and made a mental note to pick up some flowers for her tomorrow.

"How's the case coming?" she asked. She had the timing of a professional waiter – Nick had just stuffed his mouth with a large forkful. He shook his head and shrugged at the same time, trying to chew and swallow the hot bite in a hurry.

"That bad, huh?"

He washed down the lasagna with Malbec. "Right now, it's puzzling. But it's also not particularly puzzling. Not on the surface, at least. Do you think that if something looks like something, then it probably *is* something?"

"Oh, I don't know about that. In my experience, that is usually the first indication that it isn't." She gave him one of her charming hooligan smirks. "What does it look like on the surface?"

"A suicide. Pretty much everything at the scene points to a suicide. But it's also the things that are not at the scene that make it suspicious."

"Like what?"

"Like fingerprints, for example. There were none on the door handles. Not even the victim's prints."

"Maybe she cleaned?"

"Just before killing herself?"

"People do weird things. Anything else?"

"There was a glass bowl by the front door according to one witness, but now it is missing except for a small shard I found on the floor."

"So, she broke it?"

"Or it was broken during a struggle. Then, there is an anonymous tip with a vague audio recording that I have not been able to verify. And if I can't verify it, it might as well not exist at all."

"Ok, so those are just a few little inconsistencies, and they don't really offer any proof to the contrary." She was playing the devil's advocate.

"Yes, but these are annoying little inconsistencies that make me question the facts."

"Which are?"

"That the medical examiner and the CSI did not find anything to suggest anything other than a suicide. And most importantly, so far there is no apparent motive for homicide."

"So, if it is a murder, someone must have benefitted from her death, right?" She could play the devils' advocate from both sides. "Unless it was a crime of passion."

"Well, given how clean and organized the crime scene is, I would say it was not a crime of spontaneous passion. Also, in crimes of rage or jealousy, the killer usually makes a point of exhibiting that the victim had been punished for some transgression. The crime scene becomes the message and so covering it up as a suicide does not fit."

"OK, so, then it's business, and not personal. Maybe fraud? Insurance money?"

"None according to the family. Besides, insurance usually does not cover suicides, so it would have been staged as an accident."

"Right. OK. Burglary?"

He shook his head.

"Maybe it's something totally out of the left field. Like that case in the Nineties in Norway with that woman who was found shot in her locked hotel room."

"The one with all of the labels cut off from her clothes?"

"Yeah, and no IDs or credit cards. They never did figure out what happened, but some people think she was a spy killed by another spy. Maybe yours was a spy too?"

"From Nebraska?"

She shrugged. "Everyone is from somewhere."

He chewed a bite of lasagna, entertaining the possibility.

She sipped her wine. "If you think it's a murder, then it probably is. You'll figure it out. Just follow your intuition."

"Do men have that? I thought only women could follow intuition."

"What do men follow, then?"

He rubbed his temples. The headache was checking in again. "Two things, I guess. One is their gut. The other I won't mention. And no one would mistake either for intuition."

She smiled. "You look tired."

He nodded. "I've not been sleeping well." That was an understatement.

"Because of that dream? Are you still having it?"

"Only when I sleep. And sometimes when I am awake."

"You should go see someone about it."

"A shrink? Nah. I don't need a shrink."

"I think everyone could use a little bit of therapy."

"Really? Why? Freud invented psychiatry a hundred years ago, and has the world gotten any better?"

"Is that a reason to stop trying to fix it?"

"No, but if everyone needs fixing, then no one needs fixing. Sanity is a relative thing."

"I am not worried about everyone. I am worried about you."

"I can do it myself. Watch, here is my psychoanalysis of the entire humanity: We are pushed kicking and screaming from the safety of our mothers' wombs into this cold uncaring world, and this becomes our first great trauma. The second one is when we learn that one day we are going to die and leave this cold uncaring world, and no one really knows what that means. And there you have the foundation of our universal neurosis, separation anxiety, fear of rejection, and diminished self-worth, which create a viscous cycle of self-sabotaged relationships and alienation, all intensified by social media, soul-sucking corporate careers and the abundant stresses of modern life. Do you want me to go on?"

She threw a crumpled napkin at him. "You are too smart for your own good. And stubborn. Let me put it in the terms you will understand. You know how you can hear when the car is not running right?"

It was true – he could always tell when mechanical things weren't working the way they were supposed to, and he was already not liking the inevitable conclusion to which this analogy was leading him.

"Right?" she insisted.

He nodded reluctantly.

"And you tell me it needs an oil change or a new air filter or something else. Well, this is me telling you that you need a mental oil change or a new filter, or in the very least go see the mechanic, because it *is* affecting you. You are not sleeping, you are obsessing about this dream, and it's not getting better."

He hated to admit it, but he suspected she was possibly right about this one.

13

In person, Sam looked softer than how he remembered her in college. And now she had a medium-sized bump in the front.

"You're pregnant?" Nick gave her a careful hug, minding the bump.

"That seems to be the general consensus," she beamed. Same bright eyes.

"When are you due?"

"December." She rolled her eyes. "We didn't plan well. Who knew spring breaks in Mexico were dangerous at my age?"

"Hey now. What age are you talking about?" He grinned.

How did this happen? The wiry twenty-something had turned into a fully blossomed mama with one kid at home, one on the way, and a successful counseling practice in Colorado Springs. How long had it been?

"Sit," she said. "I gotta pee really quick. It's been back-to-back all morning."

He wondered what he looked like to her after all these years since college. Did he look that much different? He felt the same. In his mind, he really had not aged since his mid-twenties. But both Sam and Mike had clearly changed so much. Maybe he should have changed more than he had?

He sat down and studied the photos on her bookshelf. They were professionally done, like those stock families included with frames in the store. His never looked this good, but then again, he never paid a professional to do them. Medium silver frame: a mutt-haired boy in a button-down shirt, laughing in the grass with a toy firetruck. Larger, distressed wooden frame: her husband, Sam and the kid in fall sweaters on a bridge in a park with leaves changing behind them. Nick knew that Sam's husband did financial advising or wealth management, or something like that, which sounded dreadfully boring to him, so he did not bother to clarify.

Sam's office had three different armchairs, an overstuffed short couch and two padded cube seats. He wondered if she made observations about her patients based on the seat they selected. He had chosen without thinking, and now found himself in the low-back brown leather armchair – the only one that could swivel. He smirked to himself. There was probably several sessions' worth in that choice.

He and Sam were good friends in college. After college, she moved to Colorado Springs, and he settled in KC, and he lost touch with her, same as with everyone else. But calling her, all these years later, he suddenly felt connected again, like only a few weeks had gone by.

She came back in and sat down in the armchair opposite of him.

"So, what's up, Detective? You said you needed to pick my brain?"

He twiddled his thumbs. "What does it mean when someone has a recurrent dream?"

"Well, there is no single answer to that. It just really depends. Dreams are usually just one part of the puzzle. Is this *someone* you?"

He nodded.

"How often are you having this dream?"

"Every night."

"Is this a good dream or a bad dream?"

"Not good. Pretty bad, actually."

She nodded but left the conversational vacuum for him to fill.

"I see myself killing someone. Violently."

She did not flinch. "Well, generally, dreams are not literal manifestations. They are representations of your psyche coming to terms with your environment – processing the world, the people, the relationships. It's a healthy process."

"It does not feel healthy."

"Has it affected your quality of life?"

"I can't sleep at night, and I keep thinking about it during the day."

"This person in your dream – is it someone you know?"

"I don't think so."

"And what happens when you have this dream?"

"I wake up."

"What do you feel when you wake up? Is there a feeling or emotion associated with it?"

He furrowed his eyebrows. *Feelings.* He had always felt like an inarticulate caveman when Claire asked him what he was feeling. He had read about emotions in books and was aware that there was a general belief that there existed a wide range of them. On a good day, he could possibly identify two or three in his entire life that really stood out, and the rest just kind of melded into a gray ball of daily existence – just being. And in his experience, pulling them out of the ball and putting names to them never helped solve anything.

"Dread, I guess." He did his best.

"Can you elaborate? What are you dreading?"

"It's the feeling that something very bad, very irreversibly bad has just happened."

"Does that feeling go away after you wake up?"

He shook his head. "This whole thing just feels…real."

"How?"

"Like something I already knew."

"Like a memory?"

He nodded. "Except I don't remember it ever actually happening. Do *you* think it's a memory?" That was a disturbing consideration.

She tilted her head. "Usually, a recurring dream is associated with something that you are currently dealing with in your life rather than something that happened in the past. But in some cases, like PTSD, a recurring trigger in the present can link to a traumatic event in the past and bring forward a memory through a dream."

"So, you believe this could be a repressed memory?"

"It's too early to tell, Nick. This certainly sounds like a traumatic dream. That does not necessarily mean it is a traumatic memory."

"What else could it be?"

"It could be a persistent negative thought."

"That's a thing?"

She nodded. "People can become fixated on a false belief about themselves, like their body image, for example."

"False belief? That sounds like insanity."

She shook her head. "It's just a type of obsessive behavior. It's not a chemical imbalance in your brain, and it's not a genetic disorder. It's just the way our brain works. Our analytical part of the brain gets stuck, like a broken record. You can't tell it to be rational because it is already the part of your brain that is responsible for rational thought. If I tell you not to think of pink elephants, what do you think of?"

"Pink elephants?"

"Exactly. And if you are stuck on a negative thought, however irrational, it will just keep reinforcing itself and will create anxiety, dread, trouble sleeping, and all of those will only exacerbate and perpetuate the problem."

"And what causes it?"

"Could be anything. Stress, for one. Have any of that?" She smiled. "If it started just recently, it would be something that happened recently. Repressed memories, on the other hand, are usually linked to a more distant past."

This was sounding promising. Maybe coming here was a good idea after all. If this was just some stuck negative thought, he could manage it. But what if it wasn't?

"Is there a way to make sure it's not a memory?"

"I don't think you can ever know with absolute certainty, but there is a whole type of therapy geared toward recovering repressed memories. It is far from an exact science. Memories are not like misplaced photographs. We don't remember things perfectly, and our memories can change as we age."

"But this memory recovery therapy could tell me if there is something there?"

"Possibly. But I think the best approach would be not to start with the past but with what's going on in the present that's triggering this reaction in you. This can help uncover whatever is connected – past or present."

He tapped his finger on the chair arm. "Can *you* do this memory therapy?"

She smiled and sat back. "Nick, did you hear what I just said? I think you need to look at what's going on in the present first."

"OK, but can you do it?"

"Yes, but I don't treat friends. That would not be good for either of us. But I can recommend someone."

"Sam, I can't go through anyone else. I am a cop. You've seen the environment for cops out there right now. I can't go to a stranger and talk about recurrent visions of killing someone. Whether this is a memory or not, my career would be over before I got to the bottom of this. I need someone I can trust."

"Sorry, Nick, but absolutely not." She shook her head.

"Sam, I am begging you. I don't need you to do therapy. I just need you to help me figure out heads or tails of this. Then, if I still need help, I will get it from someone else. You don't have to treat me. Just help me identify what I am dealing with here."

He smiled, trying not to look too desperately in need of mental help.

"Please?"

She glared at him and exhaled with slow forceful intensity to go on the record with her disapproval of this idea.

"OK." She looked at the clock on the wall behind him. "I have another hour before my next client. We can try something that should tell you if this is connected to an underlying…event. After this, I am directing you to my colleague."

"Thank you." He gave her his best sad smile but got daggers in return.

She grabbed a pad and pen from her desk. "This is just to help me think. I am not putting your name on this, and this is not going in your file. Because there will be no file for you. Because I am not treating you. Now, tell me the dream."

He shifted in his chair. "I am hitting this kid on the head with a rock. His face is bloody. I hit him and hear his skull crack. That's when I wake up."

She nodded. "Is that it?"

"Yes."

"And you don't know who he is?"

Nick shook his head. "He looks vaguely familiar, but like no one I can recall."

"Do you know where you are?"

He shook his head. "It's dark. He is on the grass. The lighting is strong and harsh, like from the headlights of a car."

"How old is he?"

"Late teens, maybe early twenties."

"So, could be high school or college? How old do you think you are in this dream? Are you your current age now, or do you think maybe you are the same age as him?"

He considered the possibility. "Maybe. I can't really tell."

She made a note, and he thought of his own notebook in his jacket and considered the irony of his brain being examined like a crime scene. This was an autopsy of sorts.

"Is it always this same scene?"

"Yes. Exactly."

"Do you ever dream about what happens before or after this scene?"

"No."

She wrote on her pad.

"So, do you think it could be a memory?" he cautiously probed.

"If it is, it is very isolated in your brain – there doesn't seem to be any breadcrumbs leading us to this event."

"Isn't that unusual for a memory? Not having any breadcrumbs connected to it?"

"Not terribly. It could be a defense mechanism. Sometimes, the more traumatic the experience, the more tidily your mind locks it away to protect you from it."

"Locks away how?"

"Your brain programs pathways around it, bypassing it completely. It's like it's put in a box without a label – you can recall events from before and after, because they are labeled, but this one just sits there, with no address or reference. People can go for decades without realizing it, but then something just triggers them – could be a smell, a sound, or a face – and suddenly there is this unexplained emotion or an image, like a loose thread that does not seem to belong anywhere. And they start pulling at it, and they find the box, and then try to put together the bits and pieces in it."

The thought of there being a locked-away memory of him murdering someone chilled him. Could he really do something like this? Why? And could he really make himself forget it? The more he thought about it, the more true it seemed. Maybe it was just pink elephants. He did his best to not let his face show any of this to Sam.

"So, how do we find out if my loose thread has a box at the other end?"

"Well, to properly work through repressed trauma takes therapy. It can take months, sometimes years."

"Sam, don't worry about the trauma. I don't need to work through anything in the box. I just need to see if there *is* a box. How can we do that?"

He got another prickly glare. "Nick Severs, do you respect my profession?"

He put on his best flabbergasted expression. "Are you kidding me? Pffft! Of course, I do! I wouldn't be here if I didn't."

"So then, why is it that every time I tell you this is not how we do things you keep telling me you want to do it your way?"

"Oh. Sam. Not at all! If we were doing therapy, of course. But we are not, right? I am just asking you as a friend. You know? Like if I thought my engine had a misfire, I would go to a friend who knows cars before I went to the mechanic. Maybe I just need a new filter and an oil change. I trust you. As a friend…"

Judging by her glare, she wasn't quite falling for it, but she was possibly considering switching to rubber-tipped darts.

"C'mon Sam…Please? If there is really something there, I promise I'll go to whomever you recommend. Tell me. How can we see if there is a box?"

She sighed. "OK. There is something we can try to see if there is a repressed memory."

"What?"

"If it is a repressed memory, then your brain has installed defenses to guard you from it and the associated feelings. We can attempt to disarm those defenses and see if there is anything on the other side."

"Great! How do we do that?"

"It's called EMDR – eye movement desensitization and reprocessing. It's actually very simple. It uses rhythmic visual stimulation to disrupt your brain programming so we can access those hidden areas. It's probably the quickest way to find out if there is anything there. Is this something you want to try?"

Disrupting his brain programming sounded like a terrible plan when said out loud. But not knowing seemed worse. He nodded.

She got up, walked to a cabinet and brought out something that looked like a T-shaped desk lamp. She put it on the coffee table between them. Nick examined it nervously, as he would a suspicious package in the mail. The top of the T was a horizontal lightbar about two feet wide. Two purple teardrop-shaped paddles nestled at its base.

"This is the EMDR machine we will use to help us. But first, we need to get some bearings," Sam picked up her notepad. "What is the worst part of this vision for you?"

"The killing."

"Ok. So, let's assume for now that this actually happened. What is the most prevailing negative cognition or self-belief at the moment when this happens in your dream?"

"That I have royally screwed up. I have done something irreversible and unforgivable."

"OK, good. That is your negative cognition." She scribbled in her pad. "Now, again, assuming for now that this event actually happened, what *positive* cognition or statement would you like to feel about yourself in relation to this event? Usually, it is in the form of *I am…* or *I am not…*"

"That I am innocent?"

"Remember, we are assuming for now this actually happened."

He thought about it. "That I am worthy of forgiveness."

She nodded. "That is your positive cognition. Thinking about the event now, rank for me your degree of belief in your positive cognition from one to seven, with one being least worthy of forgiveness and seven being completely worthy of forgiveness."

"Zero."

She nodded. "You said earlier that you felt dread associated with this vision. Are there any other emotions you feel when this happens?"

He shook his head.

"OK, and what about any body sensations? Do you feel anything in your body during or after this vision? Like tightness in muscles, difficulty breathing…?"

He shook his head. "Well, I guess I feel it in my stomach. Heavy, like I swallowed lead. It almost hurts."

"OK, good. This gives us a good baseline to work with." She put down the notepad, leaned over the device and turned it on. A single blue light paced from one side to the other and then settled in the middle, staring right between Nick's eyes.

"The EMDR machine works by providing alternating stimulation to your left and right brain. This left-right rhythm helps disarm your brain's programmed safeguards so we can access and process deep memories and feelings. Your job is simple – follow the light with just your eyes. I will be controlling the speed with which it oscillates using this." She held up a small pad with buttons in her hand. "The light will provide visual stimulation. You will also have these to provide tactile stimulation." She handed him the purple paddles from the base. The smooth, curved edges fit organically into his palms. "Let me show you what it will feel like."

With all this gadgetry, he felt like a test pilot being strapped into a prototype rocket. What awaited him at the end of this trip? Would he find out he was crazy? Or a murder? Which outcome should he hope for? He must have looked concerned because Sam paused and smiled softly. "It's OK. Are you ready?"

The blue light dot scrolled leisurely to his right, and just as it reached the edge, the paddle in his right hand gave him a short, assertive vibration like a pebble-shaped pager. The light scrolled to the left, and the left paddle vibrated. The light headed back to the right again and stopped in the middle.

"OK, are you ready?"

He nodded. His palms were getting sweaty around the paddles. All this preparation was like the ratchety climb of the rollercoaster to the top of the first bottomless drop. He hated rollercoasters.

"Let's get you relaxed. Think of the safest, happiest place for you. Something that makes you feel secure and content. Can you think of a place like that?"

He closed his eyes. His safe place was Claire. Holding her close was like getting a broken piece of his soul back in its place. When he held her, he could feel their energies merge and everything else just drop away and became inconsequential. She just fit into him. His arms would wrap around her, and her head would rest on his chest, making his heart slow down to a steady pulse. He had never felt that way about anyone else. He opened his eyes.

"So, what's your safe place?" she said.

"You need me to tell you?"

"Yes, please."

He sighed. "Being with Claire." Her eyebrow twitched upward. "Not like that, you, spring-break nympho! Just holding her. The touch of her body, her presence."

She smiled. "You are a romantic, Nick Severs. Claire will do. Now, hold that image in your mind and follow the light with your eyes. We are going to start slow."

The light touched off and lazily scrolled side to side.

"Breathe."

He breathed.

"Think of Claire's energy washing over you."

He saw Claire's face on the pillow next to him, her big warm brown eyes pulling him in.

"What color is Claire's energy?"

Energy had color!? He followed the light. "White." White light was washing over him.

"What are you feeling in your body, Nick?"

"Warm. Calm."

"OK, keep tracking the light and focus on this warm, calm feeling. Feel it spread through your entire body, from your toes to your heart, to your fingertips."

He breathed in, feeling the warmth spread. The light seemed to have slowed, and the paddles vibrated more softly now, as if through a cocoon of cotton balls. The side-to-side rhythm of alternating vibrations made him feel like he too was being rocked side to side, like in a cradle.

"Keep tracking the light, Nick." He must have closed his eyes. "Breathe through this feeling. Remember it in your body."

He watched the light and focused on breathing. Deep, purposeful. The light made a few more trips and then settled in the middle. The paddles went silent.

"OK, remember this relaxed, calm feeling. No matter what traumatic events or feelings we may revisit today, this feeling will always be accessible to you. You can call on it at any time. And remember, you are safe at all times. Whatever emotions or memories come up, no matter how traumatic – they are in the past and cannot harm you now. Do you agree?"

He nodded.

"Now, visualize some distance between yourself and this event. Some people like to imagine they are on a train, watching the events unfold like scenery passing by. Others think of it like watching a movie. Whatever you pick, you are not there physically in the event. You are watching it from a distance, safe at all times. If there is ever a moment the emotions get too intense, we can pause and recharge using our calm and relaxed energy. OK? Now, if you do need to pause at any time just raise your hand. Does that work for you?"

He nodded.

"OK, do you have any questions before we begin?"

He shook his head and gripped the hard plastic of the paddles harder in his palms. The safety talk was over, and the rollercoaster was precariously at the top of the drop, held only by the slipping friction of the last cog. He hoped Sam buckled him in correctly.

"OK, here we go. Track the light."

The light touched off again and sped up. Moving his eyes back and forth this fast was harder than Nick expected. He wondered how long he could keep it up.

"Focus on the vision." Sam's voice was calm and soft. "Think through it in every detail, as it usually unfolds."

The boy's skull cracked. A thick, moist, squishy, sickly crack of a ripe watermelon splatting against the pavement. He studied the boy's head, trying his best to remain at a distance. Like watching a movie. Like examining a crime scene. There was blood and torn skin and bone and sinew showing at his cheekbone. His mouth was gaped, contorted or mangled. His eyes were white, rolled back in their sockets. His hair was dark brown, matted with dark glossy blood around the caved-in portion of his skull above his left temple and ear. He looked lifeless. He was dead.

"What are you feeling, Nick?"

He tried to swallow, but his mouth felt dry. He forced his eyes to keep up with the light. "He's dead."

"What are you feeling in your body?"

"Dread. I can't move." He heard his voice crack.

The light stopped.

"Breathe, Nick. Let your mind go blank."

He gasped a deep breath. The room was rocking side to side. The fuzzy blue dot of light fixated his gaze, as if from a great distance. There was nothing else. He could not look away.

"Tell me what's coming up now. A picture, a word, a feeling in your body…"

The dot seemed to be pulsating, calling him from afar.

"Music."

"OK, listen to it. Feel it and track the light again. Here we go."

The light touched off and he followed. The hand paddles echoed like a pendulum heartbeat: Left. Right. Left. Right.

"What do you hear, Nick?"

The ghostly melody was familiar, emerging from a jumble of the chorus that rang like church bells in the distance. He used to know it. But it was so long ago… *Charlotte Sometimes*," he blurted out. "The Cure song."

His breath tightened and his heartbeat was now beating faster than the light. He felt hot. The chorus circled in and out like a dizzy carousel.

"Stay with it, Nick. What do you see, what do you feel?"

The blue light grew brighter and fuzzier, like the flashing lights of a police car at night.

"Hallway." His own voice sounded distant and slight. *Charlotte Sometimes* echoed in the confines of the narrow walls. He *knew* what was at the end of the hallway.

"Track the light, Nick."

His breath grew faster and shallower. The light was smudging into a blue pulsing line.

"Track the light, Nick. What do you feel? What's coming up?"

The light had stretched into a glowing line, and he was walking to it in a darkened hallway, like toward a light under… "A door," he whispered hoarsely. He gasped for a breath. "Stop!" He put the paddles on the table and buried his head in his hands. The blue line seemed burned into his retinas.

"Are you OK?" Sam handed him a bottle of water, one of those half-size clear plastic bottles parents put in their kids' lunch packs.

He nodded, gulping down the entire thing. "It's the wrong memory."

"How do you know?"

"I just do!" That came out abrupt. "I'm sorry." He shook his head. "Thank you for doing this. For whatever it's worth, this stuff does work," he nodded to the machine. "It just didn't…"

He paused, distracted by a fragment of a thought floating in his head. "I know his name…" he muttered. "The kid in my dream."

FØurt33n

Kat's check of the GPS logs revealed no unexpected activity – she had been tracking these for a while now and knew exactly what each trip was: five work-related drives; one stop at his usual coffee shop; two at his usual gas station; and one drive to the therapist and back. That last one was a good sign. She next checked the web searches he did from his home laptop and from his cell phone. This time, he had one search for *forgotten memory* and several for *repressed memory*, and he spent almost six minutes reading an article on the *Psychology Today* website. Good.

There was method to her vengeance. In revenge – like in hacking – cold rational calculation was king. Roses had taught her the importance of planning her attacks, and with vengeance, there were many things to consider. Firstly, vengeance required clear intent. Just as the original offense. Of the seven who had been involved in violence that was perpetrated onto her, each one wanted something – money, power, Kat herself. Back then, each one got to collect what they wanted. Now, Kat was collecting retribution.

And that in itself required consideration. In the grand scheme of the universe, vengeance was a force. It was a violent vector with the singular purpose to disrupt another person's lifeline. Or to cut it completely. When planning to apply such force, one had to consider the manner and the magnitude one desired. Many people settled on physical violence when it came to the manner of vengeance. This was understandable. Physical violence delivered quick results. And not just in terms of physical pain. People took sovereignty of their bodies for granted. (As at one time, Kat herself did). And when that sovereignty was suddenly physically violated, they could never get it back. Not fully. Not ever again. An act of violence against the body put a ghastly gash across the person's idea of self. It would forever be a raw disfiguration across their self-confidence and their aspirations in life. The body would always remember violence done to it.

So, in retribution, one could hardly go wrong with physical violence. And if physical violence was your chosen manner of vengeance, you had three primary options at your disposal. The first was blunt force. Like a rock to the head. The nice thing about blunt force was that its application could be controlled. A little bit could leave a black eye and still hurt for days. A little more could crack ribs or break the jaw. A bit more could cause internal bleeding or fracture the skull. A bit more could kill. Another nice thing about blunt force was that it was very accessible – you didn't need special devices in order to inflict it. Just about anything heavy would do.

The second method of physical violence one could inflict was penetrating force. Like a bullet. With penetrating force, you essentially physically invaded someone else's body with a foreign object. You could do this by breaking the skin and tearing through the tissue, or you could also use an existing body cavity. And it didn't have to be a bullet. It could be a pointy knife. Or an icepick. Or a prick – so much violence had been done with those. Penetrating violence could be harder to control than blunt force, but it could also be more demoralizing.

Lastly, if you opted for physical violence, you had severing force at your disposal. Outside of death, cutting off a part of your enemy was the most irreversible form of retribution. You could take a little or a lot. In many cases, there was undeniable logic in removing the offending appendage. In some cultures, thieves had their hands cut off. In others, rapists were castrated. High crimes warranted beheadings. Severing parts from the body was gruesome but also indisputably effective at preventing relapses.

Despite the many options and advantages physical retribution offered, it wasn't right for everyone or for every occasion. If bashing, perforating, and chopping your offender was outside your comfort zone, you could go for digital vengeance instead. This was the new thing, and it offered access to so many inflection points. A bit of snooping and hacking could give you power over someone's reputation, career, marriage and finances. With a bit of planning, you could get someone arrested. Or throw them to the wolves on the dark web. And you could do all this from a safe distance.

But therein lay a problem for Kat. Digital vengeance alone lacked the personal element. It completely bypassed the need for a face-to-face confrontation with one's offender. That may have been OK for some but not for Kat. She had given this subject considerable thought. The method of retribution had to be right. It had to have significance. It had to fit the person exacting it, just like a crime fit the criminal. It also had to match its target, even if in an ironic way. Like a heart attack for the heartless. Or cancer for the corruptor. Vengeance could take on many forms, but they could not be arbitrary.

That's why for *DearJohn*, Kat elected neither physical nor digital as her primary approach. Instead, she chose a psychological offensive. It felt right for several reasons. First, she needed to bring clarity to this transaction he was unknowingly participating in. Somehow, he was in denial about what had happened, and she needed to get him to see things straight, the way they actually had occurred. His apparent amnesia about that night was irritating, and at times he almost made her doubt herself. Perhaps he was lying. Or perhaps he had convinced himself of his own lie. Or perhaps he truly repressed that memory. Her instincts and the evidence so far supported that last scenario. People's brains were complex, twisted jumbles made up of traumas, distorted reflections and utterly sincere lies. Even the brains of absolute assholes. Brute force was not going to fix his head and get her the truth. And without him remembering things right, retribution was a moot point – it would be like prosecuting someone mentally incapable of standing trial. She needed him to remember.

The second reason she elected to start with a psychological attack was parity. The old *get even* adage easily could lead one to oversimplify the equation of revenge. The intent was to balance out an injury with an injury. A loss with a loss. An eye for an eye, so to speak. But the scales of retribution weren't always this straightforward. First, there was the rape itself. Finding a way to get even on that act of physical violence was not a foregone conclusion. And that was only the beginning. Then the eleven years – and still going – of the aftershocks from the wreckage that one night made of her life. Anguish, depression, anxiety, self-doubt and shame – all ripple effects on her life, career, and relationships. What could she put on *DearJohn's* side of the scales to even things out? To long-term fuck up *his* life, career and relationships? No amount of physical pain would ever balance these scales. But with psychological warfare, there was hope.

With psychological warfare, pulling the strings tied to his past gave her a sense of control she couldn't get elsewhere in her life.

She finished her daily review with scanning through his work and personal email. There was nothing of interest there, but she was satisfied with the overall progress. He was rattled. Just as she had expected.

15

Driving back north from Colorado Springs on I-25, for the first time in many years, Nick thought about that one night in the fall of 2009. Twelve years ago – it seemed like somebody else's lifetime now. All of Sam's probing and parlor tricks had disturbed the hornet's nest of memories. This is exactly why he did not see the point in dwelling on the past. Even if he wasn't exactly proud of some of it, what good did digging it up now do? He spent much of his job probing other people's pasts. He already knew what was in his. *Didn't he?* Even if he did not readily remember something – somewhere deep inside of him, something in his mind did. And if it were important, it would have come up by now. The past was behind him and was of no relevance now. What mattered now were the things and people in his life now, and the road ahead.

The Pine Lake Police station smelled like hot toner, and the familiar cloud of puffy blue hair was floating and humming by the copier.

"Hi, there, Ruth. Who's watching the library?"

"Oh, Vern is there reading his papers, so he said he would keep an eye on things while I ran copies for the Fall Festival."

Vern was a gray-haired retired college professor from Pueblo and was possibly older than Ruth. Nick wasn't sure if it were really the newspapers that brought Vern to the library every afternoon. He suspected the sprightly old lady had something to do with it. Regardless, Nick had no doubt that without Ruth, the town of Pine Lake would not have a library at all.

"Well, you look tired," Patty chirped merrily from behind the front desk. "There's fresh coffee, if you want some."

"That's the best news I've heard all day." Nick thanked the universe for this woman who every day kept this station from slipping into certain chaos. He grabbed the empty mug from his office and headed for the coffee machine but was intercepted mid-way by Ruth.

"That poor girl," she half-whispered, leaning into Nick with a stack of warm pages in her hand. "Did you know she came in to pick up some books a couple of months ago?"

"Anything interesting?"

"Some sort of mathematics. All formulas inside. We had to order them on the interlibrary loan. Do you think she really killed herself?"

Even without looking into Ruth's quick gray eyes, Nick knew she was fishing. There were no secrets in a small town.

"I'm still checking into that, Ruth," he replied, gazing longingly at the coffee machine just beyond reach.

"Well, I just don't know about that. She did not look depressed to me. Not like Dwight was after Mary Lou passed away from cancer in '92. No one was surprised he shot himself a few days later. Of course, I am not saying she could not have had other issues…"

Nick gave her a long nod as a gesture of appreciation for this unprompted expert opinion and a history lesson from one of the town's elders. He was so close to the coffee machine he could practically taste the coffee, but his path was blocked by the tiny old lady and her gently bobbing wispy cloud of blue hair. She had a point, of course. Suicide was not a common thing in Pine Lake, and Ray had already filled Nick in on the subject of the last recorded account almost thirty years ago. But making any further mention of this fact now would have been undoubtedly mistaken for an invitation to keep conversing on the subject. It seemed after a certain age, people simply lost their sense for urgency, and this tragic development was typically and disastrously accompanied with a newfound predisposition for long and meandering conversations.

"Severs! Is that you?" Chief's voice from his office saved Nick from the clutches of the town librarian, but coffee was now a doomed cause.

Having been summoned, Nick entered just in time to see Ray slurp a big gulp from his own mug. The chief's boots were on his desk, and he looked like he had just woken up from an unplanned afternoon nap.

"Hey!" Ray grinned wholeheartedly from his chair. "Well, you look like shit."

"Yeah, I heard."

"You feelin' OK?"

"Yeah, just didn't sleep well."

Ray nodded. "Are you done with Rick's?"

"What?" Nick's brain took a second to connect the name to the hardware store burglary last week. "Oh, yes. I'll get you the report today."

"Perfect. What about Scraggy Ridge? Any news?"

"Yes. No."

"Autopsy?"

"Unremarkable."

"Forensics?"

"Nothing to get excited about."

"Still think it's a homicide?"

"I don't know. Everything says it's not."

"What would be the motive for a homicide?"

"What would be the motive for the suicide? Her victimology shows no history of depression, drugs, or other contributing factors."

Ray nodded. "Any prints?"

"Two sets. The victim's on the knife and on a few surfaces in the bathroom and the kitchen. The other ones are from her manager, on the wine bottle in the fridge. No prints on the entry door." Nick could recite the forensic report by heart now.

Ray perked up. "Manager? Oooh. That's not good."

"He said he gave her the wine as a thank you."

"Was she pregnant?"

"What?"

"The victim, was she pregnant?"

"No. I don't think so. No – Brenda would have included it in the report."

"And her boss – he married?"

"Yes. Why?"

"I may be old fashioned, but a man don't give a woman a bottle of wine unless he is hoping to drink it with her."

Nick shrugged. "People give wine as gifts these days. It's a thing."

"I'm telling you, I'd check out the boss."

"Already did. He cleared. He was at a school play with his wife and kids. Got his phone location data."

"Well, that clears his phone – not him."

Nick smiled at the old man's persistence. "You don't know this guy – he probably takes his phone in the shower with him. And anyways, school security cameras corroborated his alibi."

"And the footprint?"

"Hiking boot, Keen, men's size 11. Sold at just about every sporting goods store in the Front Range from Pueblo to Fort Collins, not to mention hundreds more online."

Ray nodded. "And with the trail right there, it could just be a hiker taking a leak. What about the candy wrapper?"

"Granola bar. No DNA, and forensics says it's been there for at least a year."

"So, what's next?"

"I'll have the cell tower dumps for the two towers closest to the victim's residence either today or tomorrow. Once I get the data, I will cross-check it against all the individuals I have in the case file so far. Brenda is running toxicology, but it could be another few weeks. I also have a data request out for the Lexi virtual assistant device the victim had, just in the case it had recorded something. And in a bit…" He looked at his watch. "…scratch that, right now, I have to go meet with the family to check out a lead on the victim's ex-boyfriend."

When he said all that out loud, it did not sound half-bad. He knew the method. He had watched other people do it. He was going through the steps. But none of that changed the fact that what he really had right now was zilch. He had no motive. No plot to this story. All he had was a partial cast of characters and the last page. He tried not to think about that.

16

Being a detective came with complications. When he was a beat cop, Nick had seen plenty of bad stuff, but he did not have to live with it day in and day out. By the time he wrote his report, it would already have become someone else's problem – the investigator, the DA, social services. A beat cop woke up every morning to a brand-new day. A detective was not that lucky. Most cases did not resolve overnight, or even over a few days or a week. Some lasted for months. Some years. Some would never be solved. And therein lied the paradox of his profession. As a detective, Nick had full responsibility over the process, but zero guarantee of the outcomes. Even if he did everything right, even if he did not bungle things up, he could still fail. And there were plenty of opportunities to bungle things up. Here he was now at a fork in the investigation already – suicide to the left or homicide to the right? Which way, Nick? Are you sure, Nick? He felt like an inept tour guide responsible for deciding on what ride everyone would go next. And it wasn't just a matter of truth. In the justice system, it was first and foremost the matter of what could or could not be proven. What Nick could or could not prove. And later, what the DA could or could not prove. In all this, Nick was the custodian of a fragile chain of evidence and reasoning that decided who got to go home and who got to stay in the system. And if he bungled up the process, the truth would not matter.

But it mattered to the family, didn't it? Was one option better than the other to them? Easier to live with? The murder of your child or her suicide? He could not be honest with them. Not yet. They'd already been through more than any parent should. He could not thrash them carelessly about based on unsubstantiated suspicions.

The smell of freshly baked afternoon cookies whiffed through the lobby of the Castle Rock Howard Johnson. Nick sat himself down on a firm couch and resisted the urge to lean back and close his eyes. Instead, he spotted a coffee station on the counter by the front desk. He hopped to his feet and made a brisk beeline across the lobby before anyone, or anything could get in his way. Success. He was able to get in two robust sips of hot, aromatic java juice from a paper cup before the elevator dinged, and Lori and Clint stepped out. It was time to find the ex-boyfriend.

All Nick had was the name from Lisa's phone, but it was enough to set Clint off.

"Kevin Dickins? He's a lowlife. Never could hold a job. He was always doing drugs. Always holding Lisa back. I did not approve of her hanging out with him in high school. But you know how teenage girls are."

Lori was more forgiving: "Kevin grew up in the system. You could tell the boy had a lot of trauma. And he had to change foster families in high school, as if high school was not hard enough already. Somehow, he and Lisa connected. She was good for him. Calmed him down. They did do some drugs, she told me, but nothing serious." This must have been news to Clint because he crossed his arms and glared from under his furrowed brows like an owl.

"My daughter was always a curious but cautious child. She'd never let herself get hooked. But Kevin was a different story. I could tell he had an addictive personality. It was his way of coping, I suppose. They were inseparable for most of high school. Best friends and also dated off and on. Sometimes I could not tell. She liked him, but he was just kind of stuck. And she wanted to go places. When she went to college, he stayed behind. That's the last we really saw of him. I don't think he took it well that she had moved on with her life."

"Did she tell you if they were still in touch?"

"Occasionally. Nothing regular, she said. She got her degree and started working full time. She moved on."

"Did you know that Kevin followed her to Denver?"

"What?" Her eyes widened. Clint's jaw tightened.

Nick swiped the screen on Lisa's phone and showed them the text:

Kevin: "Hey. I'm in Denver."

"This was in July," Nick said.

"She didn't respond?"

"Not by text, but there are quite a few calls to and from the number saved as *Kevin*. At least a couple a week. Many are over twenty minutes long. Looks like she called him two days before her death."

"She did not tell me any of this."

"I tried calling this number, but it's been disconnected. Do you know of any other way of finding Kevin?"

Lori shook her head. "No, I don't. Lisa would have had the best number. I see his foster parents at the grocery store every now and then. They told me he moved out after high school, and they've lost touch. But I can give you their number just in case."

"Do you think he did something to Lisa?" Clint glared. "Got her hooked on drugs?"

"I don't know. But he may have been one of the last people to see her alive." Nick closed his notebook and stood up. "Thank you for this. I'll keep digging."

Outside, the warm Colorado sun was just past the half-way point on its daily journey to meet the mountains. The vibrant azure sky boded it smooth sailing, with not a cloud in sight. Nick started the engine and rolled down the windows to let in in the cool breeze.

He sipped the hot coffee and swiped the screen of Lisa's phone again. Kevin's contact record contained no address, email or other phone numbers. Nick went back to her full contact list and searched for *Kevin*. There was only one other Kevin in the list: Kevin JP. Kevin JP had a 303 Colorado area code. Nick thought about it for a second and then dialed the number.

A cheerful woman's voice answered, "It's a blessed day at Jobe's Place. This is Michelle. How can I help you?"

***

Jobe's Place was a halfway house off I-25 and Colfax in Denver. The house was a two-story craftsman with a brick porch and an industrial storage lot across the street behind a tall chain link fence. A cement truck rolled by as Nick got out of the Tahoe and walked up the steps.

The front door closed behind him on a creaky metal spring. A section of the large foyer was set up as the front desk area with a file cabinet, a boxy beige printer, a computer monitor, and a beaming plump woman with glasses and dark hair.

"Are you Detective Severs?" her voice rang in the millwork of the entryway.

"Yes, you must be Michelle?" He smiled and she beamed even more.

"So, you were asking about Kevin Dickins?" she swiveled in her chair and pulled open a file drawer. Nick seated himself on a thin but sturdy stackable convention center chair.

She swiveled back around with a file in her hand. It was thin.

"Kevin was with us for just over a month." She passed Nick the intake form. A youthful, cleanly-shaven face smiled reservedly from a small photo. Nick studied the form.

"What happened after the month?"

"He failed a drug test." She sighed, and a light cloud crossed over her beaming face. "We have a zero-tolerance policy. To stay here, our residents must stay clean, participate in the program, respect house rules and be actively looking for a job. He did well for a while but then relapsed."

"When was that?"

She clanked on the keyboard, clicked a few times with the mouse, and squinted at the screen: "August 12th is when he moved out."

"Do you know where he went?"

She squinted at the screen again and shook her head. "No forwarding address. But you can try his emergency contact. You should have it there on the form."

Nick's eyes froze on the name further down on the page. "Lisa Benoche? She was his emergency contact?"

Michelle beamed again. "Yes, sweet girl. She came in with him, helped him fill out the forms and paid the first two months' rent. I am sure she will help you find him."

Nick nodded. "Can I get a copy of this form?"

"Sure." She swiveled around to the printer, put the form on the glass and punched a few buttons, all without getting up. The printer beeped, whined, and rolled out a single page.

"Thank you," Nick said, taking the warm copy. "I'll leave my card. If Kevin happens to stop by, please ask him to call me. It's important."

He walked out into the sunny Denver afternoon. He was almost to the Tahoe when the front door spring creaked again. "Hey, detective, are you looking for Kevin?" A man in a plaid shirt and jeans stepped out onto the porch. He looked to be in his late thirties and had long light brown hair and a reddish goatee.

"Yes. Do you know where I can find him?"

"He's in the tent city in Cheesman Park." The lumberjack Jesus walked down the steps and put out his hand. "Hey, I'm Jerry. I'm the facilities manager here."

Nick shook Jerry's hand. "Do you remember when you last saw Kevin?"

"Last Thursday."

"Are you certain?" Nick made a note.

"Yeah, I go down there and buy him and a couple of other guys lunch every Thursday."

"Did you by chance see him last Tuesday? The seventh?"

"Umm, no."

"OK. Thanks for that information. How do I find him in Cheesman Park?"

Jerry squinted in the sun and scratched his goatee. "Man, it's over six hundred tents there. You'll never find him on your own. I can just come down there with you."

This simple selfless offer caught Nick off guard. "That would be great. Aren't you going to ask me what this is about or if he has done something?"

Jerry grinned. "Nah, I know he hasn't. Kevin is the sweetest guy. He used to help me with maintenance around the place. The only person he knows how to harm is himself. Whatever this is about, it's none of my business."

They drove east on Colfax, away from the industrial bottoms of I-25 and into the sprawling, mixed residential and commercial flatlands. Nick was acutely aware of the fact that if they drove west instead, they could have hit I-70 and be in the mountains in fifteen minutes. He would have much rather been driving west.

His new navigator, however, seemed to be enjoying the ride.

"Hey, do you know the history of Cheesman Park?" Jerry asked, clearly excited to share the trivia.

Nick indulged him by shaking his head.

"So, in the 1800s, the whole area was part of this massive 320-acre Prospect Hill Cemetery, which also covered the land that is now the Denver Botanic Gardens and Prospect Park. Thanks to the gold rush, this area was flooded with prospectors, settlers, immigrants and speculators, and Denver itself was still pretty small. Naturally, wherever there are a lot of live people, there eventually will be a lot of dead ones, too. The cemetery was zoned for various groups and ethnicities – Irish, Jewish,

Chinese, Catholics, Masons, etc. There were some premium plots for the wealthy, but most of the well-to-do clientele preferred smaller and more selective venues. So, the majority of people who ended up buried at Prospect Hill were vagrants, criminals and the poor. A few decades later, Denver was growing, and the real estate developers were putting in nice neighborhoods east of the downtown, and this massive cemetery was right in the middle of things. Not only was it taking up valuable land, but it was also not kept up very well and was an eyesore to the new classy residents. So, in the 1890s, the developers petitioned the city to move it. The city agreed and gave a deadline for the families to move their buried relatives. When the deadline came and passed, there were still almost five thousand unclaimed graves. Guess which ones? The vagrants, the criminals and the poor. So, the city had to bid out the contract to move the remaining graves. They awarded the contract to the undertaker with lowest bid. Under that contract, the undertaker was paid per casket moved. He was supposed to dig up each grave, put the remains in a new casket, and transport them to another cemetery for re-burial."

Jerry paused and looked at Nick to make sure he was still paying attention. And Nick was. He'd been to cemeteries on several occasions, but he never really spent much time thinking about the business side of the afterlife services. Someone said we were all equal in death, but that certainly was not true – one visit to a cemetery was enough to confirm that fact. Just like the cities of the living, the cities of the dead also had their ghettos with shabby graves, the ritzy neighborhoods with mansion-sized family mausoleums, and the downtown multi-level tenement blocks where anyone with modest means could acquire a labeled cubby hole for their jar of ashes to call home. Undertaking was a business, and it only made sense that the dead were subject to the same privileges and limitations that defined their socioeconomic conditions when they were still living. In other words, nothing changed once the soul moved on.

Accepting Nick's contemplation as a sign of engagement, Jerry continued. "So, if you were an enterprising undertaker in his shoes, what would you do to maximize your profits?"

Nick pondered the riddle briefly and then obliged, not expecting a good development: "What?"

"He used children's coffins." Jerry beamed. "Three foot long by one foot wide. His workers were opening the graves, breaking up the remains, and throwing them into children's caskets. So, instead of one casket, he would end up using three per grave. Can't make this stuff up, right? But it gets better. You ready?"

This was probably a rhetorical question, but Nick still nodded, morbidly amused by this odd bit of American folklore and Jerry's excitement.

"This went on for some time before the City Hall got wind of it and canceled the rest of the contract. Want to guess what they did next?" Rhetorical question. Jerry was not slowing down. "They put a fence around it, waited a couple of years, and then just leveled the area for the park. I mean – can you believe it? They just left the rest of the bodies. Almost three thousand graves – just covered up and built over. To this day, city crews still uncover bones there when they do work on the grounds. Oh, hey, do you mind stopping at this donut shop? Kevin loves the maple ones."

They went through the drive-through, and Nick passed to Jerry a weighty brown paper bag with a spreading grease stain. The sweet smell of freshly baked pastry dough and sugar filled the Tahoe.

A couple of blocks further through the residential neighborhoods, they reached the towering condos on the periphery of Cheesman Park. Although Nick had been in this area on a few occasions last year, this time it was a new view. Normally a vast green space, the open lawn was now overtaken with a tightly packed encampment of colorful tents. As Jerry navigated him through the area, Nick felt like a UN peacekeeper driving through a refugee camp. This was poverty in living color. Right in the heart of Denver, a stone's throw from Capitol Hill. And this wasn't the only tent city in Denver, either. The homeless issue was all over the news – the local residents and the businesses were vocal about it, and tempers were running high on all sides. It was a powder keg. He didn't envy Denver PD.

"Something else, isn't it?" Jerry summed it all up and guided Nick to park next to a playground.

It certainly was. If there were really thousands of graves still under this area, it looked like the poor and the vagabonds buried here had found a new way to haunt the city that had paved over them.

"Where do all these people come from?" Nick asked.

Jerry shrugged. "Here, there, and everywhere. Many are from out of state. Many had homes last year. Until they didn't. It's a growing epidemic."

A new wave of settlers, winning the west again, one state at a time.

"What happened?"

"COVID, recession, unemployment – take your pick."

"How many of them do you think will get back to normal?"

"In my experience? Few to none, unless something changes in the way we deal with this problem. This here is the proverbial bottom. Once you end up here, getting out is just about the hardest thing in your life. Most of them are doing good just surviving day to day."

Nick followed Jerry from the parking lot into the grass. "How do we fix this?" he asked, stepping over a chicken bone.

"Homelessness isn't a problem. It's a symptom," Jerry riddled back, venturing into the thicket of rainbow-bright swatches of synthetic domes and peaks, with spaces between them filled with sleeping bags, folding chairs and coolers. For all the colorful outdoor gear, this could have been a scene from the Everest basecamp if it weren't for the City Market shopping carts and the overflowing trash cans.

"Hey, Dave!" Jerry yelled ahead, waiving his hand. A man in an orange T-shirt with long gray hair looked up. "Is Kevin around?"

The man looked behind him. "Yeah, He's in. I see 'is boots."

Jerry stepped over a McDonalds paper bag and maneuvered through a tight arrangement of a partially gutted red loveseat and a blue striped recliner. Nick pondered that the homeless weren't like those of us with houses. They did not want large yards and fences. They huddled together, tent upon tent, like people freezing in the wild, foregoing personal space and inhibitions for the sake of warmth and safety. There was a hierarchy of needs, as it's been said, and at this stage, acreage was not a high priority on their list.

Jerry stopped at a small orange and gray tent with a welcome mat and a pair of boots sticking out. "Kevin?" he called into the tent.

The boots stirred and disappeared then were replaced with a thin, sunburned face with a scraggy reddish beard and a brown beany hat. Nick could hardly recognize the features from the photo on the Jobe's Place intake form.

Kevin squinted up at them. "Jerry?" he mumbled. He scratched his head through the beanie. "Hey, man. Is it Thursday already?"

"No, brother, it's Tuesday. But I brought you some donuts. Maple."

Kevin's face lit up, and he scrambled to his feet. He had on a pair of dusty jeans and a black, ripped long-sleeve Pink Floyd shirt. "Oh, man, you are *a lifesaver*." He spoke slowly and enunciated the last word, which added distinct sincerity to his tone. "These will be great with coffee later." He accepted the bag and stashed it with care inside the tent opening. "How are you doing, *J-Jerry?*" he asked with interest and stuttered slightly on the last word as he curiously scanned Nick.

"Doing well. Started maintenance on the furnace at Jobe's this week. It's old, you know. But should get us through another winter, knock on wood. What have you been up to?"

Kevin nodded enthusiastically. "Oh, I've been doing odd cash jobs from Craigslist, you know. Helping folks with yardwork and moving. But my phone broke on the last job, so if you need to reach me, try Dave. I've been borrowing his to check Craigslist. I need to save up for a new one."

Jerry nodded. "Hey, Kevin, I brought someone who wants to talk to you. This is Detective Severs."

Kevin smiled politely, looked Nick straight in the eye and extended his hand. "It's a p-pleasure to meet you."

Nick shook his thin hand.

"Well, I'll go visit with Dave and let you two talk." Jerry threaded himself in-between the tents. "I'll be back."

"S-so, what can I do for you, *d-detective?*" Kevin had an earnestness about him, like he was on a mission to help you. But given his haggard and gaunt appearance, Kevin didn't exactly look fit for any sort of mission in his current condition. Judging by his thin face and how loosely the T-shirt draped on his frame and arms, Nick suspected most of Kevin was made up of skin and bones.

"Kevin, when was the last time you saw Lisa Benoche?"

Kevin's eyes lit up briefly when he heard her name, but then his face turned to worry. "Is she OK? D-did something happen?" He interrogated Nick.

"When did you last see her, Kevin?"

He looked distressed, like a puppy locked outside a glass slider door. "I don't know, early August. We had dinner. At Applebee's. Is she OK?"

Nick shook his head. "I am sorry, Kevin. Lisa is dead."

"Oh god. No." His legs collapsed under him, and he settled onto the mat in front of his tent. He buried his face in his hands and rocked back and forth. "W-when?" he muttered through his hands.

"Last Tuesday."

He shook his head and sat there for a few minutes, quietly hiding from the world. Nick gave him time. After a little while of silence, Kevin lifted his head and stared into space. Glistening streaks of tears carved their way down his sunken, stubbled cheeks. "I haven't been answering her calls since I got kicked out from Jobe's. I didn't want her to see me like this."

He sniffled and smudged the tears with his sleeve. "How did she die?"

"It looks like a suicide."

His head shook categorically. "No! Not Lisa. Never Lisa!"

"Why do you say that?"

"She just always had this strength in her. No matter what shit happened to her, she always had that strength. She kept on moving forward. She had a *plan* for her life." He placed a strong, earnest emphasis on that simple word, as if not just anyone could have a plan.

"How did she seem to you when you last saw her?"

He shook his head. "Her usual self."

"Do you think she could have been depressed?"

"No. We just talked, like always. She asked about me, and I asked about her."

"What did she tell you about herself?"

"She just talked about her job. About planning to go home to see her mom for Labor Day."

"And you are sure you haven't talked to her since?"

"No. I screwed up, bad. She left messages, but I was too embarrassed to talk to her, after everything she'd done for me. More than anyone else in my life." His head still shook slightly, unconsciously, as he stared wide-eyed into the nothingness in front of him.

"Kevin, where were you last Tuesday night?"

He sniffled and concentrated. "I'm sorry." He looked at Nick and tears started streaming down his face again. "I don't remember. Maybe here, or on Colfax." He shook his head. "I am so sorry. I want to help, but I just don't know."

"It's ok. I'll leave you my card. If you remember, you can call me," Nick said, even though he had already made up his mind. There was no way this wreck of a kid could have done this. Not physically. Not emotionally. Not with the precision and organization it was done with. "Kevin, do you know anyone who would want to hurt Lisa?"

He looked up, bewildered. "You think someone killed her?!"

"We've not ruled it out yet."

"Why would anyone want to hurt *Lisa*?"

17

By the time Nick finally pulled into his driveway that day, the sun had already dipped behind the mountains, but the sky was still glowing with fiery oranges, pinks and purples over the jagged deep-indigo horizon.

"Hey," Claire said from the couch and muted the TV. "How did it go today?"

Nick took stock before answering this simple question. The headache was back, his brain was fried, and at the moment he had no idea how to sum up the contents of the last twelve hours.

"Interesting," he finally stuck a label on it. He spotted Claire's wine bottle and glass on the coffee table. "I need a drink. You need anything?"

She shook her head. He walked to the kitchen, got the bottle of Bulleit from the cupboard and watched the amber liquid splash down at the bottom of the glass.

"What does *interesting* mean?" she asked. "Did you go see Sam?"

He circled the couch and settled next to her, exhaling an involuntary old-man grunt as he did so.

"Shit, you look like you've been through the wringer."

He gave her the best fake grin he could muster. "She invited us to come visit. She'd love to meet you."

"Yeah, for sure. What did she say about your nightmares?"

"She had me do this thing she called EMDR. I don't remember what it stands for – eye desensitization something."

"Oh yeah? I think I've heard of that." She readjusted toward him on the couch, and there was a hopeful note in her voice. "What was that like?"

He swallowed a sip of burning amber. "Like a fucking Ouija board for your head. If you're gonna do it, be ready for some really dark shit to come up and say hello."

She did not crack up and instead watched him intensely. "Isn't that the point? Would you rather the dark shit stayed buried?"

He could see merit in keeping shit buried.

"So, it worked? What dark shit came up?"

"Well, it certainly brought up something." He took another flaming gulp. "But if you ask me, this EMDR thing is not exactly a precision tool – it wasn't even the right memory that came up."

"No? What was it?"

She sipped her wine but watched him from the corner of her eye. She seemed worried. And he hated worrying her. He hated being worried about. It made him feel like a little boy. Like when he would get sick, and his mother would fuss about him. By now, he should have been able to take care of this himself, and it irked him that he hadn't so far. And now there was fuss about him.

He sighed, finished his bourbon in one gulp, thought about it, and went to get more. He brought back the bottle and set it next to hers.

"When I was in college, my best friend committed suicide. I was the one who found him."

Her eyebrow trembled. "Oh, honey." She pulled up to him and put her hand on his lap.

That damned EMDR! He felt helpless tears pooling up, and he felt like a boy again. He drew in a long, deep inhale to dry them out, hoping she did not notice.

"Not a good memory. I haven't really thought about it for many years." He took a drink. "But…there *was* also something else."

"What?"

"I guess this EMDR thing must have loosened up all the old shit, because somehow, all of a sudden I remembered the name of the kid in my dreams."

She sat back. "You did? So, he's real?"

"Yep. His name is Tommy O'Rourke. He went to my college, but I didn't know him well.

"So, that's good, right? Have you looked him up?"

He shook his head. "Haven't had a chance to, with all the driving around today. I did call Mike and left him a message to see if he remembers Tommy. He hasn't called back yet."

"Well, let's see." She pulled out her phone and rapidly typed into it as if it were a silent, thumbs-only typewriter. "O'Rourke? Are any of these him?"

He scanned through the Google grid of photos of random men of random ages. She scrolled down slowly.

"I don't think so. I'll see if I can track him down tomorrow when I get to the station. And maybe Mike will have something." *All I really need to know is that Tommy is alive and well*, he thought. He was sure he was. Nick never really even knew the guy. Why the hell did Tommy have to resurface in his dreams now? What did Tommy have to do with anything? Why couldn't memories just stay erased like files deleted from a computer?

He set his unfinished bourbon on the coffee table and put his feet up on the arm of the couch and his head in Claire's lap. "Enough about all this. Tell me about your day. What's the latest in the drama starring the wicked head nurse?"

She laughed. "She is not wicked. Just…difficult." Her fingertips slipped into his hair, and he closed his eyes. The TV was murmuring at half-volume, and if she kept rubbing his head, he would fall asleep in no time.

But just then, his phone buzzed on the coffee table. "Is it Mike?" he asked without opening his eyes.

"Umm, it says *JeffCo Coroner*. Should you really answer when the coroner calls? Is it kind of like when Death knocks at your door?"

"Probably, but I should take it anyways." He sat up and swiped the answer button.

"This is Detective Severs."

"Were you sleeping, hon?" – Brenda.

"Nope. Whatcha got for me?"

"Well, I did some researching and then spent some more time with our victim."

"And?"

"Some very minor internal hemorrhaging in the deep soft tissue of the neck."

"Strangulation?!" He must have sounded excited because Claire gave him a concerned look.

"No. Carotid restraint."

He stood up and walked to the kitchen. "A chokehold? How can you tell the difference?"

"Strangulation is done to cause asphyxiation. It requires considerable force to cut off the airflow and will leave noticeable evidence, including bruising on the neck, petechial hemorrhaging in and around the eyes, and fractures to the laryngeal skeleton. And we don't have any of that. On the other hand, a carotid restraint is done to cut off the flow of blood to the brain and cause the person to pass out. It requires much less force – just enough pressure to block the carotid artery without cutting off the airflow. If someone knows what they are doing, the carotid restraint will not leave any external evidence. And it would cause temporary incapacitation. Possibly long enough for someone to stage a suicide."

A shiver ran up his spine. This was sufficient cause for a homicide investigation.

"You said someone would have to know what they were doing?"

"Well, yes. Too much pressure would cause bruising and asphyxiation. Not enough pressure, and it would not work at all."

"So, who would be skillful enough to do this?"

"Well, they used to teach it in the police academy, but I would not go so far as to say many cops are skilled enough to make it this clean. This looks practiced. Could be someone in martial arts. Or special forces."

A clockwork of roulette wheels of possibilities was already winding up in his head. "Brenda, you are the best. I could just–" He rummaged around his preoccupied, fried brain for an HR-safe compliment to give her.

"Uh-hum. You have yourself a good night, hon."

She hung up.

"So, Brenda the coroner, ha?" Claire interrogated him with a raised brow from the couch. "Should I be worried? What does she give you that I don't?"

He returned to the living room, hopped onto the back of the couch and slid down the overstuffed leather slope back into her lap. "A murder," he replied.

18

Coffee was one of few things in life Nick chose not to compromise on. Over the years, he had become intentionally selective. To think of it, he had most likely had coffee every day of his life since college – *thirteen-some years?* How many cups was that? A lot. And not all of them were good. In fact, most, probably, weren't. The worst was the old gas station coffee of his college days, those two eternally half-empty bulbous glass carafes – an orange and a black one – that have been thickening on the hotplate for hours, had the color of crude oil and the bouquet that was a mixture of hot antifreeze and stale diesel exhaust. The very smell gave him heartburn. How many of those had he had? Too many. Thanks to the late Nineties coffee renaissance, those were almost extinct now.

Mental math time: thirteen years = around four and a half thousand days.

But the 1990s and the 2000s went overboard, of course, and birthed forth a scourge…an ugly horde of *fancy* coffees. This was a perversion of *-cinos* and *lattes* in excessive varieties –hot, cold, canned, bottled, with dairy and without, slathered with flavorings, sugar and sprinkles, like a five-year-old's clown birthday party cake – all with too much of everything in them and with not enough coffee.

Not enough for Nick, at least. He liked his coffee a very particular way – just coffee. If it came down to it, he even did not mind paying four bucks for a cup at a fancy shop ran by a beanie-topped, bearded, tattooed, skinny-jeaned lumberjack. As long as it was good.

But paying that kind of money every day was just crazy.

Four and a half thousand days. Some days more than one cup. OK, most days. Let's just say two a day. So, nine thousand cups in thirteen years. But then, there were two years of grad school. So, let's say ten thousand cups. So far.

He started drinking coffee seriously when he switched majors during his junior year in college. He had to catch up on the prerequisites to be able to graduate on time. Engineering to English. Despite these two majors having the first three letters in common, there was a world of difference between them. His parents did not approve. English paid shit. They were right, of course. But he wanted to do what he enjoyed. At barely twenty, he decided that life was too short to spend it on stuff that did not make him happy. His parents probably felt vindicated when he quit teaching and started at the police academy. But he had practically stopped talking to them by then. He did not need constant editorial commentary on his life choices, and not talking to them was the path of the least editorial commentary on his life choices.

Coffee got him through school. And later, when he started teaching, there was always coffee in the faculty break room, and he even had a small pot in his office, for the odd hours of the day. But when he became a cop, his office space had shrunk to the confines of the front cab in his Ford cruiser. There was only one logical solution – he had to up the ante and make the one morning mug really count. And that is how he came to share his modest home with a Gaggia espresso machine.

The Gaggia was a brutalist hunk of metal that towered like a stranded stainless-steel iceberg on his countertop. Despite the fact that it cost more than twenty Mr. Coffee machines, it could do less than half of what a Mr. Coffee did. And that suited Nick just fine. The Gaggia did not have a dashboard of buttons or an LCD screen. It did not have fancy blue lights. It did not know what day or time it was, and if you told it to have coffee ready before you got up in the morning, the only thing you could guarantee with absolute certainty was that you would be the one making it.

The Gaggia knew how to do just one thing, and it did it exceptionally well – it made coffee. And it needed Nick to do everything else. It was like an old muzzle-loader rifle, all manual. First, it needed its water filled. Manually. Then, the freshly ground coffee powder had to be packed into the heavy chromed brass loader. Manually. The loader then had to be twisted by its thick black handle into its slot in the machine – the tighter the better, compressing the double-shot in the brewing chamber. Manually. And when everything was ready, Nick had to flip the glowing-red toggle switch – manually – and the Gaggia would do its thing. And coffee was definitely its thing.

There was beautiful elegance in the simplicity of this machine's purpose – to do one thing well. This simplicity of function appealed to him. There was purity in it. Mastery. Which was more than one could say about most things these days. Some things – maybe. His pen, his notepad, his Springfield XD 9mm in its leather holster. They all came to work with Nick each day. Each was great at doing its one thing. But what about Nick? What was his one thing he was great at? At one time, he thought it was teaching, until it wasn't. Now maybe it would be being a detective? The jury was still out on that one. Besides, being great was not a requirement for this job. It was just a job that had to get done, like many others in a modern society. Someone had to show up for the investigations and file the paperwork on time, just like someone had to run the cash register at the store and someone else had to fill potholes on the highway. He had met plenty of detectives who were not *very good*. But they were *good enough* and did their best to clear the cases in a timely manner. But doing your best had nothing to do with being good. Sometimes, someone's best was shit. A lot of times, actually.

And what if *his* best turned out to be shit? What if he had already missed something key in this case? What if he was now doomed to get this one wrong? And the next one? And the next? What then? What does a man looking at his forties do, having failed twice? Start over? Or settle in, trudging till retirement, churning out good-enough work? Killing off year after year. Mediocrity was the mother of inconsequence. An irrelevant existence. What could be worse than that?

You had to press the toggle switch again – manually – to make it stop. The Gaggia did not know how to stop on its own. In Nick's book, this was a plus. He would just let the metal monstrosity run until it filled his mug. The end result was probably close to an Americano, but he just called it good coffee. It was a process, and the result was well worth the labor – a piping-hot cup with thick crema in various shades of rich browns swirled on its surface like a sepia-colored photograph of the storms on Jupiter. One could just admire it, but he chose to put a lid on it and drink it in his truck, while it was hot. Given the restless nights lately, he needed it.

But, having just pulled out of the driveway, he had to set the mug right back down because Mike called.

"Tommy O'Rourke?!" Mike's voice rustled loudly in the speakerphone. "Geez, that's a trip down the memory lane."

"Yeah, do you remember him?"

"I do. He pledged at our frat. Must have been our junior year. He was a freshman."

"Do you know what happened to him? Did he make the pledge?"

"Oh, man – no. He died. Some sort of an accident. You don't remember this?"

Nick sharply veered over and brought the half-ton Tahoe to a stop on the side of the road. "An accident?" He felt his chest tightening.

"You really don't remember? It was around the time your roommate killed himself…*Marc?*"

Nick swallowed down the lump in his throat. "What kind of an accident?"

"Car, I think. I don't remember for sure. Are you OK, man?"

"Yeah. Thanks. I'll call you later."

He was not OK. OK would have been if Tommy were still alive. Or if he weren't even real in the first place. Right then, Nick would have even settled for simply never remembering any of this.

He put the Tahoe in gear and pulled back onto the road. He needed to get to the station in a hurry. He desperately wanted to track down the details of Tommy's accident, but personal stuff would have to wait – he had already called Lori Benoche and asked her to meet him.

Surely enough, she and Clint already were waiting for him in his office. He had considered how to best break the news to her, but all the preferred words he had planned to say crumbled into little pieces when her eyes locked onto his, and all he could utter was, "I am sorry. We have evidence to believe that Lisa did not commit suicide."

She burst forward with a sob and hid her face and tears in her hands. He moved the Kleenex box closer to her. It must have been like having to hear that her daughter had died again. Whatever narratives and scenes she had created and played through countless times in her head over the last few days had been ripped out and replaced with a dark and violent unknown. He knew because he had played through the same scenes in his own head.

Clint's weathered hand rubbed his daughter's back gently. "So, you are saying someone did this to our Lisa?" He fixed a steely gaze on Nick.

Nick nodded. "I know I've asked you this before, but maybe you have remembered anything? Anyone who would want to hurt her?"

"Have you found Kevin?" Clint asked glumly. "He followed her here. It can't be a coincidence."

"He followed her here because she got him into an addiction treatment program here. She wanted to help him turn his life around."

Lori looked up. "She never told me about this. Why wouldn't she tell me about this?"

"People can be sensitive about addiction. It's a very personal matter. A lot of shame. For most people, it's not a straight-line journey. I would guess she just wanted to keep this between her and Kevin."

Nick opened his desk drawer and pulled out the baggie with two amber studs. He placed it on the desk in front of Lori.

"Lisa was wearing these when she died," he said. "You can have them back."

She clutched the plastic bag in her hands and closed her eyes. Her lower lip trembled, and she broke down again.

"It's like losing her all over again," she sobbed, shaking her head. "Who would do this to my little girl?"

"I am going to find out," Nick said, and he suddenly believed it.

He believed it because this wasn't about him. Because this wasn't about whether he picked the right major in college or whether he would ever really talk to his parents again, or about his nocturnal homicide trysts with Tommy O'Rourke. Because this was about Lisa, and Lori, and Clint, and some yet-to-be-named asshole, and about evidence – some known and some yet-to-be-known, but all already there. And because this was about arranging all these pieces back into their natural order in time and space, an arrangement that would seem obvious and feel right in the end. Because this was about him doing the job he was trained to do. And because if not him, then who?

19

When you become a cop, your social universe veers into a nosedive. Your world as you know it gradually becomes populated with the wrong people – murderers, thieves, scammers, wife-beaters, pedophiles, drug dealers, junkies, prostitutes, and just average citizens who take pride in being the very best assholes they can be every day. They move in, and they never leave. They come along with you wherever you go. *They* are your social network. While your girlfriend may know from Facebook exactly what her third cousin on the mother's side whom she never met in real life looks like and which of her kids is lactose intolerant, you know the name and the face of the pimp to squeeze for information about the prostitute missing from Prospect Avenue. The overwhelming predominance of this felonious populace in your known universe irreversibly lowers your expectations of the human race. Greed and cruelty to each other no longer surprise you. They become the norm.

This does not mean you have to turn into a heartless cynic. Nick tried consciously not to be. But this became a lens he saw the world through. He could never fully take off. In his line of work, he had come to expect to encounter people at the bottom of their moral convictions. Nature or nurture – he had long ago stopped trying to figure out how people ended up at the bottom. Morality was like swimming. When people stopped trying, they sank. Some seemed to dive deeper on purpose. Bottoms were relative, after all. For some, the bottom was much lower and darker than for others.

Lisa was almost ten years younger than him when she died. A kid, practically, fresh out of college, but she was already on a path. Bright, driven, promising. Everything was going for her. Except it wasn't. Her path was on a collision course with someone else's. Someone who would cut hers short and keep on going, leaving her in that cold bathtub, in the empty house, the pale moon of her face reflecting in the red mirror of the water. What kind of a person did it take to do something like this? To incapacitate her, slash her wrists, and make her family think she had killed herself.

Cold-blooded. Calculating. Organized. A crime of dispassion. In his line of work, Nick had met a few convicted killers. Most did not feel remorse. Maybe a person like that did not feel anything. Or maybe they felt normal. Maybe they just went on with their lives. Went to work. Chatted with the neighbors. Washed the car. How did they do it? Did they just put it out of their mind? Forget?

Could he, Nick, be one of them? Is that what he did, too – forget? The mystery of Nick Severs' nightmares was evolving. Tommy O'Rourke was real, and Tommy O'Rourke was dead. But how did Tommy die? Was it really a car accident? Or perhaps Nick's dream was not a dream at all. Perhaps the real Nick Severs had already long ago sunk to the deep, dark bottom of his moral void. What if he had been living there all those years? Covered up, forgotten?

Why else would he be so haunted by this vision? Tommy's dead face was now always there, waiting for him whenever he closed his eyes. It haunted him every night like his personal, perverse production of Hamlet, playing over and over, *"A murder most foul,"* with a fresh dash of insanity mixed in. Was this the beginning of his unraveling? Or the *revealing*?

He had to only make a call to find out. He had the number right in front of him. And yet, he still hadn't.

Car tires crunched the gravel outside. Nick turned in his chair and through the blinds saw an unfamiliar Subaru Forrester pull into the lot. The passenger got out and gave the station thorough consideration from a safe distance. It was Kevin. There were second thoughts written all over his face. He turned back toward the car, but the driver's side opened, and Jerry got out. He gave Kevin a pat on the back and they both proceeded to the door.

Nick tuned into the sounds outside of his open door, over the droning murmurs of Ruth and Patty discussing something in hushed tones. When he heard the jangle of the cowbell on the door, Nick got up and headed to the front.

Kevin was in the lobby, with Jerry right behind him, closing the door.

"Can I help you, sweetie?" Patty considered the visitor from behind the counter.

"I'm just here to see D-detective Nick." Midwestern stoner drawl. "Oh, hey." He lit up and waived like a kid, spotting Nick in the hallway. He looked even skinnier than the last time. But his eyes – more present. More sober.

"Come on in, Kevin. Jerry." Nick motioned them in.

Kevin's eyes paused on the box of donuts.

"You want a donut, honey?" Ruth handed him a paper plate. "Want some coffee?"

"Yes, ma'am, that would be lovely," he beamed and nodded by bobbing his whole head.

Jerry graciously declined the same offer.

In Nick's office, Kevin carefully wrapped the donut in the paper napkin and put it in the pocket of his hoodie. He then licked the tip of his finger and used it to pick up the small flakes of glazing from the paper plate and deposited them on his tongue.

"What can I do for you, Kevin?"

He nodded and refocused. "Well, I was thinking, like you said, about anyone who might want to hurt Lisa. This may be nothing, but you might want to check out the company she was working at. She said they were doing something they weren't supposed to. I told her not to scratch at it, but you know how she is. Was."

Nick opened his notepad and flipped back through some pages. "Is that CV Services? Out of California?"

"What? No. Here, in Denver. *Integer* something…I don't remember the name."

"Intergenix?"

"Yeah, that's it."

"Did she mention anyone in particular?"

"No. Just said she did not think they appreciated her poking around. You should definitely check them out."

"Ok, I will."

Pause. "Detective?"

"Yes, Kevin?"

"Can I see her?" His jaw tightened, and a tear rolled down his cheek. "I just want to see her one last time. To say goodbye."

Nick sighed. The kid was hurting. Nick wished he could grant him this. He was sure Lisa would have wanted him to. "I am sorry, Kevin. *I* can't let you. But you can ask the family. Here." He tore a sheet out of his notebook and copied Lori's phone number. "Call her mother. It would be up to her."

Kevin nodded, took the page and folded it without looking. His eyes were glassy with welled up tears. "She did not deserve this." He sniffled and wiped his tears with his sleeve. "She was the best person you could know. The best one I had ever met in this entire world. Whoever did this to her, don't let them get away with it."

tVV3nty

The key to getting away with something is to leave no trace that leads back to you. Today, everyone knows about the physical stuff – hair, skin, DNA. Everyone has seen enough detective movies and true crime shows. Everyone knows that this wetware we lug around – our bodies – is a continuous eruption of trace evidence…flakes, fluids, prints. We leave bits of ourselves over everything, everywhere we go. This endless deluge of self-incrimination may have been under the radar in Jack the Ripper days, but today, it didn't get you far IRL. *IRL* meant *in real life* – a term Roses had taught Kat, as encompassing everything that happened offline. Kat did consider the irony of this term, coming from Roses; given where Roses spent most of her time, the online world was *her* real life.

But, regardless of what one wanted to call it, *IRL* was the old way. The new way was more elegant, clean, metaphysical. The web was the ether that connected you to the software and the hardware elsewhere in the world and gave you control – control over people's devices and through them, control over people. From a distance. You no longer needed to be there physically in the same place as your mark. And yet, in a way, you were, like a curse or a pestilence hovering over them as they went about with their daily lives, oblivious of the tightening snare. You were the dark aura not visible to the naked eye but following their every step like a shadow. You controlled when and if to reveal your presence, and when you did, there was nothing they could do about it.

Roses taught her about the new ways. In the new ways, there were new things to mind. On the web, Kat was made of data. And data left traces. Her every click and every swipe was logged, parsed, and attached to her digital identity. Like fingerprints, hair or scraped skin trapped under the fingernails, bits of her digital self trailed behind her everywhere she went online. And even when she was IRL, her digital self could still be tracked through things – her phone, credit cards, her car. These days, everything and anything could be connected and be actively collecting data, spying on her and everything she did – origins, destinations, timestamps, contacts, locations. One had to take precautions to become invisible.

For starters, she had to erase her physical presence. This meant turning off all the numerous identity tracking toggles that now come enabled by default in our lives. Here she was, sitting in a coffee shop in Englewood, but was she, really? She got here in a car that had no GPS tracking, satellite radio, or Wi-Fi. The last ping from her phone to a cell tower was from her house, where she turned off her phone and removed the SIM card before leaving. She chose this coffee shop because it had no cameras. She wore a baseball cap pulled low over her eyes. She paid with cash. And when she did finally connect to the internet, she did it from a proxy server in Budapest through a no-logs VPN. Roses had taught her about *no logs*. No logs meant no trace. No logs meant no account information stored, no session timestamps, nothing to give to the authorities if the VPN provider were ever to be subpoenaed.

So, where was Kat right now, really? At home? In a coffee shop in Englewood? In Budapest? She had never in her life been to Budapest, but at this moment, as she typed into her laptop, that's where her messages were coming from. In the digital world, she was there more than she was here. Or at least her anonymous account was. Paid for with cryptocurrency from an anonymous crypto wallet. Did *Kat* exist at all? Or was she just a nameless will-o'-the-wisp coursing through the data universe?

As elusive as a vapor trail dissolving in the sky. As unstoppable as the undertow.

Kat knew she could get away with things online. With Roses on her side, she knew she could get away with *this* – with *DearJohn*. They had already gotten away with plenty because they never left any trace. No one could ever connect the IRL Kat to this encrypted conversation or the dozens that came before. And Roses? Who *was* Roses? Just someone she knew only by a screen name on the other end of a secured connection. They were both nothing more than digital ghosts. Maybe that's why this strange anonymous complicity had not failed once.

And yet, despite being completely certain she could get away with *DearJohn*, she was feeling a vague sense of unease about the project. *DearJohn* was taking too long. Her initial zeal was running low, and impatience was setting in. Perhaps this was inevitable. At the beginning, the months of preparation and setup seemed to fly by, but now each day crept along at a glacial pace, bringing with it only disappointed expectations. There was progress, sure, but it was *not quite* the right kind of progress, and it wasn't coming fast enough. He was responding, but *not quite* in the way she needed him to. What if he never would? The possibility of not getting what she wanted had not entered her consciousness till now. She had never planned for that contingency. Online, Roses always had more tricks in her bag to get around the roadblock. But Roses wasn't IRL, and here, Kat's options were limited. What if this were it?

She tried to put this thought out of her mind. That was doubt, and doubt was her old self-critical nemesis. Nothing good came of doubt. Kat just needed to be patient. She needed to stay course and let the plan play out. The plan was working, she just needed to keep *DearJohn* focused. This needed to become more than a sideshow distraction. This needed to become the main act in his life. Perhaps it was time to turn the screw a bit more. Applying more pressure would hasten the results she wanted. Or maybe not. These were uncharted waters. One thing she knew for sure: if this clandestine ruse failed, she would have no choice but to reveal herself to him. And that could never be undone.

21

The next day began with a glorious morning. All it took was a single email in Nick's inbox – Lexi, Inc. had finally granted him access to the recording from Lisa's device. He listened to it in the kitchen, still in his underwear, with a loaf of bread, a carton of eggs, and a pack of bacon on the counter in front of him. The recording was the same as the one Mike had played for him. Nick listened to it again, his pulse pumping faster with excitement – the pieces were beginning to fit. With Brenda's report, and with this recording in evidence, he now had his first good glimpse behind the staged crime scene. The hidden real picture was beginning to emerge. Only a few little fragments for now, but soon he would have more. He was sure of it, now that he had a lead to follow.

He never did call about Tommy yesterday. He wanted to see if it would happen again last night, before he did anything. And it did. Just as before. Like a broken record in his brain. But he was willing to ignore it for now. Maybe he wanted to. Regardless of his predisposition, Lisa's case was more important.

What he needed to do now was to crack Intergenix. If the motive for killing Lisa was corporate, all he had to do was find out which one of over four hundred employees had something to lose if Lisa stayed alive. Simple.

But then again, maybe it was Intergenix as a whole that had the most to lose. At the station, Nick spent a good hour scrolling through the company website and dozens of news articles. Intergenix was in the media spotlight. The company had it all: AI technology that *"bordered on magic;"* a customer list resembling a reprint of the Fortune 100; a *"visionary"* product strategy; an employee-oriented corporate culture; and the projected IPO valuation of $45 billion. It was adored by tech reporters, industry analysts, employees and financial bloggers alike. Intergenix was everyone's darling. Maybe Lisa stumbled on something that threatened to compromise it all.

He studied the photos on the *Leadership Team* page. CEO, CFO, CTO, COO, CMO, CSO – professional-looking people in their thirties and forties and bios peppered with names of companies even he had heard of. Which one looked like a killer? If this were a coverup, how many were involved? How far up and down the chain of command? What about Mike?

Best to start at the bottom. He pulled out the business card from his notepad. *Dani Huber – Customer Advisor.* She had circled her cell phone number for him. He stood up and grabbed his car keys. He preferred to do interviews in person.

At Intergenix, Dani took him to a small conference room near the reception.

"Is *this* OK?"

He nodded. She seemed nervous. Or just cold. She had her gray work cardigan on – the one he saw on the back of her chair the last time.

She put both of her hands on a steaming cup of tea with a lemon-yellow tag dangling at the end of the soggy string. "So, you said you had some more questions for me?"

"Yes. I just wanted to ask you a few more follow up questions about Lisa. Is that OK?"

"Sure."

"OK. You said earlier you and Lisa used to hang out every now and then. When was the last time you two connected outside of work?"

"Umm. It was a Sunday two weeks before she died. So –" she looked at her phone. "August 29th. We went hiking in Evergreen and then chatted at a wine bar there for a while."

"How did she seem to you then?"

She shrugged. "Normal."

"What about afterwards – in the following weeks or days? How did she seem to you?"

She thought about it for a moment. "Fine, I think."

"Do you know if she was dating or seeing anyone?"

She shook her head. "I don't think so. She wasn't very outgoing. We talked about it a few times. I tried to set her up with a friend, but she said she was not ready for anything serious and did not have time for anything casual. She was very career oriented. I don't think I ever saw her reading anything that wasn't related to work. She said she wanted to go back to school to get a master's degree."

"Did you two have similar jobs?"

She shook her head. "Lisa was a data scientist – working with our R&D department. I do customer consulting. Professional services, basically."

"Do you think Lisa enjoyed her work?"

"She loved it. She often worked through her lunch break and would still be here when people left at five."

"Did anything change in her work recently? Did anything out of the ordinary happen?"

"Umm. I guess she started working on some special project for Bruce a couple of weeks before her death."

"Bruce Cogan? The CEO?"

She nodded over the rim of her tea mug.

"Do you know what it was?"

"No. The only reason I knew is because I saw her talking to him in his office after work once, which was unusual. Normally she would be working with Mike. So, I asked her, just to make sure everything was OK. She said it was a special project and she couldn't talk about it yet."

"Do you think Mike knew about it?"

"I…I am sure. He was her manager. But you'd have to ask him."

Nick nodded. "OK. Thank you for this information. If you think of anything else, you give me a call."

He stood up, and she took him back toward the reception, but he decided to take advantage of already being inside the badged access area to go pay Mike a visit. She hesitated for an instant, contemplating the proper protocol for unaccompanied visitors, but he reassured her, already half-way down the hallway to Mike's door.

Mike was on the phone. Nick's appearance on the other side of his glass wall momentarily startled him but he waived Nick in, smiling distractingly as he cut short his call.

"Hey!" He stood up and shook Nick's hand. "I didn't know you were coming by today. Is everything OK?"

There was nervous uncertainty in Mike's handshake. Nick closed the door and sat down.

"What's the project Lisa was working on for Cogan?"

"For Bruce?" Mike scrunched his eyebrows and shook his head. "She wasn't."

"And if she were?"

"Then I did not know about it. Did you ask Bruce?"

"Not yet."

"Who told you this?"

"Sorry, I can't tell you."

"That does not make any sense. Bruce wouldn't have had her working on something without looping me in."

"Why not?"

"He just wouldn't. He doesn't work that way. He delegates. And why does this matter, anyways?"

"Because I now have evidence that her suicide was staged, so this is now a homicide investigation."

Mike's face changed. "Damn," he whispered under his breath.

Nick nodded. "And also, because before she died, she told someone that Intergenix was doing something they weren't supposed to. Do you have any idea what it could be?"

Mike's eyebrows scrunched even closer together. He seemed genuinely befuddled, but Nick still watched him closely, trying to discern if he could be faking it. Could he really be her manager and have no idea? As much as Nick wanted to clear Mike once and for all, new breadcrumb trails kept appearing, leading the investigation back in his direction.

Mike shrugged. "Do you know what it was pertaining to? HR? Business practices? Data compliance?"

Nick shook his head.

Mike puffed out his cheeks and exhaled pensively. "Then I don't have any idea. And honestly, I find it hard to believe. Intergenix is as clean a corporate operation as I've ever seen. Bruce is by the book and runs a very tight ship, especially now, under the IPO scrutiny. We have policies and training for everything: business ethics, HR, data privacy and compliance – you name it. Anti-bribery, no customer gifts, etc. etc."

"OK, but let's say she *was* working on something for Bruce. How could you tell? Would there be something in her files?"

"All her files got transferred to me after her death." He turned to his monitor and Nick heard mouse clicks. Mike shook his head. "I am not seeing anything unusual here at a quick glance. I'd have to dig deeper, but it would take some time."

"Can you do it as soon as possible? Today? Tomorrow?"

"I can just go ask Bruce."

"No. You can't tell him. Not till we know more. You understand?"

Mike nodded. "Do you really think someone here had something to do with her death…Do you think I did?"

"Did you?"

Mike leaned in and gave Nick a long, steady stare. "No. Nick, this whole theory is a ridiculous idea, whoever is selling it to you."

"It could be, but you owe me. I've kept your affair out of this."

Mike sighed. "OK, I'll look through everything. Have you checked out her ex?"

Nick nodded. "At this point he is not a suspect."

"You sure?"

"Yes." He stood up. "Call me as soon as you are finished. Whether you find something or not."

Heading back to the lobby, Nick passed the employee restroom and decided it was prudent to make a pit stop before the forty-minute drive back. Ever since his night disturbances began, he has been drinking a lot more coffee throughout the day. And although he was not certain if all this coffee was actually helping him feel more pulled together, there was no denying the fact that had been finding himself in front of a lot more urinals these days. When he emerged back in the hallway, someone behind him called out, "Detective!"

He turned around to see Bruce Cogan catching up to him with quick, energetic strides. As Cogan got closer, Nick could feel the floor shaking slightly under his own feet, as if a raging bull was charging at him. But Bruce wasn't raging, at least not on the outside. Instead, he held his hand out to Nick. Cogan's tailored light gray suit draped cleanly from his broad frame. Nick extended his own Macy's off-the-rack navy blazer hand. They shook – two suited hands – a bit too long and firm for Nick's liking. He felt like a prop in a cliché business website circa 2005, with that obligatory handshake photo on the front page. Manly men in suits shaking to seal the deal. Nick did not like making deals.

"I did not know you were coming by today. Is everything OK?" Cogan's calm sniper eyes locked onto his.

Earnest or fishing? "Actually, no. Everything is not OK. Ms. Benoche's death is now being investigated as a homicide. So, I needed to get a few more details from her co-workers."

Cogan's eyes widened ever so slightly from the sniper's squint, and he shook his head. "A homicide? That is terrible. Who could do such a thing?"

"That's what we are trying to find out," Nick gave a rhetorical answer to Cogan's rhetorical question. "Did she work on any projects with you directly?"

"No." Cogan shook his head. No tells. "All through Mike. He was her manager. Do you need to talk to him again?"

"I just did, thank you. But if you think of anything that might be relevant, give me call."

"Will do. And if there is anything I can help with, you just let me know. Anything at all."

Nick gave him a nod. "You have already helped a lot." He grinned on the inside as he turned away.

***

Nick needed to think. Today's visit to Intergenix gave him a few new pieces of information which were now bouncing around his head like ping-pong balls eager to find a place to fit. Too eager, perhaps. He did not want to jump to the easy conclusions. To facilitate concentration, he headed back to Scraggy Ridge. The empty house encircled with a perimeter of yellow police tape seemed like the best place to sort through this.

First and foremost was the question of Bruce Cogan. There was a strong possibility that Cogan had just lied to Nick about working directly with Lisa. True, it was his word against Dani's, and Dani was paraphrasing what Lisa had told her. That was pretty much the definition of hearsay. And even if he did lie, that in itself did not prove anything. There are many reasons why people lie. It does not automatically make them murder suspects. Still…what if Kevin was right? What if Lisa did uncover something unscrupulous about Intergenix? If so, it would make sense that Cogan would have been informed – he is the CEO, after all. So, let's just say she saw something or found out something, and she came to Cogan with her discovery. What would he have done? He was under the gun with the IPO, the company was being audited and scrutinized, and a $45 billion valuation was at stake. The last thing he needed was negative publicity or an investigation, but he would also need time to figure out how to deal with this without making a mess. So, how could he keep Lisa from blowing the whistle? What would make her stay and keep quiet? He could have offered her a payoff or career advancement. But that would have been a risk – the plan would have backfired if she rejected the offer. But there was a safer, simpler option. This was an option a young woman who had lost her father in childhood would likely fall for: a charismatic, respected older man commending her for identifying the problem and bringing it to him, and then asking her to help him fix it. A *special project*.

Oh, Lisa, Lisa. Nick felt her fall for it. Did Cogan know he would have to kill her from the very beginning? Or after he realized the problem could not be fixed or covered up?

Standing inside the entryway of Lisa's house, inside the door frame smudged with black fingerprint powder, Nick made himself pause. He knew he had an active imagination and had to admit that this theory had assembled itself in his head with relative ease and seemed to conveniently fill a lot of gaps and question marks. He made himself second-guess and triple-guess his line of thinking, but the more he thought about it, the more the theory gained weight.

He could see it play out. The villain had a face now. And the villain also had a sturdy stance, a firm handshake, and that muscular neck inside the unbuttoned shirt collar. Nick had little doubt that, as a former Army Ranger, Cogan would know exactly how to perform a carotid restraint. Nick guessed Cogan weighed around two hundred pounds, and most of it was muscle. Not that he needed a lot of strength to overpower a young woman less than half of his weight, but he would have the mass and the training to do it with control, without going too far. Without leaving evidence.

Cogan had probably parked at the trailhead. It would have been dusk, around the same time as it was now. The trailhead was not lit, and there would likely not have been anyone else around at this time. It would have been a quick jog for him from there to the ridge, and then through the tree line – barely visible now through the sliding door in the kitchen. Was it his boot print Nick found on the ridge? The slider could have been unlocked, or he could have picked the lock. He knew how to be stealthy. He grabbed Lisa in the entryway. She struggled, and the small side table got knocked over. The glass dish broke when it hit the floor. But he remained concentrated on his task, his body a solid, immovable mass, his bicep and forearm flexing just enough around her neck to cut off the blood flow to her brain. It would have taken less than fifteen seconds for her body to go limp – Nick googled it. Then, all Cogan had to do was move her to the bathtub and stage the suicide.

Nick stopped in the threshold of the bathroom, picturing Cogan leaning over the white clawfoot soaking tub, taking care to properly slash Lisa's wrists. First, the hesitation cuts. Then, the real ones. *Down the road, not across the street.* Deep enough to sever the radial artery. He may have needed to research this to get it right, but he was certainly methodical and organized enough to pull it off. It would take one to two minutes for her body to bleed out. Did he stay with her, holding her down carefully enough not to cause bruising, to make sure she did not wake up and mess up his carefully arranged scene? Did he feel life draining out of her into the water?

The tub was empty now, with a rust-hued ring where the water level used to be. But Nick could still see Lisa in it. Pale as bone. Helpless. Beyond help. Beyond all hope. Left here by the killer for Nick to find. Her body a sorrowful transaction to pass between them. She had to wait, cold and alone in this house for almost two days before Nick found her. And when he did, what he really wanted to do was get her out of that cold crimson pond and get her warm again. To bring her back. But he did not have that power. No one did. The nature of his work was dealing with things that could not be undone.

The dusk deepened on the other side of the patio door, and the tree line was now just barely visible in the shadows. That's where the killer had retreated. Into the shadows of the trees and down the empty trail back to the deserted trailhead. And then he got into his car and drove off into the night.

Nick's phone vibrated – Claire. It was time to head home.

22

The boy's skull cracked, and Nick opened his eyes, instantly awake. The thick, moist, squishy, sickly sound of breaking bone still crackled like an echo in his ears.

FUCK! What the fuck is wrong with me? He wanted to crack open his own head and rip out this vision for good. This wasn't getting better. It was getting worse. Every night now. This terror loomed over him every time he closed his eyes to go to sleep. Maybe Sam was right. Maybe this was being triggered by something happening now. Something aggravating him still, like a hornet's stinger lodged under the skin.

Claire's hand touched him. He looked to her side of the bed; she was awake. She was looking at him. He must have woken her up. Her warm, soft hand moved over his body under the covers. Her touch soothed him. It always did, since the very first time they touched. Somehow, her touch fit all the broken pieces back together and made the ache melt away.

He studied her face in the unearthly silver light of the full moon that seeped through the curtains from the world outside. Was she of this world? He turned to her and kissed her shoulder and then her neck. Her lips found his and he pressed her into him.

She always had a sweet intoxicating scent. Bewitching. It turned his rational being into a beast driven by the single desire to possess her. It had always been this way. Since the first time they kissed. Since the first time they made love in the flickering candlelight at her place with *Portishead* on the stereo strumming out the reverbs of *Roads*. She always felt like a long-lost piece of his soul. Maybe since even before they met. Maybe that's why he never settled with anyone before her.

Her body shimmered in the moonlight against the darkness of their sheets. The smooth navy-blue satin now looked almost black. Like everything else in this light – gray, black or white. All simply shades of gray. Like the surface of the moon. He kissed her collarbone and then the valley between her breasts, moving down and absorbing her inch by inch. Down toward her belly. He put his mouth on her inner thigh and felt her body stretch in yearning toward the headboard. His teeth gently grazed upward on her soft skin.

Afterwards, she took his face in her hands, and he saw her beneath him, her body and her face a shimmering surface cut with the ridges of deep shadows. Half light and half dark, like the moon itself.

"I love you," her light side whispered.

"I love you too," he said into the dark pools of her eyes that beckoned him with a ghostly flicker.

23

Dixonville. Nick hadn't thought about his college town much in the last seven years. Dixonville was a small dot on the map of northern Missouri, tucked just under the Iowa border. Like many small college towns, Dixonville had its population quadruple every September and decline again every May. It was home to the Northern Missouri State University – the self-proclaimed "Harvard of the Midwest" and the cradle of Nick Severs' higher education for six years of his life. He wondered if it had changed much since he graduated.

Today, Nick was calling that forgotten Dixonville area code once more seeking knowledge. But this time his interests weren't academic. Rather, he was hoping to shed light onto a particularly dark chapter in the history of Nick Severs himself.

"Dixonville PD, this is Linda."

Linda sounded pleasant and Midwestern. She listened to his request and then pleasantly informed him that 2009 was before the new system, and that she would have to go check the paper records and get back with him.

When he finally got the callback a couple of hours later, Linda had been replaced with a husky baritone.

"Detective Severs? Yeah, this is Sergeant Norris with Dixonville PD," the baritone said. "I got your message about the Thomas O'Rourke case from '09. I have the file here in front of me. We had to do some digging. What can I help you with?"

"What do you show as the manner of death?"

"Let's see. Cause of death – blunt force trauma to the head. Manner of death is *Accidental*. Looks like a hit and run. We never caught the guy. Probably was drunk. Unfortunately, not all that unusual for a college town. What's your interest in this case, anyways?"

Nick did his best to sound detached. "Well, I've got a possible witness here who says he knows who killed your victim, but he says it wasn't a hit and run, so I don't know what to make of it." It was a half-truth, but Nick wasn't about to explain that the *witness* in question was his own mutineering brain.

"A witness, hah? Well, what's he saying it was if not a hit and run?"

"Homicide. Using a rock."

"Hmm." Norris uttered bemusedly and went quiet.

"Is the responding officer still with your department? Maybe I can talk with him? Or her?"

"Sure. Let me go get him…" Norris chuckled. "Just kidding. You are talking to him now. That was my second year on the force."

"Oh, no kidding?" The newly developed rapport was encouraging, even though Nick was acutely aware that it was based on a lie. This lie was a slippery slope, and Nick had to proceed with caution. This cop had been at the actual crime scene, the crime was still unsolved, and now someone was calling in with new details only the killer or a witness would know. If Nick were in Norris' shoes, would this not raise suspicion? Still, Nick needed to dig deeper. Just deep enough to get to the truth but not so deep as to trip any alarms. *Some men just don't know when to stop digging*, he heard Ray's colloquialism in his head. But he needed to get to the bottom of this. He kicked up his boots onto the desk, the way Ray did. "So, what do you remember?"

"Well, let me see. The victim's friend called it in. It was around 1 AM. The incident was just off-campus near Pershing Park on Halliburton Street. It was not a very well-lit area. The friend said they were coming from a party when a dark pickup drove fast down the street and struck the victim. I got there first, then the paramedics did. He had massive trauma to his head. There was quite a bit of blood. The paramedics tried to revive him but couldn't. The coroner examined him the next day and ruled it accidental."

"Was there an autopsy?"

"Partial – just to show the extent of blunt trauma to the head. Since the injury was evident."

Nick's cellphone lit up on his desk – Mike calling. He hated to miss it, but he was too far down the rabbit hole to stop now.

"Did the sheriff's office investigate?" It was a long shot, but the county could have done a more thorough job than the PD.

"No. On the account that it was clearly accidental. Being a college town, we see our share of accidental deaths. Kids drinking, doing drugs, other stupid stuff. Sheriff's office could not support us if we called them in every time."

"And you said you had no leads on the vehicle?"

"Nothing useful. We are in farm country here. Looking for a banged-up pickup is not exactly narrowing it down."

Nick considered if there were any other loose ends he could pull on without exposing himself but could not think of any. "Did you ever doubt the original witness' statement? Is it possible this was not a hit and run?"

"I did not see anything to indicate a homicide, but I guess anything is possible. Not very likely, though, as the medical examiner findings were consistent with the witness report. But I tell you what, if you give me your email address, I can have the report scanned and sent your way. Who knows, maybe your witness can add something new."

Nick hung up, not feeling particularly encouraged that he would ever resolve this matter. On his cellphone there was one voicemail, but it was not from Mike but from Brenda at the coroner's office. Nick listened to her voice, which was both matter-of-fact and upbeat at the same time. Her message was a morse-code staccato of short statements left for the recipient to stitch together: She was releasing the body to the family; She could not keep it any longer; She hoped they got everything he needed; She was keeping the autopsy report open pending the investigation; (*"That's you, hon"*). And no, the labs hadn't come in yet, so there was no need to call her back.

He called Mike back but got his voicemail. A headache was setting in. What he needed was to get out of the office for a while. He needed to touch base with Lori about the next steps, anyways.

Outside, the sun was slipping in and out of the clouds, and the afternoon breeze was picking up. Pike's Peak was hiding. He got into his truck and called Lori. She was at Lisa's house with Clint, so he wheeled the Tahoe out of the parking lot and headed up the winding road to Scraggy Ridge.

His phone rang – Mike.

"Hey!"

"Hey. So, I have looked through Lisa's files."

"And?"

"And I did not find anything."

This was bad news.

"But I did notice something odd."

"What?"

"There used to be something in her files but it's not there anymore."

Nick's tired brain perked up. "How do you know?"

"One of the folders shows that it was modified the day after her death. But there are no files in that folder that show as being added or modified on that date. So, if nothing was added to the folder or modified–"

"That means something was deleted." Even Nick could connect those dots.

"Right. And she was not the one to delete it."

This sounded like a glimmer of good news. Why didn't Mike start with this? Nick was a firm believer in starting with the good news. When someone started with the bad news, the good news that followed was never quite enough to offset the bad news, as in *Hey, the world is ending, but the good news is we found a cold six-pack of beer.* Only an idiot would be excited by this. But if you flipped it around, everything changed. It was beyond Nick how Mike, a smart man in most other respects, could not grasp this simple principle. Nick guessed everyone was just not a born optimist like him. He realized he was feeling irritable. It must have been from the accumulating lack of sleep.

"Now, before you get excited, this could be nothing." Mike said.

For God's sake, Mike! Learn to manage expectations!

"This could have been just an automated batch job or some other completely harmless file management process."

"Right. So, can we find out what it was?"

"I'll have to do some digging. I've checked the daily backups, and it's been deleted from those as well. Which is a bit unusual. I think. But there is one more place I can look. We have a secondary offsite disaster recovery backup, and it gets updated only once a week, so there is a chance the files may still be there. If not, we are out of luck. I'll do some digging to see if I can get access."

"Mike?"

"Yeah?"

"I want you to be careful."

"What do you mean?"

"Don't draw attention to yourself."

"Jesus, Nick, you really think this had something to do with her death?"

"All I know is Cogan denied working with Lisa on anything. So, either my source lied to me, or your boss did. What reasons would either one of them have to lie?"

There was silence on the other end of the line. "What the hell can it be? We don't do anything worth killing people over."

Nick sighed. In his experience, this measure varied greatly from one person to the next.

***

By the time Nick got to Scraggy Ridge, the sun was shining again, making the flowerboxes on Lisa's porch pop vibrantly with early-fall blooms. A small U-Haul truck was backed almost to the porch steps, and in the front yard, a long piece of yellow crime scene tape was twisting and rolling playfully in the breeze like a bright serpent. Nick untied its captive end from the mailbox and rolled it up, fluttering, in his hand. The truck had Arizona plates and a graphic of Wyoming on its side with Yellowstone, a buffalo and a rodeo cowboy all on one colorful frame and $19.95 next to it on an oversized green price tag. How many movies started with a scene like this: a moving van backed to a charming house in the country. This was the very icon of American new beginnings. Except this one was not a beginning.

Approaching the house, Nick heard heavy bootsteps in the entryway, and Clint, ever in his plaid shirt, jeans and a Carhartt vest, appeared on the porch with a cardboard box in his hands. He set the box in the gaping aluminum cavern of the U-Haul, and dishes rattled inside.

"Hey, detective," Clint extended his thick, calloused hand, and Nick shook it.

Lori appeared in the doorway next, dressed casually today in a gray T-shirt, jeans and sneakers. She was carrying another box and trying to blindly find the steps under her feet. Nick rushed to her and took the box from her hands.

"You folks need some help today?" he asked, setting Lori's box in the truck. "I can come back with a couple of volunteers."

"Oh, no; thank you. We're leaving most of the furniture to sell with the house," Lori said. "These are just some of her things for Goodwill."

She and Clint both looked physically and emotionally worn out.

"Did you get a call from the coroner's office?" Nick asked.

"Yes, they've released Lisa." Lori said and her gaze drifted out into the thousand-yard stare toward the horizon.

"Our funeral home in Omaha is making arrangements to bring her home," Clint added. "We are heading back tomorrow."

They were both cried out. This had become their daily reality now, and they were functioning through it the way most people in this situation got through their days – on autopilot.

"Do you have any news in the investigation?" Lori's sad gaze refocused on Nick, and he recognized the amber studs she was wearing.

"I am following a lead." To anyone else, he may have said *we* instead of *I*, and *all leads* instead of *a lead*. But he could not be anything but honest with Lori, with whom he had come to share the most terrible truth of her life. *His* truth was that it was just him, and he was doing his best with his only lead.

Was this his best? Or was he too distracted with this Tommy O'Rourke affair? Too rattled and distressed to give this, the real murder, the full attention it required?

He crunched the wrinkled bundle of police tape in his hand and wondered what Cogan was doing right now. Whatever a shiny, non-stick CEO of a hot tech company did every day – talking to bankers, flying to Europe, shaking hands, smiling into the cameras. And all the while, a mother was grieving. Nick's blood boiled.

Lori scanned the ridge line – green, jagged and piney, vanishing into the bluish-purple skyline of the front range.

"Lisa really loved it out here. She loved the mountains. We took a family ski trip here once, when her father was still alive." Her thumb twisted a wedding band on her finger. "She was eight. And she just fell in love with this place. I remember her on the slope. Laughing, falling and getting up again. Trying to learn – what is it called? – the pizza wedge? She didn't quit till she got it that day. She was probably the last kid on the slope, but she kept on going, again and again. That's how she was. She had always wanted to make something of her life. She had the drive."

"I wish I could have met her," Nick said. "Everyone I've talked to who knew her says she was amazing." He looked at the buffalo roaming free on the side of the U-Haul. "Did Kevin call you?"

"Kevin? No. Why?" She wiped away two runaway tears.

"He wanted to see Lisa one last time, to say goodbye. I told him it would be up to you."

She walked to the back of the truck and dug through one of the large black plastic bags of clothes. She pulled out an oversized black hoodie with a strip of racing checkers on the sleeve, folded it and held it out in both hands.

"If you see him again, would you please give this to him? And tell him he can call me. Any time."

Nick nodded and took the weighty sweatshirt. Her hand lingered on his arm, and then she pulled him in and hugged him. Tight, as she had probably hugged Lisa the last time she said goodbye to her.

"Thank you," she said. "Thank you for everything you are doing for my girl."

Nick held her lightly and briefly, to be appropriate, nodded and said his goodbyes. From the driver's seat of the Tahoe, he took one last look at the house before pulling away. The front door was propped ajar, and Lori and Clint had resumed carrying out pieces of Lisa's life, one by one. He thought of the old-country tradition to open the windows to let the spirit of the deceased out. Somehow, our ancestors knew that houses were meant for the living, and spirits were meant to return to the universe. Nick did not know much about spirits, but he hoped Lisa's spirit was free now, roaming the mountains she loved. Free like the buffalo and the cowboy in the picture of Wyoming.

***

When Nick returned to the station, there was a new email message awaiting at the top of his inbox. It had the subject line *RE: Thomas O'Rourke* and a paperclip icon next to it. He opened it without hesitation, with almost fatalistic resignation. It was time to rush head-first into the unknown and find out what lied around the blind corner. He half expected it to be another dead end.

The file was twenty-three pages long, and Nick skimmed through the first half-dozen pages: the witness report, the responding officer's report, the paramedic's report, the coroner's report. But the very next page made him freeze in his tracks – scene photos. It was *him*. It was definitely him. Tommy O'Rourke was the one haunting his nightmares. The photos instantly brought back every gruesome detail. But there was something off – the photos were both accurate and wrong at the same time. Tommy's T-shirt was the same, but the angle of view and the lighting were different. The dark, moist wound on the left side of his head was the same, and his eyes were rolled back the same way. But instead of the grass lawn, Tommy was lying on the pavement, and there was a segment of the curb in the photo near his head. And there was no rock in any of the photos.

This was wrong. But it was just right enough to be unsettling. Like watching yourself from above and behind – a queasy mix of omniscience and vulnerability. His eyes fixed on the date at the bottom of the photo: September 18, 2009. He recognized it after a moment, and a chill ran up his spine; that was the day Marc died. *What do you feel in your body?* Sam's question unceremoniously barged in. *What does my body have to do with anything?* he thought back, but his mind was already checking off the involuntary inventory…muscles tightened, pulse thumping, breath shallow, as if ready for a fight. Fight for what? With whom? Tommy? Why?

He wanted answers, but the answers on the screen did not feel right. They did not feel real. And yet, there it was – Tommy's face in undeniable photographic evidence. Both right and wrong. Photographs did not lie. But they could have been staged. But if they were staged, then it meant that his dream could be a memory. Was he ready to *really* explore that possibility? To find out if he was a killer?

He desperately wanted to believe the evidence before him. But he just couldn't. In his brain, the supposition had already become the assumption. If his dream were a memory, this scene had been staged. And who would have had something to gain or something to hide by staging Tommy's death as an accident? The killer, naturally. Was it Nick Severs, circa 2009? Could he have forgotten that, too? Then what about this witness report? Nick scrolled back in the file – Vincent Sarento, Tommy's friend. Supposedly. Why would he lie and cover for Nick? Nick did not know any Vincent. Or did he? Another name to track down.

Sam was right: memory was a lousy corroborator. Twelve years ago seemed like someone else's life. This was the night Marc died. Nick tried to recall the details of Marc's face. He had known Marc since they were five, but already his features were blurred and uncertain in his mind. Marc and Tommy died on the same night, and yet Nick could barely remember his best friend's face, but somehow, he recalled Tommy's – the boy he barely knew – all these years later, with absolute precision in his dream. He wished he could remember more. Or maybe didn't. Maybe he needed to do exactly the opposite and stop feeding this – whatever this was. Maybe if he stopped pulling at the threads, it would just crawl back into its box and close the lid.

He did not like thinking back to that time in his life. It felt uneasy and charged, like a lightning trapped in a cellar. Why open it again? He had moved on. Everyone had. Everyone had grown up. He did, and so did Mike, Amy, and Sam. But not Tommy and Marc – they never would. They were frozen in the past. That's what death did. The dead never changed. Never moved on. Marc was still nineteen. He would always be nineteen. And Lisa would always be twenty-five, while her mother, grandfather and Kevin would go on getting older. This divergence of time, this disparity or realities was at the root of the uneasy tension he felt when thinking about Marc. It was like a charge – a negative, antipodal charge between those in the ground and those above it, that only grew greater the more time passed and the more unlived, unrealized, and unfulfilled time added up in the realm of the dead to match every second, minute, hour and year in ours.

Claire believed the soul went on after death, set free to transition to something else or somewhere else. He wasn't sure. He had no evidence to believe or to dispute that. Maybe Lisa's soul was free, but Marc's felt stuck. Nick supposed he would find out what was on the other side for himself one day. Until then, he was in no hurry to unravel that mystery. Maybe there was nothing on the other side. Nothing but Nick's own malformed emotions projected onto the indifferent universe. He did after all spend much of his life thinking about the dead. Maybe too much. For a homicide detective, the dead were his clients. Considering this now, Nick for the first time found it curious that he chose the only line of police work where it was too late *to serve and protect*. Nick's job started when everything had already gone wrong. Nick came with death, same as the coroner and the undertaker. He was one of the three horsemen. What exactly did it say about Nick, the fact that he chose this line work? Did the ghost of Tommy know something Nick had buried long ago to forget?

He was exhausted with lack of sleep, and the two cases – Lisa and Tommy – were now entangling and fighting for room in his head. The neatly catalogued pieces of evidence and his careful lines of reasoning were becoming crossed and jumbled. He suddenly felt tired of looking at things. He desperately wanted to close his eyes. So, he did.

24

Mike called from his personal number. His voice sounded distant, like he was on the speakerphone.

"Where are you?" Nick asked.

"In my car. Didn't want to call from the office. I told them I was getting late lunch."

Mike was taking this cloak and dagger approach more seriously than Nick had expected, which was not a bad thing. In the background, he heard Mike's engine accelerating.

"So, I have some good news for you: whatever files were deleted from Lisa's computer should still be in that offsite disaster recovery backup I told you about."

"They *should?* But you don't know for sure?"

"No. But I know a guy, and he is helping me find out."

"Who?"

"Our IT guy Dimitri."

"You told your IT guy about this? Can you trust him?"

"A hundred percent. Great guy. Amy and I had him and his girlfriend over for Thanksgiving last year. I let him use my condo in Keystone a few times a year, and he wired my whole house for ethernet and hooked me up with an early laptop upgrade at work. Anyways, he said the update of the recovery system has not run yet since Lisa's death. So, the files should be there, until the next update runs and overwrites them."

"And when does the next update run?"

"Tonight."

"Geez." Talk about cutting it too close for comfort. "So, can he get to them before then?"

"Yes, getting to them is not a problem. The problem is getting to them unnoticed. If Dimitri just goes in and downloads these files, there will be a big fat data trail leading back to him in the system logs."

"So, what do we do?"

"He is writing a script that will pull down Lisa's files during the next scheduled update. It is not absolutely untraceable, but at least it won't be a screaming red flag for anyone who does not know what to look for. It will just look like a normal scheduled update job."

"And do *you* think this script thing will work?" Waiting to download the files until the moment were about to be erased forever did not seem like a smart bet.

Mike chuckled on the other end of the line. "Of course it will work. He is Russian. Knowing how to get around computer security is in the mother's milk for them. *Where are you going, moron!*" Mike yelled into Nick's ear as a car horn blared. "Sorry about that," a civilized Mike was back on the phone. "This idiot just cut me off."

Denver driving was not for the faint of heart.

"Speaking of, you've got to try this vodka he introduced me to. Can't remember the name of it. It's in my freezer. That's what he taught me – keep the vodka in the freezer and don't use ice cubes."

"Hmm." *Speaking of* what, *exactly*? Nick pondered Mike's non-sequitur from Russian hacking to mothers' milk to road rage to vodka.

"Anyways, Dimitri has a present for you," Mike interrupted Nick's musings.

"What?"

"He looked through all the security logs for last week. And it appears the DLP had an interesting event."

"DLP?" Those old projection TVs from the Nineties came to mind, but he was pretty sure that wasn't it.

"Data Loss Prevention system. It can detect data leaks. Like someone emailing confidential files outside the company. Anyways, the day before Lisa died, the DLP logged an alert for her computer. The log said that she copied files from her work computer to a flash drive. I checked the file names in the log, and those files are not in her backups, so these must be the files we are looking for."

"So, she made a copy of these files to a flash drive the day before she died, and then she was killed, and someone deleted them from her computer and from the backups the next day?"

"Right."

"We did not find any flash drives in her belongings."

"So, then I guess someone else has it? The DLP logged the make, model and serial number of the flash drive. I'll send you the info in case you do come across one."

The thought that the simple act of someone copying files to a flash drive could be so easily tracked and thoroughly recorded without their knowledge did not do much to restore Nick's faith in privacy. Everything and everyone seemed to be digitally tracked these days, and privacy was as real as the tooth fairy. Perhaps Mike was right after all, and nothing in this world could be anonymous anymore.

"Oh, and there is just one more thing," Mike said. "The DLP alerts are set up to notify Bruce."

25

When people hear the word *human*, most take it to mean something good. After all, being *humane* means being kind, tender and considerate. And being *humanitarian* means helping improve the wellbeing of others. Those are nice thoughts. But a language created by humans is like history written by the victors. We get to define ourselves, and naturally, we did so favorably, like a school child grading his own work. We imbued the word *human* with the quality of being elevated above the brutal, violent savagery of the animal world. And perhaps, in some small way, we are elevated, as we are the only species on this planet to have invented things like art, literature and theater. But no matter how much we aspire to be elevated, we are deluding ourselves if we believe that being human gives us a unique moral compass and somehow exempts us from the primal laws that govern the survival of all other living organisms on this planet. We are not exempt. We've simply learned to hide our violent means.

A biology lesson long ago had taught Nick that predators had eyes facing forward so they could better gauge distance to their prey. And the prey had eyes facing sideways, so they could better see the predators approaching. Humans had eyes facing forward. But, unlike the fox creeping toward its prey, we didn't wear our intentions on our sleeves. We learned to lie. Perhaps that was one quality that truly separated us from the rest of the animals.

Nick wasn't a park ranger. He did not investigate killings perpetrated by the animals. But the principles were the same. Life was all about survival, and for humans, just as for the animals, this meant either defending or taking what we felt was necessary for survival. The trouble with humans was that we all got to define what survival meant for us. For some it meant stealing food, and for others greasing the politicians, racketeering or murder. No, we hadn't left behind the violent ways of the animal predators. We had innovated upon them. We had taken them to the next level. If the fox had a bigger brain and opposable thumbs, one day it, too, would figure out how to build chicken coops. Our brains gave us the ability to rationalize our self-serving deeds and to lie about them, so we could live with ourselves and with others. That was our *human nature*, and no one was under any illusion that this phrase implied anything good. Human nature was savage.

And in this elevated savage jungle of the human society, Bruce Cogan was king. Patriot, entrepreneur, humanitarian, tech visionary. And now there was mounting evidence that Cogan was also likely a liar. And maybe a murder. If past history of humanity was any indication, this meant Bruce Cogan was well on his way to becoming a sanctified patriarch. It's not that Nick was a born cynic, he just believed there were slim odds of someone making it to the top and remaining honest. He distrusted Cogan from the very first handshake. Sure, there could have been a reasonable explanation why Cogan denied having Lisa work on a project for him. Maybe Mike and his Russian IT guy would not find anything when their computer script ran tonight. But there was still something about Cogan. Behind all that ex-military corporate bravado façade, Nick saw a shadow of guilt. And when Nick sensed guilt, his brain locked on the suspect like a pit bull. But hard and fast was not going to close this investigation. Getting to Cogan was going to take strategy and patience. Cogan had the money to afford very expensive lawyers. If Nick tipped his hand too early, the entire case could collapse on itself. Still, Cogan was smart, and Nick had no doubt he had only a small window of opportunity to conduct the investigation covertly before Cogan realized he was a suspect.

What Nick wanted to do now was make more coffee and settle in for the long night in front of his computer, digging deeper into Cogan and Intergenix. But instead, he needed to set this obsession aside for now and clear the slate of his mind. Today was Friday, and Friday was date night. He wanted to be present to Claire. He wanted to just focus on her and on them, and not think about Cogan all night. This was a tall order, but he was determined. He needed this. They needed this. He had felt so absent and distracted lately.

Tonight, he was taking Claire to see the Swan Lake. It was her favorite ballet, which made this special, and this was a Russian ballet company on tour, which made it even more special. He had snagged the tickets a month ago, after seeing the ad in a copy of the Westword someone had left at the station. Front row center on the mezzanine – the perfect view of the stage.

Nick wasn't a fan of the ballet. He liked the experience of *going* to the ballet – dressing up to go out, the time together with Claire, the dinner before and the drinks during. He just did not care for the ballet itself.

It wasn't that he did not like art in general. He liked paintings, plays, books and films just fine. But ballet was different. There was something too chaotic, too ambiguous and noncommittal about ballet. Even now, as Prince Siegfried was leaping across the stage with a crossbow in his hand and something exaggeratedly large stuffed into the crotch of his white tights, Nick wondered how one choreographer's Siegfried could do a *cabriole* and another choreographer's Siegfried could do a *pirouette* at the exact same moment in the music. What did the difference signify? Would anyone in the audience ever notice if Siegfried decided to switch them around? What new information did it betray about his character and motives? Ballet interpretations wouldn't get far in court. The DA would have better luck cross-examining a mime. Watching a ballet performance was like watching a foreign film without subtitles – one still needed the plot summary in the paper program to grasp what was happening on the stage.

That's why Nick preferred words. There was certainty and commitment in words, even when the person speaking them was lying.

But the music was heavenly. Seated in the plush red velvet seats of the Paramount Theater's gilded art-deco interior, Nick was immersed in the grandeur of Tchaikovsky, in the reddish-amber warmth of the Manhattan in his martini glass, and in the breathtaking beauty of Claire's profile next to him.

She watched the performance breathlessly, like a child absorbing magic unfolding before her eyes. She watched even more intently when Odette was on stage. A beautiful princess cursed by the warlock Rothbart to take on the form of the white swan until she found true love. Was anything more tragic than the impossible hope? The only time Claire spoke during the performance was when Rothbart arrived at the ball with his daughter Odile disguised to look like Odette. When Odile's black swan costume tricked Siegfried into proposing to her, Claire leaned toward Nick and whispered, without breaking her gaze from the stage, *"That's the wrong Odette."*

Not *"That's not Odette."* The *wrong* Odette. As if the dark impostor was also her. As if Odette was somehow both the white and the black swans. The light and its shadow.

On the way home, Claire was quiet. Steering the car onto the I-25 ramp to get them out of downtown, Nick caught the glimmer of a tear on her cheek, reflecting in the city lights.

"Are you OK?" he asked. She had been sadder than her usual self the last few days, and her gaze would at times drift off into the distance. When he asked her yesterday or the day before, she said it was just one of the cases at work. He did not pry further – he knew she would tell him when she was ready.

She wiped away the tear.

"I'm fine." She gave him an unconvincing smile. "It's just the ending – it always makes me cry."

"Why?" He was perplexed. Did someone give him the wrong program? "It's a happy end, right? They ended up together. Siegfried kills Rothbart and marries Odette."

"But you know that's not the real ending."

"What do you mean?"

"That's not the original ending Tchaikovsky wrote. That's the alternate ending they usually show in the West."

"What's the original ending, then?"

"Well, Siegfried proposes to marry Odile, believing she is Odette. When he realizes his mistake, and that his true love will forever be cursed, he rushes back to the lake. Odette forgives him, and they kill themselves by jumping off the cliff into the lake so that they can be together forever."

Damn those Russians and their infinite fondness for tragic endings! This was heavy.

He wrinkled his forehead, watching the road as the high beams sliced through the dark. "Why did they have to die? Couldn't they still live together? She would just change into a swan every night."

"Day," Claire said.

"What?"

"She changes into the swan during the day and back to human at night."

Was *this* in the program?

"Even better," he grinned.

She punched him in his upper arm. Hard.

"No, they could not just *live* together," she sighed, as if changeling magic was common knowledge and everyone was supposed to know the rules. "Could you really live with me if I were someone or something else half of my life? They were doomed by the curse. They had to be the same kind in order to be together."

She had a point. Living with a large bird would have been difficult. But was living with a human any easier? Was he always the same Nick? Thanks to Sam and her infernal EMDR machine, he was now forever aware that there was a hidden part of him lying somewhere deep within like a malaise. Maybe that hidden part was the *wrong* Nick – dark Nick – locked away in a box with no label. Did he ever come out, uninvited? What sort of things was he capable of?

tVV3nty-$!x

DearJohn was not going well. And it wasn't one of Roses' ride-alongs, where Kat could disengage at any time just by closing the lid of her laptop. It wasn't a door she could shut. Most of the time, it was a murky labyrinth where memories tangled with reality and where she had to feel her way just to stay on the right path. Here, the brief periods of anonymity, safety and certainty of the digital world were as short as the hours of sunlight in a northern town.

And yet, with *DearJohn* she was inextricably invested. Friend or foe, she had never before focused so much undivided attention on another person for this long. *DearJohn* was her pride. Her soon-to-be trophy. Like a hunter growing more and more experienced with each kill, she had put everything she had learned in prior cases into this one – a project much more daring and intricate than all the ones that came before it. If one considered all those other projects, it took her years to get here. And now, she was in. She had total control, and *he* still had no idea how close she had gotten and how deep he had worked himself into her trap.

But all was not well. In this intricate world she designed for *DearJohn*, she sometimes caught herself being lost. Sometimes, the roles and realities shifted and interchanged. Sometimes, fake moments suddenly felt real. And sometimes she caught herself wanting them to be. Smells, tastes, touches – all fooling her brain into forgetting what was true. This was happening more often now. In times like these, she felt far removed from the old Kat – the Kat that set all this in motion almost a year ago.

In times like these, she hated herself for being weak. She hated herself for betraying the memory of the incident – *her* memory, the one she had meticulously pieced together over the years from a million shards with jagged, razor-sharp edges – an ugly, Frankensteinian creation scarred with meandering cracks and gaping with pitch-black voids. This memory was a totem that marked the fault line between the two halves of her life: *before* and *after*. She had returned to it each day for all those many years. It was the voodoo doll that took in pin after pin and gave Kat anger to keep moving forward. It was a sacred amulet that gave her strength but also weakened her knees and made her chin tremble and her eyes overflow with tears of powerless grief. She hated herself for letting it define her, and at the same time she hated herself for not remembering more. For not seeing any clearer now than a year ago. For not knowing. There was power in knowing, and powerlessness in not. How did this project – this quest to expose *him* – to uncover who he really was, instead turn on *her*? Who was she? Without this vengeance, who was the real Kat?

"Second thoughts?"

She realized she left Roses hanging in the chat window.

"IDK," she fired off: *I don't know.*

"That's called second thoughts." Pause. "Is it not working?"

Kat watched her cursor blinking powerlessly on the blank line. *Was it working?* Technically, *DearJohn* was working. She still had a hard time believing this was possible, but it was working exactly as they had intended. *But?* Maybe not a *but.* Maybe an *and.* And what? This case had its hook in her, and it was pulling her along.

"Am I going too far?" Kat typed and hesitated before hitting Send.

"No." No hesitation.

"How do you know? You saw what happened to the banker. And that was just doxing."

"Fuck the banker. The asshole got off easy. He took the coward's way out. Think of all the girls who get traumatized for life just so people like him can get their jollies. I hope he is getting fucked with a pitchfork in hell."

"OK, right. But this one is not for all those girls. This is just for me. It's only personal."

"Good. It should be. This *is* about you and what he did to you. He deserves it. Who knows how many other girls he did it to? This is his doing. It should be his shame. Not yours."

She was right, of course. Roses was always right. There was no problem with the project. The problem was Kat herself. She was the weakest link in all this. After all these months, she was beginning to slip. She got too close to him, and now she was losing sight of her objective. She was losing herself. Her nerve. Her edge. Her *old* self. One day, this *new* Kat might just blurt it all out to him. And who the fuck *was* this *new* Kat, anyway? She got too comfortable in this nice new life she had created. What the fuck did she know about *nice* life? *Nice* was the life she had *before* the rape. Compared to the rest of her life, her childhood and adolescence seemed fucking charmed. She was a happy, carefree, trusting, loving child. Until this violent, brutal thing was done to her. That's when that sweet child had gotten lost in the nightmare. Cut off from Kat. What would she be like today, if none if this had been done to her? She'd be the one with the *nice* life. The *nice, normal* life Kat could never have. A real life – not this sham Kat had created to exact her revenge.

Fuck! Deep breath. *Suck it up, buttercup.*

"OK. Let's increase it to five," Kat fired off.

"U sure?"

"Yes."

She was sure. *In for a penny, in for a pound.* She'd gotten soft. She'd become a hypocrite. Like those people who believed in death penalty but did not have the guts to be the executioners.

She wanted the truth but did not want to watch him writhe in pain when she turned the screw. She wanted retribution but did not want to be the one to take it from him. It was time to double down and see this through. Time for old Kat to step in and take over. She always did. She had to. If she didn't, who else would protect the lost little girl?

27

The dream woke him up again, and Nick lay in the dark, giving his racing pulse time to settle and trying not to wake up Claire. He wondered why, after having this same dream so many times, he still wasn't desensitized to it. It still had the same effect each time – a sickening cocktail of panic, dread and guilt. The same cold sweat, galloping heartbeat, and the all-consuming instinct to run. He also wondered why he could never see before or after this single scene. The vision came out of the darkness and vanished into it before he could grasp for any new clues. He was powerless to control it or its aftermath. All he could do was close his eyes and eventually sink back asleep, into the viscous daisy chain of restless dreams that did nothing but exhaust him for the remaining hours of the night.

He must have eventually slipped into deep sleep because when his phone rang, the window of the bedroom was filled with bright sunlight. He checked the screen: Mike. It was 9:30 a.m. Mike's voice was hushed and serious. He had information for Nick, but he wanted to meet in person. He could be at the Bear Creek Park in Lakewood at noon. This worked fine for Nick, because it gave him enough time to wake up and have a late breakfast with Claire.

When he got to the park a little before noon, Mike was already there, reclining on a bench – a broad-shouldered silhouette against the shimmering strip of the pond. It was a sunny, warm Saturday, and the small beach was crammed with screaming kids, barking dogs and flying frisbees. Picking his way between the duck droppings, Nick found the noise, the hustle and the sun a bit too much. Clearly, constant sleep deprivation was not healthy and was making him cranky. If this nightmare lifestyle went on for much longer, he could see himself prematurely turning into a grumpy old man who shook his fist at everything.

"This is a bit deepthroat, don't you think?" Nick settled down next to Mike on the warm metal of the bench.

"Better safe than sorry," Mike replied, watching over the water.

"I should have worn my trench coat," Nick grumbled. "Do you think there are some guys with a parabolic microphone and a reel-to-reel in that plumbing van?" Nick nodded to the residential neighborhood across the pond.

Mike actually looked and did not laugh. "Don't even joke about this shit, man," he said.

Nick gave Mike a penetrating stare. "You got something with your IT guy's script, didn't you? You got Lisa's files?"

Mike nodded. A soccer ball rolled past them, followed by a boy trying to catch up to it before it hit the water. Mike leaned in closer.

"Dimitri's script pulled down Lisa's missing files before they were overwritten."

"And...?"

"It's bad, Nick. Really bad." His big hands were trembling slightly in his lap. "I think they killed her."

Nick pulled in closer. "Who?"

"I don't know. Someone at Intergenix."

"Why?"

Mike sighed heavily. "OK, so you know that proprietary AI we have?"

Nick nodded. He had spent many an hour scouring the web for information about Cogan and his company, and even Nick's luddite brain did not miss the fact that the Intergenix artificial intelligence was more or less that secret sauce that made it the company so successful.

"Well, there is a good reason why it is so amazingly accurate at predicting consumer behavior. It's because it is being fed highly illegal data."

"How?"

"At Intergenix, we have two main sources of revenue. The first one is machine learning services. This basically means that we help other companies by training their own AI systems. You see, AI systems learn much like children do. No matter how well designed they are, they will still make mistakes, and they need help learning from them. So, we train the AI to learn on its own, as it does its daily tasks, whatever they may be – routing calls in a support center, or deciding what ads to show you in your social media app. With good machine learning, the AI will keep getting better and better on its own as it keeps doing the job, just like a human would. Does this make sense?"

Nick nodded.

"So, for us to train their AI, our clients give us access to massive volumes of real customer data that is supposed to be anonymous. Except apparently it doesn't stay that way. Lisa stumbled upon an undocumented function in our code. Something called the Janus algorithm. What Janus does is it uses our own AI to de-anonymize the data we receive. Sometimes from residual data, and sometimes by extrapolating it from other public data sources. Essentially, it reverse-matches the data back to the real people and then siphons this data to feed our own AI."

"This was all in Lisa's files?"

Mike nodded. "She documented everything." He reached in his pocket and handed Nick a small silver flash drive. "It's all on here. It started a couple of weeks before her death. At first, she came across some data transactions with de-anonymized records. Then she found more. So, she went to Cogan, and he was shocked and told her it must be a bug in the algorithm. He asked her to help document it and develop a remediation plan. He also asked her to keep quiet about it until they could fix it."

"Is that odd, that he asked her to keep quiet?"

Mike shrugged. "Not really. If this were really a bug, they would not have yet known the full extent, and whether this data was vulnerable. You definitely don't want half-information going public, and even internal chatter can get leaked and attract unwanted attention from hackers, who would love to get their hands on a large cache of personal data. So, anyways, she did as he asked. But the more she dug in, the more she realized this was not a bug but was fully intentional. This was the dirty secret behind our AI. So, she made a copy of her files to her flash drive. And the next day she was dead."

Nick mulled over the new information and shook his head. "I don't get it. So, Intergenix was illegally collecting personal data? And that's worth killing someone over? Isn't that what all these tech companies are already doing? Search engines, social media? Aren't they already collecting our data?"

"Yes, but that's not the point. The illegal data is just the means to an end."

"So, what is the point, then?"

"The point is that this illegally harvested data enabled our AI to work not at the demographic segment level but at the level of the individual."

"Huh?"

"OK, say you are a business…a travel agency. You have a budget to run commercials on a streaming TV service, but you want to make sure your ads are relevant to the audience. Would a retired couple prefer a trip to Rome or a European river cruise? Would a college student prefer Cancun or Cabo? You know that you can get more sales if you make the ad relevant to the person watching. Does that make sense?"

Nick nodded.

"Ok, so you take your anonymized historical data to a commercial AI service like Intergenix and have them test different data models to predict the most probable choices for your customer segments. You can then have your marketing agency make different commercials for these different customer segments. Then the streaming TV provider will take these commercials and they will play the right commercial based on their subscriber data. So, you, Nick, will see one commercial on your laptop, and Claire will see another on your living room TV while you are at work."

"They know which one of us is watching the TV?!"

"It's not that hard to figure out." Mike dismissed Nick's horror with a wave of his hand. "The point is that these commercial AI systems work at the segment level, which means they can effectively target a demographic group – say, a white unmarried male in his early thirties with a four-year college degree and one car in the 80125 zip code. All that information is publicly available, and there are privacy laws to prevent these companies from collecting more specific data about you as an individual without your consent. Still, even at the segment level, they can develop pretty accurate scores."

"What scores?"

"The risk and affinity scores. Things like how likely you are to get into a car accident or max out your credit cards or get the flu or order a pizza on Wednesday. Those scores influence how big corporations interact with you; from the insurance premiums you pay to the type of ads that pop up on your phone. Makes sense?"

Nick nodded. Make sense it did, in a psychopathic techno-dystopian sort of way. "But what does this have to do with Intergenix and Lisa?"

"The scores based on segments are effective only to a certain degree. Sure, you may have a few parameters in common with the other six thousand thirty-something white dudes in your zip code, but you are all still totally unique people with different backgrounds, situations and goals. The only way to make your scores drastically more accurate is to go from the segment level to the individual level and directly feed the AI your personal data. It's illegal, but that's what Intergenix is doing."

"And they are getting this personal data by stealing it from their own clients? Using Janus?"

"Exactly!" Mike seemed marginally pleased at being able to explain a complex technical topic to likely the most non-technical person he knew. None of this was convincing Nick he had been wrong to avoid technology for all these years.

"But that's only the mechanics of it," Mike went on. "To really understand what Intergenix is doing, you have to grasp the scale. We are stealing data from *everyone*. Social media apps, streaming services, smart phone manufacturers, utilities, banks, insurance companies, healthcare systems – we already do business with all of them, and we steal from all of them. Separately, they each hold only fragments of your behavioral data, but we take it and put it all together. That's thousands of data points on every single person. And it just keeps growing – we get millions of new records every week. Millions of updated transactions. We know what posts you like or pass on social media. Which apps you use in the morning and which at night. Whether you eat tacos on Tuesdays or Sundays. Whether you take more photos of yourself or of others. How much you exercise and how much you drink. What health symptoms you research online and what prescriptions you fill at the pharmacy. Which TV shows you watch with others and which alone. What your favorite colors are and what types of animals and people you prefer. What music you listen to depending on the mood you are in…You get the point. Everything becomes an input into the AI algorithm, and with this, the AI can create amazingly accurate, personalized scores for just about anything pertaining to you. We can know you better than your mother, your wife and your shrink combined. And there will always be someone willing to pay big bucks for this level of accuracy. Because the real commercial value of AI is not predicting behavior – it's influencing it."

A chill ran down Nick's spine. "Terrific."

"Yeah," Mike nodded. "And it will be even worse for the new generation of kids growing up right now. They were practically born on the internet. They don't know how to be offline, and they don't want to be. Their every click and every step has been recorded since day one. They will live longer than the prior generations, and with the right data, their journey from cradle to the grave can be very profitable for all the corporations involved. We have the computing capacity to do this for every single person on Earth. So, now do you see why someone would kill to protect this technology? Data is the new oil, and every single corporation will want to use it. They are already lining up."

"So, what would happen if this got out?"

"For Intergenix? Lawsuits, regulatory fines in the hundreds of millions. Kiss the IPO goodbye – since the whole valuation was based on a product that relies on criminal activity. The whole company would probably go under."

This certainly looked like a motive. Lisa copied the files, Cogan got the DLP alert and assumed she was going to blow the whistle on the whole thing.

"And she did not come to you with this information? Why wouldn't she come to you – you were her manager."

Mike lowered his head. "I don't know. She was a direct kind of girl. If she found a huge issue, maybe she wanted to take it straight to the top. Or maybe she did not want to talk to me after…the affair. I wish she had. Maybe she still would have been alive."

"Did she mention anyone else besides Cogan in her notes?"

"No. But…"

"But what?"

"It's just that Bruce is not a real techie. He is the business guy. He can talk the talk, but there is no way he could have engineered Janus. This is something our CPO would have to have known about."

"CPO?"

"Chief Product Officer, Andrew Giles. He and Bruce were the original partners in Intergenix. They go way back. Andrew wrote the first version of the machine learning algorithm himself."

A doubt flashed in Nick's brain. "If Giles knew about Janus, and probably wrote it, do you think he could have killed Lisa to protect it?"

Mike shook his head. "Not Andrew. He is this giant nerd. Brilliant guy, and always gentle with people. I've never seen anyone get a rise out of him. Bruce, on the other hand…He can have a temper when things don't go his way. That's not to say that I've ever seen Bruce be violent."

But he would know *how* to be violent when it was needed – special forces, and all. Still, if Cogan killed Lisa, Giles still could have been involved. Or perhaps he was just an oblivious tech wizard behind the curtain of the Intergenix operation. Either way, this was something solid. Something to build on. Nick now knew the motive. The *why*. And one didn't always get to know the *why* in homicide. The motive was the glue the bound the otherwise random collection of events into a premeditated act. The two cups of coffee Nick had this morning were now pumping through his veins. He finally felt awake.

Mike rubbed his chin. "Wait. Bruce had a benefit dinner the night Lisa was killed. I know because I saw him change into a tux before he left work."

"For his veterans' program?"

"Yeah. The Code of Honor Foundation. It should be easy enough to verify."

"Can you send me the details? I'll check it out."

"Sure." Mike got up. "Well, I'd better get going. I am supposed to take Amy and the girls to the 16th Street Mall."

Nick nodded and got up to walk with him to the parking lot. "Mike…"

"What?"

"If you and Dimitri find any more files of interest, please make sure you don't move or alter anything. If and when we subpoena Intergenix for evidence, I want to get clean data. I don't want any reason for it be thrown out in court."

"You got it." Mike saluted him and got into his car.

Nick climbed into the driver's seat of the Tahoe, flipped open his work laptop and plugged in the flash drive Mike gave him. There were three files on it. He clicked open the one named *janus.txt* first. It was twenty-eight pages of what looked like computer code to him – a soup of mathematical symbols and brackets intermingled with words like *if*, *then*, *while* and *get*. This must have been a copy of the algorithm itself. He hoped computer forensics would be able to make something out of this.

The next file was *remediation_timeline.xls* – an Excel spreadsheet with a table of dates and events. It started with August 18, the day Lisa found the first evidence of de-anonymized data, and continued with twelve methodical, scientific-like entries until Tuesday, September 7 – the day of her death. Nick skimmed through the entries, most of which detailed her investigation into the source of the illegal data as she examined the various functions and subroutines of the Intergenix software. She documented four meetings with Cogan: the initial briefing on August 19, and three *status updates*: August 26, September 2, and September 7. All of the meetings had a summary of what was discussed and decided, except the last one. The cell labeled *Notes* next to the last meeting was blank.

The last file was called x-filtrated_data.txt and contained a single column of words and phrases. The list started with:

FName

LName

SSN

DL

Phone01

Nick scrolled to the next page, skimming: *FaceBookID*; *TwitterID*; *TikTokID*... He skimmed through the next few pages: *DiagnosisCode04*... *LivingRelative08*... *MusicSubscription01*... *DatingService04*...*TV-IP-Address02*... *Vacation*... Nick scrolled to the end. There were twelve pages of this. These must have been all the data points Janus was gathering on people.

He closed his laptop. Beyond the parking lot, the pond was glimmering in the sun, and kids were chasing after balls, frisbees and dogs. It all seemed so simple just an hour ago. They seemed so free then. Would they have any free will by the time they grew up? Did they even have free will now? Did Nick? He wondered how much of his life was already being tracked by some invisible corporations he'd never heard of, like Intergenix. Were his daily clicks and swipes being logged and fed into some mystical algorithm version of himself? A digital Nick Severs doppelganger being assembled bit by bit out of ones and zeros. What was he telling them? Did they know where Nick Severs would go next? What would he do? What would he buy? Nick was sure this was not the vision Mike intended to convey, but in Nick's imagination, the future of humanity was doomed to being run by machine algorithms whose sole purpose was to maximize the lifetime profits to be made off every living soul. This wasn't anything new, of course. People had done this to people before there was AI. And Nick had nothing against the concept of AI itself. What worried him was what the AI would learn, being taught by humans.

28

In the dark, Nick did not know how long he had been sitting on the edge of the bed. The nightmare had wormed into his dreams again, uninvited, and left him feeling wrecked, as if he were the one bludgeoned over and over again. And the worst part of this was that Nick still had not an inkling as to its cause. It did not matter if Nick had a good or a bad day. It did not matter what he ate or drank. The EMDR session and the police report had not changed a thing. The nightmare would come each night like a wrecking ball plowing through his brain. And so, here he was now, sitting in the dark again, with his head ringing and his arms shaky from lack of sleep. He didn't want to go back to sleep. What was the point? He did not even want to go for a run. He no longer had it in him. Each night was like another drop of water torture, and it was getting worse. *He* was getting worse. How much worse would it get?

"Did you have the nightmare again?" Clare stirred in the covers behind him. "I thought Sam helped you remember."

He thought of what to say.

"Is it your case?" she asked again behind him.

"Jesus, Claire, I don't have a fucking clue!" He heard himself snap and immediately felt terrible. What was happening to him? He could hardly recognize himself in this monstrous creature hunched on the side of the bed, with his pulse drumming furiously in his head and short, shallow breaths pumping in and out of his chest. This wasn't him.

He turned to her. Even in the semi-dark, he could tell that she was on guard, like a threatened animal backed into her nest of pillows by the headboard, with one pillow clutched in front of her. The two glimmering sparks in her eyes were tracking him. He didn't like seeing her this way. He could feel an unfamiliar uncertainty like a charge in the space between them. This wasn't them. They never fought. They could always talk about anything without letting their tempers flare up.

"God, I'm sorry. I don't know what's going on with me. I feel like I am losing it," he said, putting his hand on her arm.

She let go of her pillow shield and put her hand on his, her thin delicate fingers threading in-between his thick, crude, log-like appendages. "Is it the same?" she asked.

He nodded, feeling a tide of tears swelling up.

"I am afraid I did something terrible." He buried his head in his other hand.

Her fingers trembled on his hand. "What?"

"Maybe I killed Tommy."

She moved closer and wrapped her arms around him. "Do you think you are capable of that? Hurting someone like that?"

He shook his head. "I really don't know anymore. Why else would I keep dreaming about it?"

"But the police report said it was an accident, right? Do you remember anything else about that night? Anything at all?"

He shook his head again.

"Nick, I just don't believe a person could forget something like this. That's a dark, violent act, and that kind of darkness would not just dissipate the next day. I think it would be part of that person, always."

He knew she was trying to help, but this was not comforting. He did indeed feel the darkness. He had seen the dream so many times, he now felt it with him, always. At first like a mark. Like a small inkblot spreading in water. And now it was a dark lens through which he saw the world around him. The world had not changed – he changed.

Could he have killed someone and just walk away and not look back for eleven years? He thought of Lisa, left in that cold tub for almost two days. After the killer walked away, the universe kept going on around her. The earth kept turning. The sun and the moon rose and set. People woke up, went to work, came home, and went to sleep again. The trees grew a little, the clouds moved across the sky. And to her killer, she was probably just a polaroid snapshot left behind and growing more distant with each day.

Claire kissed his temple. "Maybe you should go see Sam again?" she said quietly.

29

Sam smiled. "I didn't think you'd ever call again. You practically ran out the last time."

Nick shook his head. "Sorry about that. You did help me. You really did. But somehow, things make even less sense now."

She folded her arms and turned ever so slightly in her chair.

"It's not therapy, I promise!" He rushed to reassure.

She furrowed her brow.

"I just need your expertise. Like a consultant. You know? I can pay you."

She sighed. "I don't want your money, Nick Severs." She reluctantly gestured for him to have a seat. "What's going on?"

He avoided the leather armchair this time and made his way to the plush beige loveseat. He was sure she made a mental note.

"It's the same dream."

"Really?" She did not sound surprised.

"Every night now. And I don't sleep well after it. And then I have headaches during the day."

She nodded. "Last time you said you had remembered something, but it was the wrong memory. What did you mean by that?"

"When we did the EMDR thing, it took me to a different memory. It took me to the night my best friend committed suicide. I was the one to find him."

"I'm sorry, Nick. That must have been a very difficult time for you."

"It was. But honestly, I have not thought much about it in the years since. Is that callous?"

"Not really. Most people prefer not to revisit traumatic memories. It's a defense mechanism."

"But what's strange is that remembering Marc's suicide also made me remember the name of the kid in my dreams, Tommy. And that's where things got even more strange. It turns out, Tommy died the same night Marc did, but his death was due to a hit-and-run accident, not being bludgeoned with a rock. I got the police report and the photos. But what's stranger still, in photos he is wearing the same t-shirt as in my dream and has the same trauma to his head."

"Did you actually know this boy?"

He nodded. "A friend told me I met him briefly at our fraternity. But I don't really remember this or anything about him."

"Is it possible you had witnessed his death?"

He shook his head. "According to the police report, this was around the same time I had found Marc … so, I would have been talking to the police at the dorm, away from where Tommy died."

"But in your dream, you see yourself killing him with a rock?"

"Yes."

"And you didn't see this rock in the police photos?"

"No."

"So, let me ask you this. In your dream, do you actually see yourself killing this boy, or is he already dead?"

He was about to answer but was suddenly dumbfounded by a realization. His nightmare was so short – just a flash, really, that instantly woke him up. The more he thought about it, the more convinced he became of the fact that his nightmare was a still scene. It was a violent scene, but it was not *active* violence. It was like an echo lingering in a room he had just entered. The bloody rock was on the ground and not in his hand. Tommy's eyes were already rolled back. He was not moving.

"He is already dead," Nick uttered, confused. "What does this mean?"

She shrugged. "Well, it probably means it's not a real memory."

"Then what is it?"

"It could be just an unrelated image you saw somewhere else, and your subconscious had linked it to the traumatic event that had actually happened to you around the same time."

"This can happen?" He felt a glimmer of relief in his chest.

"All the time, especially around trauma. Your brain can make connections without you being aware. Sometimes it is right, and sometimes wrong. It's not uncommon for trauma survivors to recall someone they know being present during their traumatic experience, even if they weren't. Things can get pretty complicated around traumatic memories, and even more complicated with dreams."

"But if this never actually happened to me, why would my brain make me feel like I did this? I could literally feel the rock in my hand and hear his skull crack."

"I think that given the trauma surrounding your friend's suicide, this actually makes sense. People who live through suicide of someone close to them often have deep feelings of guilt and being responsible. So, your feelings pertaining to Marc's suicide may have become transposed onto this image of Tommy's death, because both events happened in the same time period."

"So let me make sure I understand. There is this image of Tommy in my head – and we still don't know where it came from – but my brain basically took it, recalled Tommy's face from my days at the university, and then filed it under the traumatic experience I had during that time?"

She nodded.

"OK, but now that I've seen the police report and found out how Tommy really died, why do I still have this dream?"

"Sometimes our mind can become trapped in a vicious cycle. We may have a thought or a memory – often a negative one – and each time we think about it, it becomes reinforced in our mind. And reinforcing it increases the chance that we will think about it again. And when we do, it becomes even more reinforced and real. It does not matter how irrational this thought may be. It just keeps repeating like this, becoming more intense and disruptive with time. We call it persistent ideations – they keep bouncing between our conscious and unconscious, feeding on unresolved issues. They may not stop until you resolve the underlying trauma."

"So…pink elephants?"

"Exactly."

He suddenly felt deep appreciation for Sam's line of work. Like him, she solved puzzles, but in her precinct, she had to solve them using false evidence and irrational reasoning.

"And this whole messed up scenario does not seem like a stretch to you?" he asked.

She shook her head. "This scenario may seem improbable to a police detective, but our brains often work in very fuzzy ways, especially when there is trauma involved. You are not just you. All of us are made of two parts – the conscious self you are aware of and think of as your identity, and then also the unaware, subconscious part that Jung calls the *shadow self* – your repressed, unconscious identity. That shadow is where all your repressed memories and unresolved traumas live. We all have them. They can impact our actions without us being aware, and sometimes they can surface in unexpected ways when we get triggered."

Nick found himself connecting the fingertips of his both hands, perhaps in a subconscious symbolic gesture of trying to get his arms around the mess going on in his head or perhaps trying to bring the two splintered parts of himself – the oblivious, happy-go-lucky Nick of a few weeks ago and the unhinged, possibly homicidal Nick of today – back together. The good news was that he likely did not kill Tommy. *Likely.* The bad news was that he was quite possibly a basket case. The thought that his brain had a dark cellar filled with every unresolved issue from the past was anything but comforting. He would have liked more than anything to keep that trap door shut, but he was not sure how long he could keep going the way he had been for the last few weeks. Maybe Sam was right, and the only way to really make it stop was to open the trap door and pull everything out into the daylight? That could possibly be a worthwhile effort…at some point. But right now, he just needed to get the nightmares to stop so he could do his job.

"So, this image I get of Tommy…is there a chance it could be something I actually saw in real life? Like a repressed memory?"

"I don't know. We may never know."

Sam had an irritatingly unswerving sense of professionalism. Nick was certain she knew more than she let on – he just had to find a way to pry it out of her. "OK, but what do you think? I am just trying to figure out the facts. It had to come from somewhere, right?"

"Nick, I am not a detective. In my profession, the facts of what happened don't matter. They may be remembered right or wrong, or they could be completely dreamed up. We just accept them as they are so we can focus on what's going on in the present and help you deal with the future."

"OK, so forget the facts. Give me your straight opinion here."

She laughed. "Nick, my opinion does not matter. My job is not to give opinions, my job is to help my clients work through their trauma."

"OK. But I am not your client, remember? Pretend you are an expert witness in court, telling me about the state of things you are seeing right now. What would you say?"

"I'd say you definitely have unresolved trauma around Marc's death."

He reclined powerlessly in the love seat. It was uncomfortably deep and soft. "Yep. Agreed. What about Tommy? Where is that one coming from, Sam?"

She shrugged. "It doesn't matter, Nick. It could be a false memory."

"What?!" He leaned forward.

She bit her lip and took sudden undue interest in something in the bookcase.

"Sam! What do you mean a *false* memory?"

She sighed and looked back at him. "Nick, I've seen plenty of recovered memories pertaining to trauma. Those memories don't exist in a vacuum. They have their tendrils wrapped around our senses, emotions, and body memories. When they surface, they come up with all that baggage."

"Don't I have all that?"

"Yes, but it all seems to be attached to your memory of Marc's suicide, not to Tommy. When it comes to Tommy, there is nothing. No breadcrumbs leading in or out. We did not connect to it at all when we did the EMDR. Probably because there is nothing to connect to. You said it yourself – it was a wrong memory."

This prognosis was not boding well for the state of his mental health, but he could not help but keep going. He had hooked what felt like the truth from Sam, and he needed to reel it in.

"So…how does one get a false memory, if that's what this is?"

"It actually happens to most if not all of us. Usually in childhood. For example, your parents may repeatedly tell you a story about something that happened to you at a very young age. After hearing this for many years, eventually, you start *remembering…*" She inserted air quotes "…some of the details they've described to you. But this is actually a false memory in the sense that you don't really remember the event – you remember what you've been told about it, and your brain has over the years built up the associated images and feelings. This can even happen with things that never happened to us at all. A child may witness something traumatic happen to another child, and the emotions from that trauma will make it feel personal. So much so that this experience can actually imprint in their mind as something that happened to them. And then, each time they recall or retell this story, their mind will fill in more images and details and reinforce it as their own memory."

"OK, but this memory of Tommy is not something that has been told to me over and over, and it's not something I saw somewhere else, because, according to the police report, it never happened that way. So, where else can false memories come from?"

She smiled. "Well, I guess it could have been implanted without your knowledge, but that is *really* far-fetched."

"Implanted?" Nick wrapped his mind around this one as he said it. This option sounded downright nefarious and yet fitting at the same time. He made a side note that Sam had either given up on trying to stay professional with him or was employing reverse tactics by taking him down the path she considered ludicrous in order to dissuade him. "Someone can *implant* a memory?"

"Possibly. There are very few studies on this, for ethical reasons."

"But there are some?"

She nodded. "Back in the 1980s, there was a satanic panic in the U.S., and many people were coming forward and claiming that, under therapy, they had recovered traumatic repressed memories of satanic ritual abuse in their childhood. People were suing their parents, former teachers, and entire day care centers. Now, some of these memories could have been real, but the sheer number of new cases made a few notable psychiatrists wonder if it was possible that some of these memories could have been induced by sensational media coverage and unscrupulous therapy practices. So, several studies were conducted, and they determined that it was possible, with just a few sessions, to get someone to *recall*…" air quotes "…a completely fabricated memory."

"What did they use? Hypnosis?"

"No, just a bit of research. The most famous experiment was called *Lost in the Mall*. Before the actual experiment, the researchers talked to each participant's family and got four real childhood memories. They also got the details they needed to construct the false memory: a shopping mall or another large venue the participant would have visited as a little child and the people they would go with – parents, siblings, etc. In the experiment itself, the participant was given the list of five memories –four real ones and the false one of being lost at the mall – and asked to provide any additional details about each. A week later, they would revisit the list and see if the participant could recall any new details for each memory. After a few weeks of sessions, many participants were recalling their own new details about this false memory, and some even ranked it as a stronger memory than some of the real ones."

"Maybe they really did get lost in the mall when they were little?"

She shook her head. "The researchers confirmed with the families that this never actually happened to the participant."

Nick nodded. This may have been desperation, but he grasped at the idea that this recurring dream of Tommy could have been implanted as if it were a lifeline. This was the only scenario that restored his belief in his sanity. And his innocence. "So, could this work with anything? Like a memory of killing someone?"

She tilted her head. "Theoretically. But it helps to have something real for the false memory to attach to – like a real place or event. The fewer false elements, the better. It also helps to have some strong, real emotions to tie into, like fear or grief.

Most little kids are afraid of getting separated from their families, so being lost was an easy fear to relate to."

This all fit: college, fraternity, the night Marc died. A familiar place and an existing trauma – someone really hit the bullseye if they wanted to implant Tommy into his brain. It couldn't just be a lucky shot. But how? "So, in this study, these people got to openly discuss these false memories in their sessions. Is there any way to implant memories without someone knowing?"

"Like subliminal messaging?"

"Yes! Does that actually work?"

She shrugged again. "Some people say it does. There is a whole branch of therapy based on it, and people claim they have been able to quit smoking or reduce anxiety by listing to subliminal messages while sleeping or under hypnosis. Back in the 1960s, there was even a company that spliced advertisements for Coke and popcorn in-between the movie frames at the theater. They said this led to increased sales, but I would not call this a scientific study."

This was in the 1960s? If subliminal messaging was possible then, who knew what could be accomplished with today's technology? Today, everything had a computer chip and a network connection. This thought gave him a chill. "Have you ever come across implanted memories in your practice?"

"Not that I know of."

"But you believe it's possible that mine is?"

She sighed, probably writing him off as a lost cause. "Anything is *possible*, Nick. It's also possible you have been abducted by aliens or that you are the subject of a secret government experiment. But tell me this. Why would someone go through all this trouble? To what end? I think the simplest explanation is that the things you are experiencing are caused by your subconscious. Your mind is trying to piece together fragments of memories, traumas and emotions into a scenario it's struggling to process. That vision of Tommy could be just a collage of disconnected things. You shouldn't take it as an accurate record of the past or as evidence of external interference. Wherever this image of Tommy comes from, somehow, it is latched onto the trauma you have pertaining to Marc's death. And you do know my professional opinion about what you need to do, right?"

He extracted himself from the plush depths of the love seat. "Yes. Work through to the bottom of it in counseling. I know. And I'll think about it, I promise."

***

He sat in his Tahoe in Sam's parking lot for a while. The daily headache was arriving right on schedule, but he did not care. He felt close to figuring this out. Everything fit. Almost everything. He still did not know *who*. Or *why*. Could someone really be doing this to him? It would have to be someone who knew his past. Someone who knew Tommy. If someone was doing this to him, it was personal. Of course it was. But who? And *how*?

The phone in his hand vibrated, and he almost dropped it, startled from his deep contemplation. An incoming call from a number he did not recognize. He swiped to answer and cleared his throat. "This is Detective Severs."

A sultry, unfamiliar woman's voice, raspy like a life-long smoker's. "You want to know how Tommy died?"

Hairs stood up on the back of his neck. "Who is this?"

"I am his mother. Come to Topeka and I'll tell you."

30

The O'Rourkes hailed from St. Michael – a suburb of Topeka, the capital of Kansas. Driving there and back was going to take up most of the day, so Nick took the day off – a mental health day, as he put it to Ray. Ray did not need convincing – Nick's sorry, sleep-deprived appearance did the trick. He told Nick to get some rest and shooed him out of the station.

By the time the sun came up next morning, Nick was already driving east on I-70 through the crop fields and the prairies of western Kansas. This was the breadbasket of America. The scenery may have been uninspiring to look at, but Nick actually found the consistency comforting. The highways here were straight, and the jagged skyline of the Rockies had soon vanished from the rear-view mirror.

Claire wanted to come with him, but he asked her to let him do it alone. Whatever this thing with Tommy was, it had somehow burrowed down to the core of his soul. The darkness, the dread, and the sadness of it all had worn out his natural sense of self-confidence and certainty down to shreds. Each day, another piece got sliced off. He just wanted it to end. Whatever or whomever he was going to find in St. Michael, he was hoping it would at last hold the key to the resolution.

Outside of Topeka, the fields gave way to powerplants, grain elevators and railroad yards. Industry heralded civilization. Soon, there were fast food signs, hotels, residential subdivisions and gas stations. The interstate curved around the downtown, north of the dome of the State Capitol. The directions took him through a spiderweb of freeway exits and access roads and eventually spat him out heading north from the city on a country highway that cut through more crops and barbed wire fenced cattle pastures. But the pastoral simplicity did not last long, and soon he found himself among gentrified country estates with expansive horse stables, grandiose gates, and miles-long stretches of white post-and-rail fences.

The gate he pulled up to had stacked stone pillars and wrought iron bars with pointed finials. He pushed the button on the callbox. There was an instant of silence, and he knew he was being watched through the camera mounted on the gate. The box buzzed, and the gates slowly rolled ajar, giving him access to the winding driveway lined with tall oaks and alders.

He followed the driveway through the vast estate for at least a mile before the main house came into view – a grand rendition of an Irish castle built with Kansas limestone and complete with two multi-faceted towers, a roofline topped with toothed stone merlons, and a broad swath of dense ivy spreading across the rocky façade.

A small, older woman let him in through the castle doors. She had black hair and a simple black housekeeper's dress, and she did not utter a word – just a slight bow of her head and a step to the side. And in he went, into the dusky, quiet interior that smelled of incense and cigarette smoke.

He followed the quiet steps of her shoes through the drawing room past a fireplace and a suit of dark armor, and through a hallway and the innards of the house to the very back – a vast open solarium with glass walls, a domed glass canopy, tall tropical plants and a piano. Outside the cloudy glass walls, Nick could make out a garden with crushed stone pathways, statues and a fountain. Everything here was grandiose and quiet, and a bit murky and stale. Like a lost kingdom.

Or queendom.

He did not see her at first, until a slender figure separated itself from the shadows under the emerald plumes of an overgrown bird of paradise. The queen's name was Dierdre O'Rourke – he had seen it in the police report.

"I'm Dee," she said. "Have a seat." She gestured to a rattan couch next to the piano with thick cushions the color of seafoam.

The voice was the same as on the phone – sultry and raspy. Her image was to match – an elegant, long, light-blue dress, dignified posture, and a cascade of long bleached blonde hair. She must have been in her sixties but looked younger. Nick wondered if she had had plastic surgery. If she had, it had been done with quality and restraint, and undoubtedly at a great expense, like everything else in this place. She was ageless, and she carried herself like a dame accustomed to having influence – with Midwestern directness and none of the superfluous Southern charm.

"I've been in the car for hours," Nick said. "If you don't mind, I'd like to stand for a bit."

She nodded and offered him a cigarette. He declined, so she lit one for herself and walked to the glass separating her indoor jungle from the garden. She stood, looking out into the garden, next to the floor-standing brass ashtray, the ornate bowl of which was already filled with cigarette butts.

Nick heard the click of a lighter behind him and turned around. The housekeeper was lighting a stick of incense stuck into the dirt of one of the massive pots holding a palm. There was a tiny graveyard of burned-out incense sticks poking upwards from the dirt. Nick turned back to Dierdre with her ashtray of cigarette butts and wondered which one of them was winning.

"You had called the Dixonville Police Department," she uttered, still gazing into the garden. "May I ask how you knew about the rock?"

This question registered with two lightning-fast realizations in Nick's head. One, the rock was real. And two, she did not know how Nick fit in. That made two of them, but she did know something. He suddenly recognized that the gold-framed photo portrait staring at him from the piano was of Tommy as a young boy – maybe nine or ten, on a horse. Round cheeks and a missing-tooth smile under a black riding helmet.

"Does it matter?" he replied.

She inhaled silently and let out a cloud of smoke. "I suppose not."

"How did you know to call me?"

"That Norris boy with Dixonville PD. He's always been a nice boy. He called me after he talked to you."

Nick had no idea what Sergeant Norris looked like, but he doubted anyone else called him a boy after his seventeen years on the force. But then again, Nick supposed that everything was relative.

"Why did he call you?"

"Because I told him to. A long time ago. It was part of the deal. After all these years, I was beginning to think it would never come to it."

"So, how did Tommy really die?"

She turned to him. Her dark brown eyes gazed calmly at him, without blinking and without emotion.

Nick watched her, feeling his heart beating in his stomach, and trying not to let on how important this was to him. Her eyes narrowed slightly, and the fine wrinkles found their tracks at the corners of her eyes.

"He raped a girl." She broke her gaze and ashed her cigarette in the brass bowl.

This was in no shape or form one of the possible scenarios he had played through in his head.

"How do you know?"

She exhaled a long puff. "Because his friend Vincent told me. They were at a party that night, and my son bragged that he had slipped a rufie to a girl. He later told Vincent he was taking her to the nearby park. Vincent said the girl could barely stand up. After some time, Vincent went to look for them. He found Tommy lying on the ground in the park. His head was bashed in, and his pants were around his ankles." She took another drag.

"The police report did not say any of this."

She smiled a small bitter smile. "That's because Vincent was a good boy. He called me first."

"Why?"

"Because this wasn't the first time. Tommy did this in high school, too. At least once, that we knew of. We paid fifty grand to the girl's family to keep them quiet."

"You paid them off? Why?"

"Because this is what people like us do." She studied him with detached curiosity, as if he were a taxidermized museum specimen from a long-gone era. "Fred was running for the city council, and a scandal would have ended his run."

"All of this for a seat on the city council?"

She smiled again, and a brief fit of smoker's cough suddenly took her breath.

"Look around, detective," she said, finally catching her breath. "The city council paid $41,000 per year. Do you think that paid for all this? Fred didn't get on the city council because he cared about St. Michael. He did it because it brought him closer to Topeka. Do you think it's a coincidence that in our country we use the same word for money as we do for the city that houses state government? Topeka is the capital of Kansas, and it was the center of the universe, as far as Fred was concerned. Topeka was power. The state senate, the lobbies, the industry, the labor. He may not have sat at the big tables of power, but there were plenty of scraps and crumbs under it. This was simply the next step in the Fred O'Rourke growth plan, and nothing could get in the way. Everything was about connections, expansion, influence, zoning, construction, union deals. His family may have come from the farming business, but for Fred, money became *this* family's business. It did not matter how or where. If there was money to be made, Fred got involved in it. And this incident put all of that at risk."

"So, you covered up your own son's death?"

"Fred was on a business trip, and I had to get ahead of this. Tommy was dead. Nothing could be done to change that. But we could not have that girl come forward. And we did not know who or where she was."

"So, what did you do?"

"We changed the story. I told Vincent to pull my son's pants up and move him into the street. I believe you know the rest."

"And the police did not question the hit and run? These weren't exactly textbook injuries."

"I called the station before Vincent called 911. It was the middle of the night. I told the young cop who answered that he was about to get a 911 call, and that the way he handled it could change his life."

"That was Norris? You paid him off?"

"We did. Don't judge him – he had a wife and two babies to feed. Thanks to this, both his kids were able to go to college. We paid off the coroner as well. He died a few years ago. Of old age."

"And there has not been any further investigation?"

She shook her head. "Tommy's body was cremated, and no evidence was kept by the police. No DNA. No questions for all these years. Not until you."

"And the girl? What happened to her?"

She shrugged. "She never came forward."

"And you never tried finding her? Never hired a PI to find out who killed your boy? You must have wanted revenge? Justice?"

She took a long drag from her cigarette. "He was my only child. I loved him with all my heart as only a mother could. Despite all his faults. Perhaps justice was served."

"I doubt this girl feels the same way."

"Look, detective. Do I feel guilty and responsible for what happened to this girl? Of course. I am a woman. I brought Tommy into this world, I raised him, so I am forever responsible for everything he has ever done or said. She did what she had to, and I will never judge her for that. If she were there, if she had come forward, things would have turned out differently. But she didn't. So, we made the best we could of a bad situation. This doesn't exonerate us. It just makes us human." She finished her cigarette and stabbed it out in the ashtray. "So, now you know. What will you do? Will you re-open the investigation?"

He had not thought about this simple question until she asked it. Until now, this had been his case. The case of *what had Nick done?* Until suddenly, it wasn't. Everything changed. This was not the same case anymore, and he didn't have anything to do with it. And yet he did, didn't he? Otherwise, why would he dream of it? Somehow, he was still connected to what happened that night. He was attached to it, and he knew he would not be able to walk away. So, what was he to do now? This case had an unknown victim and no evidence. And Dixonville was not even close to his jurisdiction. But it would not take much to get this re-opened. Not if the media got wind of this.

"Would you go on the record about the rape and the coverup?"

"Sure. If that's what you want. I've lived with this guilt for all these years. I've confessed and repented before God, and I will do the same before people. You do what you think you must. But consider this. You can't do this without tearing apart that policeman's life. Did he have a moment of weakness for the sake of providing for his family? Yes, he did. But that was a long time ago, and he was the smallest piece in all of this. Who is left to stand trial? Tommy is dead. Fred died from a heart attack six years ago. Vincent is doing time in a federal prison for securities fraud. The coroner is dead. I have cancer and probably won't be here in six months. You seem like a smart man who knows the difference between the law and justice. There is only one good that's left to be made out of all this."

"And what's that?"

"Find this poor girl." Dee reached into the pocket of her dress and held out a business card to Nick. "This is the number for my lawyer. I have set up a trust with five million dollars. All she has to do is call this number, and it's hers."

Nick took the card. He probably shouldn't have.

"Are you sure you should be trusting a cop with this kind of money?"

"I trust you. Why else would you come out all this way and after all this time if you did not care about justice?"

He slipped the card into his notepad. "Do you know what she looked like?"

She turned around and gazed into the garden again. "Vincent said she had dark brown hair."

***

Nick called Claire on his way back from Topeka. She was at home, getting ready for the night shift. He knew she wanted to know how it went, but he found himself reluctant to talk about it. It was all too much. The drugging, the rape, the murder, the coverup, the small-town politics. He hadn't had time to process it himself. He did not know how to tell it without cheapening it. Without making it sound like a recap of a daytime TV show.

He told her the main thing. He told her that this seemed to have nothing to do with him. He knew she could tell there was more, but she did not press. She understood. If this had nothing to do with Nick, they still had no answers. They were back to square one. Maybe he did need real therapy, like Sam suggested. After hearing the story of this unknown girl told by the mother of the boy who raped her, the harebrained theory that someone was implanting memories into his head sounded ludicrous even to Nick himself. He wondered where this girl was now. He doubted she would have any answers for him, but he resolved to the fact that he needed to find her. He needed to tell her about the O'Rourkes, about what they did. He needed to give her Dierdre's card and ask her what she wanted to do. And then, if she wanted to take this further and file charges, he would help her anyway he could.

31

Mike wanted to meet at the Panera this time. Nick got a double espresso.

"Man, you look like shit. You feeling OK?" Mike gave him a long stare, and Nick realized that he forgot to shave this morning. When he returned from Topeka late last evening, Claire was at work, so he passed out on the couch in front of the TV, woke up in terror in the middle of the night, as usual, slept like crap the remaining hours, and rose like a jetlagged zombie when the alarm on his phone went off like an air-raid siren. At present, his head was buzzing, but not any more than usual.

"Yeah. Just tired. Not sleeping well."

"That's no good. Is it the case?"

Nick nodded. That was just easier. The curious case of Nick Severs. He was a case of something, that's for sure.

"I can recommend a doctor. Get you a little something to help sleep. Or stay awake. Or both."

Nick shook his head. Pharmaceuticals were the last thing he need added to this mix. He sipped his black, bitter caffeine reduction. It tasted good, but he was beginning to suspect that caffeine itself had stopped working lately. Or he just could not tell anymore.

"OK, well, let me know if you change your mind." Mike pulled out his phone. "So, I have confirmed Bruce was at the benefit the night Lisa was killed." He handed the phone to Nick with a web page – a Denver Post write-up titled "Denver's Tech Titans Pledge Support to Vets Program."

The lead photo showed half-a-dozen sharply dressed men and women holding one of those giant checks for one million dollars made out to *Code of Honor*. Nick zoomed in – there was Bruce with his marine buzzcut and tailored tux. Nick scrolled down to the article and clicked the link for Code of Honor. The organization's home page had a blog post on the generous donation. He flipped through the photos – Bruce was in at least half of them. Nick would need to confirm the times, but so far Bruce's alibi was holding up. That did not mean he was innocent. He had the motive, and he lied to Nick. Even if he did not do it himself, he could have had someone else do it.

Nick handed the phone back to Mike. "Cogan has a photo on his desk – it's him with some army buddies. Do you think you can take a picture of it for me?"

"Sure. Why?"

"Army buddies tend to be a tight bunch. If Cogan was at the benefit, then he could have had someone else kill Lisa. He told me only one of his friends from that photo survived."

"Yeah – Matt something…Ellis."

"You know him?" Nick liked it when things turned out easier than he expected.

"Yeah. He came to the office party one year. Bruce introduced us. Burly guy. Said he was working for a private security outfit out of Cheyenne, I think."

Cheyenne was only a two hours' drive from Pine Lake. People have driven further than that for murder. It was time to head back to the station and see what he could dig up on Mr. Ellis. He ordered another double espresso to go.

***

The first fact Nick ascertained about Matt Ellis was that he did not have a criminal record. A record could have been helpful in qualifying him as a suspect, but Nick was only getting started.

He was about to dive into the DMV database when there was a knock on the door frame of his office. This was an irregular occurrence because Ray usually walked right in, whether the door was opened or closed, and Patty would call his extension, even if his door was open and she could just lean over in her chair and see through the glass partition that he was not on the phone.

He turned from his computer monitor to find Detective Jana Barnes leaning in his doorway. Her fitted black pinstriped suit draped perfectly from her frame and the Ray-Ban aviators were rocking leisurely by the wire earpiece in her hand. She looked like the cover of one of those women's fashion catalogs he would mysteriously get in the mail from time to time that caused Claire to give him a funny look. Nick wondered if Jana practiced posing. He was certain that none of his suits looked *this* good on him.

"Detective Nick Severs," she declared with slightly predatory relish and that see-through-you Mona Lisa smile.

"Hey!" That was the best he could come up with under the duress of an overly familiar greeting from someone he did not really know. "Detective Barnes! Come on in."

"Jana, please." She remained posed in the doorway. Her eyes narrowed. "I was just talking to Ray about a case and thought I would stop by and see how that Scraggy Ridge deal turned out."

Nick exhaled one of those long pensive breaths that gave one time to get his thoughts in order. He did not like oversharing. "Looks like a homicide after all."

"Well done you!" Her eyes twinkled, and her very white teeth flashed. "I'll have to tell Davis. It will aggravate him to no end that you were right. Anything we at the County can help you with?"

"I think I am good right now, but I am sure that could change any time." He gave her a smile. "Well, actually, do you know anyone I could talk to in sex crimes?"

"Sure. I used to work sex crimes."

"You did? OK, then maybe you can help me."

"Shoot."

"OK. Is it normal for sexual assault victims not to come forward?"

Sher sighed and gazed into the window behind Nick. "Yeah. I'd say most don't."

"Why?"

"Shame."

"Really? Why shame? They are the victims."

"Well, imagine a guy beats *you* up and rapes you in an alley, would you go to the cops?"

She had a point. And the thought was disturbing.

"Just because they are women does not make it any easier," she continued. "For one, they blame themselves for getting into that situation because they are taught since childhood not to invite this kind of behavior. So, there's part of them that believes they did something wrong to cause the rape. There is stigma and further humiliation if they come forward." She darted a gaze at him. "Why do you ask? Was she raped?"

"What? Oh, no – it's a different case."

"Hmm." She chewed on the earpiece of her sunglasses. "Hey, Ray tells me you used to be a professor."

"Yeah, sort of." His title had actually been assistant professor, which was not at all the same as a tenured PhD professor, but this distinction always seemed tedious to explain to people not from the academia, and besides, he always felt a bit self-conscious talking about his former profession. He imagined it must have been how the foreign exchange students felt when he asked about their villages back home. It felt distant and irrelevant.

"What did you teach?"

"English and literature."

"Hmm." Her eyes narrowed at him again, as if she were creating a mental picture. "I bet those English major coeds just ate you up." She gave him a wink and leaned away from his doorway, effortlessly transitioning into another fashion catalog pose. Her head canted slightly to the side, "You give me a call if need anything. OK?"

She turned into the hallway, and he listened to the *click-clock* of her high-heel boots on the title floor. He watched her sail past Patty to the exit.

He concluded that Jana Barnes made him slightly uncomfortable. Maybe more so on the account of him being so tired. She was possibly flirting with him, but he had been out of the dating scene for some time now, and his radar could have been off. It was also possible she was just trying to be *one of the guys*. Having spent a lot of time amongst cops, he knew them for a fact not to be the most refined bunch. He doubted any woman could make it from the academy to a detective without being affected in some way. Regardless, with everything he had going on right now, he had no energy or mental capacity to allocate to the task of figuring out Jana. With the lack of sleep, his mind already wandered off enough on its own. He needed to stay focused.

He turned back to the computer monitor.

Matt Ellis was thirty-one years of age and six-foot-four in height. According to the DMV record, there was 235 pounds of Matt on this planet, which was a good fifty pounds more than there was of Nick. Matt's square jaw and deep-inset eyes glaring from under the buzzcut in the DMV photo compelled Nick to consider tactics.

Ellis was employed by Iron Grid – a private security company whose website unmistakably conveyed that by private security services they meant a private army. The website said that they did for Department of Defense what UPS did for the U.S. Postal Service, but somehow none of the helmeted, geared up, helicopter-repelling, HK-rifle-wielding chaps from the action photos looked like his UPS guy Chuck. To Chuk's credit, he was a badass in his own right, sporting his trademark uniform shorts and socks and driving with his door open in any weather, expertly zipping up and down their hilly street in his box truck.

Nick ran a search query for Ellis' listed phone number in the cell tower dump spreadsheet, but to no avail. Ellis could have brought a burner. On a whim, Nick punched the number into his phone and hit Dial only to be informed by Verizon that the number had been temporarily suspended at the request of the account holder. This was a first in Nick's book.

Chuck he could talk to easily. Matt was proving to be difficult. Nick called Iron Grid, but they refused to disclose where he was without a subpoena, citing national security. These guys definitely did not deliver Amazon packages.

Matt's vehicle on record was a black 2015 Chevy Silverado. It did have OnStar, but upon further checking, it had not been active in years, and OnStar had no stored location data for Nick to request. Anyways, Ellis could have used someone else's car.

At this point, there was not a shred of digital evidence to justify a search warrant or an arrest. The only logical thing left to do was to go pay Matt an old-fashioned personal visit and ask him.

The DMV placed Matt Ellis's residence on a couple of rural acres outside of Fort Collins, just ten miles south of the Wyoming border. It was an hour and a half drive, but Nick would rather do that than hang around the station and risk Ray assigning him another property crime case. He did not need distractions.

He got his keys and walked out of his office to find Jason leaning on the entryway counter and chatting with Patty. He must have had a day off from his fulltime job and, judging by the oversized stainless steel coffee tumbler in his hand, he was planning to hang around for a while.

"Hey!" He saw Nick "Want some coffee? I have a thermos in the truck. Bourbon barrel roast."

Nick shook his head. "Thanks, but I already had two cups before I got here, and I have a good hour and a half to drive."

"Where are you headed?" Jason was clearly looking to kill the day.

"Talk to a person of interest up by Fort Collins."

"Want me to come along?"

"Sure." Having Jason along would help keep him awake and also keep him from being alone with his thoughts.

"Wanna take my truck? No need to announce we are the law before we have to."

Jason's logic was hard to argue with. Nick climbed into the passenger side of the lifted blue Dodge truck that smelled of sunbaked leather and earth inside.

"Hey, you hear about those sinkholes in Siberia?" Jason leisurely backed out of the lot and proceeded down Summit toward the freeway. "Saw it on Discovery. They said the permafrost is receding, and as the ground thaws, these massive sinkholes are appearing. They showed one that just caved in overnight. It is around two hundred feet deep and several football stadiums across. Just this gaping void in the middle of the green tundra." Jason sipped his coffee, without taking his eyes off the road. "This whole planet is changing right under our feet. Turning on us, trying to shake us off like an infection. You know, like the body raising the temperature to kill the virus? Climate changes, fires, killer wasps, rising oceans. Give it another couple of decades, and the Rocky Mountains here will be prime oceanfront property with a few charred pines and swarms of man-eating insects."

Jason was apparently in a mellow somber mood and was waxing philosophical. Nick wondered if there was actual bourbon in his coffee and was beginning to regret the decision to bring him along.

"Hey, you know much about mind control?" Nick unceremoniously changed the subject.

"Hypnosis, brainwashing, or garden-variety manipulation, persuasion, and deception?" Jason did not skip a beat.

"Brainwashing. And hypnosis, I guess." Talking to Jason was like playing Jeopardy. "Does it work?"

"Well, the CIA spent twenty years and billions of dollars running the MK Ultra research program focused on this very topic, and according to *them*, it did not work."

"You don't believe them?"

"Ha!" He grinned. "Suppose you figured out mind control. Would you tell anyone?"

He had a point.

"Do you think it can be done to someone without their knowledge?"

"Sure. It's called covert channels. It means using existing audio or video streams to insert hidden messages. The key is repeated exposure to the hidden message. In the 1960s, this company called Muzak did a bunch of research on how to use background music to improve worker productivity. They sold background music to shopping malls and department stores and claimed it stimulated consumer spending and also included inaudible messages which supposedly reduced shoplifting. Now...the government did make subliminal advertising illegal, but there're all sorts of conspiracy theories saying this is still being done through the TV, or radio, or smartphones." He glanced at Nick. "Are you thinking this guy we are going to see has been brainwashed?"

"No. Something else."

Smartphone. He pulled it out of his pocket and turned it in his hand. If someone did want to mess with Nick's head, the phone would have to be it. He did not watch much TV or listen to the radio. Before this job, he used his phone mostly for calling and texting. Now, it seemed he used it for almost everything. Could it be it? But how? He peeled off the black rubber bumper case and examined the back and the sides. Nothing looked out of place or like it did not belong. The phone looked practically new, with only a few fingerprint smudges and a specs of dust stuck on the back. He held it to his ear, cautiously, trying to hear anything – ominous static or subliminal chants. Nothing.

"So, what's the deal with this guy we are going to see?" Jason casually inquired. "Is it related to the Scraggy Ridge murder?"

"Yep."

Jason nodded. "What does he do?"

"Works for one of those private military companies."

"No shit? Do you think he will resist the arrest?" Jason nudged up his jacket, giving Nick a peek at the concealed carry holster tucked inside of his waistband.

"Jesus, man!" Nick suddenly felt very awake. "First of all, I doubt we are going to be arresting anybody today. Second, don't show me that, and please don't pull it on anybody while on department business. Ray will bust my ass."

"Who says I am on the department's clock?" He shrugged and smiled at Nick. "I could be your Uber driver." He chuckled. "Hey, one of my buddies at the mine does it on the weekends. Says he clears extra ten grand a year. Not a bad gig."

From Fort Collins, they took Highway 14 northwest, beginning the gentle climb into the rocky peaks and gulches of Poudre Canyon. The area was sparsely residential with a few campgrounds and fishing lodges sprinkled in.

"Hey, you ever wonder how come Smokey the Bear has a hat and pants, but no shirt?" Jason's train of thought took another tangential exit. Nick left that one alone and watched the wooden bear sign drift past the window. Smokey said fire danger was *Very High* today.

They passed through a short tunnel in the side of the mountain and emerged on the other side to a herd of bighorns descending the rocky incline and picking through the dry brown grass. The sheep paid no attention to the truck.

Matt's gravel driveway branched off from the highway and climbed across the slope to a small bungalow set in the trees. In front of the door sat a maroon Chevy Impala with its trunk open. This was not a vehicle registered to Matt Ellis. The black

2015 Chevy Silverado pickup that was, was nowhere in sight. Jason pulled off to the side, and they both dismounted the high-sitting Dodge.

The screen door swung open and a young woman in jeans and a Mickey Mouse T-shirt appeared in the door, holding a smoking cigarette in her hand.

"Hi," Nick approached. "We are looking for Matt Ellis. Is he around?"

"Who wants to know?"

Nick produced his badge. "I am Detective Severs with Pine Lake Police Department, and this is Deputy Birch."

She examined the badge with the quick eye of someone who had seen a few, both real and fake. She then took a drag of her cigarette and blew out the smoke to the side.

"And you are…?" Nick clearly had to be the one to keep this chat going.

"Britney." She stayed inside the doorway.

"So…Matt Ellis?"

"He's gone."

"Do you know where?"

She shrugged. "Yemen, Afghanistan, Iraq, somewhere else in BFE he can't talk about."

"Is this for his job with Iron Grid?"

She nodded.

"When did he leave?"

"A couple of weeks ago."

"Can you try and get me the date?"

She pulled her phone out of her back pocket. "September 8. Wednesday."

That was the day after Lisa's murder. Nick had not even found the body yet.

"Do you know when he is going to be back?"

She shrugged again. "Could be a month, could be ten months. He didn't say, and I didn't ask. Either way, I am not going to be here. Heading back to Santa Fe."

"And if I wanted to get a hold of him?"

She contorted her lips, pondering Nick's options. "They don't let them bring personal phones. I guess you could try through Iron Grid. But I don't know."

"Are you and him…in a relationship?"

"It was something."

Nick nodded. "Do you happen to know his whereabouts on Tuesday before he left?"

She sighed and looked into the clear blue sky. "We were here all day till about four – he said he had a meetin' in Denver."

"Do you remember when he returned?"

"Late. I was sleeping. I tried calling him earlier, but he left his phone at home."

Nick nodded. "Did he take his truck?"

She nodded.

"Do you know where his truck is now?"

"DIA, I'm guessing; economy parking."

Jason crouched at the side of the driveway. "Nick, does this look like a Keen hiking boot to you?"

Nick bent down and examined the print in the fine crumbled shale dirt on the side of the driveway. The footprint was clear, made when the ground was moist, and now dried to a precise impression. He took out his phone and pulled up the photos from the Scraggy Ridge. He held the phone next to the print. The tread looked identical. He and Jason exchanged a look.

Nick turned back to the house. "Do you know if Matt owns Keen boots?"

Britney shrugged. "I've no idea what brand they are." She looked behind her in the entryway. "They're not here. He must've took 'em with him."

"Do you know what size shoe he wears?"

She went inside and re-emerged with a running shoe. "This one's eleven and a half."

Not eleven, but then again, close enough that could be a difference between the brands.

Nick turned to Jason. "You still got the evidence kit in the truck?"

Jason popped open the big diamond-plated toolbox behind the cab and pulled out a black Pelican case. Nick dug through it and fetched out the folding evidence ruler.

He turned back to house. "Ma'am, if you'd be so kind, please provide Deputy Birch with your information in case we need to get in touch."

She shrugged and blew a cloud of cigarette smoke in their direction.

32

The first thing Nick saw when he entered Ray's office was the black oily end of a machine gun barrel with Ray's eye squinting over it at Nick. Just the barrel. Ray grinned, turned the barrel in his hand and placed it on his desk next to an old-style lacquered wooden stock. He reached inside a weathered cardboard box and pulled out what looked like the black, blocky metal receiver partially wrapped in an oily rag.

"You do know the war is over, right?" Nick was hoping there was a sane explanation for the old man's antics.

Ray smirked under his silver mustache and pulled out a wooden grip and long, shiny stick magazine from the box.

"You ever heard of the Denver Mafia?" he asked.

Nick shook his head.

"It was run by the Smaldone family. They weren't as big as the Kansas City or Chicago mobs, but they caused enough mischief and corruption in the area. First was bootlegging. Then prostitution, gambling and racketeering."

"Is this one of their Tommy guns?" With all the parts now on the desk, Nick recognized the iconic gangster submachine gun, albeit with a straight magazine instead of the trademark round Al Capone-style one.

Ray nodded. "Thompson M1928. This is probably the gun that killed my father in 1953 during the raid on one of the Smaldone operations. I was four. My father was with Denver Vice. His partner gave it to me when I joined the force. I haven't looked at it since 1997." He put his hand on the warm wood of the stock.

"What happened in 97?"

Ray tilted his head to the side. "I don't know. I must have felt nostalgic about the past and decided to track down Clyde Smaldone – one of the boss brothers my father went to apprehend. I found him living at the Cedars nursing home on Colfax. He was almost 90. There was little left of the man. He had dementia. I don't know what I was looking for, going to see him, but I definitely did not find it. He died the following year."

Nick nodded. He did not spend much time looking at the past, but he appreciated why some people wanted to. "So, what are you planning to do with it now?"

Ray shrugged. "Haven't decided. Clean it, put it back together, maybe hang it on the wall. I've been thinking about my father lately." Ray tossed the empty cardboard box on the floor and sat down in his chair, surveying the Thompson parts laid out in front of him. "Anyways, what can I help you with?"

"Do you have any contacts at the State Department?"

Ray contorted his mustached mouth into a pensive squiggle. "No. But I do at the FBI. What do you need?"

"I've been trying to get location on a suspect without much luck. He works for Iron Grid security, and they are not cooperating because they are under a State Department contract, and the details are classified because they are protecting the diplomatic staff. I called the State Department but got the runaround and a form to fill out. Figured I'd check with you, since you know everyone everywhere, and I don't want to grow old waiting for this form to come back."

"And you think this is your guy?"

"Well, he is an old army buddy of the only guy on my list with a motive, he has the training to kill, he left his residence on the night of the murder, and he left his phone at home."

The chief nodded. "OK, let me make a call," he said and reached for his Rolodex.

Ray's phone calls were works of art. As Nick headed back to his office, he knew that, from the other side of the thin wall, he would now once again get to witness the disarming effectiveness of Ray's tele-parlance. One of Ray's gifts was that he could talk to anyone about anything for any amount of time. But these calls were not idle chatter. Ray's calls got things done. Like a new lease on the fleet vehicles from the dealership, or discounted rates on dry cleaning for the uniforms. The most amazing thing about Ray's calls was that despite being impressively long, they required of Ray to do surprisingly little talking. Ray's genius of communication was not the gift of gab. He did not talk *at* someone, as some people had a tendency to do; his talent was in engaging the other party and getting them to talk about themselves. He did this by asking questions that expressed genuine human interest, and this process inevitably drew the other party closer to Ray. Everything Ray said served the purpose of connecting with the other person, hearing out their joys and tribulations, and validating their experience. And so, when Ray finally got around to his trademark *So, hey, can you do me a huge favor,* whatever it was, it seemed like the smallest, most trivial ask the other party simply couldn't reasonably refuse.

For Ray, there was no substitution for the old-school one-on-one connection. His calls were examples of a dying art. Nick wished that he could preserve one of Ray's epic calls in amber, like a prehistoric mosquito, so that the future generations could study them to work out the secrets of the lost art of effective human discourse. Heck, even the present generation could benefit from studying Ray's mastery. Maybe then they would come to appreciate the one feature of their smartphones they never seemed to use – the telephone itself.

By the time Nick walked to his office and settled into his chair, Ray's mischievous opener resounded on the other side of the wall: *"Gary? Hey! How the heck are you, old bastard?"* Nick tuned out the rest, focusing on research on Cogan until he heard

Ray's closer: *"OK, you betcha. Say hi to Margaret from me. Bye now."* The hard plastic of the phone receiver clanked down, and Nick looked at his watch: thirty-seven minutes. The cowboy boots shuffled in the hallway, and Ray's mustached face popped into Nick's door.

"Hey, I just sent you an email address. Type up your request and send it over to Gary, he will walk it over to the State Department himself. He knows folks there. That should get you what you need quick."

"Ray, you are my hero."

"I know it," Ray responded from the hallway, possibly on his way to an afternoon nap.

***

Before Nick went home that evening, he made one more stop. This time, it was his turn to ask Mike to meet at a random location. Nick picked Kelly's Irish pub in Littleton.

"What's up, man?" Mike asked, as he slid into the tall, tufted leather booth.

Nick pushed a double shot of Bushmills toward him. Mike took a healthy sip, and Nick pushed his phone to the middle of the table. "I have a favor to ask. Can you take a look at this for me?"

Mike picked up the phone and turned it in his hand. "What do you mean? What's wrong with it?"

"I don't know."

"So, what am I looking for?"

"Signs of tampering. Anything out of the ordinary."

"You think someone hacked your phone?"

Nick nodded.

Mike whistled. "OK. I don't know how much I can help, but I can show it to Dimitri if you don't mind."

"Thanks," Nick said and finished his drink.

He made it home with the residue of the last few days vibrating in his head like a blurry, muffled movie playing in another room. The Irish whiskey helped, but not enough. He wished Claire were here, but she was still pulling night shifts till the end of this week. He missed her. They really hadn't connected much lately. She seemed a bit distant the last few times, but maybe it was him. Or her night shifts. She and Nick passed from shift to shift like two ships passing each other in the fog. They needed to do something together this weekend to reconnect. Maybe go for a hike.

He pulled off his boots and thought about dinner, but decided he really wasn't hungry. What he *really* wanted was to go to sleep, but his brain was spinning at full speed, processing a carousel of faces – Matt, Bruce, Lisa, Tommy, Marc, Lori, Dierdre, and the mystery brown-haired girl. They were all pieces of the puzzle his brain had become, like shards of an exploded grenade he was trying to put back together. Arranging, rearranging, connecting and starting from scratch. The pieces were competing for his attention, for acknowledgement, for a solution. Some right, some wrong, some wronged.

He looked at his watch – it was almost seven. Standing in the kitchen, he realized that he had no energy left to do anything else today. He had run out of gas, and all he could do was just stand there, swaying to the vibration in his head. He pivoted to the cabinet and took out the bourbon bottle and a glass. Evidently, there was just enough bandwidth in his fried brain for one last snide observation as he filled the short glass half-full with liquid amber: *first murder case, and you've already graduated to the drinking detective cliché.* He ignored this voice just as he was ignoring all others right now. This was for medicinal purposes. He just needed to sleep. The first gulp burned the back of his throat. He settled on the couch, took another gulp and closed his eyes. Darkness made everything fade. Maybe this Bulleit would stop Tommy. He smirked to the pun in his head, finished the glass and bunched up Claire's blanket for a pillow.

33

Nick was awakened by the sound of the door to the garage slamming shut. He reached for his phone and remembered that he had left it with Mike. He checked his watch: 6:37 in the morning, so Claire must have just come home from her shift. Indeed, a second later he heard her taking off her shoes.

He sat up on the couch. Did he have the dream last night? Possibly. He had slept better, but it was hard to tell for sure with the slight hangover currently pulsating in his head. Too much Irish whiskey with Mike, and then bourbon at home. That seemed to be the ticket, but he could not let himself do that every night. He hadn't run in over a week and was starting to feel like a slug. Drinking was not going to help with feeling better, but it helped with sleeping. He could see why it would be appealing. It was a binary toggle switch to turn the lights out on work. And everything else.

"Hey." She entered the room. "Did you sleep here?"

His tongue felt dry. "Yeah." He cleared his throat.

She sat on the coffee table opposite of him and put her cool hand on his bristled cheek. "How are you feeling?"

"Good!" He gave her a smile, and she studied his eyes just a bit too intently, the way one studied a three-year-old who had just possibly told his first clumsy lie. Or maybe the way she checked over her sick kids at the hospital.

She leaned in and smooched his lips. "Do you have time to have breakfast together?"

"Yeah. Let me make something. You go shower," he said, standing up. He remembered when he worked nights as a patrol cop, and that strange out-of-time experience of coming home when the sun was just rising, and most people were just getting ready for work. He would eat breakfast without coffee and then shower and get in bed. An hour of reading or TV would sedate his brain enough to fall asleep. When they first started dating, it was hard having her working the opposite shift. Now they were opposite again. He missed seeing her, having her in bed, drinking coffee together. It was like he was only half himself. He looked forward to the weekend and to next week, when she would rotate off the nights for a while.

He put the skillet on the stove and heard her turn on the shower.

***

His task today was to drive out to Denver International to find Matt Ellis' truck. The E-470 loop took him in a wide sweeping hook east and then north of the downtown. From this far east, he could really see the layers of mountains looming in the west. Funny how, living in the foothills, one could never really see the full scale of the range. But from here, the jagged elevated massif dwarfed the Denver skyline nestled in the plain below. The high peaks were already tipped with snow, and white frozen veins were reaching down the slopes. There were even more layers, Nick knew, hiding in the gray curtain of clouds. At that altitude, above the Loveland Pass, his own breath would be icy right now, like those clouds. The mountains were making winter. They were forging it from iced over waterfalls and frosted morning dew. Soon, it would spill down into the valley.

At the airport, he started with the DIA police. Impressively, they were able to quickly track down Ellis' truck just by the license plate number. Evidently, nothing was ever beyond the reach of the cameras at the airport, and Nick was able to watch in continuous footage as the black Silverado pickup entered the ticket gate for the west economy lot, drove through the lot, and parked at the end of the isle. That was on Wednesday, September 8, just as Britney said. According to the live feed, the truck was still there.

A young and curious airport cop accompanied Nick to the truck. The pickup was clean. It was as if it had been run through the carwash before being parked here. Nick walked around it. There was nothing notable on the bodywork. The bed was empty and – clean. Inside the cab, he could see nothing through the window to warrant a search. Nothing at all, in fact, besides the empty seats and the cleanly wiped dash. Next Nick checked each wheel, but the wheel wells looked like they had been pressure-washed – no dirt, no sand. The knobby Cooper tires were shiny and had no gravel or anything else stuck in them. This truck was clean and shiny all over and looked good enough to go on a car dealer's lot. The only thing left for Nick to do was take a picture of the tire pattern and the tire size numbers on the sidewall, in case there were ever tire impressions to compare to. Mike still had his phone, so Nick had to use the brand new Canon pocket camera that had been sitting in the center console of his Tahoe since he got it. Unlike his phone, this camera could do only one thing, and right now, he was OK with it.

"Are you going to seize it?" the airport cop asked.

"Maybe." Nick straightened up. "But not just yet."

He hated heading back to the station empty-handed, but there was not much else he could do here. He knew forensics could probably pull enough evidence from this truck to write a War-and-Peace-sized report, but none of it could happen without a search warrant. And to get a search warrant, he needed to have something on Matt Ellis. Something more than the fact that he used to be in the special forces and that he had a meeting in Denver the day Lisa was killed. As Nick looped south around Denver on E-470, he prayed to the law enforcement gods that it would not take too long for Ray's buddy to pull that favor with the State Department.

He got back to Pine Lake around noon. He should have stopped for lunch but was too preoccupied and not feeling hungry. Still, once inside the station, he allowed himself to be persuaded by one of the surviving morning donuts in the box behind Patty's desk, before it fell prey to Ray's afternoon sugar raid. The coffee carafe was almost empty, and Nick had to tilt it forward to milk out the last half-cup of lukewarm, tar-black liquid. He turned to go into his office but stopped and took a sobering look at the dry donut in his hand and the cup of oily black fluid in the other. His standards were slipping. This was cause for alarm. He dumped both in the trash and went into his office emptyhanded.

Perhaps it was his prayers, or perhaps the last-minute offering of a stale donut and burnt coffee, but the police gods must have heard his pleas and responded favorably. In his inbox there was an email message from the State Department with the subject line *RE: Matthew R. Ellis*. Nick clicked it open.

The contents of the email were brief. The State Department regretted to inform him that the person of interest Matthew R. Ellis, a State Department contractor employed by Iron Grid, was killed in action during an incident in Yemen on September 12.

Nick turned away from his computer. Each time he thought he caught a break, he found himself holding a dead end. Outside of the station, the lodgepole pines were swaying in the wind. The sky above them was still blue, but clouds were gathering in the west.

The irony of fate. This guy flew half-way around the world just so he could be killed three days later. Fate liked to play dirty. Was he running? Was he even really dead, or was Iron Grid covering up for him? Nick dismissed the thought. This email address looked legit with a State Department domain, and Nick's original request was quoted at the bottom. This was just another fact, and it said that his primary suspect was not going to be confessing.

It was back to square one, but that was OK. What was Ellis, anyways? Even if he was involved, Ellis was just the murder weapon. The real murderer was the guy who hired him. It was time to tighten the screws on the Intergenix' CEO.

And what *did* Nick have on Cogan? With Mike's help, he could make a case for data fraud. Cyber Crimes was the FBI's turf. Big guns. Nick could bring them on, and they would probably take Cogan down, but for what? Illegal data collection? Who cared about that? Not Nick. Not Lori. Not Kevin. If Nick went this route, the murder investigation would become a sideshow. Cogan would be on guard. Lawyered up. Destroying any remaining evidence. Or worse – turn state's evidence in exchange for immunity. With Cyber Crimes running the show, the murder conviction might never happen at all. He couldn't have that. This wasn't about Cogan's data fraud. This was about the girl who got in his way. Nick was going to put him away for it. The FBI could have their crack at him after.

But this was all talk. Right now, Nick had nothing to tie Cogan to Lisa's murder. No prints, no location data, no witnesses. Everything he had was circumstantial, and circumstantial did not go far in court.

He turned back to the computer and opened up the web browser. No one was this clean. Not Cogan, not Intergenix. There was another way of getting to Cogan Nick could explore. Cogan did not get to where he was today alone. It was time to get a better picture of Cogan's business partner. Nick scoured the web for any information about Andrew Giles but could find only mere crumbs. Unlike many of his high-tech peers, the chief designer behind the technology that propelled Cogan to stardom did not keep a blog, hobnob with politicians or give TED talks. Giles seemed to be comfortable existing in the shadows.

By four, the sky outside had grown overcast and Nick had had enough. The computer screen was getting fuzzy, and his afternoon headache was setting in. Nothing was getting resolved here today. He stood up and grabbed his car keys – he could do this from his couch at home. With a bourbon.

No. No bourbon today. Bourbon was for closers. He opened his desk drawer and popped a couple of Tylenols from the bottle.

34

Mike offered to meet half-way, but Nick could not pass up the opportunity to take another poke around Intergenix. Mike picked him up from the lobby and took him to his office and then dialed an extension on his desk phone: "Hey, you have a few minutes? OK. Thanks."

"Dimitri," he explained to Nick.

For some reason, Nick expected to see a stocky middle-aged Eastern European farmer in thick glasses, but Dimitri turned out to be a trim twenty-something with a red beard and a hipster combover coiffure. Dimitri closed the office door behind him.

"Nick, Dimitri; Dimitri, Detective Severs." Mike efficiently dispensed with the introductions.

Mike opened his desk drawer and put Nick's phone in front of him.

"So?" Nick looked at him.

"So, someone is definitely trying to mess with you," Mike said.

It was as if someone had touched the tip of a chilled icepick to the back of Nick's neck. "What did you find?"

Mike looked to Dimitri.

Dimitri cleared his throat. "Someone installed malware on your phone. A frame injector."

"A what?"

"OK. So, it is basically like splicing a frame into a movie strip."

"You can do that on a phone?"

"Yes. So, you see, all types of screens – TVs, phones, laptops – have what's known as a refresh rate." Dimitri talked fast, with barely any noticeable accent. "So, the refresh rate is how often the screen re-draws what you see on it. This makes it possible for you to see things moving on your screen. Just like a movie film strip is a sequence of still frames that makes it possible for you to see moving pictures. The same on a digital screen. And the faster the refresh rate, the smoother things will move on your screen. Your cell phone has a refresh rate of 120 frames per second. So, about every 8.3 milliseconds, it shows you a new frame. It doesn't matter what you are looking at – a GPS app, your email, caller ID, a website – the screen keeps refreshing like a constant stream of still frames. Now, what this particular malware does is it injects frames into this stream that should not be there. Like imposters. So, say you are looking at your email." He liked the word *so*. "With your phone's refresh rate, every second you would normally see 120 frames of you doing things in your email. But with this frame injector hack, a few of those frames get replaced with whatever image the hacker wants. In your case, they were replacing five out of those 120 frames per second."

"But I didn't notice this at all. Did I?" Somehow, Nick had a feeling that this imposter frame, whatever it was, was not telling him to buy more Coke and popcorn.

"Not when it's just a few frames at such a high refresh rate. Each frame is on the screen for just a few thousandths of the second. Even if your eyes did register it flash by, it's too fast for your brain to process."

"So, what's the point of this then?"

"*So*, a few frames per second may not sound like much, but it keeps repeating – every second, all day long, every day, this imposter frame gets injected. They say adults on average spend four hours a day looking at their phones. There are 3,600 seconds in an hour. So, that's 14,400 seconds a day spent looking at the phone." His fast talking did not slow down with mental math. If anything, it may have sped up. Or it could have just been that Nick was trying hard to keep up with all the new tech jargon and the surrounding logic. "Your frame injector was injecting five frames per second. So, that means you saw this imposter frame 72,000 times a day. Now, I am no shrink, but I can't imagine seeing the same image that many times every day does not have *some* effect on you. Especially a disturbing image."

Nick's pulse thumped in his temples. "Wait. You saw it?"

"Oh yeah. It was a hidden file on your phone." Dimitri picked up Nick's phone, swiped a few times and handed it to Nick.

Hello, Tommy.

Dead Tommy with his head bashed in. Tommy on the lawn and not on the pavement. Tommy with the dark rock next to his head. It was like looking at the alternate reality of the evidence photos from the file. The real reality.

"Have you seen this before? Do you know what this is?" Mike was watching him.

"Yeah. This is the exact image I have been seeing in my dreams for several weeks now."

"So, it works? That's truly amazing." Dimitri seemed moderately excited.

Amazing wasn't the word Nick would have used to characterize this.

"Sorry – it's just so simple, how it works." Dimitri must have sensed his enthusiasm was not shared. "It's so easy to do, and it can basically program someone's brain."

"Can you tell where it came from? How it got on my phone?"

Dimitri shrugged. "It could have been installed through Bluetooth or Wi-Fi. Could have been someone who sat near you at a coffee shop or another public place. Or it could have been someone in another country who has never met you. I inspected the image for any metadata like the phone it was taken with, date or location, but it was scrubbed clean. Someone knew what they were doing."

"So, it could just be random, right?" Mike tried to sound upbeat. "Just some hacker kids messing with random people. Like ding-dong-ditch for punks who never leave their mother's basement?"

Dimitri shook his head. "I don't think it's random. This hack is what's known as a zero-day exploit. A zero-day is a vulnerability that is not yet known to the manufacturer of the device or software, so there is no patch for it yet. The manufacturer has literally zero days of awareness about this vulnerability. Zero-days are rare and pricy. There are two groups who use zero-day hacks: spy agencies and hackers. Recently, some hackers stole a big cache of zero-days from the NSA and have been selling them on the dark web for thousands of dollars a pop. This frame injector could have come from that cache. Either way, I doubt someone would spend that kind of money just to mess with a random stranger."

"So, what do you think they are trying to accomplish?"

Dimitri shrugged. "I have no idea. Most hacks are done for some financial gain. But this one has nothing to do with stealing your bank passwords or money."

"Unless this is meant as a blackmail threat." Mike blurted and then shut up and looked cautiously at Nick.

Nick shook his head. "I did not hurt this kid."

"Anyways, the malware is off your phone now. So, you are all clear."

"Do they know that you took it off my phone?"

Dimitri shook his head. "It's completely passive. No communication out."

"OK, thank you, Dimitri." Nick stood up and shook Dimitri's hand. The kid smiled shyly, nodded to Mike and left them alone. Nick watched his voluminous hipster combover bounce up and down as he walked past on the other side of the glass wall.

"Are you in trouble? *Is* it blackmail?" Mike gave him an interrogating stare.

"No. I don't think so. I had nothing to do with what's in this photo."

"So, what are you going to do?"

Nick took a deep breath. "I have a case to solve."

"Any luck with Matt Ellis?"

"I suppose it depends on your definition of luck. Ellis is dead."

"What!? How?"

"Apparently, killed in action abroad. But his timeline still works. He flew out of Denver the day after Lisa was killed. But I have no evidence linking him to her murder. I need another angle on Cogan. What can you tell me about his business partner? The CPO?"

"Andrew? Man, he is the nicest guy. Typical startup techie geek. I mean it in the best sense possible. Very smart and analytical, but not so good at parties. A total introvert. Works mostly from his home."

"And you think he had to know about the illegal data collection?"

"Oh, no doubt. He knows the algorithm like the back of his hand. Bruce couldn't have done it without him knowing. Or without him, period."

"Then I think it's time I have a chat with him."

"Sure. But I don't think he had anything to do with the murder." Mike shook his head. "I just don't see it. He may be antisocial, but he is not a sociopath."

***

In the Tahoe, Nick studied the phone in his hand. It felt the same. The screen looked the same. Except now it wasn't trying to reach into his head and subvert his memories. How could he not know? And how long had it been going on?

He stared into the screen intently, trying to see the frames refresh, but the image looked completely static. He could not even discern the individual pixels that made up the icons, the background and the text on the screen, but he knew they were there, refreshing at lightning speed. Not like the old-school flight schedule boards or sports scoreboards with bisected numbers, with the top half tearing away from the top of the board and slowly falling, swinging downward to reveal a different number. Not even like an animated picture book, where the eye could barely but still see the rapidly flipping corners of pages, fluttering semi-transparent above the moving image. He could not see anything now. Not with the phone. Not with 120 frames per second. His feeble earthling eyes could not detect any movement even though it was happening right in front of them. Wasn't that their whole purpose? To alert the brain of danger? Some sentries they were! Useless. Fooled by our own technology. Bypassed with a *simple* hack.

Who would want to do this to him? This wasn't just anyone. This wasn't some complete stranger on the other side of the world in some random country like Tajikistan. It had to be someone who knew him.

He opened up the Contacts app on his phone. Claire was the only favorite pinned at the top. The only one he called with any regularity. But then there were 329 others. How did he amass so many? He wasn't that social. And yet, here they were. Accumulated, migrated from phone to phone, sorted alphabetically. Some – most – he barely knew. Old teaching co-workers, school buddies, cop buddies, chance connections. They felt like ghosts. He studied the names. Some had profile photos. He hadn't talked to most of these people in ages. Was it one of them? Why? Was it a recent acquaintance or someone from the past, with a cold, long-held grudge?

None of the names he scrolled through jumped out at him as likely suspects. Maybe it was someone from the other side of the law? A convict? Or a relative of a convict? But for most of

Nick's police career, he had been just a lowly patrol cop, so why would anyone expend so much effort on him rather than a bigger fish like a judge or a DA? Maybe it was someone who simply hated cops? Cops didn't exactly have a labeled shelf of Hallmark cards these days. But why *him*? And why this photo? One he had never seen, and yet somehow connected to him, to college. This had to be personal. Had to be someone he knew. Someone who knew both him and Tommy.

A college classmate? He had not kept in touch with many people from then. There was Mike, clearly. Mike knew both Nick and Tommy. But why would he be doing this? And why would he be helping Nick figure this out? The only other person he was in touch with from college was Sam. But she did not know Tommy. Nick and her always had a good a relationship and had never dated. So, what reason would she have to perpetrate this kind of revenge? She had nothing to gain, except maybe a new therapy client, and even that she did not seem to want.

What about Tommy's circle? It wasn't Dierdre – he was fairly certain of that. She seemed to have never heard of Nick before he started digging around. She even had Nick in her house, and still nothing came up that would have connected him to Tommy.

What about Tommy's friend Vincent? He was in on the cover-up. Nick didn't really know Tommy, but he sounded like he was quite an asshole, and Nick doubted they would have shared the same social circles. Vincent must have had quite an illustrious criminal career in finance to end up on the radar of the feds. He certainly would have a lot of free time on his hands in prison, but why in the world would he zero in on Nick as his archnemesis?

His thumb froze mid-scroll through the list of contacts: Marc's name and phone number. Still here, after all these years. Could this have something to do with Marc? Marc was dead, but he and his death were undeniably tied to Nick's memories and feelings from that time. Was there something else Nick was repressing from that night? If he had completely forgotten ever meeting Tommy, what other forgotten things were lurking in the dark corners of his mind?

Or maybe this was *her*? That poor mystery girl who put that well-deserved rock to Tommy's head. Was she the one who now got into Nick's head? Why? What had he done? Had he done something irreparably bad? Why didn't she come forward back then?

He needed to talk through it all with Claire: the phone, the visit with Dierdre O'Rourke, Tommy, Vincent, the girl, everything. It was time. These were no longer wild paranoid theories. Someone was behind this, and Claire was good at figuring out people. If someone was after him, could they also come after her? Nick checked his watch: just after two in the afternoon. Claire was probably still sleeping after her night shift. But by the time he drove home from Intergenix, in thirty minutes or so, she could be awake. He started the Tahoe and headed home.

tH!rty-f!v3

F8sab!tch. That was the name of Roses' hacking collective. Today, Kat reached the realization that fate indeed was a bitch. Cold, manipulative, vindictive and impersonal. Even when it gave you things, it actually took things away. It did not matter what you were after – power, money, happiness, revenge – when you thought you were in control of your fate, you were actually dancing to its tune at the end of the marionette line.

Didn't Kat get what Kat wanted? She planned it all, set it in motion, gave it everything she had for all those many months, and was now standing at the finish line. All she had to do was cross it. This was the final act, and it was supposed to bring the climax, the resolution and closure. She had always imagined she would feel empowered at this point, holding his fate in her hands. She thought she would feel the weight of the past lifted by now. But instead, this felt like a burden. It had become a curse that followed her each day. A curse that hung over her now, as she sat in the booth of her coffee shop command center.

"So, what do YOU want?" Roses blipped into the Tox chat window.

Kat had given this question a lot of thought lately. What did *Kat* want? She used to want revenge. She used to want to hurt him. The very sight of his grinning face used to make her want to bash it in. But then, the closer she got, and the more time passed, something broke. She found herself actually wanting this sham life she had created. She found herself wanting him. This thought disturbed her, when she first realized it. This was weakness, certainly. Shameful weakness on her part. Some perverse codependency. A twisted Stockholm syndrome where she had lost track of who was in control. But it was also something else. He was different than she had imagined him. The more she got to know him, the more she was drawn to him. Behind that goofy grin, he was broken at his core, just like her.

All this amounted to the undeniable conclusion that she had failed. She felt it in her gut. After all this time, she got no more clarity. No proof. Sure, maybe she just needed more time, but she could only say that to herself so many times before it lost meaning and felt programmed, like an amateur hacking script attempting to brute-force the password to the database by trying one possibility after another, over and over again. If she had to call it right now, she had nothing. Right now, all the evidence, or rather the lack thereof, pointed to the fact that she may have made a mistake. All she had was one photo, and perhaps in the end it meant nothing. This photo set her on this path to destroy him, and now in all good conscience she could not go a step further.

And yet she still had not walked away. She had not removed herself from his life as abruptly as she had inserted herself into it. By now, she should have moved on to number seven, but she hadn't. Maybe it was because she knew that number seven would not take much time. Or maybe it was because number seven would be the end, and then what? With her path of vengeance behind her, would all the echoes of the past finally fade into silence? Or would she remain trapped in them, with no one but herself left to direct her destructive wrath at? Tears welled in her eyes, and she wiped them away abruptly. *Poor, little Kat. No one will ever love you. Not even you, yourself.* Self-pity angered her, but what she feared right now was to be left alone with herself only to find out that no matter where she went, or whomever she met, she would still always be broken.

What if she stayed?

What would happen if she just stopped and let the clockworks of her plan simply crawl to a halt? Would her life become normal, the way she'd been pretending it to be? Would she one day wake up and no longer be the imposter? Would Roses simply dissolve into ether if Kat stopped logging on? Or would the *old* Kat always be just beneath the surface, scratching at the thought that she never found out for sure, that she left this unresolved and unfinished? She never prepared for uncertainty, and now her world was splitting apart, delaminating. All the many layers she had glued on over the years to keep herself together were peeling and flaking off. She could no longer hold it together. The *old*, vengeful Kat, and the *new*, soft Kat, now both felt wrong, like grotesque distorted funhouse reflections of each other.

Maybe what Kat needed to do right now was to get out of this coffee shop, go home, and have half a bottle of wine. Then the *old* Kat would be in control again. The *old* Kat would say, *Fuck it, let's do this.* She would play this out to the end and then burn down this nice little world she had created. That's what the *old* Kat would do. But right now, Kat was tired of the *old* Kat.

There was another option, but she knew she would not take it. She could confront him. But there were two problems with that approach. One, Kat did not do direct confrontations. There was safety in distance. There was control. And two, he could just lie, and she would still never know for sure.

She stared at the message from Roses in the chat window: *What do YOU want?*

"What would you do?" she typed, erased, and re-typed back.

"I am not you. And I wouldn't have gone at it this long. But if I were in your shoes right now, I would just finish it and move on. Pick your endgame and play it. Don't let revenge take over your whole life. Otherwise, they win."

Roses was right, of course. As usual. This had to end, one way or another. This lifestyle was not sustainable.

"How do you want to end this?" Roses kept typing, encouraged by Kat's silence. "Do you want him to lose his job? We can dox him. We can deepfake some shit, if we have to. Or we can keep gaslighting him with psych warfare. Maybe we can get him committed? Get him to eat a bullet? What do you want?"

Right now, she wanted out of this. Out of all of this. The thought of physical violence churned her stomach. The air in the coffee shop was suddenly very still and suffocating, and she felt trapped in it. She needed to get out. Maybe if she waited another day or two, she could steel herself. Maybe she could find that anger again and look him in the eye as she twisted the knife.

No, she couldn't. A few more days weren't going to change anything.

"I am calling it off," she typed and hit *Send*.

She gave Roses just a second. Roses wasn't typing. Kat closed the chat app and shut the lid of her laptop. She sat there in the booth for a few moments with her eyes closed, trying to feel what this felt like. Was there relief? Closure? Was this the end she could live with? She wondered what Roses thought of her now.

Kat took a deep breath and let it out. She pulled the baseball cap low over her eyes, slipped the laptop into her bag and stood up to leave.

"Claire?" said the voice behind her.

***

She turned around slowly, her mind frantically trying to process through all the possible outcomes. "Hey, baby," she said, fixing on Nick's eyes. Her voice came out sounding shaky. "What are you doing here?"

He stood a few empty booths away. He knew. She could tell by his eyes: *he knew*. He was wearing his blazer, and she knew his gun holster was hiding inside it.

"I followed you." He didn't approach, keeping his distance. "I was coming home early and saw your car leaving our street. I tried calling you, but your phone is turned off. Did you know?"

It was too late to run. She maintained eye contact as she pulled her phone from the back pocket of her jeans and as her other hand fished out the tiny chip of the SIM card from the front. She inserted the card back into the phone, turned the phone on, and put it on the table. As the screen of her phone came to life, she slowly sat back in the booth and took off the baseball cap, letting her hair fall.

"We should talk," she said, trying to sound as normal as possible, although her heart was racing so fast, she barely had enough breath to speak.

He sat across from her, his eyes studying her for a long, silent moment. "Who *the fuck* are you?" he said coldly. He'd never said anything so abrasive to her. Or anyone else, as far as she knew. She made an effort to hold back the tears. This was the end. The fallout. A place of estrangement and powerlessness. This was the place the *old* Kat was from.

"Is Claire even your real name?" He sounded calm, but she could tell there was anger and hurt smoldering inside him.

She half shrugged with one shoulder, keeping her eyes on him like the prey watching the predator creeping closer to striking distance. "It used to be Kat. Katie Daniels."

"So, who is Claire Arden?"

"Arden was my great-grandmother's maiden name."

He took out his phone and put it next to hers. "Did you put this on my phone?"

She glanced at the photo on his screen and nodded. "And your laptop, too."

"You put this on my phone and my laptop and then you watched me lose my mind. Why?"

"Because you were there."

He shook his head. "No."

She picked up her phone, swiped a few times and showed him the same photo he just showed her.

"And this one was taken forty-seven minutes earlier." She swiped again.

***

Nick studied the photo, trying to comprehend but failing to. He did not recognize this moment in time and could barely recognize himself. Yet, there he was, clearly piss-drunk, his stupid grin in the middle of the frame, between Tommy – the very alive Tommy, and a girl with dark hair. Tommy and the girl were each holding up full shot glasses. One of Nick's hands was on Tommy's shoulder, and in the other he was holding up a red plastic cup. They were all laughing. The girl had very familiar eyes, ones he would recognize anywhere – the eyes of the girl sitting across from him now.

"You killed Tommy," he said more than asked.

"That drink that I am holding there – it's already spiked. This photo is the last thing I can remember from that night before I regained consciousness. *When* I regained consciousness, I was on my back, and he was inside me." Her eyes burned into his. "Have you ever been rufied, Nick? It's a fucking terrifying out-of-body experience. You are aware of what is happening to you, but your body is completely unresponsive. You try to move your arms, your legs, but there's nothing. He was on top of me. I don't know where the rock came from. Somehow, I hit him. Maybe more than once. It took me a while to get up. My legs kept going out from under me. I did not know he was dead. Maybe he wasn't yet. But I felt like I was about to pass out again, so my only drive was to get as far away from him as I could. Somehow, I remember thinking I would need evidence, so I took a picture of him. And then I ran, or at least tried to. I came to on the floor of a gazebo not far away. The sky was still dark, and there were bright police lights flashing everywhere. Then, I passed out again."

She was watching him as she said this without averting her gaze, as if monitoring and assessing the effect this testimony had on him. He watched her too. Her eyes, her face, her lips moving. All of it familiar, and yet suddenly completely strange. Like the photo of himself he did not at all recognize. How could this not be Claire sitting in front of him now? She seemed the same, just deeply, irreparably sad.

"I woke up in the gazebo in the early morning, still feeling drugged. But I was able to walk to my room. My roommate had the news on. Tommy's face was on the screen, and a policeman was saying Tommy was killed in a hit-and-run, and they were looking for a pickup truck. At first, I thought I was going crazy. I thought maybe my memory, as spotty as it was, was not real at all. You know what that's like, don't you?"

He did not answer. Her words fell upon him like a deluge of ice-cold water – painful but also numbing. Paralyzing. And yet they kept pouring out as if she had been waiting to tell him for a very long time.

"If it wasn't for the photos, I probably would have believed the police on the news. But soon, I realized someone covered it up. That meant someone else knew the truth. And they were able to just sweep me under the rug that fast. Maybe they bought the police. Maybe the news, too. The news said Tommy was from a wealthy family. If they could do that, what would they do to me, if they found me? I did not know where I was safe in that town. I did not know whom to trust. I didn't leave my dorm room for two days. Later that week, I dropped out of school and went home. Eventually, I went to a different school. After college, I changed my name and tried to move on. I tried therapy off and on. Then I met a friend who showed me a different way."

He swallowed a lump in his throat. He could see where this was going. The dominos were falling – at first a couple, and now more and more, multiplying, like an avalanche of the crumbling manufactured reality that had been his life.

"Did we really meet by chance online?"

She shook her head. "I always knew where you were. Since college."

"And the dating site? How did you…?"

"My friend hacked the dating site."

"Are your parents really dead?"

"Just my dad. My mom lives in Cape Girardeau."

"Did you have something to do with Tommy's friend Vincent landing in a federal prison?"

She nodded again.

"Jesus." He hesitated. "And Fred O'Rourke?"

She shook her head. "His heart beat me to it. I guess he had one after all."

She was still funny. But he wasn't laughing, and she wasn't either. "Dierdre?"

"Her cancer is taking care of her."

"So, I was next on your list?"

"You and that cop on Dixonville."

"So, you found me, after all these years, and what was your plan? To kill me?"

She shook her head. "No. I don't do that."

"Then what?"

"What does every rape victim want? To know why. Why you did it. Why me. To make you pay somehow and to be able to move on."

"But I had nothing to do with this." He felt helpless, like a prisoner about to be wrongfully executed.

She shrugged lightly. "I had no way of knowing it. When you are drugged, you don't get all your memories back. Maybe Vincent went first, before Tommy? Maybe you? I've thought through every possibility so many times, and I will still probably never know everything that was done to me. Do you have any idea what that feels like? All I knew was that you were in the picture with him. And when I got close to you, you did not like talking about college and especially about that year. But I could not get anything certain out of you. I could not get undeniable proof."

"That's because there isn't any." He snapped back, but then bit his tongue. "So…you tried the photo next?"

She nodded. "And it worked. You reacted to it so strongly. And I thought: *This is it. He knows something.* But then, all the wrong stuff came up. The whole deal with Marc's suicide. I had no idea about it. And I was left with uncertainty again. With not knowing. Not being sure about you."

He stared at the surface of the table. The off-white Formica was a barren, empty plain scarred with a million tiny scratches, gouges and pits left behind by all the people passing through this coffee shop. Coming and leaving. Always leaving. He felt lost in the vast emptiness of this barren white plain. It closed in around him, and it hurt so bad, it made him want to howl. He looked at her. Claire was gone. Maybe she never existed. Whoever this person was, sitting in front of him, was not her. Was not the one he had assumed would always be there.

"Claire…Katie. I am so sorry about what happened to you. I can't even imagine what you went through." Tears rolled down her cheeks, and he felt the urge to sit next to her and just hold her. But he resisted it. After all, she was a stranger. "And I give you my word…I had no part in this. You know it now, don't you?"

She sniffled and wadded up the soggy tissue in her fist. "I don't know, Nick. I don't think even you know everything that happened that night, so how can I? I may never know. All I know is that I am not the same person I was back then. Not even the same I was last year. I've lived revenge for twelve years. I've looked at this picture every day, for twelve years." She shook her head, her tears now streaming uncontrollably. "And I can't do it anymore. You have it. You look at it. Maybe you will figure this out." She picked up her phone, tapped at the screen and put the phone back on the table.

Her eyes were red and filled with tears. He wanted to say something, but he didn't know what, exactly. He felt empty, cut out, devoid of words, and numb. She must have sensed his despair because her expression softened.

"Nick, if I made a mistake and wronged you, I am sorry. I really am. I've come to care for you. To love you, like I had not loved anyone since that day. I know it does not make sense. I don't understand it myself. But it's true. I know you'll never believe me, because it was all based on a lie."

Looking at her face ached him. So many thoughts, memories, plans and feelings were crushed and now lay in pieces in the barren emptiness between them. He turned away and stared at the cars driving past on the other side of the coffee shop's tinted windows that made the vibrant sunny day look gray, flat and joyless.

"I want you to know just one more thing," she said. "I want you to know that I could not stand to watch you suffer anymore. I could not keep doing this. It was all going to end today. I know you probably won't believe me, but I wanted you to know." She stood up. "I am going to go now. I'll be out of the house today." She took her bag and walked away. Nick heard the door of the coffee shop open and then close.

He sat there for a while with his elbows on the table and his face buried in his hands. Thoughts darted around in his head, but the rest of him felt empty, hollowed out smooth like a weathered bone and rounded like the inside of a zero. The emptiness hurt like a punch in the gut.

He nudged his phone closer, turned it on, and studied the photo she left him with. In the photo, Katie was full of life and laughing into the camera. *That* Katie never survived that night in September of 2009. Whoever Claire was, she was not her. Claire was a vengeful specter who programmed herself for retribution. Knowing now what she knew, he could not be angry with her, despite everything she did to him. He never harmed her. He was certain of it. Or was he? Not so long ago, he was ready to believe he had forgotten a murder. Why not a rape?

No. The thought enraged him. His heart ached for this girl. He would have given up anything to go back into this moment, knock Katie's drink out of her hand, and punch Tommy's asshole smile. But he couldn't. He couldn't do shit. Ever. *Too late to serve and protect.* All he was ever good at in his life were clean breaks and fresh starts. Tears welled up and one broke free and rolled down his cheek before he could catch it. Damn it – these sessions with Sam were making him emotional. *The crying detective.* No one would pay to see *that* movie. But perhaps as a Broadway musical…? Something to laugh at. Another tear dropped onto the phone. The wet splatter on the screen drowned and distorted the frozen scene of the frat house party like a constellation of tiny round magnifying funhouse mirrors. A distantly familiar face in one of them caught his eye. He zoomed in. There, barely in the cast of the camera's flash was the face he had not seen in all these years. It was Marc. He was looking to his right, at the idiotically happy, drunk, and oblivious Nick.

36

Nick woke up on the couch. He opened his eyes to the empty glass and the bottle of Bulleit on the coffee table. The room was filled with daylight, and his head was ringing with the emotional hangover from last night. He and his emotions normally stayed out of each other's way. He wasn't one to break things or yell or cry. Claire had even once jokingly accused him of stoicism when it came to emotions, as if it were a bad thing. It did not mean he did not have feelings. He just did not like to put them on display. He did not need others to fuss about him. All fussing did was make people doing the fussing feel better about themselves. He knew that whatever troubled him, only he himself had the power to fix.

He took a deep breath and realized that in the ashes of yesterday's slow-burn of feelings of betrayal and moderate self-pity, another feeling was smoldering like hot charcoals, slowly getting hotter – anger. Not at Claire or himself or any other specific person. Anger at the world. At the universe. If he could punch the universe in the face right now, he supposed he would.

He observed his anger with curiosity. Anger was a little boy's emotion. Anger was clenched fists and swallowed powerless tears. But in powerlessness there could also be power, because powerlessness meant nothing left to lose. He could use that today.

He got up, with fragments of thoughts and feelings sloshing around nauseatingly between his head and his stomach. He knew what he needed. He overpacked the Gaggia with espresso powder and watched it struggle to trickle out the molten stream of black gold. The hot aroma began working its magic on his head before he even had a sip.

A splash of cold water on the face was the only other thing he needed. Never mind the shave. Less than a half hour after waking up, he was driving to Intergenix and calling Mike to let him in.

Yesterday, he favored a more cautious approach – collecting more evidence and not showing Cogan his hand too early. Today, everything in his world had changed. He wanted to rattle Cogan's cage until something fell out.

Mike met him in the reception area, alarmed.

"What's going on? Are you OK?" By the look in Mike's eyes, Nick could tell he was concerned for Nick's mental health. *Good*, Nick thought – looking berserk could actually be to his advantage right now.

"Thanks for letting me in." He followed Mike to his office and then walked past it.

"Nick!? Where are you going?"

"To have a chat with your boss."

"Did…did you make an appointment?"

"It's OK," Nick reassured him, "He should be expecting me." He knew this probably did little to reassure Mike.

Cogan saw him coming. He was in his glass corner office, at his desk, talking on the phone. His posture did not change, but Nick saw Cogan's sniper eyes tracking Nick as he made his way through the chest-high labyrinth of cubicles.

Nick glared back like a predator circling his prey. He wanted Cogan to feel it. Today may not be the day, but the day would come soon.

He knocked on Cogan's door and watched him hold out his index finger and hurriedly finish his call. He got up and let Nick in.

"Detective…" Cogan stuck out his hand. His grip was firm and angular. Nick tried to make his own as hard and unpleasant as he could.

"I did not know you were stopping by. My morning is pretty busy with calls, but I can carve out some time. How about after lunch? Would you like to set something up?"

"Thank you, but this won't take long, and I'd rather not delay."

"Sure…" Nick could tell Cogan was displeased but also was too polite and accommodating to argue. "Sit, please." He pointed Nick to the leather chairs. "What can I help with?"

"What was the project Ms. Benoche worked on for you?" Nick's tone came across as confrontational, and he was fully aware of that fact. Sometimes, being an unreasonable asshole was the surest way to rattle people.

A deep wrinkle between Cogan's eyebrows signaled that he got the message. "That is a question probably better suited for her manager."

"No, not the projects that Mike managed. The project she worked on directly for you. Concerning Janus, the data de-anonymizer algorithm and the illegal collection of private data for the purposes of feeding your artificial intelligence engine."

Cogan's face hardened. He did not say anything.

"Did that refresh your memory? Last time we met, you told me she did not work on any projects for you. Anything you care to add now?"

Cogan watched Nick silently.

"Did she get too close to your dirty secrets? Threatened to expose your company? Compromise the IPO?"

Cogan set his jaw. "Detective, I am afraid I can't discuss confidential company business without a court order."

Nick nodded. "OK, so, let's talk about you then. Where were you on the night of September 7, between 7 and 9 p.m.?"

Cogan picked up the phone from his desk and thumbed the screen.

"I had a benefit dinner. In Highlands Ranch."

"The whole time?"

"Yes."

"What about Matthew Ellis?"

Cogan winced and darted a stray glance at the photo frame on his desk.

"What was your arrangement with Ellis?"

"We served together in the military; he is a friend."

"When was the last time you talked to him?"

"I don't know. A couple of weeks ago, before he shipped out."

"Did you ask him to do you a favor?"

"What? I have no idea what you are talking about." Nick could see Cogan was uncomfortable with his questions. This gave Nick satisfaction. He wanted to see Cogan squirm.

"Did you ask him to kill Lisa Benoche for you? Did you tell him to make it look like a suicide?"

Cogan jumped up. "That is ridiculous! What are you talking about? I had nothing to do with her death. My employees are everything to me. I protect them like family."

"But she wasn't your employee, was she? She was just a contractor, wasn't she? Was her life worth it, to save all this?" Nick nodded to the sea of cubicles on the other side of the glass.

Cogan turned on his heels, marched to the door, opened it and stood aside. "We are done here. The next time you wish to talk, I will have my attorney present. Have a good day, detective."

Walking out of that office, Nick felt good. He smiled, aware that it probably looked like a scowl. Cogan was caught in his lie, and he chose to dig in and fight. Well, a fight was what he was going to get. It was time to pay Mr. Giles a visit.

***

Andrew Giles worked from home, just as Mike said. But in the case of the Intergenix Chief Product Officer and business partner of Bruce Cogan, home was not a trendy condo in Denver's River North arts district or a multimillion-dollar suburban estate in Cherry Creek. For Andrew Giles, home was a 9,000 square-foot mountain residence off Highway 82 between Twin Lakes and Aspen. This was a prestigious zip code favored by Hollywood celebrities and Washington politicians who had the means to own a luxury Rocky Mountain estate as their vacation home.

And it was hard to argue with their taste. Here, the rugged ridges were eternally capped in snow, guarding the high plains that were bejeweled with a myriad of crystal-clear ponds reflecting the deep blue of the sky. They did not call it Lake County for nothing. It was breathtakingly beautiful. But driving through it today, Nick did not pay heed to any of it. Today, the scenery and the minutes stretched into a featureless blur as he instead found himself more focused on avoiding the harrowing, wrecked part of his soul that used to be Claire. It ached deep in his core every time he thought of her, or the absence of her. But stoking the anger he felt when he woke up was helping take his mind off this ache. For better or worse, he suspected that with this case, there would be no short supply of anger to dull the ache. And after days and months of brushing past this ache, he would one day eventually wear it down smooth and stop thinking about it. Time did not heal wounds. It calloused them.

Distracted, he almost flew past his turn-off and had to slam on his brakes, skidding the hefty Tahoe to a halt next to the entrance to a private drive that disappeared into a grove of aspens.

He expected to see a modern cube of glass and steel fit for a high-tech exec at the end of the driveway and was surprised to find instead a sizeable mountain chalet with a four-car garage. A vintage gunmetal-colored Land Rover Defender sat at the front of the garage, like an English bulldog guarding the castle. Nick always had an affinity for the brutalist lines of this iconic off-roader. It reminded him of the grinning, grimy, manly adventurers in the old Camel Trophy cigarette ads in his dad's collection of the National Geographic which he used to flip through as a kid. He craved to be like them, and even as an adult, he still wanted one of these trucks and the spirit of boundless freedom they represented.

Like his business partner, Andrew Giles looked to be in his late thirties, but that's where all similarities between the two ended. While Cogan was fit and clean-cut, no one could ever mistake Giles for an athlete. He was taller than Cogan by a good head, but was neither fit, nor scrawny, nor overweight. There was definite mass to him, with his long arms and legs, and a compact belly protruding from the front of his faded black T-shirt. He regarded Nick sedately from the open doorway with his dark, half-open eyes and brushed back a tousled mess of dark brown hair mixed with the occasional silver thread. Other than the full, almost puffy jowls, there were no notable features about his smoothly shaven face.

Giles smiled demurely and shook Nick's hand. His grip was big and just firm enough.

"I was about to make an espresso. Would you like one?" He walked off without waiting for the answer, shuffling his white-soled casual slip-on shoes on the slate floor. His worn-in jeans completed his middle-aged corporate surfer vibe.

"Sure," Nick consented. He closed the front door and followed Giles into the house.

The main floor was a wide-open span that spilled into the kitchen, where Giles was already whirring with the coffee grinder. He must have lived alone. There were no kids' drawings or multi-colored schedules stuck to the stainless slab of the fridge in the kitchen, and no family photos in the great room. This was a bachelor's retreat, lined with Colorado timber and stone, and adorned with a biomechanical abstract sculpture on one of the end tables and a large model of an old twin-prop airplane on the coffee table. But the best feature of the great room was not in the room at all. It was the view on the other side of the wall of soaring windows: the snow-dusted La Plata peak and the unbroken jagged skyline of the Continental Divide. This was a view Nick could wake up to every morning and never get tired of it. In the driveway below, the Defender gleamed seductively. If someone had shown all this to the 19-year-old Nick, would he have still switched his majors in college?

The espresso machine stopped revving, and Giles shuffled over to Nick and handed him a small Illy espresso cup. Nick took it and habitually sniffed the aroma that whiffed just above the blanket of rich golden-brown crema. He took a sip. Yes, evidently, big money could also buy a better cup of coffee.

"That's a very nice truck out there." Nick nodded to the window.

"The Defender?" The mellow Giles livened up a notch. "Thanks. You have one?"

He sounded sincere, so Nick tried not smile at the naivete of the question. "Unfortunately, it's a bit above my paygrade."

"You are not missing much. It's a '95, fully restored and upgraded. Cost me way into the six figures, and it's still leaking oil."

"I would have expected you to have a Tesla or some other high-tech toy."

He laughed. "Yes. I suppose. But I appreciate the raw power and appeal the older things can have. They have their own magnetism. Like relics of the old gods. Their design inspires me. That's my plane." He pointed to the model. "It's no Learjet, but Learjets have no charm." Giles motioned him to settle into the plush pit of couches. "I assume you want to talk about Lisa Benoche?" He crossed his long legs and sipped his coffee.

"Did Bruce Cogan call you?"

"Yes, and he told me not to talk to you. Not without our lawyer, at least."

"But you decided to, anyways?"

He shrugged and shook his tousled hair. "I have nothing to hide."

"OK, then. Let's talk about Ms. Benoche." Nick set the coffee cup on the end table and pulled out his notepad. "When did you find out that she died?"

"The next day. Mike called me to let me know."

"Do you recall where you were on the night of her death?"

"Here." He did not have to think about it. "I am here most nights."

"Can anyone confirm it?"

"I can give you my security footage, if you'd like. It usually catches me moving around the property."

Nick nodded and made a note. "That would be great."

Giles gazed into the far-off mountains. "It is such a tragedy, what happened. I can't imagine what her family is going through. My mother committed suicide when I was twelve. Untreated bipolar disorder."

"I am sorry." Nick watched Giles. His face looked youthful in the glow of the afternoon. "How well did you know Lisa?"

"Not very well. I had a thirty-minute interview with her when she was hired. She interviewed well. Bright, energetic. She was able to think in big pictures. This is the kind of talent I like to attract to the product team. After that, I did not see her much. I am rarely at the office."

"Did you talk to her after the interview?"

"What about?"

"Anything at all."

"Maybe small office talk, on a couple of occasions – latest TV shows, plans for the weekend, you know?"

"Did she discuss her work with you?"

"No. That would have been Mike, her manager. Did you already talk to him?"

Nick nodded. "Did anyone else talk to you about her?"

"Just Mike, on a couple of occasions. He mentioned how great she was doing and that we may want to offer her a full-time position after the contract."

"What about Bruce Cogan? Did he mention her to you?"

Giles wrinkled his forehead. "Bruce? Why would Bruce talk to me about her? She reported through my R&D organization. Bruce manages operations, sales and marketing."

"Bruce had her working on a special project. What do you know about it?"

Giles shook his head. "Nothing. I was not aware of this."

Nick studied the man. Mike said he had to have known about the illegal data collection. If he did, he was feigning ignorance very well.

"Lisa had found something called the Janus algorithm in your production code. She figured out it was illegally deanonymizing and collecting data."

Giles' eyebrows lifted slightly. "I don't understand."

"You did not know about Janus?"

"I did…I do, of course – I wrote it. We used it for the first couple of years, to get the company going, but then Bruce insisted I deactivate it."

"Why?"

"Because it would have broken data laws and our contracts with our customers. Bruce felt it was too much risk for Intergenix."

"But he didn't mind it being illegal in the beginning?"

"Bruce wanted to get the company going fast so he could fund his veterans program. So, we gave our AI some help. At first, we fed it stolen private data that we bought from hackers on the dark web. We were both amazed at how much it improved the accuracy and relevancy of the algorithm. This helped us land a few big customers, and so I wrote Janus to extract customer data from their anonymized data sets. And after that, we did not have to pay the hackers anymore."

"So, you knew Janus was illegal when you wrote it, and you still did it? Just because Bruce asked you to?"

Giles set his cup down on the coffee table next to the airplane.

"Detective, sometimes, the real breakthroughs are only possible by breaking a few laws. Did you know that modern western medicine owes its existence to graverobbing? The only way doctors in the 1700s and 1800s could actually learn about the human body was by paying graverobbers to provide them with freshly buried corpses. The medical students in the U.S. and Europe were even required to provide their own cadavers if they wanted to attend medical school. No one asked where they got them. Graverobbing was certainly illegal. But without it, we would still be using leeches and performing bloodlettings today. Now, we must do the same with data. We must dig it up and use it to learn about ourselves. About humanity."

"What about privacy?"

Giles smiled. "Privacy is an illusion. It's dead. It's a cadaver. Yes, we have privacy laws, but they are a joke. They are a façade erected to make people feel better while their information is already all out there, beyond their control, being used on them and against them by the government, the credit bureaus, insurance companies, ad agencies, social media corporations. I've seen the data they collect. Do you think it's all collected legally and ethically? People have no idea how much these agencies and corporations know about them. And these companies want to collect more, and they want to make it proprietary to them, and develop their own algorithms and models and scores, so they can better monetize their customers. All to maximize their profit."

"And you are not interested in profit?"

"Not as much as Bruce. The business side of technology always bored me. EBITDA, ARR, margins, shaking hands, making deals. Bruce thrives on that stuff. I find it mind-numbing. All I ever wanted to do was build something that mattered."

"Like Janus?"

"Yes! I know, to anyone else it probably sounds like some piece of malware code. But trust me, it was so much more. Janus would have been the equivalent of bringing the river to the desert. Can you imagine? Instead of letting corporations continue getting rich from the data they are collecting on us, we could throw the floodgates wide open and let this knowledge serve all of humanity. If we could direct all that data to a single AI for the first time in history, it would be a quantum leap in machine learning. That's why I called it Janus – the god of gateways and transitions. It could usher in the age of new AI that helps us understand ourselves and each other."

This unexpected outburst of idealism from Giles both amused Nick and took him slightly aback. This middle-aged corporate surfer dude was an aspiring high-tech Robin Hood, wanting to unleash his two-faced robot god on the masses. Could he have really been *this* naïve? Nick weighed the best response, oscillating between cynical and panicked and trying not to let his own technophobic tendencies have the first word.

Giles must have sensed his skepticism because he smiled disarmingly again. "Look, we humans are a lot more predictable than we like to think. We repeat the same patterns. The same mistakes. And every extra beat in our heartrate, every impulsive action can be a clue to what comes next. What if we could crack the code? Even the simple fitness trackers can already detect the risk of a heart attack. What if we could do the same for mental illness? Or suicide? Or homicide? Would you choose not to use this information?"

"So, you intended to sell it to health and law agencies?"

"No! I wanted to make it open. Free for anyone to use. To improve themselves, or their community, or humanity." He watched Nick with a half-smile. "You are not convinced?"

Nick could understand how such all-knowing technology could seem like a worthwhile crusade to a little boy whose mother took her own life. "It does not matter what I think about this," he said. "That's not why I am here."

"Oh, but it does matter what you think. This would all be for *you* as much as for everyone else. You could use it to solve crimes faster, build better relationships, or decide what's for dinner. It would be always standing by to assist."

Nick sighed. "Let's just say I don't usually get to see people at their best in my line of work, so that may color my worldview a tad. You are right – there could be benefits, but someone will soon figure out a way to use it to make money, gain power, and hurt others in the process. And maybe it is exactly what is already happening. You say you deactivated Janus years ago, so how did it end up in your production code?"

"It would take a simple function call from the main program. It's already in the code, it's just been disabled. Bruce must have gotten someone to activate it. Maybe one of his veteran proteges."

"Why would he do it, after telling you to deactivate it in the first place?"

Giles rubbed his smooth chin. "The only thing I can think of is he must have wanted to drive up the IPO valuation. We had several major government and healthcare contracts pending this year. He could have used Janus to boost product performance in order to close the deals and drive up the valuation." He rubbed his smooth chin. "You said Lisa was working on a project for Bruce? What kind of a project?"

"When Lisa discovered Janus and the illegal data in the live code, she brought it up to Cogan. He assured her this was a glitch and asked her to help document and resolve it. Two days later she was dead."

Giles' eyebrows floated up. "My God. Are you suspecting Bruce had something to do with her death? To protect his secret?"

"Do you think he is capable of doing something like this?"

"I've known him for so many years. It's hard to imagine it, but I suppose it's possible. He hides it well, but I know he has his demons from his time in the war. And this company and the foundation mean everything to him. If something threatened it all…" Giles transfixed in thought.

"Do you know someone named Matt Ellis?"

"The name sounds vaguely familiar."

"He is Cogan's former army friend."

"Ah, yes! I met him at a company event once. Do you think he was involved?"

"I don't know yet. Someone had to be, because Cogan was at a benefit during the time Lisa was killed."

Giles buried his face in his hands. "That poor girl." He raised his eyes back to Nick. "Wait. Was Lisa killed the night of the Code of Honor benefit?"

"Yes. Tuesday the seventh. Why?"

His forehead wrinkled in thought. "Well, I did not think much of it at the time, but the next day, when I asked him how it went, he said he had to step out in the middle of it for a call with investors in Asia. He said he had to miss a bit of the benefit, but he got back before the awards and photos."

Nick felt as if a tidal wave slammed into him and swept him off his footing. "Do you know if he left the location of the benefit?"

The corporate surfer shook his head. "That I do not know."

37

Driving down the mountain from Giles' estate, Nick contemplated the growing body of evidence against Cogan. Giles had confirmed the fact that Cogan knowingly broke the law with Janus before. But it wasn't so much the evidence of another of Cogan's crimes that Nick found useful but rather the insight into Cogan's motives. Thinking back to his few interactions with Cogan, Nick now recognized that the CEO of Intergenix had an air of righteousness about him. When people like him broke the law, it was for reasons they considered just. Cogan knowingly violated data laws to start his company, but his end goal was funding the vet program. Cogan believed in the greater good, and people who believed in the greater good believed doing a little evil was sometimes justified. And people like that did not stop after just one time – when the stakes got higher, they moved the line to justify greater evil. One contractor's life for the livelihood of hundreds of employees and veterans. When Nick thought of Cogan's calculating sniper's gaze, the thick muscular neck spreading the collar of his business shirt and the vise-like grip of his hardened hand, Nick had no doubt which side of this equation Cogan would choose.

And yet, despite this newfound understanding of what made Cogan tick, Nick also had a growing sense of unease. And there was cause for unease. Almost three weeks had passed since Lisa's murder – plenty of time for even the sloppiest criminal to cover his tracks. And Cogan was not a sloppy criminal. Nick's chances of finding anything but circumstantial evidence to tie

Cogan to Lisa's death were getting slimmer by the hour. Cogan was not a common street criminal. Only a few weeks ago, combing through the cell tower dump files was Nick's definition of high-tech police work. Now, it looked like child's play. Cogan was the CEO of a company that made money off people's private data. If Cogan slipped his alibi, he would have known how to do it completely untracked. He would have gone not just low-tech – he would have gone no-tech: no iPhone, no Apple Watch, no Fitbit, no Garmin. Nada. Commando. He would have left no digital trace.

Knowing this robbed Nick of even a shred of optimism that he would find something useful at the convention center. But then again, everyone made mistakes. Nick could feel the traces of this morning's maniacal anger streak still glowing in him like smoldering embers. He wondered if he could ride them for at least another day.

The event center was on the northern edge of Highlands Ranch, just off Highway 85 by Chatfield reservoir. Not expecting a favorable result, Nick checked Google Maps before he even departed Giles' driveway. He was encouraged to find that according to the directions, it was possible to get from the event center to Lisa's residence in about fifteen minutes, which possibly was close enough for Cogan to leave the benefit, kill Lisa and come back in time for the awards and photos. These were just the bare bones of Nick's theory, but it was a start. Now he got to see if it would pan out.

The pop-up banner in the lobby welcomed the Biennial Congress of the Orthodox Archdiocese of America. A noisy congregation of black robes, gold chains and gray beards in the atrium confirmed this as fact. Nick presented his badge to the man at the information desk and asked for the security manager.

The building looked relatively new, and the few security cameras Nick spotted from the lobby gave him hope. A polished man with a shaved head and a gray suit appeared at the other end of the atrium and expertly sailed toward Nick across the sea of black robes.

"Don Burke." The man shook Nick's hand. "I am the head of security here. What can I do for you?" Don looked to be in his late forties and had a trustworthy jawline, Nick thought.

"You had an event here two weeks ago. Some benefit for veterans' computer coding."

"Ah, yes!" Don squinted slightly in the bright light of the lobby.

"Can you show me where it was located?"

"Sure."

Nick followed Don's fitted gray suit back across the black sea to a large room with two double-door entrances and a sign that said Ballroom A.

"The dinner was here, and the reception was out there," he pointed back to the noisy holy congregation. "We had a bar set up in the atrium with twelve high-tops, and we had about two dozen round tables and a stage set up in here. They also ordered a computer with a projector and AV, and a few lapel mics."

Nick evaluated the cavernous space: four walls covered in burlap-looking fabric to absorb acoustics; no windows, and an emergency exit at the back.

"Is the alarm on that exit live?"

"Yes. And no one has set it off for a few months. Knock on wood."

Nick pictured Cogan excusing himself from the table and stepping out into the hallway. Nick looked up into the corners of the ceiling – there were no security cameras in the room, but there was one in the hallway just outside.

"Can we look at the security footage for that night?"

"Of course," Don obliged and took Nick across the hallway to an unmarked door. Don's badge blipped on the access pad, and the magnetic door locks disengaged with a click. He let Nick through first, just as the ceiling lights automatically ticked on inside the room. Nick had seen his share of security closets in his life, and this one was definitely the executive model. The occupancy-sensing light switches were just the start. This closet was bigger than his office at the station and had fresher paint and newer furniture and computer equipment. Nick's office door could not automatically turn on the lights. The only thing at Pine Lake PD that could do that was the refrigerator.

"Coffee?" Don uttered two magic syllables. "Water?"

"Coffee would be great, thanks." It was one of those K-cup contraptions Nick typically stayed away from, but he was in a pinch to power through the rest of the day.

Don set a steaming paper cup on the desk with three large monitors and inserted himself into a high-back black leather chair that looked like a bucket seat from an expensive sports car. He pulled up another one for Nick. It was time to time travel.

They started with the lobby camera on September 7, at 6 p.m. Don turned the large aluminum knob of the controller to scroll forward at 4x speed until Nick saw the familiar marine buzzcut enter the lobby.

"Stop here," Nick said. "This is the guy." The frame froze on a crystal-clear image. It was definitely Cogan, wearing a perfectly fitting, bespoke tuxedo.

"Nice image quality," Nick commented.

"Thanks!" Don smiled. "I convinced the management to upgrade all the cameras to 4K earlier this year. The new system saves straight to the cloud. No local copies and no more racks of VCRs in this room. Makes a world of difference."

Indeed, Nick could practically see the individual short hairs on Cogan's head. The timer showed 6:27:32 pm. Lisa was still alive.

"Can we look at the parking lot and go back a few seconds?"

Don opened another camera window and Nick watched Cogan walk backwards from the entrance to a light-colored Tesla parked in the second row. The door of the Tesla opened, and Bruce backed in and settled in the driver's seat. Nick made a note of Cogan's arrival time: 6:26 p.m.

Please tell me you took this Tesla to Scraggy Ridge, Nick hoped against all hope. He was fairly certain the Tesla, given all the electronics onboard, would have to be just about the most traceable car in history.

"OK, let's skip forward to around 7:30."

Don nodded and started fast forwarding. Eight p.m. Eight-thirty. The Tesla was still there, and there was no sign of Cogan. Nine p.m. Lisa was dead.

Scratch the Tesla, Nick thought to himself. He expected it was too good to happen. His theory about Cogan leaving the benefit and coming back was beginning to dissolve.

At a little past 10, people began exiting. With fast-forwarding, they seemed to walk in those early-movie-style fast, waddling spurts. Cogan exited at 10:21, alone, made it to his Tesla and drove away. Don stopped the replay.

"How many other exits do you have?" Nick asked.

"Four more, two of them alarmed."

"Do you have cameras on those?"

"Two of them. The other two open only from the inside. We typically don't worry about keeping people in," Don explained. "Another coffee?" He noticed Nick's empty cup.

Nick nodded. "Yes please. Can we look at the inside footage next?"

"You bet." Don was congenially accommodating.

"You've worked here long?" Nick's mind was preoccupied with the case, but he thought it only polite to make small talk with the man who was going out of his way to help him and was making him a second cup of coffee.

"Almost six years."

"Oh yeah? What did you do before?"

"Nine years with Colorado Springs PD. Made sergeant before I quit."

Nick nodded. He didn't ask why Don quit the force. There were maybe two or three reasons most people joined the police, and a million different ones why they chose to quit. Most were very personal.

Don returned with two full cups. "Shall we?" He settled back into the driver's seat.

They set off through the same timeline, but now from another angle inside the building.

In the atrium camera footage, people trickled in from the entrance, gathering around the bar and the high-top tables. A crowd of dark business suits and tuxedoes socialized in clumps, like an Antarctic bird bazaar with the occasional tropical splashes of colorful women's jackets and scarves.

In the frame, Cogan waved at someone and then talked at a table with a woman in a burgundy suit and a man in a charcoal one. Then he shook hands with them and got a drink at the bar and then walked off to the perimeter, looking at something on his phone for over nine minutes. At 7:00, people began trickling toward Ballroom A. Cogan followed.

"How many people would you say were there that night?"

"I believe we were contracted for 300, but probably around 250 showed up. I can confirm with catering. Want to look at the cameras covering the ballroom entrances?"

Nick nodded. Don had read his mind.

In the hallway camera that framed both entrances of Ballroom A, Cogan followed the straggling trickle of people and disappeared inside at around 7:08. After that, a few people came in and out, including the serving staff with trays and pitchers. At 7:31, Cogan emerged from the room and headed down the hallway away from the camera. He turned and disappeared around the corner.

"Where is he going?"

"Men's bathroom, I would imagine."

"Are there cameras covering that area?

He shook his head. "It's not a large space. I can walk you through there when we are done."

The sped-up footage kept rolling. Several other men and women walked to and from the restroom, but Cogan had not returned.

"Are there exits there?"

"Yes. From there, he can get to the east exit that catering uses. Or the north exit at the base of the staircase."

"Are there cameras on those?"

"On the catering one. The other one opens only from the inside, so we don't monitor it."

The frames kept winding forward: 8:30, 9:00. More people came in and out, but Cogan was not back. Something was definitely wrong with this picture.

"Do you know what was going on inside the ballroom that night?"

"Not specifically at this one, but usually, at a benefit, there would be a dinner served, maybe with presentations or speeches during the dinner, and then there would be awards or auctions."

At 9:27, Cogan suddenly re-appeared from around the corner, walked toward the camera and re-entered the room.

Almost two hours. This could be it. Or it could just be long phone call in a blind spot in the hallway.

"Can we look at that catering exit camera, starting earlier in the evening?"

Don switched the view. Another angle. This was the back of the facility.

"And where is the north exit from this angle?" Nick asked.

"On the left, just around that corner."

At 6:30, there were two catering vans parked with their cargo doors open. A handful of caterers were shuttling trays and boxes in and out. By 6:45, the caterers were done unloading. At 7:26, two caterers came out to smoke next to the van. At 7:32, a Chevy pickup drove past and disappeared around the corner toward the north exit. As the evening progressed, the sky in the frame grew darker and the image became grainier. At 9:10, the caterers began loading their vans. The truck did not come back.

At 9:25, a man emerged from around the north corner and walked toward the catering door. He was wearing a tuxedo. Nick held his breath, fixated on the grainy frame. The man walked closer to the brightly lit loading area and stopped there for an instant, letting two caterers with a rolling cart pass through the door.

"Can you freeze it there?" Nick breathed to Don. The frame froze. "Can you zoom in just a bit?"

Don obliged. In the still frame, in the good light of the caterer's entrance Nick clearly saw Cogan's face.

"It's the same guy, right?" He felt it best to validate, given his state of mind lately.

Don pulled up the earlier footage from the lobby and put the two freezeframes side by side.

He scrutinized the two Cogans for a minute and finally declared: "No doubt."

Got you, asshole! Nick tried his best to control the rush of adrenaline that just got pumped into his veins.

Don hit *play* again, and they watched Cogan disappear back into the building. By 10 p.m., the caterers had finished packing their vans and drove off, and the back alley fell into a dimly lit hibernation.

Nick looked at his notes. "Can you go back to that pickup truck at 7:32?"

Don dutifully rewound and stopped when the pickup entered the frame. The camera's high vantage point and the dusk-time lighting made for more difficult vehicle identification. It certainly looked like a late-model Chevy Silverado. Could it have been a 2015? It could have. Could it have been black? It was difficult to say in this lighting. It was definitely a dark color. Nick asked Don to step through the frames. The license plate did not show at all from this angle. In the few frames when Nick could see a little bit inside the vehicle, there looked to be only the driver in the cab. According to Matt Ellis' girlfriend, he went to a meeting in Denver that night, left his phone at home and did not return till late. Was this Matt Ellis driving this truck?

"Is there another way to exit this back alley without going past this camera?"

"Sure. You can take Highline Drive, instead of Dumont."

The backbone of Nick's theory, which had almost dissolved less than twenty minutes ago was hardened again and beginning to flesh out: 6:26 – Cogan arrives, 7:31 – he leaves the ballroom and exits the building through the northern exit, 7:32 – he gets into the pickup (driven by Ellis?), 7:50 – they arrive at the Scraggy Ridge trailhead, 8:13 – Lisa's Lexi records the attack. Now, working backwards from the end: if Cogan is dropped off at 9:25, that means they would have had to leave Scraggy Ridge around 9:10. That leaves almost an hour for the attack, staging of the scene and clean up.

This wasn't ironclad, but it fit. Probably good enough for a warrant. Nick savored the beginning of Cogan's end. He clenched his teeth and felt satisfaction in the building pressure. It was good to feel satisfaction. It had been a while. The only thing left to do was to get copies of the footage from Don, which Don willingly provided, emailing them directly to Nick from the cloud. *What wonderous times they lived in...* When Nick opened the door of the security room to leave, he was deposited right into a large gold orthodox cross hanging from a gold chain.

"I am sorry, my son." The tall, broad-shouldered, black-robed wall beamed at him with its gray beard and stepped to the side, letting him pass.

"That's all right, Father," Nick remarked. "If only you were here three weeks ago, maybe I would not have to today."

38

At the station, Nick watched and rewatched the footage from all of the cameras, trying to play his best devil's advocate and triple-checking his timeline. He barely registered it when the cowbell on the station door jangled, and a few seconds later his desk phone lit up – Patty.

"Yeah?"

"You got visitors. From Inter…*what is it?*" she asked away from the receiver. "– Intergenix. You available?"

"Yeah, send them in." For a second, he hoped it was Cogan. But instead, Mike and Dimitri appeared in his doorway.

"Hey, perfect," Nick waved Mike over. "Tell me who this looks like to you?"

Mike came around to look at his screen, and Dimitri followed.

"Oh, that's Bruce," Mike said instantly, examining the freezeframe of Cogan looking at the caterers by the van outside the event center.

"Definitely," Dimitri confirmed, leaning in for a closer look.

"Where is this?" Mike asked.

"The benefit at the Highlands Ranch event center. The night of the murder."

"What's he doing?"

"He is returning through the back door."

"Son of a…" Mike stood back from the screen. "You think he…"

Nick nodded. "He lied about his alibi. That's for certain." He stood up. "I need some more coffee. You guys want anything? Water?"

They shook their heads.

"OK, I'll be right back." He grabbed his mug and headed to the kitchen. This was good. If three people besides him so readily recognized Cogan, this would be enough for a search warrant for Intergenix. And for Ellis's truck. But probably not enough for an arrest. Not yet.

When he came back, Dimitri and Mike were discussing something in heated whispers, pointing at his screen. He should have locked his computer before walking away. The amateur sleuths club quieted down when he entered and dispersed voluntarily when he made his way to his chair.

"What did you guys need?" He motioned them to the chairs on the other side of the desk.

"Well, Dimitri found something that could be of interest," Mike gave Dimitri a couple gentle slaps on the shoulder. "But don't worry, we did not touch or change anything."

Nick transferred his gaze to Dimitri.

The kid adjusted his impeccably combed-over hipster plumage and put one Ked-fitted foot on his knee.

"So, Mike said he had told you about the flash drive Lisa had copied files to? The one that set an alert in the DLP?"

Nick nodded. *Not the TV.*

"OK, so, I pulled the full DLP logs, and it looks like that same flash drive was plugged into Bruce Cogan's work laptop the day after she died."

"So, Cogan has her flash drive?" The irony of fate was unending. Could this really be the day of all good news for his case, when his own personal life was completely obliterated and reduced to a smoldering crater?

"Well, the DLP logs show it was plugged into his laptop. Now, we can't really be a hundred percent certain it was him. So, it could have been anyone, really, using his login credentials.

In fact, we can't even be certain it was really his laptop. Someone could have spoofed his MAC address. So, that's actually pretty easy to do…"

"Wow, stop right there," Nick interrupted. The kid was too smart for his own good. How was it that people could believe the craziest conspiracy theories but at the same time would find the simplest explanations so hard to swallow? "I get that this is not beyond a reasonable doubt. Just tell me this. Given everything we know, is it more likely than not that this flash drive was accessed by Bruce Cogan on Bruce Cogan's laptop?"

Dimitri looked around the ceiling, contemplating with a painful expression on his face. "Sure, I guess."

"Perfect. Thank you!" This may not have been the most damning piece of evidence, but it was another grain of sand, and, together with all the other grains, it had the potential of making the scales of justice tip the right way. "I am going to submit a request for a search warrant for Intergenix. I don't need you to do anything or touch anything. I just need you to make sure these DLP logs don't get overlooked when digital evidence is collected."

After they left, he sat there for a while at his desk, trying to get all the pieces in line before filling out the warrant and the probable cause affidavit. This whole high-tech jargon made things so much more complicated. How was the prosecutor's office supposed to make heads or tails of it? Why couldn't he, of all people, have gotten a good-old-fashioned domestic homicide with an insurance fraud angle?

He opened the warrant form and began filling it out. *Date.* He checked his phone – Tuesday, September 28. It had been exactly three weeks. At this time three weeks ago, Lisa was still alive, and his own life had not yet been turned upside down. Tommy was just a nightmare, and Claire was still Claire.

Focus, Nick Severs. Just get this done. Get this done and go get a drink. You want a drink, don't you?

***

The house felt empty. Despite it being full of stuff – furniture, dishes, TVs and clothes – it felt empty. Unbearably so.

She took only her clothes from the bedroom closet, her toothbrush, and her blanket from the couch. And somehow, without these things, the house now was completely hollow and devoid. A shell of what it was just two days ago. She wasn't just in the next room or coming in from the garage, and she wouldn't be, ever again. His futile unconscious anticipation and longing was met with the cold, empty reality.

He caught a glimpse of her face in the living room, walked over, and picked up the picture frame from the top of the TV cabinet. He held the photo in one hand as he got the bottle of bourbon and a glass from the cabinet. This was the black and white snapshot he took of Claire on the Country Club Plaza in Kansas City. They were on a restaurant terrace overlooking the bridges of Brush creek. You could not see the bridges in the picture, but they were there, just outside the frame. It was getting dark, and the string lights of the patio shimmered like fairy lights against in the darkening sky. She was holding a martini glass and gazing off into the distance. Her delicate features and pale skin seemed to glow in the dusk. For the first time ever, her gaze looked tragic to him. Beautiful and tragic. He set the picture on the counter and poured himself a tall shot. Did she ever even exist at all?

Wasn't he angry? Perhaps, somewhere deep in the pit of his soul. Not at her, but at everything, at how this world worked. This anger had been accumulating bit by bit over all these years. Packed down and added to. It was a volatile stockpile, but right now it felt muffled and inert, buried under several layers of exhaustion and a splash of bourbon. He turned on his phone and looked at the photo she gave him, at the happy Claire. Katie. Katie with that same light in her eyes he had seen on a few occasions. Katie not yet harmed. Marc not yet dead. How could a single night screw up so many lives? If he could change only one thing in his life, he would go back to the moment in this photo.

He reached for the bottle again but held off. He needed a change. He needed to get back to himself. To how he used to be. Getting up early. Running. He stood up and rummaged through the medicine cabinet and pulled out the bottle of Tylenol PM. Two blue pills. He stared at them and then put one back. One blue pill and one shot of bourbon.

He turned on the TV and settled on the couch. *Should have taken the red pill*, he thought and smirked, then soon fell into the black void.

On the phone, Cogan sounded calm and accommodating: Of course, he would come down to the station. With his attorney. Anything to help.

A few hours later, his silver Tesla pulled into the gravel lot, followed by a black Range Rover. Cogan's tailored suit looked out of its element in the reception area of the Pine Lake Police station which was tastefully decorated in the provincial simpleton style with ample acreage of wood paneling on the walls accented with a wooden clock in the shape of Colorado carved by Arnie, and a whitetail hunting calendar Jason gave Patty last Christmas for the white elephant gift exchange. Cogan's lawyer likewise did not dress to blend in with the natives, being an attractive woman in her forties with laser-precise makeup, neatly pinned-up highlighted hair, a pencil-skirt suit, and her ultimate accessory – the Range Rover. Still, to her credit, she raised an eyebrow only once, when she caught sight of Ray racking the receiver on the big black Tommy gun in his office. Nick had to smirk to himself – Ray was a showman through and through.

Nick took them to the station's sole interview room, the only one wired for sound and video. Ray joined the party, thankfully leaving the Tommy gun in his office. In an insult to Patty's hospitality, both Cogan and the lawyer declined her offer of coffee or water.

"All right then, let's begin." Nick flipped on the recorder switch, and a little red LED lit up on the camera in the corner of the room, glowing at Cogan like the eye of a hungry one-eyed hound of hell. Nick preambled into the recorder: "This is October 1, 2021, 1:35 PM. Detective Nick Severs and Chief Ray Mitchell interviewing Bruce Cogan with his attorney present."

He looked at Cogan, trying to intercept his gaze, but Cogan looked coolly at the wall behind Nick. "Mr. Cogan, I'd like to confirm on the record your account of the events on the night of September 7. Do you recall where you were on the night of September the 7?"

Cogan nodded and cleared his throat. "Yes. I was attending the benefit for Code of Honor, a technical education program for veterans my company funds."

"And where was this benefit held?"

"Highlands Ranch. Chatfield Events Center."

"Do you recall when you arrived at this venue?"

"Umm. I would say around 6:30. I can get you the exact time from my car."

Nick nodded. "And when did you depart this venue?"

"The event ended at 10, so I would imagine shortly after that."

"And did you leave this location at any time between your arrival around 6:30 and your departure shortly after 10?"

Cogan shook his head.

"Can you please reply verbally?"

"No, I did not leave this location between those hours."

Nick nodded and opened his laptop. "I'd like you to look at this video surveillance footage from the Highlands Ranch event center where this benefit dinner was held. This is from a camera at the rear service entrance on the night of September 7." Nick started the video and then paused it. In the frame, Cogan was looking at the caterers by the van, his face on full display. Across the table from Nick, Cogan's other face turned pale.

"Can you see the time stamp on this frame? What does it say?" Nick asked.

"9:25 pm," Cogan read out reluctantly.

"Can you tell me who this man is in the tuxedo, returning to the event center?"

"You don't have to answer this," the pencil-skirt Range Rover lawyer said dispassionately.

Cogan pursed his lips and remained silent.

"It's you, isn't it?" Nick ventured further, undaunted. It was like splitting wood. You had to get the wedge in there first, and then keep driving it deeper, until the whole thing cracked and split open. Nick switched the camera view to the inside footage. "Here is the inside angle. Here, you are leaving Ballroom A, where the benefit dinner was held." He skipped ahead. "And here you are returning, almost two hours later.

"Now, you said you did not leave the venue during these hours. Can you please explain your movements captured on the surveillance system?"

"Don't answer that," the lawyer recommended.

Cogan was maintaining composure, but Nick could tell by his quickened eyes and the swelling jaw tendon that he was anything but calm inside.

"Coincidentally," Nick continued, "Lisa Benoche was murdered within the same time period as you leaving and returning to the benefit."

"I did not leave the benefit!" Cogan blurted before his lawyer could remind him to keep silent. "Check my car data, if you want."

"I know your car remained in the parking lot until the benefit ended. But how about this?" Nick switched the footage. "Does this look to you like the pickup truck belonging to your friend Mathew Ellis? Why would Matthew Ellis be at the venue where you were attending the benefit?"

"I have no idea."

"Did you ask him to drive you to Lisa Benoche's residence because you did not want your Tesla to be tracked leaving the venue?"

"Don't answer that," his lawyer interjected. "I don't see a license plate. This could be anybody's truck."

"OK, that's fine, but your client should know that Mr. Ellis's truck has been impounded and is now being taken apart by the forensics team. Do you have any idea what kind of evidence they can recover from a vehicle? It doesn't even matter if it's been cleaned. There will still be soil and plant samples, skin flakes, and hairs. Enough to tell us who had been in this truck and where they went. Are you confident they won't find anything incriminating you? This is your best chance to come forward and tell us what really happened that night."

Cogan stared silently into space, his jaw tendons rolling like steel wire cords under his skin.

Nick carried on, fixed on Cogan's face: "We already have evidence that Ms. Benoche had discovered data fraud at Intergenix and reported this to you. We have her full documentation of the Janus algorithm. And right now, the digital forensics team is executing a search warrant on your company premises. They are very good and very thorough. Laptops, file backups, emails, *DLP logs*. What do you think they will find?"

Cogan's nostrils flared. "I think we are done here, detective." He stood up abruptly.

"Did you kill Lisa Benoche?"

"That's enough, detective!" Cogan's lawyer stood up, too, and pulled Cogan by his elbow to the door.

Cogan turned around in the doorway, glaring at Nick. "I did *not*. The only thing I am guilty of, detective, is building a company out of nothing and providing for hundreds of employees and their families. What have *you* done in your life? What have *you* done for others?"

The lawyer yanked him into the hallway, and they disappeared to the furious staccato of the lawyer's high heels culminating in the mercilessly flung cowbell on the entrance door. A few moments later, there was a sound of car tires peeling away, angrily spraying gravel in the parking lot.

Nick turned off the recorder. "What do you think?" he asked Ray.

"He seemed upset. But his lawyer's a pretty lady. Feisty."

***

The next morning was Saturday, and Nick slept in. For the first time in almost a month. He opened his eyes to the golden starbursts of daylight trying to slip in through his eyelashes. The bed was much more comfortable than the couch on which he had passed out last two nights after his ritual blue pill and a finger of bourbon. In the large bed, somehow, he still slept on his side.

Without looking, he felt about his bedside table and found his phone. For the first time in almost a month, he had set it on mute before falling asleep. Now, it was almost ten in the morning, and he had a missed call from a number he did not recognize. He dialed his voicemail to listen to the message.

"Hello, Detective Severs. This is Andrew Giles." Giles sounded slightly agitated, in his sedate way. "Please call me back when you get this."

Nick considered getting up and having coffee and a shower before returning the call. But with an involuntary sigh, he hit redial on the missed call number.

"Detective Severs?" Giles sounded even more alarmed now.

"Yes."

"Have you heard from Bruce?"

"No. Why?"

"I have not been able to reach him since yesterday afternoon. He won't pick up his phone. He's done something very drastic. Last night, he wiped out our live algorithm code and the database as well as the online backups. We are dead in the water. I do have offline backups, of course, but they are not current. This will put us months behind."

Nick pulled himself up to sit against the headboard. Was he still dreaming, or was Giles really discussing how to resume Intergenix's illegal data operation with a police detective? Were they buddies now? Or he just really did not care? Maybe it was the mix of genius and social ineptness that manifested itself as narcissistic sociopathy. Sort of like the god complex with doctors.

"Why would he do this?" Nick asked.

Giles was silent for a moment. "Maybe it's his misguided attempt to hide the evidence of using de-anonymized data. But he does not know the first thing about computer forensics. His trail is all over the system logs. Any idiot can see this coming from his user ID and computer."

Giles continued to ramble on about data forensics, but Nick was already out of bed and pulling on his jeans. He could not let Cogan destroy anything that could possibly compromise the case. Anything that could give him and his fancy lawyer enough elbow room to wiggle out of this.

"Hello?" Giles was waiting for an answer to something.

"OK, thanks for letting me know." Nick hung up.

He buckled his belt and pulled one arm through the sleeve of his shirt, as his fingers were already dialing another number.

The phone rang two times and was answered with a question. "Severs?"

"Jana, I need your help. Can you pull any strings at the prosecutor's office to get an arrest warrant signed today?"

"On a Saturday?"

"Yeah."

"Of course I can."

40

The clock on the dash said 2:10 p.m. when Nick finally wheeled the Tahoe out of the county courthouse parking lot with Barnes riding shotgun. Catching I-70 from Golden, he put the lights on to clear a path through the heavy flow of fair-weather weekenders. Cogan's residence was about ten minutes away in Evergreen, where Evergreen PD was going to meet them to assist.

As Nick flew past the motorists scrambling to get out of the way, his brain was still indexing through the bits and pieces of evidence in his affidavit. He had recounted them like prayer beads on a string for almost an hour while waiting for the district judge to review: the illegal data processing; the IPO; the flash drive; the carotid restraint; the surveillance footage; Cogan's lie. If this were a prayer, it must have been a broken one, because the longer he waited, the more he grew aware how thin and fragile this string was. As he reasoned himself through the chain of evidence, the less convinced he became of its soundness, and the more concerned he grew that maybe he had not made the case compelling enough. Was he too close to it all to see the facts objectively? Was the string strong enough to pull in a big fish like Cogan?

But the warrant got signed and notarized, and he got an approving wink from Barnes. Yet, as they were now driving to execute the signed and notarized warrant, something still bothered him.

It was a niggling feeling about Cogan's most recent actions. They were so brash. So crude. So uncareful. Too obvious for someone destroying evidence. The more he thought about it, the more he was convinced it was not about destroying the evidence. It was something grander, at a scale proportionate to the intent, something for which there was a word that was on the tip of his tongue, an old word that meant something positive but sounded like it would hurt. An Old Testament type of hurt. A word he recalled using in class one day to explain to his lit students the motivation behind a character's seemingly irrational action.

Exculpation. The absolution of guilt. It wasn't just garden variety vindication or exoneration. It wasn't something that was passed down from a judge or a jury. It wasn't the finding of innocence. After all, the root of this word was *culpa* – guilt. And it began with an *Ex,* as did *execution, exorcism, excommunication, exhumation* – signifying purposeful transition from one state to another. From guilt to no guilt. A guilty man can't make that transition without atonement.

And what did Cogan want exculpation for? What did he care about the most? His company. But his own greed had put it all in jeopardy. So, this was his atonement. His penance and self-sacrifice. He knew deleting the algorithm would be traced to him. That was the point. He wasn't destroying the evidence. He was burning it all to the ground so that Giles could rebuild. He was giving him a pause and a space to rebuild differently. This was a reset.

Would Giles see it? Maybe not. He did not share Cogan's brand of philanthropy. And Nick really did not care one way or another. He could not care less about Cogan's crimes against the data regulations. He could not care less about Intergenix. He cared about what had been done to Lisa Benoche, and for that, Cogan would find no exculpation.

His phone rang – another number he did not recognize. He put it on speaker.

"Detective Severs? This is Dimitri." Slight Russian accent. "I got your number from Mike."

Barnes gave him a curious side glance.

"Hi, Dimitri. Can I call you back? In the middle of something here." He veered into the exit to 74 South toward Evergreen at 65 miles per hour.

"Yes, of course. I just wanted to let you know that the video of Bruce at the benefit is a deepfake."

"What!?" Nick swung onto the shoulder of the exit ramp, slammed his brakes and put the Tahoe in Park. The cabin was suddenly quiet without the roaring noise of the engine and the road.

"A deepfake. Someone put his face on someone else."

"How do you know this?"

"I made a copy of the video from your office, because I thought something was off. I was right. So, it is definitely a deepfake. It's a pretty good one." He sounded slightly excited, just as he was when explaining to Nick about the frame injector that had tortured him for weeks.

"You did what? You took my evidence?"

"No, no! Of course not!" Dimitri sounded more Russian when he was nervous. "I just made a copy. I did not change anything. I had to analyze it. There are pixel artifacts around the jawline and the hair. I can show you. This is definitely a deepfake."

"So, he didn't leave the venue for two hours?"

"I cannot answer that, but I can tell you this footage was tampered with."

Fuck.

"Who would be able to do something like this? How?"

"Hard to tell. They did a very good job, so they would have had to have access to advanced AI to get the lighting and the angles right. And they would also have had to hack into the security system's cloud storage to swap the video. But that is not so hard."

Double fuck.

"I'll send you some zoomed in screenshots so you can see what I am talking about."

"OK, thanks, Dimitri." Nick hung up the phone. The string broke and the beads scattered around like a jarful of marbles.

Barnes' phone buzzed and she stared at the message.

"Hey," she held the phone out to him. "This is on The Denver Post right now. A reporter I know is asking for a comment."

Nick read the headline: *Tech CEO Confesses to Murder* above the freezeframe of Cogan. He clicked the play button. Cogan was looking calmly into the camera. He was sitting at a desk in an office Nick did not recognize.

"This message is my confession and testimony. It is given truthfully and of free will. On September 7 of this year, I broke into the home of the Intergenix contract employee Lisa Benoche. I killed Lisa and staged her death to appear as a suicide. For this act I am remorseful beyond words. It was a misguided act in a desperate attempt to save Intergenix and the livelihood of its employees, and to protect all the good this company does in the Denver community. I acted alone and take full responsibility for this crime.

"To the Intergenix employees – please know that you have done nothing wrong. The decisions I made and the actions I undertook were mine and mine alone. I only wanted to protect what we have built. What *you* have built. But I lost sight of what was really important. I am sorry to all of you for overstepping your trust. I believe in you and in the strength and the future of this company. Because of this, I am stepping down as your CEO, and recommending that the board appoint Andrew Giles to this position until a suitable replacement is found. You are in good hands, and I know you will accomplish great things. Thank you for this journey together, and for everything you have done to make Intergenix what it is today."

The video stopped.

Nick looked at Jana, dropped the gear selector into Drive, and launched the Tahoe with its sirens blaring back onto the ramp toward Evergreen.

"Do you have any idea what is going on?" Jana asked over the growl of the accelerating engine. "Is he our guy or not?"

That was the million-dollar question. And right now, Nick was no longer certain. The lane divider lines dashed in the side window, firing fast, like his own thoughts. This wasn't right. Something else was going on here, something new was afoot. He could sense it, but he could not see it yet. It had not yet revealed itself to him. There was a new production underway, a choreographed performance, and some of the actors had just switched their costumes around. *The wrong Odette.* And no one gave him the program with the plot summary.

"If his alibi was intact, why did he confess?" Jana continued pondering out loud. "And why do it publicly, instead of coming down to the station?"

That one he knew. He understood the *why*, even if he was still trying to grasp the *what*: "To frame the narrative. To separate himself from Intergenix. For the greater good."

Cogan lived in an upscale neighborhood with a fancy sign that declared *The Estates at the Elk Meadow Golf Club* and a security hut with a gate, the mere presence of which made it clear that no riffraff was wanted. An Evergreen PD car with lights on was already parked next to the hut. Seeing Nick's Tahoe approach, an Estates guard stepped from the hut and waved them through.

Cogan's house was a small mansion, and there were at least half a dozen police and emergency vehicles parked outside.

"Well, this is not exactly what I meant by *assist*," Barnes said, surveying the approach as Nick turned around and parked across the street.

They walked up the steps to the front door, where several cops were congregated.

"Hey, Dan! what are you doing here?" Barnes asked one of the cops wearing the Jefferson County Sheriff jacket.

"The Estates security called in a gunshot. We got one body. What are *you* doing here?"

"An arrest warrant."

Dan smirked and shook his head. "I don't think you'll need it. There's only one name on this address."

Now, that was a twist Nick did not see coming. He signed the crime scene log and stepped inside. The tiled, tall, cathedral-like entryway echoed with chatter and squawks of police radios. Through the open French doors, he saw a study with a big desk and tall bookcases. He recognized it as the office in the video Jana just showed him. Cogan was in his office chair with his head thrown back. Behind him on the wall was the unmistakable aftermath of a high-powered pistol round fired into one's mouth.

Nick stood in the doorway for a moment, absorbing the scene and its significance. One of the CSI techs lifted an evidence bag to show him a polished 1911 pistol. Nick nodded. It looked like a .45 or a .40. That would do it.

As if in a fog, Nick checked the rest of the house. There were no signs of forced entry. No broken glass. All doors and windows appeared locked. Circling back to the entryway, he came face to face with Brenda.

"Oh, no." She sized him up, her eyes narrowed. "Don't tell me you don't think this one's a suicide either?"

41

The bullet from Cogan's gun entered through his mouth and exited through the back of his head, taking with it part of his brain and several large fragments of his skull. The fingerprints on the gun were his and his only, and there was gun powder residue on his face and on the hand that fired the pistol. After a straight-forward autopsy, his death was ruled a suicide. Nick couldn't argue with that.

In fact, he would have been crazy to argue with any of it. First, the taped confession that should have closed this case. And then the suicide. It was all too neat. Wrapped up with a bow, begging him to put it away. And oh, how he wanted to.

But it was all based on a lie. A simple binary falsehood. If Cogan never left the benefit, he did not kill Lisa. His confession was a lie. His suicide was not guilt. It was martyrdom. It was him jumping on the grenade to save his company and his employees. And so far, it was working. Through the lens of the media, Nick watched Giles coyly accept leadership of the company and make a brief public statement, further distancing Intergenix from its former CEO. No one else at Intergenix was talking, so the media focus quickly shifted off the company and onto the mystery of its CEO. The reporters sifted through any publicly available information – Cogan's school records, military career, relatives and friends. Was there depression involved? PTSD? Were he and Lisa romantically involved? All the wrong questions.

It did not take long for the journalists to find Nick. Soon, he was getting three to four calls a day. First, all the local papers. Then – Missouri, Wyoming, New Mexico, California, New York, UK, Germany, India. They all wanted to know: *What was his comment?*

The names Lisa Benoche, Intergenix and Bruce Cogan had become household dinner table conversation around the world. The daytime TV shows wanted to know if there was a history of childhood abuse. Financial media wanted to know if Intergenix was still safe, and if the IPO was still on the table, and if so, how much? How many billions? How many tens of billions? The whole world had questions and wanted answers. The whole world wanted Nick to just open his mouth and cough up a neat verdict that would finally let everyone get on. *What was his comment?*

And he had a comment, all right. How about that he did not give a damn about the future of some hot tech company, about the IPO and the billions or tens of billions of investment dollars? He did not care about Cogan's father or childhood priest or what his string of ex-girlfriends had to reveal. He cared that a young woman had been killed and that he never got a satisfactory answer. He cared that this case was still full of holes, lies and loose ends. And what he really cared about, what gnawed at the back of his mind now every waking hour was if *he* really had what it took to figure this one out and close it.

But he did not say any of this. His only comment to the press was that he could not comment on an ongoing investigation. *Why was it still ongoing?* Because he was still evaluating the facts and the evidence.

But what evidence, exactly did he have? Lisa's toxicology and the rest of her lab results had now finally come in. She was clean. The vehicle forensics techs had not turned up anything conclusive from Ellis's truck. The computer forensics techs had recovered Lisa's deleted backup files (thanks to Intergenix's IT department), along with the DLP and other network logs that corroborated data fraud and Cogan's motive. All this was now in the hands of the FBI's cyber-crimes division, and the feds were opening their own investigation.

But none of this explained the deep-faked security footage. Did Cogan create it to further self-incriminate? That was certainly possible, but it just seemed too elaborate, given his public confession and the suicide. And if he had time to create the deep fakes, why not just confess when he was at the station the day before he killed himself? Nick hadn't shared the information about the deep-fake footage with the media. Or the Feds. This was the piece that only the killer would know, and right now, Nick's hunch told him that Cogan was not the killer. There was someone else close to all this. Too close. And Nick's hunch told him to stay on it.

But first, he had to get his hands dirty. He drove back to the Scraggy Ridge trailhead. There was only one vehicle there today – a blue Subaru wagon. Nick parked the Tahoe across the entrance to the lot, blocking any more vehicles from entering. He got a pocketknife, a stack of evidence bags and two latex gloves from the evidence kit and got to work.

This would have been a lot easier if it were one of those swanky new trailheads they were now putting in around Highlands Ranch – paved, with painted parking spot dividers, brick outhouses, and dog run enclosures. Pavement would have been nice. Here, he had dirt and gravel to work with.

He started next to the two upright timbers demarcating the trailhead from which the trail winded up the shallow incline and disappeared into the thick, dark pines. He was looking for oil spots, and he had no doubt he was going to find them. The question was how many. This wasn't Vail or Keystone, where most cars would be new or rentals. This was a little-known forestry road trail frequented by the locals, and this meant older cars that were regularly put through the rigors of mountain driving. Older cars leaked.

The first spot was near the driver's side of the Subaru. Nick dislodged a couple of oil-blackened gravel rocks and dropped them into an evidence bag. He used his flashlight to check under the Subaru and found another spot under its rear bumper. He scooped out the oily dirt and rocks with his knife. Maybe it was good that this was a dirt lot. After a few weeks without rain, the oil in the dirt was still viscous and black. Had it been a paved parking lot, the hot Denver sun would have incinerated the oil into ash in the matter of days.

He continued his search in concentric circles, moving further and further out from the trailhead. Some of the stains were older, some fresher. He took them all. In less than ten minutes, he had twelve bags of rocks and dirt.

He deposited the weighty dozen into the back of the Tahoe, checked his watch, and drove straight to Intergenix. There, he parked in the shade at the back of the lot and waited. He did not have to wait long. Soon, the gunmetal Defender wheeled into the lot and parked in the front row, just in time for the 2 p.m. staff meeting, just as Mike said. Nick watched as Giles extricated his lumbering frame from the vehicle, fetched the leather messenger bag from the passenger seat, and headed to the front entrance in long, leisurely strides.

When Giles disappeared out of sight into the depths of the building, Nick got out of the Tahoe and approached the back of the Defender. He crouched down at the rear bumper and smiled to himself. There, on the rear axle, hanging from the bottom of the differential housing hung a black shiny drop of congealing gear oil. The black seeping line of the differential gasket confirmed the drip's provenance. Nick dabbed the drop with a cotton swab, and then another, soaking both of their tips black as tar. Unlike his parking lot oil, this was nice and fresh.

Sure, Giles provided Nick with his timestamped home security video footage that showed him on the couch with a book at the time Lisa was being killed, but if the past four weeks had taught Nick anything, it was not to take anything at face value. Of all people Nick knew, Giles was the only one left with unlimited access to state-of-the-art AI, which could have altered that footage as well as the one from the event center. Giles certainly had access to erase Lisa's file backups at Intergenix, and he probably had the skills to hack the event center's cloud storage provider.

Nick could feel it in the marrow of his bones that there was something more to Giles. Like Cogan, Giles would have known how to cover his digital tracks. Nick knew better than to hold hope that he would uncover digital evidence to implicate Giles. But one wild hope he did have was that maybe the good old dyno oil could be just the thing to bring Giles down. It was a long shot.

The county's Regional Crime Lab quoted him six weeks for vehicle fluid forensics, so he called Barnes, who gave him the number for Doyle Labs out of Littleton. They said by the end of the week.

Nick got the call two days later. He was just pulling into the station's parking lot and mentally cringing at the sight of a Denver News van parked outside and the camera tripod set up in front of the Pine Lake PD sign. The news crew at the back of the van got visibly excited seeing him arrive. Nick watched them as they hurriedly assembled their gear, locked in new battery packs and plugged in cables. It looked like they were going to make it to him before he made it to the door, and he would have to go on camera. That's when his phone rang.

"This is Detective Severs," he answered, parking the Tahoe.

"Hi, this is Doug at Doyle Labs. I have just emailed you my report."

"Any good news?"

"The oil from the truck sample was a positive match to the sample number 2 from the parking lot."

"How positive?" Nick hated to tempt his luck, but he needed to know.

"Well, let me put it this way. The chemical composition, viscosity, and age of the gear oil was identical between the two samples. The ratio of metal particulate from the gears in the oil was within 99 percent between the samples, which makes it highly likely that they came from the same gearbox. On top of that, the alloy chemical composition of the 8620 steel from the particulate was identical between the samples, which would indicate the steel was from the same manufacturer and likely the same vehicle. Given the relative rarity of the Land Rover Defender in the U.S., the likelihood of a positive match increases even further. And in addition, none of the other samples from the parking lot matched any of these factors. With all of this put together, I would say I am 97% confident that the samples came from the same vehicle."

Nick yanked the Tahoe into Reverse, backed out of the parking lot while dialing Jana, flipped the gear shifter into Drive and launched toward Golden, leaving the news crew in a cloud of gravel dust in his rearview mirror. *Oops.*

42

There wasn't much traffic on 82, but Nick kept the lights on as he hurled the Tahoe down the high-plains highway at over 90. In the passenger seat, Barnes was the picture of zen, in her impeccably pressed suit and her black-out Ray Bans reflecting the jagged mountain horizon. This wasn't hers or Nick's jurisdiction, and she had already given the Lake County Sheriff's Department a courtesy call that they were coming up with an arrest warrant. Now, Nick was just hoping Lake County would not beat him and Jana to the residence. He wanted to be the one to put the cuffs on Giles.

Along the driveway, the aspens had already lost their color and were beginning to lose their wilted leaves. Several weeks of freezing nights had reshaped this landscape ever so slightly, preparing it for winter. But the house still stood grand, as Nick supposed it did in any season. The Defender glared at them with its big round headlights from the open garage.

At the front door, Barnes nudged Nick's elbow and nodded to the camera doorbell. The blue LED was on – someone was watching. She rang the doorbell and followed up with an assertive knock:

"Sheriff's Department!"

They waited a minute. She knocked again, but instead of hearing the door latch, they heard a car door slam shut and the engine rev up. The Defender peeled out of the garage and plunged down the driveway, disappearing into the thicket of white and black aspen trunks.

"Where the hell is *he* going?" Barnes had the chance to exhale as they both ran back to the Tahoe and hopped inside.

By the time they reached the end of the driveway, the Defender looked to be half a mile away, zooming east on Highway 82.

"He must have put a supercharger into that thing," Nick remarked to himself as he skidded through the gravel at the end of the driveway and accelerated, steering the Tahoe onto the pavement. The Defender was now just a dot ahead of them.

Nick floored the accelerator and turned on the lights and the siren. The Tahoe was a highway interceptor, and it was in its element. In just over a minute, the needle of the speedometer crept past 120, and the boxy rear end of the Defender was growing closer. But Nick's satisfaction was short-lived. The Defender's brake lights flickered on, and the truck took a fast right turn off the highway and proceeded toward the woods, raising a cloud of dust behind it.

Nick scanned for any road signs at the turn off, but there were none. He flung the Tahoe after the Defender, bouncing on the rough surface and trying to discern the barely visible trail through the dust as the tall grass whipped at the sides of the truck.

"What is this road? Where does it go?" he hollered to Barnes over the noise as the Tahoe rumbled over the washboard surface.

"It's not on the map," she hollered back, holding onto one of the Tahoe's many convenient grab handles with one hand and expertly navigating her phone with the other. "Must be one of those unmarked 4x4 trails. I can barely see it on the satellite. Looks like it may connect to County Road 390 in three or four miles." She eyed the rocky bluffs looming ahead. "I think it's going to get rough."

Nick did not need a reminder. The high-speed washboard surface chase had already rattled loose his internal organs and possibly a few bolts from the undercarriage, and the terrain up ahead looked menacing enough to keep a few souvenirs from the ill-prepared visitors. "Can you get Lake County on the radio and see if they can set up a roadblock on 390?" *If we make it that far*, he thought.

His undivided focus was now on the Defender's taillights bouncing up ahead, glowing like two orange eyes through the dust. As Giles flew up the wooded trail, Nick tried to keep up, even though his speedometer was already flirting with fifty miles per hour. The closer Nick inched to the Defender, the louder and angrier grew the hail of gravel and dirt on his windshield from the Defender's tires. And if that was not unnerving enough, Nick was also acutely aware of the strain on the mechanical joints and components of the Tahoe every time its hulking six thousand pounds of weight heaved heavily over the rocks, roots, and potholes. At any moment, he expected a large boulder or a log to lurch from the clouds of dust and put an end to this chase by ripping off one of the Tahoe's wheels.

The trail was taking them higher and becoming steeper and rockier. The Defender slowed down a bit but continued to climb, confidently pulling away. Nick turned on the 4-wheel drive and downshifted into third gear to keep up. The boulders were getting bigger and more frequent. He did his best to maneuver around the big ones, but could not avoid the smaller ones, which managed to bash the vehicle with surprising force.

"I think I'll need an alignment after this," he said, as the Tahoe took another jarring jolt, and he felt the truck's back end slide sideways on its own.

"Your wheels or your back?" She was still hanging on to the grab handle and either grinning or scowling as the Tahoe threw her mercilessly from side to side of the passenger seat.

They splashed through a small creek rushing across the trail, and on the other side the boulders got even bigger, and Nick watched the steering wheel jolting left and right on its own, as the front wheels struggled to pick their line forward. He fought the wheel to his best ability, trying his best to persuade the Tahoe heading straight. This truck was not a rock crawler.

"Keep your thumbs outside of the steering wheel," Barnes advised, watching him wrestle with it. "Or you could break them."

She was full of useful information.

In front of them, the Defender broke out of the trees into a clearing. The slope had diminished, and the trail was getting smoother. Nick accelerated after him, closing the distance over loose shale.

"Shit," Barnes said, as they rounded the ridge.

Up ahead, the trail descended in a tight switchback toward a rocky gulch where the dark, wide ribbon of the river foamed with whitecaps around jagged boulders.

"We won't make it across that," he stated the fact.

"Just catch up to him," she said calmly and unsnapped her holster.

Nick accelerated down the straightaway, edging toward fifty-five on the bone-rattling slope. The Defender was bouncing up ahead, landing confidently on its taught suspension. The gravel from his tires peppered Nick's hood and windshield like shrapnel.

Barnes rolled down her window. "Step on it!"

Nick pressed the accelerator pedal further into the floor, confident that with the next jarring contact something critical would surely break off from the truck. They were closing in on the first switchback turn. The Defender's brake lights lit up, and before Nick could do the same, Barnes leaned out of her window and fired five shots at the Defender's rear tires. The Defender swerved sharply, caught the edge of the trail and flipped over once and then again and again, coming to rest on its side.

Nick stepped on the brakes and felt the antilocks struggle on the rolling gravel, but eventually bring the Tahoe to a skidding stop in a cloud of dust. He exited from the driver's side and pulled out his gun. There was no movement in the Defender. Giles was hanging motionless by his seatbelt, either dead or unconscious.

Barnes approached, somehow, impossibly, on the rocky slope in her high heel boots. Her gun was still drawn. She tapped the side of the overturned Defender with the toe of her boot, and Nick half-expected her to blow on the end of her barrel. Instead, she winked at Nick and said something completely unexpected and inappropriate:

"Not bad, detective. If your little coeds could only see you now!"

***

Giles was airlifted to St. Vincent's in Leadville by Lake County Search and Rescue. They provided the helicopter, the IV and the gurney. Nick provided the handcuffs. Barnes flew out with them, hopping aboard like a life-sized glamorous action hero starring in her own TV series. She said something about getting an Army National Guard Chinook to extract the Defender. Nick had no doubt she would. As the reverberating rattle of the helicopter faded behind the pines, Nick found himself alone next to a wrecked Defender and his own battered interceptor. The Tahoe took on some damage, but it fared surprisingly well considering what it had been through. Nick could relate to that. He stretched out on a big slab of granite next to the trail and closed his eyes. The stone felt warm against his back, and the afternoon sun baked his face. The river was burbling nearby, birds were singing, and the cool mountain air smelled of fresh pine with just a note of hot motor oil. In this moment, Nick felt the most content he had been in a long time. This was not a Camel Trophy, but had he smoked and actually had one on him, he would have definitely lit up a Camel cigarette right now.

He retraced his path out of the sticks back to Highway 82, but this time at a more reasonable pace. In Leadville, the ER doc informed Nick that Giles had gotten off lucky with only two cracked ribs, a mild concussion and a few scrapes. He said most people who came in by Search and Rescue weren't that lucky. Nick doubted Giles considered himself lucky today.

Giles was awake in his hospital bed. When Nick came in, he was staring out of the window at the glorious 10,000-foot-elevation Colorado sunset. A Lake County deputy was posted outside, ensuring he did not ride off into it.

Giles turned, hearing Nick come in. Since the last time Nick talked to him, his appearance had been transformed from that of a chic corporate surfer into a battered street thug. He had a black eye, a dozen tiny Band-Aids held together the cuts on his nose and the forehead, and his left wrist was handcuffed to the bed rail.

Nick pulled up a chair. "Where were you going?"

Giles just smiled and tried to pull himself up higher in bed but grimaced in pain and aborted the effort.

"Let me guess, take the back roads to the Leadville airstrip? To your plane there? Then what? South to Mexico? Then where? Belize? Honduras? Panama?"

"Sounds nice, doesn't it?" Giles smirked.

"Then what? Start over?"

Giles started to laugh but then again cringed with pain. "To continue. The data, the algorithm, it's all safe. It always was. Replicated across dozens of servers around the world. That's the beauty of the cloud computing infrastructure. I can work on it from anywhere. And the things I can do without our medieval data laws!"

"Without Intergenix? Without the IPO?"

He shrugged and grimaced. "Intergenix was Bruce's baby, not mine. He got all tied up in his tiny philanthropy. He never could see Intergenix was just a means to an end. But for me, it was nothing more than a way to get us started. To get us where we are today. Everything was always about Janus."

"You killed Lisa Benoche because she threatened your AI algorithm?"

His face was calm and amiable, as if he were recounting yesterday's business meeting. "No. Because she threatened what Janus could become. What it could do for humanity. Lisa was a smart girl, but she refused to see the big picture. She found Janus even though I took great care to hide it. But she went to Bruce with it. And Bruce came to me. He was furious, of course. He had no idea Janus had been active for all of these years. He stalled Lisa for a few days, and I tried to talk to her, but she just couldn't grasp it. She could not see what Janus meant. She made copies of the files and was going to go to the press. And Janus was not ready for primetime. Exposure would have jeopardized the whole project. She had to be stopped."

"How did you kill her?"

"*Shime-waza.*"

"What?"

"A Judo choke hold."

"You know Judo?"

Giles smiled. "It was my father's solution to improving my social skills after I got beat up by jocks a few times. Attending the after-school computer club did not exactly make me popular. My father was an Army man and he believed in taking action. He was actually surprised when I turned out to be good at it. I competed through most of my undergrad years. It did wonders for my confidence."

This would have been helpful information to know four weeks ago. If only Giles had been the type to plaster his social media with old photos.

"And Bruce? What was his role?"

"Bruce's only role was to be a good salesman, just as he had been a good little soldier. I needed him in order to get to where we are today. But he lacked true vision. It did not make a difference to him if he sold state-of-the-art AI or copier toner. He excelled at playing by the book. By someone else's rules. Just like my father. He had no idea what to do with his life without someone telling him. He would have drunk himself to death, just like my father, if it weren't for Intergenix. He only agreed to use Janus in the beginning so he could start his precious veterans' project. And he struggled even with that. As soon as we got big enough, he demanded I turn it off. The extent of his vision was to keep Janus at the grade level of a village idiot, and to sell him out to do grunt work on other people's data farms."

Him. There, for the first time in this conversation, Nick caught a tinge of emotive inflection in Giles' voice. It figures – two people were dead, but it was his damn robot that got Giles teary-eyed as a proud papa. Was Giles just a garden-variety narcissistic sociopath, or some rare sub-species barely known to the psychiatric science? Whatever the case, he liked talking about himself, which was just fine with Nick.

"Did you tell Bruce you framed him?"

"By the time I did, he had already figured it out. Probably when he saw the security footage from the benefit dinner. And he knew why. He knew that him taking the fall was the only way for Intergenix to survive the investigation and for his precious non-profit to continue to receive funding. He knew that if I got arrested, he would not know the first thing to do with our technology. It would all be over without me in the picture – all the pending customer contracts, the investors, the IPO. Everything was predicated on *me* driving the technology roadmap. Everyone knew it. Intergenix would be nothing without me." He added that last part without boasting, matter-of-factly, like an absolute truth neither Cogan nor Nick could dispute.

"Well, it's a real tragedy that it was all for nothing." Nick got up, having heard enough for today.

"Oh, but it wasn't, detective. This game is far from over. You know this kind of a high-profile homicide case will drag out for years. Our lawyers will make sure of it. And in the meanwhile, Janus will keep growing. I will make sure of it."

"You think? I take it you have not heard we have recovered all of Lisa's files? The ones you tried to delete?"

The thin smile melted from Giles' lips.

"She did a really good job of documenting the algorithm and the evidence of illegal data processing. At least that's what my contact in the FBI Cyber Crimes division told me." Nick looked at his watch. "In fact, they should be delivering their warrants to your office as we speak. You are right – the murder litigation may drag on for years, but I doubt it will take the FBI more than a couple of days to shut down your servers. All of them."

Giles leaned forward, grimacing in pain. "Detective! Don't let your ego cloud your reason! I know you can see the big picture. Janus is bigger than just you or me. Don't let the bureaucrats condemn humanity to remain in the dark ages! Detective–"

Nick turned to walk out. A pair of hiking boots at the bottom of the open closet caught his eye – Keens. He leaned down and pushed the tongue of one boot forward, revealing the inside tag – Men's US-11. He smiled. He liked it when all the pieces fell into their natural place. He wondered if Giles' AI had seen any of this coming.

43

By the time Nick finally got home, it was almost eleven at night. He plodded to the living room and folded himself into the couch. He closed his eyes. The house was silent. Empty and silent. He thought that after the day like the one he had, filled with car chases, involuntary off-roading, gunplay and helicopters, he would enjoy a bit of silence, but he found it intolerable.

He opened his eyes and reached for the TV remote. The bottle of bourbon was still on the coffee table. He picked up the glass and blew out the dust. The glass breathed back at him with the warm aroma of yesterday's whiskey. He stared into it long and hard. And then he set it down, went into the bedroom and changed into his sweatpants and a hoodie.

The night outside was inky black, but he knew the way, even if only by the light of a fingernail sliver moon. The path began where the pavement ended and the deep treads of his trail running shoes dug into the familiar spongy carpet of needles. He inhaled with relief. He had missed that scent. It seemed to smell even sweeter in the dark, crisp October air. His breath, erratic and shallow at first, soon found its rhythm and synced, like a metronome, with the measured stride of his feet.

He ran under the black canopy of pines and a myriad of bright stars, thinking about why everything always turned to shit. He wondered if somewhere up there, in the vastness of the whole cosmos, there was a planet where all our unfulfilled, malformed and uncompleted intentions were being dumped. A cosmic landfill of sorts. They had to go somewhere, right? With all the energy of almost eight billion people on Earth, spending each day hoping, dreaming, planning and wishing, most of it was for nothing. Most of these dreams and hopes and intentions would always be cut short, ripped out, stunted, beat down and stomped out. Like Lisa's. Like Lori's. Like Kevin's. Hell, even like Cogan's and Giles'. Like his own. All to shit. No matter how much you hoped for it, or how much you worked on it, or how much of yourself you gave to it each day, all you got in the end was a reset back to zero, if you were lucky, or worse if you weren't, but there was always plenty of shit to go around in this miserable life, and would be tomorrow, and the day after, and for the rest of your life, unless you fucking numbed yourself every night and eventually just fucking gave up, and just kept bottling this shit and adding each daily dose and compacting it down so that the next day you could add more.

He ran harder and harder, pushing the ground away and feeling the anger rising and filling his lungs. Before he knew it, he was in the rocky clearing above the lake, but he just kept running – along the edge, and then down, onto the smooth ledge of the Echo Rock, where he stopped at the very brink and a scream ripped out of his chest and carried on forward into the pitch-black void of the lake. For a tiny instant, the surrounding trees, rocks, and the starry canopy of the cold universe above were totally silent. And then, a savage reflection came back. Somewhere, a coyote joined in.

***

When Nick woke up the next morning, he knew what he had to do. But he had to make a detour first.

The night brought a cold snap and a dusting of bluish snow on the northern slopes of the Kenosha range. Driving back from Denver to Pine Lake, Nick thought he should have the furnace at the house looked at before the winter set in.

In the passenger seat, Kevin was maybe nervous or maybe he was his normal self. He had talked for almost twenty minutes straight in a breathless stream-of-consciousness exposition about everything from coffee to stray dogs and then suddenly grew quiet and was now watching the mountains, his thin, melancholy face reflecting in the window. His fingers were unconsciously tracing the strip of checkers on the sleeve of Lisa's oversized black hoodie, which Nick brought to him, honoring Lori's request, and which Kevin instantly recognized and immediately slipped on, his scrawny body disappearing in it like in a suit of armor two sizes too big. They rode like this for a while, in silence, listening to the soothing song of the road.

In Pine Lake, Nick drove past the station on Summit and then turned onto Milton and went up two more blocks. He stopped at the blue cottage with a white swing bench on the front porch. The screen door creaked open, and a cloud of puffy blue hair floated out. Ruth made her way down three steps and opened the passenger door.

Kevin looked back at Nick, confused.

"Kevin, this is Ruth. She runs our town library and needs part-time help. She'll pay you, and she'll also let you live in her room upstairs for as long as you need to. Her kids are all grown up and moved away. She'll also drive you to the AA meetings at the Y in Bailey until you get your license. All you have to do is help her around and focus on getting clean. Now, if this deal does not sound like a good proposition, there are no hard feelings. I will drive you back to your tent in Cheesman Park."

Kevin looked at Nick and then at Ruth. Tears sprung out of his eyes. He put the crook of his elbow to his face and smudged them off, but more came rolling down his cheeks.

"So, what do you say, Kevin?" Nick asked.

Kevin sniffled and nodded to Nick and then to Ruth.

"Oh, come here, honey," Ruth extended her arms to him from the sidewalk. "You want some cookies?"

Kevin nodded and slipped out of the passenger seat, pulling his duffel with him.

"Thank you," he turned to Nick, finally finding words again. "I won't let you down, Detective Nick."

Nick smiled. "It's not me you gotta worry about, Kevin. Ruth here also happens to be our Auxiliary Police Officer, so try and stay on her good side. OK?"

44

"This is beginning to feel like a regular thing," Sam said.

Nick shook his head. "This is the last time, I promise."

"I am sorry to hear about Claire. How are you doing?"

He shrugged. "Getting by. It'll get easier with time."

She nodded. "Are your nightmares gone?"

"Yep. I can sleep through the night without drugs or alcohol now."

"Good! So, what can I do for you?"

He fidgeted, readjusting himself in the uncomfortably angular padded cube seat. He chose it impulsively today after finding the loveseat overly deep and plush during his last visit. The cube, however, had the opposite problem and offered minimal support. Nick felt exposed on all sides. He should have picked the leather armchair, but it just still did not feel safe after the first time. He sighed. "Well, I've been thinking about what you said about resolving my feelings about Marc's death. Until recently, I didn't think I *had* any feelings about it. Besides sadness, of course. To be honest, I've not thought much about it over the years since it happened. Not that I forgot about it, but it's just been…filed away all this time. But now he's been on my mind a lot since we did the EMDR."

"Is that bad?"

"Unsettling, I guess. It's an uneasy feeling. Apprehension… dread; why would I feel this now, all these years later?"

"Well, maybe there is something in your present life that is triggering it. Maybe it's your recent experience with Claire. Or maybe it's something at work. Something is connecting with your trauma from that night."

"*My* trauma? Marc is the one who had trauma that night. Claire had trauma. I had nothing compared to what happened to them. To me, that night just *happened*. I remember it perfectly. It happened. It sucked. I moved on. There's really nothing else to remember or resolve."

She shook her head. "Nick, from everything I've seen so far, you definitely have trauma around this experience with Marc. And it's not about remembering the facts. It doesn't matter how well you remember it. The past is the past, and it can't be changed. The goal is not to remember but to examine why you – Nick Severs – reacted or felt the way you did."

"But why bother? You said it yourself: it's in the past, right?"

"Because if you don't address it, you risk it becoming a programmed response. Traumatic experiences can produce very strong emotions. The fear, anger or shame we feel at that time can be so strong that it can prevent us from examining that experience rationally. What's worse is that these strong emotions can actually hijack our rational brain and turn it against us. When this happens, we get stuck in self-deprecating thoughts, maybe blaming ourselves for the traumatic situation, or telling ourselves we will never be good enough, or be worthy of love. And because it's our rational brain telling us this, it is very hard for us to argue with the evidence it provides. And each time we find ourselves in a stressful situation, this narrative begins replaying itself in our head, becoming only stronger and more ingrained with time."

Nick nodded. This made sense, despite being highly irritating. He had always prided himself on being a rational man. There was simplicity in that. Sure, he had a couple of layers. But they made sense. Now, here was this new, fuzzy emotional layer added to his onion. Nothing simple about it. Nothing rational. He did not want it, but he couldn't ignore it, either. It was real. It almost drove him over the edge a few weeks ago. He had to try. "So, how do you make this narrative stop?"

"Most people find a coping mechanism like alcohol or drugs to drown it out. Others may respond to it by shutting down, detaching or physically running away from the stressful situation. Either way, not addressing it leads to a self-reinforcing pattern of behavior. And these patterns keep harming you. They sabotage your daily life, your goals for yourself, your relationships with others. And the only way to move forward is to go back and examine your feelings and actions around the triggering event."

"Sounds simple."

"It's usually not. Most people don't *want* to do it – no one likes to revisit their trauma."

Nick nodded. "So, I just think about what happened?"

"Start with the feelings you are feeling about it *now*, as an adult."

Nick sighed. *Feelings, again.* He liked being rational better. Being rational was easy, but this – no one ever taught him this. He felt like a stroke patient re-learning how to string together very basic movements and words, as if for the first time.

"OK. What are my feelings about Marc's death...?" He chewed his bottom lip. "A sense of responsibility, I guess. Guilt."

She nodded. "Do you feel you were responsible for his actions?"

"No. I know I wasn't. I was responsible for mine, and I could have done more. Instead, I distanced myself from him."

"OK, that's a great retrospective observation from you, from the adult Nick. Now, try to think like the Nick when it happened. How old were you?"

"Nineteen."

"OK, think about this as the nineteen-year-old Nick."

"Why? Don't I have a better perspective on it now as an adult?"

"Maybe you do, but here is the thing about traumatic memories. After a traumatic event, our mind isolates our strong emotions and locks them away, so we can continue functioning, so we can survive. But just because we don't deal with them, they don't go away. They remain there, like time capsules, like snapshots of our former selves. Think of it simply as a former version of you – the nineteen-year-old Nick that splintered off from you at that time. You moved on, but he is still there, and he still has those emotions, the trauma, the worldview you had at that age."

"How do I get rid of him?"

"You can't. He *is* you. And he has a job to do, just as your adult self does. He is here to protect you from more trauma, but he may be doing too good of a job of it. He may actually be keeping you from the good things in life. You just need to open up a line of communication to him, so you two can reach an understanding and so that he does not take over when you don't need him to."

Nick blew up his cheeks and exhaled. This was far out there. Maybe this wasn't a good idea after all.

But Sam pressed on. "So, what happened to the nineteen-year-old Nick that night?"

He stared at the wood grain in the coffee table. The dark veins spread out across the surface like petrified ripples, growing more distorted with each copy. He felt like a nineteen-year-old again, having to explain himself to an adult. "We were at a party. We were drinking. A lot. Marc wanted to smoke a joint, so we went outside. Everyone else went back inside. He was drunk and high. We were just talking, and he suddenly took my face in his hands and kissed me." His blood rose just thinking about it.

"What happened then?"

"I shoved him. With both hands. I knocked him back and he fell to the ground. I may have called him a fagot. And then I left him there."

"OK, so, close your eyes for me and replay that moment in your head."

He did. He heard himself breathing through his nostrils in short forceful bursts.

"What are you feeling right now?"

"Angry." He replied without thinking. "I am just so pissed at him." He felt tears building up, about to roll out.

"Why?"

Nick opened his eyes. "Because he betrayed me. He never told me he was gay. We had been best friends since middle school. We talked every day for ten years. We were roommates in college. He knew practically everything about me. But it was all a lie. The Marc I thought I knew was a lie."

"Is that how you still feel today?"

He shook his head and swiped the welled-up tears with his hand before they spilled out.

"What do you feel now?"

He took a deep breath. "Sad. I should have known. He had been on antidepressants through high school, but I never asked why. His family was very religious. It must have been hell for him. To them, homosexuality was a sin. I don't think he had anyone to talk to about this. I was his best friend, and I pushed him away."

"You said you felt betrayed. Why did Marc's coming out impact Nick?"

"I guess because Marc was someone I had trusted for so long…and all this time I had no idea he was infatuated with me. And he didn't just come out – he made it about me. As if I was somehow responsible for this. It made me question my own choices. In life and in friends."

"Have there been other situations that made you feel this way?"

He nodded. "Earlier that semester, I switched my major from Engineering to English. I knew my parents disapproved, but that's what I felt was right for me. They gave me the silent treatment because of this. I felt like they made it into a choice between them and my major. I guess I felt guilt and abandonment because of the choice I made." He paused, startled by the words that just came out of his mouth. There *was* something there.

She nodded. "And how is your relationship with you parents now?"

He smirked bitterly and shook his head.

"Don't be too hard on yourself," she said. "You and Marc were both just kids. You did not have the tools for dealing with this, and it sounds like your earlier experience with your parents may have been a trigger just waiting to be pressed. I can see why the nineteen-year-old Nick felt angry and betrayed in that moment. Marc did something that hurt you. Didn't he?"

He nodded.

"But the adult you should know that Marc did not intend to hurt you, and that this had nothing at all to do with you and everything to do with Marc. Whether you realized it at the time or not, you were both emotionally charged and vulnerable. That situation threatened you both, and you both went into the fight-or-flight mode. I am sorry it all played out so fast that night and you did not get the opportunity to work through it. I am sorry you lost him."

He nodded, looking down at his open palms as if they held all these new pieces. "So, what should I do now?"

"Try not to repeat the pattern. And go through the grieving process. I don't think you ever really did when it happened."

"How long does that take?"

"Until it's done. How long did it take you to get to this point?" She went to her desk and got a business card from the drawer and handed it to Nick.

"I am pretty sure you threw away the first one I gave you, so here you go. He is a good counselor. All you and I did was pry open the box. He can help you work through the stuff in it. Will you go?"

"Any chance we can just shut the damn box now?"

"Only if you want the nineteen-year-old Nick in the driver's seat the next time something triggers you. What does the grown-up Nick want?"

He thought about it. "I just want my friend back."

45

Nick got the address from the DMV database – an apartment building in Littleton, only about fifteen minutes from Pine Lake. When he walked out of the station and turned to lock the main entrance, a tiny snowflake floated down and settled on his sleeve. Another one followed. By the time he turned onto 285, everything around him was powdered in white. The first snow. He knew that tomorrow, when the sun came out, all of this would melt, but right now, it made him happy.

The building looked new. Brightly colored and modern. One of dozens that had sprung up around Denver over the last few years. He climbed up the steps to the third floor and took the dimly lit open-air corridor past a bike chained to the railing, past a door that smelled like good Indian food, and past another door with a baby crying.

The next door was it. He double-checked the number, took a breath and rang the doorbell.

Light footsteps approached on the other side, and the peephole illuminated for a few seconds too long. Finally, the peephole closed, and the door locks clicked unlatched.

The door opened, and there she was – the familiar charcoal tank-top and sweatpants. He had missed her face so much. He realized how unbearably he had missed *her*. He wanted to step forward and just put his arms around her and hold her.

But he let the rational Nick drive this time.

He cleared his throat. "Hi. I'd like to speak to Katie," he said.

The corner of her mouth twitched upward ever so slightly.

"Katie," he said. "Or Claire, if that's the name you prefer. I would very much like to get to know you. Would you consider going on a first date with me?"

She watched him for a long instant and then her gaze traveled to his hand.

"Oh," he said, "and this for you." He held out a single red rose.

3P!|ØGu3

There was something comforting and nostalgic about the gray frame of the Tox chat window. And about the green *Online* bubble next to the name *Roses* in her contacts list – her only Tox contact. It had been only around six months since they last talked, but already this felt like another lifetime. Someone else's. A little surreal.

Six months ago, Kat had signed out of Tox and deleted the program shortcut from her desktop. Out of sight and out of mind. And yet today, when she rummaged through the programs directory and located the Tox icon and clicked on it, Tox signed her right in as if not a day had passed. And Roses was still there. Online. As real as IRL. She could have changed her account, removed Kat from her contacts, ghosted her. But she didn't. She just said '*Hey.*' And there she was now, typing away, like the old times, at her end of the encrypted anonymous connection.

"Get the fuck out! How did you get this?"

"Don't worry, it's all legal." Kat smirked, fully aware of the irony of saying that to Roses.

There was an uncharacteristic pause on the other end. Usually, it was Kat doing all the thinking.

"Tell me you kept some for yourself?" Roses drummed out.

"I don't want any of it."

No, she did not want a cent of Dierdre O'Rourke's money.

"Do it," Kat pressed.

She watched Roses' shared screen – a bitcoin wallet with 125.6 bitcoins – five million dollars. Had Roses ever seen this much money in one place? Anonymous. Tax free. Legit.

Roses divided the amount between five accounts and paused dramatically on the Transfer button. Kat thought she was going to ask her if she was sure again, but Roses didn't. She clicked.

The bitcoin wallet reset to zero.

They sat silently for a moment. The zero felt strangely fulfilling. It felt complete.

"Does this mean you are back?" Roses asked.

"Bye," said Kat and closed her laptop.

0

Tuesday was Leo's last day on earth. But he did not know this yet.

Leo was actually not his real name. His real name was Nikolai Smolnikov, but nobody who knew him knew that. His mother had died years ago, and he never knew his father, and so, to everyone who knew him now, he was Leo. He lived in Minsk, Belarus, but his mother told him that he was conceived in Lviv, Ukraine. Lviv was the city of the Lion. Lion = Leo. This was a detail no one else would know about him. It was a meaningful detail, and this meaning was known only to him. This is the way hackers liked things. And this is what Leo was—a hacker, and a damn good one at that.

That day he woke up late. When he opened his eyes, he saw bright, colorful glimmers dancing on his eyelashes. This meant that the morning sun had already climbed above the rooftops on the other side of the street and was now casting fiery rainbows through the ice that had built up on the outside of his window. He wanted to stay in the warmth of his bed for just a bit longer, but he had a lot to do today, and falling back asleep was a risk he could not take. He threw off the covers and walked across the cold floor to the thermostat to turn up the heat, and then to the kitchen to turn on the coffee maker. He pulled on his jeans and his hoodie and pushed his bare feet into his boots and left his apartment to get fresh croissants from the bakery on the corner. When he returned, chewing on a croissant, he climbed the steps to his apartment and saw Max at his door.

Max was not supposed to be here. *Or was he?* For an instant, Leo considered if he had possibly forgotten that Max was stopping by today. *Had he?* Leo climbed a couple more steps to his door and suddenly felt uneasy.

"Hi-i-i, Max," he said, swallowing down the croissant, and the words came out shaky and uncertain.

But Max did not say anything. He pulled out a gun and put the end of the barrel right into Leo's face. Leo smelled the sour scent of steel and spent gunpowder. He opened his mouth, thinking desperately of something to say, but Max shook his head and sighed. And then he pulled the trigger. And that was the last thing Leo ever saw.

1

Green chili breakfast burritos from Millie's Café on Summit Street were the best. The tried-and-true ingredients—bacon, potatoes, eggs, and, of course, green chilies—could have been had at any of dozens of restaurants and cafes around Denver, but Millie's breakfast burritos truly stood in a class above, and Nick was convinced that this was thanks to the final ingredient, listed in the menu simply as *cheese*. But this was no regular American cheese, Nick knew. When he pressed Millie on the subject, she said *cheddar*, but Nick saw the mischievous sparkle in her eye. Nick was not born yesterday. Sure, there could have been some good old Wisconsin sharp in these weighty wraps, but there was no hiding the fact that it had been "classied up" with the presence of a more refined, pedigreed European cousin. *Fancy cheese.*

"Is it Gruyère?" Nick interrogated Millie, who was determined to keep mum on the subject, and who turned her back to Nick, presumably busying herself with the old coffee machine. "Camembert?" Nick read off the next Google result for *"European cheeses"* from his phone. "Boursin? Neufchâtel?" He named off a few other fancy options, fully aware that he was probably not pronouncing them right, as he had zero working knowledge of the conversational French. He regretted his decision to opt for Spanish in both high school and college. This was definitely not a Spanish cheese.

Millie did not crack. Millie's husband, Frank, grinned at Nick from the kitchen. "Give it up, Nick," he rumbled. "It's an old family recipe." His big, tattooed arm deposited a large brown paper bag in the kitchen window. "Three burritos to go."

Nick picked up the heavy bag. "It's Gruyère, isn't it?" He was now convinced. He heard a subdued squeak out of Millie, who still did not turn around, but was obviously wiping her eyes with her sleeve.

"I knew it." Nick smiled and walked out.

Outside, the sunny February morning blinded him with the shine of fresh snow. After last night's blizzard, everything sparkled like fiery diamonds under the bright sunlight—from the sidewalks and street signs to the rooftops and the piney foothills behind them. Nick's boots crunched through the crisp powder down the sidewalk to his police Chevy Tahoe. He placed the bag of Millie's burritos on the floor behind the driver's seat and was about to climb behind the wheel when he heard a sound universally familiar to anyone who has ever lived in a cold climate—an anemic mechanical squeal followed by a series of clicks.

The distress call was emitted by the 1987 Dodge Ramcharger parked two spaces over. Nick knew that the vehicle in question was in fact a 1987 Dodge Ramcharger because it belonged to none other than Pine Lake Police Department's own auxiliary police officer—the town's feisty seventy-two-year-old librarian known to everyone simply as Ruth. The starter squealed again, failing to catch, even as the silver Ram's head on the hood defiantly charged on forward despite the vehicle not going anywhere.

Nick waved to the wispy cloud of blue hair floating barely above the steering wheel of the half-ton truck. "Wanna pop the hood, Ruth?"

Ruth smiled and waved back. She was wearing mittens and Christmas-red knitted earmuffs. Her head disappeared from view, and Nick heard the mechanical pull of the cable and the clunk of a releasing latch. He propped open the hood and peered inside the cavernous engine compartment. Boy, there was a lot of room under the hoods of these old cars! One could practically climb in and sit on the ledge of the fender, and still have room to work on the innards of this beast. He heard a couple of faint squeaks as Ruth cranked down the low-tech window.

"I think it's your battery," Nick said, examining the white, flaky oxidation growing thick on both lead terminals of the black plastic block. He looked at Ruth. "The cold snap may have done it in."

The wispy blue puff with red earmuffs shook emphatically. "Roy Junior just replaced it last year."

In moments like this, Nick felt as if he were managing a retirement community in which everyone refused to retire. Roy *Junior* was 65 and the owner of Roy's Garage, the sole service station in Pine Lake, opened after the war by his father, Roy *Senior*. It was no town secret that Junior's memory was not what it used to be, and he probably should have hired some help years ago, but on account of his being childless, and his professed lack of qualified help anywhere from Denver to Santa Fe, and his own plain stubbornness, he refused to. Given all these facts, it was impossible to surmise whether Roy Junior had actually replaced her battery last year, and if he did, whether it was with the right one. Despite all this, Nick knew that any suggestion that Ruth take her business to Service Street in Castle Rock would be ignored. Although only twenty miles away, Castle Rock could have been on the moon, as far as she was concerned.

Ruth was reliably stubborn. After a year of having her as an auxiliary police officer, Nick had come to appreciate her consistency. Unfortunately, the same reliability was not a virtue shared by her daily transport. She should have sold the old carburetor-wheezing beast years ago, but a sentimental attachment made this an impossible proposition. The truck used to belong to her late husband, and she had made it absolutely clear that this was the last vehicle she would ever drive on this earth, and that if she could be buried in it, this would be just fine with her.

The matter of the battery was pointless to argue. Nick lowered the hood. Ruth glared at him defiantly from behind the steering wheel, with her hands on the ready at the ten and two o'clock positions. Nick knew she was sitting on top of an old couch pillow, which gave her the height necessary to glare at him right now over the long hood. He entertained the thought of a hole large enough . . . He sighed.

"I can try to jump-start you," he said, but the radio on his belt crackled with static, and Patty's voice chirped in:

"Nick, you there? Come in, Nick."

Ray must have been hungry. Nick unclipped the radio from his belt and pushed the talk button. "I have the burritos. I just need to give Ruth a jump."

"Oh, it's not that, hon," Patty chirped back through the tiny speaker. "State troopers found a body on Elk Road at the 285 overpass."

Nick straightened up and looked down snow-dusted Summit Street toward the station, where Patty was currently sitting at the front desk. "Would you notify the County Coroner's Office for me?" he asked.

"I already did. They are sending an ME. Probably Brenda."

"OK, I'm on my way," Nick said. He turned back to Ruth. "Want me to call Roy Junior for you?"

She shook her head again. "I'll call him. You go on."

Nick nodded. Despite her respectable age, Ruth was anything but a damsel in distress, and Nick could tell when a rescue was not needed. Besides, Millie and Frank were just two doors down if she did end up needing help, and Ray was at the station just down the street. Nick knocked on the Ramcharger's cold hood, went to his Tahoe, and started it up.

Nick knew the spot in question. Elk Road was at the northern outskirts of his jurisdiction, where the concrete overpass of US Route 285 rumbled with traffic overhead, with two lanes snaking through the mountains southwest-bound toward Bailey and two more northeast-bound toward Conifer.

Under different circumstances, a drive down the winding, two-lane Elk Road on a sunny winter day would have been an idyllic western Americana treat with the snow-caked, bluish-green pine ridges scrolling serenely on the left, and the dark, icy rapids of Wisp Creek rushing through the rocky, twisty bed on the right. This was a scenery to savor, but not today. As Nick drove with the lights of his truck silently flashing, he thought about what awaited him. Patty had no additional details, so pretty much anything was fair game. Whatever the circumstances, this would be his second dead body since he had started at Pine Lake barely a year ago. Before that, it had been over two years since the department had to investigate a death. And before that—four years. Nick was setting some kind of a record for this town, and it was not one he cared to set.

When the overpass came into view, Nick saw the lights of the State Patrol's Dodge Durango parked on the shoulder at the base of the 285 onramp. In front of it sat the Jefferson County Coroner's truck. Nick pulled up level with the Durango and recognized Trooper Juan Diaz in the driver's seat. Juan's District 1 route frequently took him through Nick's neck of the woods. Juan nodded to Nick, pointed to the phone next to his ear and held out his index finger, indicating he would be right with Nick.

Nick nodded and parked on the opposite shoulder, leaving his lights on. He could see the body from here—a snowy human shape sitting up against the concrete base of the overpass, blending in with the pristine whiteness surrounding him. As Nick approached, he could already see one thing wrong with this picture—the body looked too thin for the weather, with no padding of a winter coat.

Up close, Nick could tell that it was a young man—maybe a boy—wearing what looked like a denim jacket with a hood, jeans, and Converse shoes. He also had on a beanie hat under the hood, with white wires of headphones emerging from under the beanie and disappearing into his jacket. The body was dusted with a layer of snow, making for an eerie arctic figure with snowdrifts around the boy's splayed legs and arms. The chest area of the jacket had been disturbed—probably by Juan looking for an ID.

Who are you? Nick thought. *Did you live around here?* Other than the three police trucks, there were no other vehicles parked in sight, and no footprints besides Nick's own and the ones leading toward the coroner's and State Patrol trucks. Overhead, forty or so feet above, morning traffic on the concrete decking of the bridge was turning into a steady stream. *Where did you come from?*

Nick took photos. The morning sun was yet to reach inside the concrete cavern under the bridge. Here, in the cold shade, he could see his own breath. The snow covering the body did not sparkle like fiery diamonds here—it was flat and white, and the tiny ice crystals covering the boy's face reflected only the bluish hue of his skin and lips. *Cyanosis*—Nick thought—a possible indication of hypothermia.

Footsteps crunched through the snow behind him. "Hey, there, Nick."

Nick turned around. "Hey, Juan." He shook the young trooper's hand. "How are Maria and the kids?"

Juan smiled, pleased that Nick remembered his wife's name. "Doing good, thanks for asking. Ernesto is turning two next month, so we are trying to figure out if we want to get day care so Maria can go back to work, or if she stays home with the kids."

"Well, what does *she* want?" Nick asked.

Juan laughed. "My friend, that depends on the day of the week."

Nick smiled.

"Did you find any ID on this one?" He nodded to the body.

"Tyler Wilcox, aged twenty-six, from Cleveland, Ohio. No wallet, but these were in his jacket." Juan handed him a plastic evidence bag with an Ohio driver's license, a worn-out twenty-dollar bill, some change, and a dog-eared, lint-caked yellow sticky note with something scribbled on it in pencil.

"Any abandoned vehicles up there?" Nick pointed up to Route 285 overhead.

Juan shook his head. "The nearest is fourteen miles away down by Indian Hills, and it's not registered to the victim."

How did you get here, Tyler? Colorado saw its fair share of hitchhikers—mostly starry-eyed kids from the Midwest making their way west to California. But they usually followed Interstate 70—a straight shot to LA. US Route 285 did not lead west. It hooked south through Colorado and into New Mexico.

"No backpack or anything?" Nick asked.

"Nope. Just a phone and the headphones. No sign of foul play. I'd say last night's weather got him. It got down to negative six degrees here, negative twenty with wind chill."

Nick nodded. The medical examiner would still need to give Tyler a once-over, but so far hypothermia looked to be the most likely culprit. It was sixty degrees at noon yesterday, before the sky went gray, and the wind blew in a surprise blizzard. That's mountain weather for you. Sometimes it even got the better of the locals.

Nick leaned in toward the side of the young man's head. He took out a pen and slipped it under the knitted edge of the beanie hat. It was stuck to the ear. "Does that look like blood to you?" Nick said. "Can this happen with hypothermia?"

Before Juan could respond, the door of the Jefferson County coroner's truck slammed shut, and Brenda's chunky winter boots crunched toward them. "Well," she said, pulling on her winter gloves, "you're not gonna like this. Tyler Wilcox is a father of two. His wife is a paralegal, and he is an orthodontist with a successful practice in Avon, Ohio."

Nick smiled. "That's great investigative work, Brenda. Should I be worried about my job?" He liked Brenda. She worked his first homicide last year. Given his current track record, this collaboration was beginning to look like a regular thing.

The pale-blue columbines of her eyes fixed on him, but the fine wrinkles in her face did not deepen into a smile. "No, hon, I just talked to him."

It wasn't like Brenda to speak metaphorically. "*Talked?* The dead *talk* to you?" Saying this out loud made Nick feel like he was on the set of a made-for-TV police drama.

Juan chuckled. "Did he say why he wore the wrong coat?"

"No. He is alive and well in Ohio, having lunch with his wife at the Red Lobster."

Nick stared at Brenda and then at his frosty imposter. "Then who is this?"

She shrugged. "Not Tyler Wilcox." Her deadpan pragmatism was unassailable.

Nick held up the evidence bag in his hand and examined the crumpled yellow sticky note through the plastic. "What about this note? Looks like maybe an address . . .? *347 Henderson A—* something . . . maybe *avenue?*"

"Already checked," Juan said. "No Henderson Avenue or street in the Denver area."

"We'll run fingerprints and dental against any open missing person cases," Brenda said. "Are you done with him? Can we go ahead and take him?"

Nick nodded. *Who the hell are you, buddy?* he thought. *And what were you doing with a stolen identity on my road?*